A GRIFFIN DOWELL
SUSPENSE NOVEL

BODY POLITIC

BY

GLYN J. GODWIN

BARBOUR
PUBLISHING

© 2003 by Glyn J. Godwin

ISBN 1-58660-600-X

Acquisitions & Editorial Director: Mike Nappa
Project Editor: Beth Rowland
Art Director: Robyn Martins
Cover design: Robyn Martins

Scripture quotations are taken from the King James Version of the Bible.

Scripture quotations are taken from the New King James Version. Copyright © 1979, 1980, 1982 by Thomas Nelson, Inc. Used by permission. All rights reserved.

Published by Barbour Publishing, Inc., P.O. Box 719, Uhrichsville, Ohio 44683, www.barbourbooks.com

ecpa Member of the
Evangelical Christian
Publishers Association

Printed in the United States of America.
5 4 3 2 1

DEDICATION

To the 1.4 million—and counting—
innocents who were denied the right
God gave them to live their life

What is crooked cannot be made straight,
And what is lacking cannot be numbered.

I communed with my heart, saying, "Look, I have attained greatness, and have gained more wisdom than all who were before me in Jerusalem. My heart has understood great wisdom and knowledge." And I set my heart to know wisdom and to know madness and folly. I perceived that this also is grasping for the wind.

For in much wisdom is much grief,
And he who increases knowledge increases sorrow.

KING SOLOMON, IN ECCLESIASTES 1:15–18 NKJV
And the last earthly thought
of Avraham Frederick Hegel, M.D., Ph.D.

PROLOGUE:
The seedling

Why are you crying, Grandma?

Keondra Johnson could hear her grandmother moaning. "Oh, Jesus! My little grandbaby."

Keondra couldn't see her grandmother, but Ms. Johnson was more than an apparition. She appeared in Keondra's mind as she always did: the thin plume of gray hair, those large dark brown eyes, that handkerchief.

But Grandma was away from her apartment, the cocoon she hazarded to leave only in daylight, suffering the glares of the young predators, fearing they would take her weekly tithe from her, a ten-dollar bill crumpled in her bra.

No, Grandma wasn't where she usually was, in the kitchen with its yellow-white linoleum floor.

And Keondra couldn't see the Formica-topped table, where Grandma sat enduring the heat rising from the stove-top flames, escaping the old scorched oven door, as she wiped her thick, wrinkled forehead with that handkerchief she kept in her bra.

Why do you always keep that old handkerchief in your bra, Grandma? Grandma, where am I?

Keondra felt stiff, clean sheets pulled tightly across her chest.

I'm not in my bed. Grandma, why can't I move my arms? What's covering my eyes, Grandma?

Keondra sensed bright light all around her, brighter than the two naked bulbs in the ceiling fixture in her and Lekeesha's bedroom.

Why did they cut off my hair, Grandma? When will they bring my baby to me? I know he's alive. Grandma, I have to tell you what Uncle John did before I—

"We can do nothing else, Ms. Johnson. The wounds are too grave," a man said.

Grandma? What does he mean?

"Not my daughter and her baby, too! Oh, Jesus! Why?" Ms. Johnson said, then plopped her face in her hands. She rolled her head. Her moans filled the room.

The death of her mother came to Keondra; that image of her mother's body lying on the small square of grass floated in Keondra's wandering memory. *Get up, Mama, get up, please! The kids are laughing at your body. They're holding their hands over their mouths, giggling. Not you, too, Jerome! Not you, too!*

Mama, get up. You said you wanted to come back home, remember? But that man, he won't let you. You said you loved me and Lekeesha, remember? You said to listen to Grandma and pray. Oh, Mama, you're shot, too! He shot you, didn't he? They're dancing, mama. Giggling, singing "Ring around the rosy. . ." Oh, Mama. You're dead now, too, aren't you?

"Listen to the doctor, Mama." Uncle John said.

Ms. Johnson rolled her head in her hands. From the muffled groans and tearful heaves, the words "Oh, Jesus! My precious baby!" emerged.

Run, Jerome! I've scooted over to give you room. Run to your apartment, Jerome! Run through the door, up the stairs to your auntie. Run, Jerome. Jerome! He has a gun!

"Ms. Johnson, you should consider signing this so we can shut off the ventilator," the doctor said, extending a legal form in one hand and a pen in the other toward Ms. Johnson's face.

Ms. Johnson lifted her head from her palms, then glanced at the form, then at the pen. She pushed them away. "Oh, Jesus," she said. Then she laid her head on Keondra's bed again. Her thin gray hair rested against Keondra's shoulder. She moved her hand toward Keondra's forearm. The doctor lowered the form next to Grandma's head. He laid the pen on the form.

"Keondra's brain is dead, Ms. Johnson. She has only minimal brainstem activity. Nothing can be done," the doctor said softly.

"Oh, my baby. My poor grandbaby." Ms. Johnson rolled her head again; she tightened her grip on Keondra's forearm. She wailed.

No, Grandma. Don't!

Uncle John picked up the pen, held it upright next to his mother's head. He gripped her shoulder with his other hand and shook her. "Do what he says, Mama. Sign the paper; I want to get outta here," he said.

Get up, Jerome! Get up! You got blood all over me.

Oh, please! You don't have to shoot me, too. I won't tell any—

Pop! Pop!

"I'm with you. I will be in the light," the Voice said.

I heard You in Grandma's church. Tell Grandma what Uncle John did to me. Tell her he came into my bedroom. Tell her I told Lekeesha to turn away, that I put a pillow over her head so she wouldn't see him do it. Tell her I tried to stop him, but he was drunk with that beer he drinks. Grandma knows Uncle John's mean when he's drunk. Tell her! Tell her that after, he jerked the pillow off Lekeesha. He grabbed his bottle of beer, then pointed at her and me. He showed his teeth and squinted his eyes like he always does when he's going to slap us, and then he said, "Tell, and you both be dead on the lawn like your mama."

"No, Keondra, I will not tell," the Voice said. "Even now you must forget those things that are behind and reach to those things that are before you."

It's You! I heard You at the altar of Grandmother's church. I heard You after that boy shot me, after I heard him say, "You betcha you ain't tellin' nobody."

Why can't I move?

Hmmmmm. . .beep. . .beep.

Those machines. I can hear them now. The girls in the projects say babies by relatives are always sickly, Grandma.

7

"It's the right thing to do, Ms. Johnson," the doctor said, after taking the form and pen from Ms. Johnson's hand.

What do you mean, you can't do it today? I gave you Uncle John's money. He's mean. He said he would do it himself! You have to! Girls come here and you just take it out, and they're not pregnant no more. Why do I need a shot? Why do I have to come back in three weeks? They were right, weren't they? Babies by relatives always cause trouble.

Whose baby's crying?

"They'll be here any minute," the director of the Anticipating Parenthood Clinic said. "He's a big male. Label him 'B/M0012.' Get him into the incubator. Make sure the particulars—weight, length, disease-free—are on the invoice. I want all the specs listed; I can negotiate on this one."

It's my baby! My baby boy! Give him back! I don't want to do this no more. I want to name him Michael, not B. . .B. . .02. . .10. . .0M! I want him back!

Oh, I hurt.

"Keondra, sugar," the nurse said, "you're coming around now. You're hearing things, sugar. All our girls have that problem. The doctor says you'll be all right, sugar. Take this. Come on. Swallow. There, there. That's a good little girl. Rest a few minutes. I'll drive you home to your grandma as soon as you can walk."

Grandma! Stop crying and listen! I need to tell you about Unc—the humming, the beeping. . .the machines. They stopped. Grandma! It's getting dark, Grandma. Grandma? I can't brea—

Keondra's chest heaved. She gasped, hard once; then a softer gasp. Then she lay still.

"Oh Jesus. Precious Jesus!" Ms. Johnson hollered.

"Come on, Mama. She's passed," Uncle John said. "Let's just go."

⌞ ⌟

Keondra opened her eyes. She felt different. Weightless and floating, as if she were being supported by a soft breeze. She gazed downward.

Her body lay on the bed below her, her shaved head wrapped in surgical gauze. She saw her grandmother's head facedown on the bed, rolling side to side. Her grandmother moaned through her tears. The moans rose up to Keondra. She could hear soft whispers in them. "I love you, baby."

I know, Grandma. . . .

A doctor stood on the other side of the bed, across from Keondra's grandmother. He leaned over the body. He lifted the right eyelid, then lifted a bright silver penlight from his lab coat pocket. He shone a small, bright light in the corpse's eye. He stood and slipped the penlight back into his pocket as he moved his gaze slowly to Keondra's grandmother.

"She's gone, Ms. Johnson," the doctor said.

Keondra's grandmother quieted. She lifted her head and wiped the tears from her face with the wrinkled white handkerchief. She stared at Keondra's body as she stuffed the handkerchief back into her bra. She let out a soft moan. "I love you, baby," Grandma said softly.

Oh, Grandma, I wish you could see me now.

Ms. Johnson stared at the doctor, then shifted her gaze to Keondra's body. "Jesus. Oh, my dear Jesus, my grandbaby's with you now. I don't feel nothing inside me; I can't cry no more," she said.

Keondra felt the soft breeze getting stronger, but for now, she hovered. Watching, listening.

Another doctor came into the room holding Keondra's chart. He spoke each word as he scribbled the last entry: "The patient expired at twelve-eighteen hours. Primary cause: respiratory failure secondary to massive brain injury secondary to gunshot wounds times two." The doctor stabbed his pen into his lab coat pocket. "This child killing has to stop. Three this month," he said to the other doctor. Then he moved his gaze to Uncle John.

Uncle John lowered his head when the doctor's gaze caught his eyes.

Keondra remembered the night he came into her and Lekeesha's room, but the recollection caused neither pain nor sorrow.

Uncle John shook his head. "Just fourteen," he said as he reached for the doorknob. "What a shame."

———|———

Nothing but light. No ceiling in the room, no roof on the hospital. No sky. Just that powerful, pleasant light. The breeze turned warm and balmy, then intensified to a wind, turning Keondra's flawless body away from the characters in the scene below: Her grandma, trying to remain calm so she could register the last images of her grandchild's body before its final gurney ride; the frustrated physicians, wondering when the children would stop killing each other.

And Uncle John, his hand gripping the doorknob. He fidgeted. Keondra knew. He craved his own comforter, his gold-labeled forty-ounce bottle of Colt 45.

"It's time, Keondra," the Voice said. "Someone waits for you beyond the light."

Keondra looked hard into the light. She could barely make out the silhouette of a familiar woman with a bright glow spreading glistening rays behind her.

"It's Mama!" Keondra shouted. "I'm going to hug Mama!"

"Soon," the Voice said.

"My baby? My baby boy? Where's Michael?"

"He must stay. As long as he is on the earth, he shall not stand on his feet; he shall not see the sun or the stars. But with a gaze of his only eye, he will fulfill his purpose, and on the seventh day thereafter, your baby, Michael, shall be with you with a new body. Now come."

The wind turned and lifted Keondra into flight toward the center of the light, away from the drama of her death below. Keondra flew through the light, into her mother's arms.

WEDNESDAY, JUNE 19,
SEVERAL YEARS LATER

CHAPTER 1

The first time she saw him, he was leering at her through the windshield of a white Ford Crown Victoria that reminded Amanda Collins of her father's unmarked police cruiser. Then she'd locked a defiant stare on his eyes. Even from the distance, she could tell the driver was Italian. Neat, late fifties. He kept his gaze on the building, but the passenger's beady look surveyed the contours of Amanda's body. She glimpsed four, maybe five, gold teeth gleaming in his smirk made crooked by a deformed jaw.

Amanda jerked her gaze down and looked toward the steps leading to the heavy metal door of the Science and Agriculture Building. Boys on the campus of the University of Rhode Island, even professors, stared at her all the time, but the passenger's attention made Amanda uncomfortable in a way those other men hadn't.

She picked up her pace toward the building and ran up the outside stairs. She lunged toward the door handle and breathed deeply when the metallic clack of the door latch sounded behind her. Being inside chased away the feeling of vulnerability brought on by the passenger in the white Ford. He surely would not follow her into this building. If he did, Dr. Hegel would have a few words to say to him. Amanda felt better when that thought passed through her mind.

The second time Amanda saw the Ford parked in the lot, she glanced. Once. The passenger inspected her again, but Amanda looked down as she walked from her staff parking slot to the entrance door.

But this time Amanda parked her gray Toyota Camry in the

students' section on the far south side of the lot. Even now she couldn't avoid being seen as she walked to the door. She could feel the passenger's leer crawling on her. She knew he had straight, thick black hair. She realized she didn't remember seeing his hair, that she had completed his full, frightening features subconsciously. Now, his entire grotesque face reconstructed itself in her mind at the sight of the white Ford.

Clack.

Once inside, Amanda regained her composure and bounded up the stairs in the Agriculture and Science Building to laboratory 214, known as the "BioSysTech lab." Under the terms of the private grant awarded to Avraham Frederick Hegel, M.D., Ph.D., and the University of Rhode Island by Biological Systems Technology, Inc., only Dr. Hegel and Amanda were permitted to enter lab 214.

Out of hundreds of applicants, Amanda had been hired nineteen months ago as Dr. Hegel's research assistant. How fortunate she had felt when he chose her! After all, this was *the* Dr. Hegel. Even before he pioneered work in embryonic brain stem cell transplantation, he had developed a complex lipoprotein that accelerated development of fetal lung tissue when injected into the mother before the tenth week of gestation. It was a treatment he had demonstrated statistically to be over ten times more effective than steroids, but without the dangers steroids posed to the mother and fetus.

Still, Dr. Hegel was best known for his Alfa Alkaloid, an emulsion he formulated to help laboratory animals endure pain while scientists infected and poisoned them and then studied their progress to their deaths.

As she drove to the building to interview for the position of Dr. Hegel's research assistant, Amanda recalled watching members of Brothers and Sisters in Fin, Feather, and Fur on national news, picketing this very same Agriculture and Science Building. She remembered watching CBS News *Reality Check* when the anchor agreed with Brothers and Sisters, reporting that Dr. Hegel's procedure could potentially kill more animals than the test protocols themselves. Looking solemnly into the camera, the news anchor had said, "The procedure used to administer the alkaloid robs the animals of their individual personalities and diabolically diminishes their opportunity to socialize with their fellow animals during their short, cruelly unfortunate lives."

In preparation for her interview, Amanda had read Dr. Hegel's article about the Alfa Alkaloid in the *Journal of Modern Research*. Probably every person involved in pure research using animal studies had read the article. Dr. Hegel had written:

"After determination of the appropriate concentration by means of the footpad prick threshold test, when injected into the frontal lobes of primates or anterior aspect of the brain of lower animals, the alkaloid emulsion maintained the animals in a permanent docile state. Thus, pain associated with gathering data regarding either the induced disease being studied, the toxin being administered, or the allergen being tested was believed to be substantially reduced or virtually eliminated.

"Anesthetic results were remarkably predictable. On a species-to-species basis, based upon weight of the individual animal, with corrections for percent fat, and the concentration of the alkaloid injected into the brain, the effect was virtually straight-line."

Amanda had asked Dr. Hegel about that straight-line phenomenon.

"My dear," he'd said, "I will take time to tell you." Dr. Hegel spoke in perfect English, accentuated by a slight German accent. His intense blue eyes fixed on Amanda's through his gold wire-rimmed glasses and riveted her to her seat.

"The reason the effect is virtually straight-line, I can only speculate. But I believe when the emulsion is injected into the anterior aspect of the animal's brain, the cephalic cells absorb the alkaloid from the emulsion directly and incorporate it into the DNA. The similarity in certain structural building blocks of DNA to those cells and the alkaloid itself supports this mechanism. Incorporating the alkaloid into the DNA strands of the cephalic cells at appropriate levels renders the DNA proportionately inactive. The cells are debilitated, of course, but yet viable. Direct absorption at the molecular level, rather than an indirect intoxication response, I believe accounts for the straight-line response."

"What about the footpad prick threshold test, Dr. Hegel?" Amanda had asked, fully engrossed and realizing she was conversing with the sole individual on the advancing front line of this discipline.

"If you read my paper, you understand that the frontal aspect of the animal's brain controls consciousness, among other things."

One Flew over the Cuckoo's Nest. Amanda wondered why that movie popped into her mind. She drifted a bit.

"Am I boring you, my dear?"

"Oh, no, Dr. Hegel. Please!"

"If the researcher injects too high a concentration of the alkaloid into the brain, the animal will not respond noticeably to the protocol. It will lie limp. It must exhibit some response. So if the animal exhibits pain in his footpad when the researcher pricks it, then the level is fine, as long as the next level of dosage gives little or no instinctive response at all. That, my dear, is the threshold."

"I saw a movie, Dr. Hegel, called *One Flew over the Cuckoo's Nest.* It was about treating the hopelessly insane or unmanageable by destroying their frontal lobes."

Amanda couldn't believe she had just blurted out her thoughts. Confused emotions billowed in her, anger at herself, embarrassment. *He's going to think I'm so immature. A movie! I'm talking about a movie in an interview for the most sought-after postgraduate position in the country!* Amanda remembered that she had wanted to apologize or just die.

Dr. Hegel stiffened in his seat behind his desk. He intertwined his fingers, then lowered his head.

The interview is over, Amanda had thought. *You blew it.*

Dr. Hegel sighed. He acted like he had a lump in his throat.

"What a dark time in the history of medicine," he said, his gaze not quite on her, not quite on anything. Then, a quick question: "In your studies, my dear, did you happen upon the name Dr. Egas Moniz?"

15

The first temptation of the interview. *Make up for lost ground, Amanda. Tell him you have.* Amanda felt like kicking herself.

"No, Dr. Hegel, I haven't. I'm sorry."

"It's not because you didn't study well," Dr. Hegel said. "Physicians and medical historians see to it that Dr. Moniz and his followers are never mentioned in the literature. It is good for you to know that Moniz was a Portuguese neurologist who treated the insane or the chronically unmanageable, or, I should say, those he diagnosed as such. He performed surgery on their brains as treatment."

"You mean like lobotomy?" Amanda asked.

Dr. Hegel nodded, then remained quiet for a moment. "In the 1930s Moniz devised a procedure to destroy portions of his patients' frontal lobes where he believed brain malfunction took place. He published his work in 1936," he said softly, shaking his head slowly.

"An American neurologist, Walter Freeman, improved on Moniz's technique. Freeman developed a simple, in-office procedure. He shocked his patient into unconsciousness with cardiac pads. As the patient lay on Freeman's examination table, he thrust a sterilized ice pick through the soft space between the eyelid and the eye, up though the eye socket of the skull, into the front of the patient's brain."

Dr. Hegel lifted the tip of his right index finger, almost touching the right lens of his glasses. "Then Freeman jiggled the handle of his hardware-store surgical tool." Dr. Hegel paused. He stared at Amanda as he continued. "The sharp point of the ice pick tore the frontal lobe tissue." Dr. Hegel lowered his head. "It's difficult to believe that Freeman's patients left his office at all when they regained consciousness, but God knows they did not leave the same as they had entered."

"Freeman's ice pick procedure became an acceptable treatment?" Amanda asked.

"He called it 'transorbital lobotomy,' " Dr. Hegel said.

Amanda wanted to say something to express outrage, but thought it better to sit still and listen.

"Neurologists refined Freeman's procedure. They didn't use an ice pick; they just went in directly through the skull, leaving X-shaped

16

scars on their patients' foreheads, not unlike my article describes for research animals."

"That's what they did in that movie," Amanda said.

"Hundreds of people were lobotomized," Dr. Hegel said. " 'Psychosurgery' they called it." Dr. Hegel chuckled once, but with a look of disbelief in his eyes. "Moniz had introduced an era of murderous surgery." Dr. Hegel's gaze shifted to nowhere again. He shook his head slowly. "Moniz received the Nobel Prize for his abominable procedure."

"Murderous?" Amanda asked. She had only a vague recollection of the movie, Louise Fletcher as the wicked nurse, Jack Nicholson's mischievous character R. O. McMurphy. But in the last scene, when Nicholson's character lay on the bed, just before the big Indian smothered him with a pillow, those two X-shaped scars below Nicholson's hairline came to her mind. "Psychosurgery." Had she ever encountered the term anywhere? In her studies? In that movie? No. Dr. Hegel was right. They did keep the era quiet. *Politics in everything.*

Dr. Hegel swallowed past another lump when Amanda turned her attention back to him. "I cannot tell you a great deal about the frontal lobes of humans," he said. "No one can. . .not really. I can only say they are developed far beyond primates and that comparable lobes are barely evident in lower animals. In humans, the frontal lobes are the source of a higher order of thinking. This is not only where mere consciousness resides; judgment, creativity, imagination, and emotion reside there as well. It's where the 'person' who we are lives."

Those scars on the forehead of R. O. McMurphy floated into Amanda's mind again. The character was a living corpse, with glazed, unregistering eyes, a human eviscerated of personality.

"Destruction of the frontal lobes leaves a shell of a human with no depth, unable to separate himself from his environment, unable to form bonds with other humans," Dr. Hegel said. He took a deep breath. "I know about the film you saw, my dear," he said softly, his lips quivering. "I could not watch it."

He's going to cry! Amanda thought.

17

"No more, please," Dr. Hegel said. "You must learn some things you will be doing for me. We will discuss those on your first day. . . ."

———

Though nineteen months had passed, Amanda had not forgotten the complex emotions she felt during that interview with this powerful, sensitive man.

Amanda brought her thoughts back to the present. She ran her hand over the black countertop of the lab bench to her right. She had managed to clear her mind of the white Ford and its disturbing passenger during the climb up the stairs from the building entrance area to the BioSysTech lab, just as she had done after the other two encounters with him.

Representations of complex biological molecules entangled with each other had been drawn on the green chalkboard attached to the wall to her left. As she walked to her desk, she passed clean chopping blocks and dissecting pans stacked on the countertop to her right. Soiled chopping blocks and dissecting pans had been piled in the galvanized sink that sat against the wall opposite Amanda's desk, out of her view, but the stench of the residual fetal brain tissue that had adhered to the blocks and pans filled the lab.

Amanda pulled the chair from under her desk and tossed her canvas book satchel under it. She walked along the back wall, along the row of windows that had been nailed shut and painted with thick coats of gray opaque paint. She washed the chopping blocks and dissecting pans, then drenched the sink and drain with Lysol spray. The lab took on the odor of a hospital ward.

On the way back to her desk, Amanda stopped at the file cabinet just a step away from her chair. She unlocked the bottom drawer of the file cabinet and removed the log in which Dr. Hegel had transferred the newest group of patient test data.

Amanda sat down, opened the center drawer of her desk, and grabbed an elastic hair tie. Then she filled her hands with her thick black hair and secured it into a ponytail, feeling coolness at the nape of her neck. Now, except for one more thing, Amanda was ready to work.

She moved her gaze to a gold-framed snapshot sitting to the side of the CPU. Narragansett Bay, Rhode Island, almost a year ago. Geoffry Reagan sat on the sand behind Amanda, his arms around her, his chin on her shoulder. Geoffry's cheek rested against hers, the pale, vulnerable skin of an Irish lad contrasting with the light brown skin of a young black American female.

Can this work? The question intruded on her daydreams every time she looked at the photo.

It can. I know it can! Dr. Hegel was right. If we love each other, backgrounds shouldn't make a difference. We will overcome our difficulties, our differences. Even my father. Amanda had never expected to be so much in love.

She pulled herself from her daydream to the heavy task before her. She turned on the computer, entered her password, and then clicked on the icon labeled "Notes/Reminders to AsstOne.214."

The most recent note read:

> *From AFH:*
> *After today, I shall be out of town and unavailable to everyone, including Mrs. Hegel, until Thursday. On Thursday afternoon, I will be at my usual hotel in D.C. Mrs. Hegel is scheduled to meet me there. She will be attending the White House reception with me. Please read the outline of Monday's seminar. Note the projection slide sequence and load the proper slides in their proper order into the projector. Perhaps you will practice a few times so you will know when to show the appropriate slide without my having to cue you. Please check the brain stem cell viability plates. After you have entered the most recent data, you may take the rest of the week off.*

"Perhaps you will—" Amanda could hear Dr. Hegel's tone when she read those words. He really meant: *"You'd better. . ."* He was just too

polite to say it that way. Or was he? He used to be. Dr. Hegel had changed over the last several months. He was under a lot of pressure. That had to be it. They used to talk, sometimes about the faculty, sometimes about the most important things in Amanda's life: her father, Geoffry, her work. The politicians who had crept into Dr. Hegel's life seemed to have something to do with his becoming more distant.

Okay, Amanda. It's time to get to work. This entry session will take all day.

She cupped the mouse then double-clicked to access the data entry matrix. The hard drive ground its way through the database section of the program, giving Amanda time for a last glimpse at the perfect couple in the photograph. A smile. The matrix appeared. Amanda opened the log and began pecking keys.

Seven states and thirteen hundred miles away, in one of the thirty or so cities in the United States named Columbia, Jackson Griffin Dowell drove his maroon BMW 740i to his office on West 6th Street. He had moved his law practice downtown into the Executive Plaza Building six months ago, away from his comfortable little office near the county courthouse.

Most of Griffin's cases were in federal court now, and even in the posh leather and walnut trim of his BMW, the drive through traffic from his golf course condominium to the heart of downtown Columbia had become hectic.

Griffin's clients, a sort he had never expected to represent, demanded the prestige of a downtown location. When he stopped at West 6th Street and Ardenwood Boulevard, he looked at the Executive Plaza from its base all the way up to its flat roof. How odd the building looked. An eleven-story, black reflective glass office building with its five-level, concrete parking lot. To Griffin, the Plaza looked like two different structures stuck together: the top, warm, shiny black, reflective, and showy; the bottom, cold, dull gray, utilitarian, and plain.

Sometimes when Griffin sat at his desk early in the morning, he was sure he could hear the tenants' cars driving on the narrow concrete driveway of the lot and braking in the reserved slots. Maybe hearing that noise would be reasonable if his office were on the first few floors above the lot. But on the ninth floor? Griffin blamed flimsy construction materials, or perhaps it was because this building was the first in Columbia with an integrated parking lot. They just hadn't known how to do it right back then.

Then again, perhaps during his tour of duty in Vietnam he had honed his sense of hearing to the unusual level needed to keep sane in the pitch-black Southeast Asian forest during the third watch. *"Jesus, are You still with me?"* Griffin had asked so many times, gazing at the stars that gleamed against a cloudless sky.

The front of his BMW dipped and then popped up as Griffin braked into his reserved slot on the fifth parking level at 7:40 in the morning. He walked across the narrow driveway to the parking lot elevator.

When he reached his ninth-floor office, he hung his suit jacket on the antique coat tree just inside the door of his office and then sat behind his desk. Deposition transcripts sat on his desk, one open with a yellow marker resting in the center. Another politician in trouble, looking to J. Griffin Dowell to help him escape what he deserved, at four hundred dollars per hour.

At 8:20 Jennifer Taylor walked into Griffin's office, steadying a cup of coffee in front of her.

"Good afternoon," Griffin said.

"Grumpy this morning, are we?" Jennifer asked. "You might work like a mule, but I have a life outside the stables." Jennifer set the cup on Griffin's desk within his reach, smiled, and strutted out of his office.

Griffin loved Jennifer's quick wit. She would have made a good lawyer, and he had learned to take advantage of that, too. He had found that the best way to analyze factual circumstances surrounding a case was to discuss them with someone else. If the other person was a good conversationalist, pieces would fall into place like a jigsaw puzzle. And

Jennifer was a good conversationalist.

She'd also put up with Griffin's insistence on perfection for four years now. That same obsession had been responsible for his commission as second lieutenant in the marines and for his elite clientele. And no doubt it was the reason seven secretaries over seventeen years had told him, in one way or another, "I quit!"

Griffin returned his attention to the deposition he had been outlining. These inquisitions in the Senate subcommittee chambers were all alike. His client—this time Darion P. Zellars—would be sitting next to him, trained and obedient. Five dapper senators would be peering down on him, television camcorders set on tripods on the sides and at the back of the room, and two microphones in front of each senator. When the cameras rolled, the senators would lean their heads closer to the microphones in front of them. They'd glare at Griffin's client as they questioned him, hunched like stalking lions, growling inane, open-ended questions typical of incompetent, unprepared trial lawyers. But no matter. They'd sound regretfully impolite, and the photo-op was good, too.

Griffin had sat through enough of these ceremonies to know the reasons these senators were there: the publicity and, perhaps, the diminution of the opposing party by destroying the career of one of its members. Their images would come across wonderfully in television news bites, like righteous statesmen, intimidating cross-examiners, attempting only to cull an unworthy one from their privileged and honorable ranks. After hours of this showmanship, with Griffin's coaching, and with a few of his strategically placed objections and soliloquies, the senators elicited little more than confused innuendo. Griffin was well worth his fee.

"Senator Zellars on line one," Jennifer's voice blurted over the intercom.

Griffin picked up the phone, wishing the call had not come so early in the day. Dealing with arrogance wasn't so bad, and contending with ignorance was just part of the job. But arrogance and ignorance residing together in the same person—that took time and effort.

Having politicians such as Zellars as clients provided much practice.

Griffin leaned back in his tan leather chair. "Hello, Senator," he said.

"This is a setup, Dowell. I want to countersue that bimbo."

"I'll set out the strategy, Senator," Griffin said. "We have a lot to talk abou—"

"You bet. They served my wife with that stupid lawsuit, and I want their—"

"Senator, I have a bargain for you."

"A bargain?"

"You're on the clock right now, Senator," Griffin said.

No reply.

"I have important things to learn from you and for you to learn from me. Do you want to do that? Or do you want to whine about your feelings?"

"Obviously you didn't learn bedside manner in school," Zellars said.

"I didn't go to medical school, Senator; I went to law school, just like you. Listen to me when I talk. When I finish, you can speak. I promise I'll listen to you."

"I was just—"

"Senator." Griffin paused, waiting for an interruption. Silence. "You can spend your money on my teaching you conversational theory, or you can spend your money on my learning the facts so that I can defend you. Do you have a preference, Senator?"

"Okay, okay," Zellars said.

"Fine. Now, a sexual harassment suit has been filed against you in federal court in addition to the same charges being brought by the Senate Ethics Committee. What you must do is come to my office so that I can tell you what to expect. I have some ideas we can discuss in your defense. Do you understand?"

"Yes, Mr. Dowell, I understand."

"I'm going to get some preliminary information from you now. When you come to my office, bring your wife. That's important."

"Do I have to?"

23

"Have you ever seen a male politician in real trouble and in public without his wife holding his hand, Senator?" Griffin asked.

———┴———

About twenty minutes into the phone conversation with Zellars, Jennifer stepped quickly into Griffin's office with a Post-it note in her hand and a "you're-not-going-to-believe-this" look on her face. While Griffin continued to talk, she pressed the note to the top of the deposition Griffin had been studying, then jabbed her finger toward it. Griffin lifted the note to eye level.

"The girl was a trap," Zellars said during the lull in the conversation. Griffin returned his attention to the telephone.

"I was set up," Zellars said. "How was I supposed to resist the little bimbo?"

Even though he felt a pang of anger when Zellars said that, Griffin did not respond. He moved the mouthpiece away from his lips, then cupped it and looked up at Jennifer. While Zellars rattled out excuses, Griffin said to Jennifer under his breath, "I don't have Warren on my calendar today."

Jennifer poked at the hold button on Griffin's phone.

"Hold on, Senator," Griffin said. "My secretary will make an appointment for you. Don't discuss your case with anyone, and stop calling the girl 'little bimbo,' even to me. To others it's 'no comment.' Got that, Senator?"

"Yeah, yeah."

Griffin pressed the hold button. He looked up at Jennifer.

"It's something to do with the president," Jennifer said. "He's hard to understand, and, well, I think he might be drunk."

"Send him in," he said.

Warren Jennings suddenly appeared at his office door, unshaven and red-eyed, one front shirttail hanging over his pants under his wrinkled suit jacket.

"Come in, Warren," Griffin said.

Jennifer walked out of the office, appearing to Griffin as if she were trying to avoid looking at the disheveled Jennings. He sat in one of the client chairs in front of Griffin's desk. Griffin wasn't sure, but he thought Jennings might be in some kind of mental shock, even near tears. But his best friend wasn't drunk. There was no sour alcohol smell floating around Jennings, and Griffin knew the smell well. He remembered when that foul air floated around him. Often.

"Well, whatever it is, let's talk about it," Griffin said.

Jennings stared in a way that looked anxious, even frightened. "It's June 19. Seven months after the election," he said. "The Fryes won't let me put their holdings in blind trust. I'm their CPA. I have a right to insist, don't I?"

"Of course you do, Warren, but you know Ashton Frye."

"I tried to talk to President Frye about it, but I can't get past that policy advisor of his, that Redden. Arrogant jerk." Jennings shifted in the chair and ran the palm of his hand across his mouth. "They're testing the media's bias on this one."

"I haven't seen you at the club for weeks," Griffin said. "You're not going to deal with that weight problem sitting behind your desk."

"Are you listening to me, Griffin?"

Good, Warren. Get mad. Get frustrated. Tell me why you popped into my office like this. "You're not in this shape because Ashton Frye is uncooperative with you. He's uncooperative with everyone, except Constance. You know that. Everybody in the country knows that." Griffin leaned back in his chair. "So what's the real problem?" he asked.

Jennings took a deep breath. "They're following me," he said. "They intend to keep me quiet. Kill me, I think. Maybe even Carolyn and the kids, too."

"That partner of yours?" Griffin meant it as a joke. *Bad timing, Griffin.*

"It's not Walter. It's Ashton and Constance, or whoever does things for them. Maybe you're the president's personal attorney and you think you know him better than me, but that's true, anyway."

"Talk, Warren. Stop the sniveling and make sense."

25

"Have you heard of Biological Systems Technologies?" Jennings asked.

"The Hegel matter? Baby brain research?" Griffin asked.

"How much do you know?" Jennings asked. His voice cleared. Griffin sensed hope in it.

Griffin quickly ran his impression of then Governor Ashton Roosevelt Frye through his mind. Governor Frye had asked him to look into Dr. Richard Landcaster and this new company called Biological Systems Technologies. The governor wanted Griffin's opinion as to whether he should invest—secretly, of course. After Griffin read the investigator's report, he recalled his advice to the governor: "How can you invest in a company that won't tell you what they do? Especially a company headed up by this Landcaster?" he had asked Frye.

A few days later, Constance Frye had telephoned Griffin. "I'll be investing myself, Dowell," Constance had said. "Call off your snoop. And don't discuss this with anyone. Attorney-client privilege, counselor. Remember that, or I'll be using your license as a place mat."

"The company's name has come across my desk," Griffin told Warren. "More than that, I'm not able to say."

"Landcaster lost his license to practice medicine. They use him," Jennings said.

"I know about Landcaster," Griffin said. The photographs Griffin's investigator had taken of Landcaster flashed in his mind: a sixty-something Don Juan with a gray, sprayed-stiff Elvis coiffure and a little diamond in his ear. Griffin recalled that Landcaster had telephoned him at least twice in the last two years. "Take a message," he had said to Jennifer. Jennifer explained that he wanted to discuss retaining Griffin to help get a state license to practice. "Not interested," Griffin had told Jennifer. *Not for a thousand an hour,* he had thought. Representing politicians who gave into the winks and pawing of pages was one thing. Serving as an attorney for a doctor who performed abortions at any term of a pregnancy—how could he explain *that* to God?

"Tell me everything you know about BioSysTech," Griffin said to Jennings.

The accountant drew in a big breath, clasped his hands, and rested his elbows on the arms of the chair. "BioSysTech is the general managing partner," he said. "It takes a percentage of profit off the top. Constance Frye owns twenty-five percent; she's the plurality shareholder. It's none of my business who the other equity owners are, but I usually find out with other clients." Jennings paused, then ran his fingers through his hair.

"Is there more?" Griffin asked.

"I don't think they want me to know that much about BioSysTech, Griffin," Jennings said. "I don't think they want me to know anything about BioSysTech anymore."

"Who are the silent partners?" Griffin asked.

"There's only one, Biological Systems Technologies, Inc., incorporated in Delaware about nine years ago. Constance is the plurality shareholder there, too."

"Who set up the corporate structures?" Griffin asked.

"A New York lawyer," Jennings said. He paused and furrowed his brow. "England. . .I'm not sure. . ."

"Kristina England," Griffin said.

"How did you know?"

"I'm the president's private attorney," Griffin said. "You need only be remotely connected to Washington, D.C., politics to learn who the major players are. Keep talking."

"I haven't learned much about these companies in the time I've been the Fryes' CPA. The returns weren't impressive, not until four years ago. Sixty thousand that year; a hundred thirty-seven the next," Jennings said.

Griffin hunched his shoulders. "So far, Constance is a smart investor," he said.

"The companies are big on charity, too. Ever hear of Anticipating Parenthood, Inc.?"

"Go on," Griffin said.

"The companies donate a lot of money to Anticipating Parenthood and other nonprofits, all politically aggressive. Committee on

27

Children's Rights. Brothers and Sisters in Fin, Feather, and Fur. And an environmental group. . .I can't think of the name," he said.

"Go on," Griffin said.

"They're all represented by England," Jennings said, then stared at Griffin.

Griffin had to think about that. Did a connection exist between BioSysTech's donations and England's representation? Of course a connection existed. But so what?

"A lot of companies donate to charity," Griffin said.

"Griffin, they're following me."

"Who, Warren? Who's following you?" Griffin asked in a tone that he knew sounded out the frustration that had been welling up in him.

"Three months ago the Fryes sent me their latest income information," Jennings said. "They sent other documents, too. Reports, readouts, and financial statements of the BioSysTech companies."

"That's how you discovered the donations?" Griffin asked.

Jennings wiped his forehead and then ran two fingers under his collar. "They couldn't have wanted me to see those documents," he said.

Griffin waited, saying nothing, while Jennings gathered his thoughts, or, it occurred to Griffin, his courage.

Jennings clasped his hands and rested his elbows on the chair again. He leaned slightly toward Griffin. "There are no transactions," he said. "The BioSysTech companies are doing something, performing services, maybe selling things, but there's no record of activities, no inventory, no services in exchange for money." Jennings fixed his gaze on Griffin's eyes and waited.

"What about records you don't have?" Griffin asked.

"The corporate records they sent are the ones that would show that information," he said. "Trust me on that, Griffin. I'm the CPA." Jennings shook his head slowly. "So much money is being grossed."

Griffin leaned forward in his chair. "How much?" he asked.

"Millions. Ten, twelve, annually." Jennings paused. "Do you know how much the Fryes invested in this venture, Griffin?"

Professional ethics prevented Griffin from saying what he knew.

The last he had heard of BioSysTech was during that telephone call from Constance, years ago. This was going to be interesting.

"Seven thousand dollars," Jennings said in a tone resounding with disbelief. "The records they sent show that was loaned to them."

"Was Ashton governor then?" Griffin knew the answer, but he had to ask.

"Constance did the signing, but I didn't come here to—"

"Why did you come here, then?"

Jennings clasped his hands again. "Have you heard rumors about Landcaster?" he asked.

"Tell me."

"About suicides or people who know too much disappearing?"

"I said I know about Landcaster," Griffin said. Nothing in the investigator's reports suggested that Landcaster arranged killings. Griffin couldn't imagine this pinkie ring–clad libertine arranging hit contracts.

"You're going to the White House Friday, to Dr. Hegel's reception, right?"

Griffin nodded.

"Tell Constance that I won't talk—that she doesn't have to worry about me. Tell both of them! You've got to tell them!"

"Warren," Griffin said softly. "If someone's following you, Constance Frye has nothing to do with it, I'm sure." Then he remembered her comment about his license. *Am I sure?* he thought. *Come on, Griffin!*

Jennings folded in the seat. "You've got to believe me!" he said.

Griffin waited for Jennings to settle down. "Before I say anything to the president, I need to see the documents they sent to you myself. I'll send a courier to your office Monday morning."

Jennings lifted his head and wiped his nose with the back of his right hand, then stared at Griffin with his swollen, red eyes.

"I want a copy of your entire BioSysTech file with the documents, too," Griffin said. "Make the copies at one of those copy places; I don't want Walter to know. We're taking a risk here. I don't have to tell you those documents are confidential."

Jennings nodded.

"I'll decide whether I should talk to the president. I won't mention this at Hegel's reception," Griffin said.

"Please, Griffin. . ."

"On Monday, if I decide nothing's there, that's the end of the matter as far as I'm concerned."

"Monday might be too late, Griffin."

⌐ ⌐

President Ashton Frye leaned against the headboard in the bedroom of the Residential Wing of the White House. Constance Frye sensed excitement in her husband's voice as he explained his new tax plan. She set her gaze on the crooked smile that he showed when he spoke with confidence.

The first lady fluffed her pillows with a few slaps of her palms. She leaned into the softness and shifted her shoulders, then positioned herself so that she could look directly into her husband's eyes as he spoke.

He can't really mean what he's saying, Constance Frye thought while the president explained his new tax plan. Under this plan, organ recipients would have to pay a tax of 75 percent of the amount charged for the new organ, maybe more if it were a heart.

"The investment would be paid into a new federal agency in exclusive control of organ distribution," the president said. He threw up his hands. "We could levy any tax we wanted, the recipients are so desperate." The president smiled that crooked smile again. "And it's only fair to move money from those who happen to have a lot to those to whom fate has given so little."

The first lady inspected her husband's face as he continued his verbal musings. His tan was gone, she noticed, and a double chin was forming. All of those dinners with prime ministers, kings, and such, without the chance to exercise like he did when he was governor—all of that was taking its toll on his once lanky form. Being president was more difficult than being governor. More people to maneuver, and the national press watching, not to mention the self-righteous right-wingers. She moved her gaze from her husband's hazel eyes to the streaks of gray that seemed to glisten against his near black hair. *The fundamentalist religious right will move this country back into the Dark Ages, Ashton. That's what you need to worry about.*

"Sure, there will be some opposition. But when it comes down to it, most people will accept this tax," the president said. "After all, few people think of themselves as organ recipients. It's a classic 'someone else has to pay it so I don't care about it' kind of proposition."

Constance remained quiet while her husband continued to justify the tax. While those in the poverty class were alive, he reasoned, the federal government had nurtured their organs, grew them sort of, especially organs in the young, chronically unemployed. Even though the people were dead now, their organs still possessed value, particularly the organs from the estimated 60 or so percent of the dead folks who—according to the statistical demographic studies by the Center for Disease Control in Atlanta—had no disease or systematic bacterial venereal infection or AIDS virus contaminating their organs. Maybe only a bullet screwing up the transplantability of a heart or liver.

While they were alive, the president explained, their organs had grown from the embryonic stage to full adulthood on federal entitlements—Medicaid, Aid to Families with Dependent Children, Section 8 subsidies, food stamps, school breakfast and lunch programs, Head Start, and a host of other federal government handouts. So a federal excise tax charged to recipients who benefited from that subsidized organ growth was only fair. The federal government was like a farmer, he told Constance.

"Let's talk more about it in the morning," Constance said.

"You can introduce the idea as a part of your own agenda, if you like," the president said.

"We'll talk about that," Constance said.

The president reached to his bedside table and turned off the lamp. He scooted to a prone position and pulled the covers to his shoulder.

Constance pondered her husband's idea under the soft glow of the bedside table lamp as his breathing turned into soft snores. The folks weren't taxed too much; that wasn't the reason there would be no federal excise tax on human organ purchases anytime soon. Her husband's justification seemed far-fetched—but was it philosophically correct? If a citizen had been supported by the federal government during his or her life, could the government claim implied ownership of that citizen's organs upon death, simply by virtue of the benefits the federal government had provided while the citizen's organs grew at the government's expense?

Of course, the government had to wait for the citizen to die first, Constance mused, even if the citizen contributed nothing to the federal treasury—unless, of course, the citizen would agree to higher federal benefits for a shorter life span; the shorter the life span agreed upon, the higher the benefits. A chuckle came. *Just which way would Senator Jeremiah Gators vote on that!*

She shifted, reached under the lampshade, and turned off the light. She slid under the covers and turned on her side, her back toward the president. The new tax would bring organ transplantation to public discussion, she mused. Radio talk show hosts, conservatives such as Jeremiah Gators, the op-ed page debate, cable news shows, the religious right. All of that would lead to scrutiny of the human organ industry by some journalist she might not be able to reach. A few newspaper editors who did not worship her still worked out there. Not all journalists were like Andrea Rue.

Even considering the new source of federal revenue and whose money would be redistributed by her husband's proposed tax, she couldn't allow anything that might raise public curiosity. She had worked too hard and had come too far. Nothing could be allowed that might tip the supply-and-demand scale for human organs toward the supply side. Not yet. Not until her Reproductive Rights Products Reform Bill passed Congress and her husband had signed the reform into federal law. Everything was so close, so fragile. She saw herself pacing in front of him, her hands clasped behind her back. "Now,

Ashton, let's discuss your new tax," she would say.

We can't allow religious fundamentalists like Gators to set our society back—not now, not ever, the first lady thought. She closed her eyes and slept.

THURSDAY, JUNE 20

CHAPTER 2

Kristina England tried to work out the grogginess the short sleep had caused. As she stepped out of her bedroom and slipped on her robe, she remembered Becky Ingram leaving at, what was it, 1:00 in the morning? Later, maybe?

Becky had complained that she'd had no idea such institutions and positions existed: honorary chairman of the National Academy of Sciences, head of the Institute of Medicine of the National Research Council, chairman of the Committee on Fetal Research, fellow and chairman of this society, board member of this one and that one. Becky had flopped on the white leather sofa in the center of England's Manhattan penthouse living room. "I want to speak every word from memory without glancing once at my outline," Becky had said.

England chuckled as she walked to the kitchen. *It's only the introduction, Becky.*

The national press would be there. The final speaker, the first lady herself, the darling of the media, demanded a perfect ceremony. Public perception—or misperception, if need be—was perhaps the most important element in the effort to change federal law, to pass Constance Frye's reforms that would legalize the secret business of BioSysTech.

England stepped into the kitchen. She opened the refrigerator and pulled out four carrots, six apples, and half a package of precut celery stalks. She set the vegetables and fruit on the counter next to the juicer and reached for the knife block.

The telephone rang. She stepped quickly to the wall phone next to the kitchen door and lifted the handset.

"Hello?"

"Kristina?"

"What do you want?" England asked. "It's six o'clock!"

"We had a problem at the facility," Richard Landcaster said.

England paused. "Just tell me what you mean," she said, then moved the handset away from her ear to move strands of hair.

"Hegel didn't take the visit well," Landcaster said. "Jacqueline said he was all right until he saw the Alfa Alkaloid injection scars on B/M0012's forehead. That's when he retched. She sent me surveillance videos by special courier. We definitely have problems."

"Tell me what happened and when so I can deal with it," England said. "Don't try to impress me with medical jargon. Start at the beginning; don't jump around in time and space. This is too important." England braced the receiver between her jaw and shoulder. The coiled receiver cord slithered, following England's stroll back to the knife block and juicer.

"The guy got there yesterday about ten in the morning. He spent the night in Ozark," Landcaster said. "I told Jacqueline, you know, I wasn't sure how he would respond because of his religious background and to watch him closely. I left the judgment up to her. Like you told me."

"Good." England drew the butcher knife from its slot in the wood block.

"Jacqueline took him on a vanilla tour at first: the quality control lab and shipping room. She decided not to show him the incinerator. You know, the guy being Jewish and all." Landcaster paused.

England slammed the blade of the butcher knife on the chopping block. "Get on with it!"

"Even in the operating room, the guy seemed fine to Jacqueline. She thought he'd be all right after that. So she took him to Level 2." Landcaster paused, then said, "You can see it all on the tape; he paled as soon as the computer opened the growing area entrance door."

"Well?" England said, wondering what she would do with the great Avraham Hegel the Squeamish.

"Jacqueline walked with him along the incubator wall. She stopped at B/M0012," Landcaster said. "On rare occasions she's pretty smart."

Come on, Landcaster, get this over with.

"B/M0012's incubator is directly in line with a mid-wall camera. She told Hegel it was our oldest conceptus. Even behind his glasses, you can see the guy's eyes glazing over and sweat beading on his forehead."

As Landcaster spoke, England remembered the impression that had shot through her mind when Constance Frye introduced Landcaster to her. "Kristina," the first lady had said, "this is our CEO, Dr. Richard Landcaster."

This peacock? He'll spend more time chasing skirts for his two-hundred-thousand-dollar salary than anything else. England had shaken Landcaster's hand and forced a smile.

Landcaster began chuckling in his description of Hegel's reaction to B/M0012 stretched out in its incubator. *Where did you find this man, Constance?* England reached for an apple and cut it in half, then in quarters.

"Jacqueline pointed out the two surgical X scars on B/M0012's forehead left by the injection of Hegel's alkaloid. When she told him she had made adjustments in his emulsion to compensate for, you know, the rapid metabolism and high body fat not encountered in other laboratory species, the guy dry heaved again. Hard. . .twice," Landcaster said through more chuckles.

England finished chopping the apples and shoved them aside with the knife blade. She started on the carrots.

Landcaster continued, "Jacqueline began discussing his footpad pain threshold test. She was testing him, you know. She told Hegel it was better to prick the roof of the conceptuses' mouths rather than the balls of their feet. The tissue is thinner at the roof of the mouth, the pain-sensing nerves closer to the surface, she told him, and—"

"Is that so?" England asked.

"Yes," Landcaster said. "Then Hegel looked at B/M0012 again, and you know, I never would have believed it, but I swear it happened."

England stood rigid. "What?" she asked.

"B/M0012 opened its remaining eye and moved it until it fixed its gaze on Hegel. Looked right into the guy's eyes. It almost seemed like B/M0012 recognized Hegel. Like it tried to say something to him. That's impossible, of course. But Jacqueline saw it, too. She said it does not make sense for the conceptus to open its eye, to have an interest. . . . The orbital lobes. . .they weren't affected by the alkaloid lobotomy, but the consciousness part, you know, the. . .cognizance. . .because of the alkaloid, you know, chemically lobotomizes. Jacqueline said B/M0012 is an exceptionally strong conceptus. . . . I don't underst—"

"I don't care about all that," England said. "You're beginning to ramble." England braced the phone hard, then dumped the chopped apples, carrots, and celery into the colander and walked over to the sink, the cord slithering behind her. "Just tell me what happened next."

"Hegel froze stiff, in a fixed stare at B/M0012, like he went into a coma for thirty seconds. All his color left him." Landcaster chuckled. "He turned and ran toward the door, slapped the growing area exit button. The doors opened just in time."

"He vomited?" England turned the rinse water off. She stepped two steps to the juicer.

"Not right then," Landcaster said. "He made it to the hall rest room, jerked his surgical mask under his chin as he ran in the bathroom. We have two surveillance cameras in that bathroom. The tapes are worth the price of admission."

England couldn't understand Hegel's compassion for an undefined mass of throbbing, profitable tissue. She turned and leaned her back against the counter. She felt weary of this conversation, of Landcaster's wallowing in it.

"He took off his glasses, splashed cold water on his face, and then wiped up. Then he pulled wads of paper towels out of the wall dispenser. The guy went back into the stall, got on his knees, and wiped the toilet rim and stall floor." Landcaster burst out in laughter, then stopped. "The great Avraham Hegel," he said, catching his breath, "the world's greatest medical researcher, wiping his own vomit off the bathroom floor and toilet rim. It's something to see—"

"What next?" England cut him off.

"Jacqueline waited in the hall. When the guy came out, he said he must have caught an intestinal virus, that he better not go back to the growing area or he might, you know, contaminate the conceptuses. That's when he told Jacqueline he wanted to get back to Ozark so he could catch the next shuttle."

"What time did he leave?" England asked.

"Eleven. Maybe a few minutes after. Would you like a copy of the tapes?"

England halted. "If you don't destroy those tapes without copying them, you'll find yourself dating a few inmates, or maybe you won't find yourself at all," she said.

"All right, all right."

"That car we gave Hegel—is it working properly?"

"Perfectly," Landcaster said.

"And the Cayman account?"

"There, just like, you know, you said."

"Do nothing," England said. "Tell Jacqueline to forget the episode. Tell her I'm taking care of it." England lowered the receiver to her side.

"Kristina. Kristina. You there, Kristina?" She could only take so much of Dr. Richard Landcaster. She lowered the receiver slowly into the cradle and stepped to the juicer. *I should telephone Becky. No need for her to worry about looking at her outline now.*

Constance Frye had been awake for about thirty minutes and was already sipping her second cup of coffee before the president stirred. Ashton Frye turned toward his wife and opened his eyes. She leaned toward her bedside table and pressed the intercom button.

"The president would like his coffee now, Rosalie," she said.

Constance turned toward her husband. "I've been thinking about your tax, darling," she said.

The president yawned and stretched. He sat up and moved his pillows against the headboard, seeming to fight grogginess.

"It isn't a good idea. Not now," Constance said. She turned and leaned over again to the intercom. She poked the button hard. "Rosalie, did you hear me? The president would like his coffee. Now!" She turned back to the president and said softly, "Kareem Jukali and his caucus would object to the racial implications."

As Constance set her cup and saucer on her bedside table, Rosalie scurried into the bedroom holding a tray. On the tray sat a silver insulated carafe embossed with the presidential seal and a cup rattling on a saucer. Rosalie stopped on the president's side of the bed and set the tray on the bedside table, then poured coffee into the cup.

"Anything else?" Rosalie asked, trembling.

Constance glared at her and motioned her away with her arm. Then she aimed the remote control from her bedside table at the television. Time for Cable Political News Network's seven o'clock news headlines. Thirty-something Andrea Rue sat behind the news desk looking directly into the camera, brown eyes, neat hairdo, pretty in her blue business suit with a crisp white blouse.

"A *New York Times* poll taken yesterday shows that people don't trust home schooling," Andrea said. "By a margin of—"

That's my next reform, Constance thought disdainfully. *Home schooling. What they really mean is Sunday school classes!* She turned to her husband, ready to say something about those foolish women who stay at home with their children, but the president appeared still lost in his musings about his new tax. Lyrics from John Lennon's "Imagine" passed through her mind, Lennon's smooth voice evangelizing the world that Constance so often contemplated: people living life in peace, meditating upon their karma, owning no possessions, and carrying on without the opiate of some almighty fantasy of God. *Why don't people see it? If only they could see.*

"Experts say we should think of children as all of ours," Andrea said.

Constance turned to the president. "An organ tax based on a justification that the organs had been grown by government entitlements carries racial implications," she said softly.

"The Black Caucus isn't a problem, honey. Jukali owes me," the president said.

"Ashton," Constance said, forcing a soft tone, "don't you think payback for my going around the country lobbying for Jukali's precious Hate Crime Handgun Disarmament Act should be support for my reforms, not for this organ tax of yours?"

The president paused.

"Remember when we talked about your running for office?" the first lady asked. "Remember you promised me we would share in policy making, that I would do more than making appearances in first-grade classes or making up trite slogans against smoking or drugs for kids to babble in the school yard? Remember, Ashton?"

"Honey—"

"You know who we have to fight to get my reforms enacted."

"Well, I think—"

"What is Senator Gators going to say?" Constance asked, contorting her face and wagging her head, " 'Getting government involved inside people now, hey, Mr. President?' He'll use your tax against you in the reelection campaign. I think you should save it for your second term." She turned away from the president and looked toward the television.

The president threw up his hands. "I don't understand where Jeremiah Gators gets his power," he said, more to himself than to the first lady. "You might be right, honey. I'll—"

"Shhh!" Constance lifted the remote toward the television and raised the volume.

"Dr. Hegel reported in the *American Medical Research Journal* that embryonic brain stem cell transplantation will be used routinely for such diseases as Parkinson's disorder, Alzheimer's disease, and even cloning," Andrea said. "Hegel wrote that the most formidable obstacle isn't the unknowns of medical science. Fellow researchers are rapidly finding answers." Andrea paused, then presented a particularly stern look into the camera. "The uncertainties arising from politicizing the procedure and misplaced, narrow moral values are the real obstacles," she said. "The scientific community is nearly united in the opinion that Hegel's research is vital for the children of this country."

"Good, Andrea. Good!" Constance said softly.

"The first lady is expected to announce tomorrow night at a White House reception that Dr. Hegel will be the science advisor for her reform bill. CPNN has also learned from reliable sources that Dr. Hegel will likely be the next U.S. surgeon general after the first lady's reform bill passes Congress. CPNN attempted to interview Dr. Hegel, but he could not be reached.

"We'll have more on this important medical development at three-thirty this afternoon. Our medical correspondent, Dr. Cynthia Kennedy-Welmeyer, will discuss Constance Frye's reform bill with attorney Kristina England, the first lady's reform policy advisor."

Andrea Rue spun her chair toward the sports anchor. "What an impressive list of special people trying to look out for the children, Barton," she said.

"You bet, Andrea. Too bad the Mets don't have the first lady to manage their team." He turned and showed a perfect grin to the camera. "Yesterday, the miserable Mets were embarrassed by none other than. . ."

Constance jumped out of bed, not bothering with her slippers. She hurried to her dressing area and began undoing the buttons on her pajama top. *Good report, Andrea. I want to hear my name and "for the children" in that interview over and over again, just like Madeline told you.*

"Okay, honey, I'll hold off on the organ tax," the president said.

CHAPTER 3

Nine forty-five.

It was late in the morning for Amanda to begin her lab chores, but few would know. She'd seen only one faculty member in the building, Professor Paul Treadaway, a tenured professor with questionable competence and unquestioned resolve to do nothing but hone his Shakespeare. He was stumpy with late middle-aged male pattern baldness. Only a few days after Dr. Hegel had hired her, Amanda acquired the notion that Treadaway would not be satisfied without causing a soap opera in the department and then steering the plot from the shadows. Best avoided, Amanda had resolved.

Most of the graduate students didn't bother showing up today, either. As the week progressed, a relaxed attitude toward work was becoming evident. What would it be like on Friday? Probably like the day before the Christmas holidays begin.

Dr. Hegel had predicted this holiday atmosphere. "The mediocre are always at their best," he had said with a hint of cynicism in his tone. Amanda had to admit that Dr. Hegel was changing. He wasn't the man who had interviewed her for this job. He'd had a kind, spiritual nature then. But now, he was just—just different.

By 10:30 Amanda had finished entering the latest patient test data in the BioSysTech program and had completed the preliminary observations for growth of brain stem cells in the nutritive medium of the petri dishes. Even without the dyes, she could see signs of cephalic cell growth. Amanda would send the new batch of fetal cells to surgeons in the New England area after Dr. Hegel prepared them.

He always prepared them alone. The surgeons transplanted the fetal cells in the brains of patients with confirmed Parkinson's disorder and Alzheimer's disease. They then sent original studies showing bimonthly results of neurological readings, muscle coordination tests, and cognitive studies back to Dr. Hegel. Pages upon pages of numbers. Dr. Hegel transferred the raw data to the log. He insisted that only he transfer the data.

Amanda understood why. Dr. Hegel had explained it during training: "If, my dear, you enter just one incorrect datum in the log, that small factor could skew the results." Dr. Hegel trusted no one else with the data for just that reason, and his transferring the raw data into the log was fine with Amanda. What would he do now if she committed just one fundamental error?

On more than one occasion, Amanda had thought about the source of the cells. She had never seen the brains, only the bits and the stains of dried juices that stuck to the chopping blocks and dissecting pans she washed for Dr. Hegel. He chopped and dissected alone, usually on Sunday nights. Neither Amanda nor anyone else, as far as she knew, saw the scraps of skulls and unusable fetal tissue. *What does he do with them?* She never asked.

Dr. Hegel, at least lately, likened his research to war. "We are foot soldiers," he said, his German accent intensifying, "taking one portion of land, then another."

"The enemy is ignorance," Dr. Hegel now said often. "Ignorant people all around me do not understand that this battle must be won so that the new battle may begin."

Just last week, while Amanda sat at her desk, Dr. Hegel had talked to himself during the final rinse of the harvested fetal brain stem cells, lifting and tilting the flasks, swirling them, then staring at the turbid, twirling contents. "Sometimes we march for evil generals," Dr. Hegel had said softly as he poured the contents onto a filter.

What does that mean? Amanda had wondered, pretending she hadn't heard him.

But today Amanda had other things, wonderful things, to think about. It was a beautiful day, too. There'd been no sign of the white Ford this morning, and she and Geoffry had planned to have lunch at his work, the microbiology and med-tech lab at Hope Valley Community Hospital.

Amanda decided to take Dr. Hegel's outline, the projector, and the slides to her apartment directly after lunch. She couldn't rehearse in the lab or even in the building. Telephone calls interrupted this virtual holiday—perhaps ten or more an hour—all for Dr. Hegel. Physicians, philosophy students, pastors, reporters, pro-life activists, pro-choice activists called, all wanting to attend Monday's seminar.

Amanda had heard Dr. Hegel talk about Dr. Landcaster, the head of BioSysTech. Landcaster had snarled at the thought of any public seminar and only grudgingly relented after Dr. Hegel wrote him a letter insisting that prepublication seminars be permitted. "You may do prepublication seminars, but the seminars are restricted to department faculty and graduate students," Dr. Landcaster had ordered. The URI administration didn't mind the restriction. Amanda had heard the administration dreaded another demonstration. Brothers and Sisters of Fin, Feather, and Fur fretting about animal research was one thing; nobody cared but them, really. But an on-campus clash between pro-lifers and pro-choicers, anti-fetal part research and pro-fetal part research, was another matter.

News about the seminars had reached all the way down to the student body. The university president had ordered crowd control plans for Monday involving campus police. "The ignorance is out of hand," Dr. Hegel had told Amanda when he learned that college administrators had notified the Rhode Island State Police, too. Amanda envisioned riot police with their shielded helmets, long nightsticks, and tear gas launchers surrounding the building.

Monday's seminar was titled "Mechanisms in Repair or Regeneration of Traumatized and Genetically Impaired Human Brain Cells by Fetal Brain Stem Cell Transplantation." It would be the third and last in a series of prepublication seminars.

Amanda had sat in the front row during Dr. Hegel's first seminar as he discussed the healing effects after transplanting fetal brain stem cells in humans suffering from Parkinson's disorder and Alzheimer's disease. She remembered him strutting behind the lab bench, with its slate-black top and curved chrome faucet. He always wore a white lab coat in the building and for his seminars. Amanda could feel the students and professors staring at Dr. Hegel from behind her, all the way to the high last row in the huge sunken auditorium known to the graduate students as "the Pit."

Dr. Hegel strode from one end of the blackboard to another, sometimes moving his gaze all the way up to the top row, then to the side, then down to the bottom row. One time during the first seminar, he had glanced at Amanda with a smile. Amanda's pride swelled.

Dr. Hegel pointed with his worn wood pointer; he drew on the chalkboard, then erased, then drew again. He showed overheads of streams of numbers, explaining the significant differences between the test groups and controls. The fetal brain stem cells were the new wonder. They defied conventional wisdom of cellular physiology. They were not predestined to be a particular kind of cell. No! They could differentiate into the very sort of nerve cell the patient needed to replace his defective ones. From the beginning to the end, not an attendee so much as whispered. Amanda knew they all felt as she did; it was an awesome privilege to listen to the sword-wielding, five-star general of the cutting-edge army of medical researchers slicing the silent air in the Pit.

In his second seminar, Dr. Hegel described the implications of transplanting fetal brain stem cells in patients whose nervous systems were damaged not by disease but by trauma. Amanda had arrived early so she could sit in the same seat she had in the first. Just like before, she couldn't take her eyes off her general, couldn't allow her attention to wander. She was a part of it, after all.

In Monday's upcoming seminar—the last—Dr. Hegel had promised to present his theories in plain, narrative language and colorful slides, rather than an hour or so of chalk and blackboard, projected charts and graphs, correlation coefficients, and standard deviations.

He promised to explain these miraculous healing responses with an emphasis on how they would lead to the eradication of nerve disorders in humans, or even to the regeneration of spinal cords. Those condemned to a wheelchair would walk again; Alzheimer's disease and Parkinson's disorder would follow polio, scarlet fever, and diphtheria into the faint memories of past generations.

And Monday's seminar would also mark the end of Dr. Avraham Hegel's career as a modern pioneer research scientist and the beginning of his life in national politics. "On the leash of the first lady," Professor Treadaway had mumbled. *He's so envious*, Amanda thought when his murmuring reached her.

Finished with her work, Amanda shut down the computer and then shot a glance at the photograph. She jumped from her chair and tossed her satchel over her shoulder, then picked up the projector and exited the lab.

Even with her heavy load, she skipped a few times along the way to her Toyota, ponytail bouncing in rhythm with the satchel. Now she had only one more thing to deal with—a meaningful talk with Geoffry Reagan—the most important conversation in her life, Amanda believed.

⌐   ⌐

Jennings paced in front of Jennifer's desk. He pushed his hands in his pockets and then pulled them out. He ran his right hand through his hair.

"Please, Warren, calm down," Jennifer said. Goose bumps popped up on her arms.

Jennings suddenly lunged toward Jennifer. He slammed down his palms and hunched over her desk.

"You have to tell me how I can reach him!"

Jennifer couldn't believe this was the same man who, when he had called over the years, had always had a joke to tell her before getting down to business. She felt her hands trembling but forced herself to present a calm, firm front.

"Warren, I told you, Griffin's in a Senate subcommittee meeting. When I tell you he has arranged his luggage to be sent directly to the airport, I'm not lying," she said.

Jennings straightened. He strode to the window and stared out over Columbia. She watched Jennings run his hand through his hair again and then lower his head. "What am I going to do?" he said.

"Everything will be all right," Jennifer said. "Just get those copies ready for our courier Monday morning like Griffin asked you."

Jennings whirled around. "They're really following me, Jennifer. I saw them. And they know I saw them."

CHAPTER 4

The plates of hot food at Hope Valley Community Hospital cafeteria reminded Amanda of the TV dinner she saw Lucy serve to Desi on an old rerun, except the dull white multisectioned plates were microwavable plastic, not gleaming aluminum. And the large Styrofoam cup Amanda had filled to the brim with water didn't help, either.

The glossy white linoleum floor reflected the bright fluorescent lighting. Seven fake walnut-topped tables, each with four black plastic contour chairs with chrome-plated legs, crowded the small eating area. Not a girl's idea of a cozy, dimly lit place for a romantic lunch.

Still, the thought came to Amanda that maybe this place was appropriate for Geoffry to tell her the truth about his feelings. That thought caused her heart to thump and her throat to feel a little dry. She lifted the cup carefully, sipped, and then set it back down, listening to her boyfriend prattle on about things that failed to generate her interest.

"Is Dr. Hegel really going to be the next surgeon general after the first lady's law is passed?" Geoffry asked.

"Geoffry," Amanda said, feeling a twinge of disappointment that their time together was focusing on this subject, "Dr. Hegel has reached the peak in his field. He's gotten everything but the Nobel Prize, and no one would be surprised if they gave him that, too. Younger, aggressive researchers at big university hospitals financed by copycat grants are catching up with him. Some researchers refute his theories, even his results. They're eager young gunfighters like in those old westerns, showing up to challenge the fastest man in town."

"I under—"

"Doctors in hospitals like this walk around in their green scrubs and starched lab coats, stethoscopes coiled around their necks. Nurses ogle them, patients worship them, while they rule out this and that, ordering critical diagnostic tests designed by pure researchers who receive only a pittance of a salary. Believe me, Geoffry, I know—"

"Amanda—"

"No, Geoffry, you have to hear this. These doctors are as far away from the intellectual and mental rigors of pure research as their golf balls are from the stupid hole when they plop in those dumb sand traps. . .pits—traps, whatever they call them—"

"Amanda," Geoffry said softly. "Hey, take it easy."

Amanda realized she had to calm down. So few people—in fact, no one, not even Geoffry—realized how much she respected Dr. Hegel. She always would, no matter what. Now, when everyone seemed to be attacking him, he needed help. She would help him become himself again.

"I know he helped you about us. . .our differences," Geoffry said.

So this is how the subject is to come up. Calm down, Amanda. Drink some water. "We need to talk about those things," Amanda said. She watched Geoffry's response. She'd been so confident when she left the lab, skipping like a little girl, certain that she'd come away from this conversation happy.

"Dr. Hegel will be winding down his work after Monday's seminar," she said. "We've taken the last batch of samples." Amanda pushed her plastic plate toward the center of the table, then slid the Styrofoam cup in front of her. She wanted so much not to sound angry, to restrain that competitive nature she had grown up with. "Geoffry, it won't be long before I have to begin looking for another job," she said.

"And what about us?" Geoffry asked. "Is that what you're going to ask me?"

Amanda stared at him for a moment. She felt her lower lip

tighten, her mouth dry. But she dared not pick up the cup, afraid it would betray her trembling hands.

"What have we been to each other?" Amanda asked. "Do I leave, go to another research assistant position somewhere maybe a thousand miles away?" Amanda paused. "Do we write or e-mail once a week about how we're getting along?"

She managed to get that out calmly, at least outwardly, but she could feel herself losing control, and she wanted so desperately for that not to happen. Amanda swallowed the lump in her throat. She looked at the cup of water but didn't pick it up.

"And what will you tell me, Geoffry? Do I get a telephone call from you? 'Oh, Amanda. I met such a nice girl today. She's smart and cute just like you. Don't worry, though. We're just friends.'"

Geoffry leaned back in his chair and stared at her when he heard her words. It occurred to Amanda that Geoffry could have any woman he wanted. The former college quarterback had had cheerleaders pawing and gawking at him all through school.

Amanda felt stupid.

This isn't a game, Amanda. Geoffry's not a goal, some sort of prize that you win. So what if he's about to end it? You shouldn't have humiliated yourself like that! You'll survive. You can get a research position at any university you want. Meet hundreds of people. Start over. Thank Dr. Avraham Hegel for that.

Geoffry smiled. "Women," he said, shaking his head. He flipped his lab coat off his hip and reached his right hand into the front pocket of his green scrubs. He pulled something out of his pocket and held it in his fist. Then he sat up straight, leaned toward Amanda, and set his stare hard on Amanda's eyes. "Don't you think I realize what will happen when Dr. Hegel's grant is done?" he asked softly.

"Well, I. . ."

"Do you believe I would watch you go off to some university a thousand miles away? Do you really think all the things I said to you were lies?"

"Geoffry, it's just. . ."

Geoffry reached over the table and set a small black velvet box in front of Amanda.

Amanda glanced at the box, then jerked her gaze to Geoffry's eyes. She looked down, clasped her hands, and dropped them in her lap. She glanced at the Styrofoam cup; then she stared at Geoffry again.

Reality rushed through Amanda's mind. Geoffry had done nothing to deserve distrust. She remembered the talk they'd had just a few weeks ago.

"Amanda," Geoffry had said, "you remember I told you about that guy Jimmie at work? Well, he finally talked me into going to one of his church services. Something happened there. I want us both involved as a couple there." And Amanda remembered what she had said: "I have to tell you about my father, Geoffry. I don't know—I just don't know."

Geoffry never once gave her an ultimatum about joining with him in his new beliefs, only saying that he believed one day she would understand. And it was always his desire for her to be with him in that little church.

What will they think? Why is it so hard for me? Amanda asked herself. *Why do I think this way?*

"Open it," Geoffry said, a thin smile on his face.

Amanda's hands trembled as she lifted the top off the small box. Joy ran through her when she saw the diamond solitaire ring. . .with a rush of realization that a new era in her life had just begun. She looked up at Geoffry. Even though her bottom lip quivered, she managed to say something: "I feel so stupid."

"You should," Geoffry said.

Amanda pressed her head against her hands and cried. She tried to say, "It's beautiful," but she wasn't sure if her words were audible through the sniffling.

"I have a question," Geoffry said.

"What?" Amanda asked, confused.

"Will you marry me?" Geoffry asked. He took the ring from her hand and slipped it on her finger.

Amanda tried to sort her conflicting emotions, tried to chase away the doubt that this was happening.

"Does this mean I don't have to send out résumés?" she asked, feeling relief in the laughter that followed. And, finally, feeling the courage to lift her Styrofoam cup.

CHAPTER 5

Senator Jeremiah Gators knew he was entering his enemy's war tent for this inevitable meeting. He stepped into the Oval Office feeling confident, nevertheless. A marine in full dress closed the door behind Gators as he walked in, then stationed himself inside the Oval Office in front of the door, as if he would not permit the senator to leave.

The president's spokespeople publicly blamed Senator Gators and those like him who disagreed with the administration's philosophy for every domestic and foreign problem facing the country. But Senator Gators knew he represented a fissure in the foundation of President Frye's view of social change for the country. The senator believed Constance Frye steered much of the president's domestic policy, and that caused him to pray often.

"This is an honor, Mr. President," Senator Gators said. "I appreciate your invitation."

"Have a seat, Senator." The president remained seated in his blue leather chair behind a piece of furniture-art called the Resolute Desk. The name came from the HMS *Resolute,* a wrecked British frigate from which the desk had been hand carved and donated to the White House in 1880.

The moment Senator Gators saw the desk, he recalled Larry King's interview with the first lady a month after the inauguration. "John F. Kennedy himself used the desk," the first lady had told Mr. King. "People need to know that my husband and I have a spiritual connection to the great presidents and their first ladies," Constance explained to an adoring Larry King. "That's why I chose that desk for my husband." The first lady had leaned forward then, softening her voice and squinting at King as if she were approaching the end of a ghost story. "And I believe, Larry, that's why it's more than coincidence that my husband's middle name is Roosevelt. Have you ever read *The Celestine Prophecy*, Larry?"

A new breed has gotten hold of the White House, Senator Gators had thought as he watched that interview.

The president gestured to one of the two blue-and-white-striped sofas that sat parallel to each other and perpendicular to the Resolute Desk. The senator sat and found himself facing Chief of Staff J. Scott Wootan, J.D., Ph.D., Professor Emeritus of Modern Political and Governmental Philosophy at Yale University and author of dozens of papers on governing theory. Wootan nodded but said nothing. Senator Gators leaned back, then turned to his right toward the president.

"May I call you Jeremiah, Senator?" the president asked.

"Of course, Mr. President," Gators said. He glanced at Wootan. Gators reminded himself why Wootan was there. The president would never speak critically of a black senator, even though he and the senator agreed on nothing. Professor Scott Wootan would be the president's spokesman regarding what happened at this meeting, at least from the president's point of view. As chief of staff, Wootan could criticize Gators, or anyone else if need be: "Well, Senator Gators has been bought by the religious right," or "I heard the conversation between the president and the senator; I was there. Typical religious fundamental rhetoric; today is not the time for such fundamentalism." Gators had seen this tactic often in President Frye's administration and in other administrations, too. But it was especially amusing in Wootan's case, because when Wootan was the subject of the press's photo-ops, he was so short he usually stood on a box or anything else he could find to stretch himself and the truth.

But there was something even more uncomfortable about Wootan. In the real political world, the one Senator Gators had studied so hard to learn and strived so hard to open to his constituents,

Professor Wootan's theory of government crippled individuality. In the professor's model, the president and select federal officials, including, of course, himself, possessed a duty to guide the ordinary working "folks," who ran frantically, stupidly, through life's maze. Only the president, the chief of staff, and federal legislation could help the folks, and, never forget, the children.

Senator Gators took every opportunity to warn that the professor's government model, with its regulations and redistribution of income, would stifle self-reliance, levy confiscatory taxes on economic individualism, and increase the population of the government-dependent. A fine outcome if you look at it from the perspective of the politicians who poured more entitlement slop in the federal feeding trough to maintain power.

"He's protecting the rich," the senator's white opponents would say on *Meet the Press*. "He's the newest Uncle Tom," his high-profile "reverend" critics would bark on broadcast television news. And the first lady, when asked about the senator, would say, "He wants to starve the children and keep them crippled and diseased." Senator Gators expected that; it was this administration's basic strategy: class division through class envy.

Gators prayed after that Larry King interview with Constance Frye. *Give me peace, Lord.* This president and this administration were evil. *God, use me, but keep me mindful that the fight is Yours.*

"I hear your dad's a Baptist preacher?" the president said. He smiled, but not with the familiar crooked smile the political cartoonists used in their caricatures. This smile was forced, both ends of the mouth lifted slightly.

"That's right, Mr. President. He's with Jesus now." Gators watched the president blush in anger and then shift his hazel glare at Wootan. Gators knew the president had ordered his senior policy advisor, Gordon Redden, to compile a dossier on him. Redden did, and then he leaked what he had been told to do. Redden was doomed to the trash heap of failed political opportunists, Gators thought.

"I'm Baptist, too," the president said.

"That's good, sir. That's real good. What's your favorite Scripture, Mr. President?" Gators asked.

"Where it says that we have to care for the children." The president's hands moved around some, but only a few strokes, as if he had conducted an extraordinarily brief, unfinished symphony.

" 'Suffer little children, and forbid them not, to come unto me: for of such is the kingdom of heaven,' Matthew 19:14," the senator said.

"Yeah, something like that," the president said. He paused, then said, "Jeremiah, we're in the same party, aren't we?"

"We are, Mr. President."

President Frye sat back in his chair. With his elbows on the armrests, he lifted his hands and opened his palms. "Then why do we differ so much? We have the same religion, the same desire to help your people." The president's hands, with his elbows still on the armrests, conducted another, though longer, symphony.

Gators leaned forward. Wootan shifted a bit. That move caught Gators' eye. *Lord, nudge me when You want me to talk.*

"And do you know you're the only colored not in the Black Caucus?" the president said.

"Yes, sir. I do." Gators hadn't heard "colored" used like that in decades. He wondered if that was a slip, or did the president mean for him to emote some emotion, perhaps anger? The word and the tone Frye used reminded Gators of how hard it was to have grown up in the '50s and '60s as a black man in America. But he was fifty-seven now, a respected United States senator. God had been good to him, and he had declared that to many, so many times. Then Gators felt that familiar impression that always came when he prayed silently and the confidence that always followed.

"Men like Representative Jukali have come a long way," the president said. "Don't you want to help them help your own kind?"

"They're all my brothers and sisters, Mr. President. You're my brother, too. I don't suppose I have a favorite Scripture, Mr. President, but one of my favorites is Jeremiah 1:5. You remember that one?"

"Senator—"

"God said to Jeremiah, 'Before I formed thee in the belly I knew thee; and before thou camest forth out of the womb I sanctified thee.' Now, what do you think about that, Mr. President, you being a good Baptist and all?" the senator asked. "That tells me God knows us before we're even born."

"It's a wonderful story, Senator." The president leaned toward Gators. He put his elbows on his desk and started moving his hands again. "An important seat will open on the Ways and Means Committee after the midterm elections, Jeremiah."

Wootan cleared his throat.

"I'm grateful, Mr. President, but I'd like to tell you a little about myself before you say anything to anybody about me and that seat," Gators said.

"Go right ahead, Jeremiah," the president said.

"I know Representative Jukali worked hard," Gators said. "His New York civil rights lawyer daddy must be proud of him, now that his son's the speaker of the house. What's his father's name? Cooper? Elliot Cooper?"

"Senator—"

"God knows I'd be hurt if my son changed his name like that. A name's history, it seems to me, is a living heirloom showing what God has done for the family."

"It's a spiritual thing," the president said. "Representative Jukali desires association with his spiritual Afrikaner past."

"Suppose so," Gators said. "Anyway, with that seat, I'd be on C-Span a lot. Don't get invited much to television nowadays. Probably because I don't look like much, Mr. President. Chubby, white hair— what's left of it, anyway." Gators chuckled.

The president smiled. He displayed a confidence of being in control of the conversation, Gators was sure. Gators glanced at Wootan. *You're the stiffest little man I've ever seen, but you'll be moving, shifting around pretty soon.*

"You know, Mr. President, my great-great-grandfather was a slave on one of those plantations down in Houma, Louisiana. His name was Lukandee. I have a real photograph of Lukandee. One of those brown-and-white pictures. It's priceless."

"That seat, Senator—"

"Lukandee did three men's work. His owner was afraid he would run north. So Lukandee always had a personal overseer during the day, and the owner kept him shackled at night."

"Senator Ga—"

"The overseer called Lukandee 'Gator Bait.' Every morning he told Lukandee that if he didn't do three men's work, that's what he would be: gator bait. Funny, when I was young, they called me Gator Bait a few times, too."

Professor Wootan shifted.

The president sat up. "Senator, I don't think—"

"When they freed Lukandee, he refused to take the name of his owner or one of the dead presidents, like most of the slaves did. He called himself Luke Gator. Short for 'gator bait.' "

"Senator, I have—"

"Luke Gator probably should've hated every white man in the South. But he didn't. He could've beaten the tar out of any of them, but he preached God's Word to them instead. Learned to read the Bible all by himself. I guess he was the first Negro preacher in Louisiana." Senator Gators couldn't help grinning when President Frye widened his eyes when he heard the word "Negro." Whatever emotion President Frye tried to evoke with the word "colored," Gators wanted to show it didn't work. Gators was certain the president realized a strategy was being played out. The president would interrupt, stop the conversation some way.

"Our family is so thankful for Luke Gator." Gators shook his head. "With Jesus as my witness, Mr. President, that's a true story."

"That's a fine story, Jeremiah," the president said.

"There's more, Mr. President."

"Sena—"

"Great-great-grandfather Gator had a bunch of children, and his children had a bunch of children. A few generations later, my grandfather and grandmother built a church in St. Tammany Parish. They don't have counties in Louisiana, you know. They call them parishes. My grandfather's name was Jeremiah Gators, too. I think he liked the sound of the *s*, so he just added it," the senator said with a chuckle.

A sound came from the other sofa, the professor clearing his throat.

"Senator," the president said, glancing at his watch, "I don't have—"

"No one knows how he got into St. Tammany Parish. Family rumor has it my grandfather left Houma because there were too many Negro churches and not enough lost Negro souls. He met my grandmother in St. Tammany Parish. Grandma and Grandpa Gators called their church Ebenezer Baptist Church."

The president glanced at his wristwatch again. "About that seat."

"Anyway, a bunch of white men in white robes and pointed hoods burned down the church. They were going to string up Grandpa Gators, but I guess God gave them second thoughts. They left a burning cross on the church's front lawn. They were hollering as they drove away, 'Nigger preacher, teach your nigger kids to pray and sing, but not to read.'"

"Bet they're still down there," the president said through his familiar grin, "driving their pickups with gun racks in the back window."

"It's mostly good people now," Gators said. "There's some bad whites, some bad blacks, too." The senator paused, then said, "I own a pickup, Mr. President. So do a lot of my friends, gun racks and all." Senator Gators paused again while he watched the president tighten his lips and study him. "Don't you think it's about time we all forgave each other, Mr. President?" Gators asked.

Professor Wootan cleared his throat again. The president shifted. He was going to say something.

"Grandpa Gators rebuilt the church," Gators said. "When he passed, my father took it over. My father and mother raised me and my seven siblings in the little parsonage. They taught the older ones to read and write. The older ones taught the younger ones when our parents got old and tired."

"That's a fine story, Jeremiah. Now, about that seat," the president said.

"I have a fine family history, Mr. President. But you know what? We didn't take anything from the government. No welfare, no stamps. My parents didn't want anything except what the family earned."

"That's a wonderful story, Jere—"

"But you know what, Mr. President?" Gators focused on the president's eyes and smiled. "The descendants of the men who wore those robes and hoods that night, who burned down my grandfather's church and almost hanged him, now head up my campaign headquarters with the descendants of the poor folks nearly killed in that fire. What do you think about that, Mr. President?"

"That's a fine story."

Wootan shifted. Senator Gators looked at him. Wootan pushed his palms on the cushion and shifted again.

No one spoke. Gators turned to the president. "There are no more cotton fields as far as the eye can see," he said. "That Houma mansion is a tourist attraction now, Mr. President. But there's still a plantation, sir. The overseer doesn't ride a horse with his rifle across his lap. The owner doesn't sit on the porch in his rocker, sipping mint juleps, but the overseer is still here, Mr. President. He's the caucus. He's the men who call themselves 'reverends,' who keep their Bibles closed and our wounds open. And the slave owner? Why, it's this federal government; it's you and the professor there who don't understand that God intended the human spirit to grow in self-reliance and self-esteem. And the plantation, with its free money and services, enslaves those you call my people, enslaves them in dependence as powerfully as that overseer's rifle did Lukandee during the daytime and the shackles the owner clamped on his ankles at night."

"What are you talking about?" the president asked.

"Now, Mr. President, what do you want me to do for that seat?" Senator Gators asked.

"You're out of line, Senator," the president said.

Wootan cleared his throat and shifted.

"You want me to campaign for your wife's reforms?" the senator asked. "Is that the price, Mr. President?"

The president said nothing.

Wootan shifted again.

"Maybe you want me to get up there next to Dr. Hegel tomorrow night, as your token religious colored man. Maybe you want me to get on CPNN with the first lady's friends and say a lot of stuff about helping the children."

The president sat still. He gazed at Wootan with a befuddled look. He threw up his hands. "What's wrong with helping the children?" he asked.

Senator Gators stood up. "Funny how our government works, Mr. President," he said. "Most senators don't even read the bills, do they? I read your wife's bill, all two thousand fifteen and three-quarter pages. Your wife's reforms kill children. They legalize selling their flesh, but you know that, don't you, Mr. President. I will fight your wife's reforms until I'm in my grave."

"You know, Gators, some good people are looking for your senate seat in the next elections. Maybe I'll go down near your headquarters in that dog patch in Slidell, Louisiana, and campaign for one of them," the president said in a calm voice and with his familiar crooked smile.

Wootan cleared his throat louder this time.

"When was the last time you took a poll in my district, Mr. President?" Gators asked.

Silence.

"Every human being is sacred, Mr. President," Gators said in a soft voice. "You, your wife, too. But I've been around a long, long time. I've heard these marketing lines, sir. Don't believe I think your wife cares about children, President Frye. I suppose a lot of the folks think she does, though. God bless them all."

"Sit down, Jeremiah. Let's talk about this," the president said.

"I don't think I will," Senator Gators said. "When you come down to Louisiana, visit my church. My brother pastors there now. I even preach sometimes. I'll even preach a special sermon on that Scripture you love so much."

Senator Gators turned and walked toward the door. Then came the familiar impression again. He stopped behind the sofa, behind Wootan. He turned and pointed at President Frye. "God works in ways our minds can't know, Mr. President. You might believe your and the first lady's plans are unshakable, but you're wrong. God moves as He pleases, beyond time, beyond events, from life to life. He is a common, everlasting thread in all men, and nothing happens but what He knows will happen."

The president rocked in his chair but said nothing.

"I will pray; the congregation in my church—black, white, young, and old—will pray. And we will pray for you, too, Mr. President. Just as His Word says we must."

The president stared at Gators; he appeared fixed on the senator's words.

"His hand opposes you, sir," Gators said. "Get away from your advisors and seek Him first, and He will draw close to you."

The president stopped rocking.

"Senator, I resent that!" Professor Wootan said.

"Get away from your wife and her people. Ask God for help. He will hear you; He will answer. You will have an opportunity to show you have courage to turn back the first lady's dark laws."

Senator Gators lowered his hand. He felt the perspiration under his collar. A quiet loomed over the office for several moments.

"Good day, Senator," the president said.

"Good day, Mr. President." Senator Gators turned toward the door, seeing first the marine in full dress, standing at the door that was already open.

As Senator Gators stepped across the threshold into the hall, he heard Professor Wootan chuckle and say, "The old man ought to leave his religion in his church, where it belongs. That's the problem with these more-holier-than-thou people."

The Chicago winds blew as they always did, especially forty-two stories above the stalled traffic below. Richard Landcaster scooted another ashtray in front of Yashimiro.

Otto Goethe popped up from the conference chair, his face so red the thick hairs of his blond eyebrows turned orange at their follicles, and his blue eyes widened. He raised his fist. He screamed in rage, "It is only fair!"

Clap!

Goethe's slapping his hand on the Chinese rosewood conference table jerked Landcaster from his musings.

"Yashimiro san! You don't trust me!" Goethe hollered.

Landcaster sat at the end of the conference table, just in front of the built-in bar. He turned his head toward Yashimiro, who sat directly across the table from Goethe.

Yashimiro lifted his cigarette to his lips. His cheeks caved in for a length of time Landcaster thought remarkable. The end of the cigarette glowed red hot, the redness reflecting in Yashimiro's horn-rimmed glasses. Landcaster couldn't determine the actual size of Yashimiro's eyes, but they had to be larger than the green-pea size they appeared to be behind the thick lenses.

Yashimiro blew the smoke out through his nostrils. "Tell me when your palm stops stinging, Herr Doktor Goethe," he said. "As usual, you make a fool of yourself with your tantrums."

"Guys, guys," Landcaster said. "Cool down. Sit down, Otto. We need to talk this out."

Yashimiro took another long draw on his cigarette. "You think you are smarter than us, don't you, Herr Doktor," Yashimiro said. "Well, I know what you really want. Don't be so cowardly, my friend. Come right out and say it."

Landcaster was determined to settle the issue Goethe had called this meeting to address and to do it without losing business. Maybe he could prove to Kristina England that he was worthy of being

CEO. The situation was perfect. Neither of these men would discuss business with a woman, not even with England.

When Landcaster briefed her about Goethe's insistence that whole conceptuses be supplied to him, England had made it clear. "The Nazi's crazy," she had said. "What does he think we are? Idiots? Tell him to forget it. I don't care how much territory he controls."

"Look, you guys," Landcaster said, "we have a lot of territory to cover. Let's cool down."

A quiet settled in the conference room.

"Okay, Otto." Landcaster realized he had raised his voice. Not a good idea. *This lunatic makes millions for the company, distributing pieces into his underground network of European buyers.* Landcaster made sure the next words came out in an apologetic but firm tone. "Supplying them whole for the new market you propose just isn't feasible right now, Otto," he said.

Yashimiro smiled. He took another long draw, snuffed his cigarette in the ashtray, then reached in his pocket for another one.

Goethe drew a deep breath. "You do not understand," he said to Landcaster. "Many researchers tell me how valuable the conceptuses would be to them. Think of it! No more speculation. Animal-human variations in reactions and testing statistically eliminated. Don't you see? The conceptuses are a perfect test species."

"Otto, I'm a physician, you know," Landcaster said. "I understand your buyers' position."

"It's a ploy, Richard," Yashimiro said. "A trick to encroach on my territory. I have researchers, too. If we ship them whole, then my territorial rights must be honored."

"It's a new market!" Goethe slapped the table again, though not as violently as before. "I thought of it, not you!"

"Hey, Otto. I said it's not feasible. Not yet," Landcaster said.

"What is it that makes it not feasible?" Goethe asked.

"Well. . ." Landcaster tried to think of something to say without offending Goethe.

"It's much less expensive for you," Goethe said. "No need to take them apart. Selling them whole cuts out the butchery. And we could charge so much more whole than in pieces. What are the values of pieces now? Prices have fallen. Donations are interfering. Live systems are the new product for this 'new market.'"

"Everyone seems to be donating something, you know. That's true," Landcaster said, nodding his head, still attempting to explain Kristina England's position, but a touch more diplomatically.

"Precisely my point," Goethe said. "We must seek out new markets now."

"Otto, you said 'live systems,'" Landcaster said. "What do you mean?"

"Why, Richard," Yashimiro said, pulling his cigarette from his mouth. His yellow teeth showed as he grinned. "Hasn't Herr Doktor Goethe explained that to you? No? Well, permit me."

Landcaster glanced at Goethe, expecting another tirade. None came.

"It's a marketing strategy," Yashimiro continued. "The pieces are not sold separately, like in a parts store. They are sold like an automobile, all components in place, working. Buying an automobile by the part is very expensive—better to buy the whole automobile. But an automobile is a system of component parts, is it not, Richard? Like a conceptus? But a conceptus, now—that's not only a system of component parts."

Yashimiro took a drag on his cigarette. Landcaster and Goethe waited for him to finish his analogy. As the smoke curled from his nostrils, Yashimiro continued, "A conceptus is a system of component parts with life. Addition of that particular item as standard equipment costs. Herr Doktor and I would have to pay your company more. A lot more."

What is this guy getting at? Landcaster asked himself.

"Of course, our distributors pay us more, and the customers, they pay much, much more," Yashimiro said. A wide grin wrinkled Yashimiro's yellowish, leather-like facial skin, accentuating his beady eyes.

"Very good, Yashimiro san," Goethe said. "You are a man of intellect and understanding, unlike our American host."

Yashimiro looked toward Goethe and bowed his head slightly. He took the opportunity to draw another long drag from his cigarette, turned again to Landcaster, and continued. "You see, Richard, the 'live-system' slogan is an advertising gimmick Herr Doktor Goethe will use in his negotiations. It reminds his scientist-customers that he realizes the value of his wares." Yashimiro took another drag, then snuffed out his cigarette and reached for another. "You should pay more attention to marketing techniques than to your faded knowledge of medicine, Richard," he said.

"Our customers are parents of dying children. We help them when the government enforces its stupid laws," Landcaster said to Yashimiro. Confusion came to Landcaster. Yashimiro seemed to be taking both sides. How could he? This guy Goethe wanted to move into his exclusive territory with his "new market."

Goethe spoke directly to Landcaster, softly for a change. "The market I propose involves corporations doing research. There will be little or no infringement on my fellow broker here. For the most part, his territory produces electronic trinkets and, as you heard Yashimiro san demonstrate with his clever analogy, mediocre automobiles, not medicines."

The words "We intend to change that" entered the air with a puff of smoke.

"Of course you will, Yashimiro san," Goethe said. "You are a resourceful, determined people. Not at all lazy and corrupt like Americans. But my country and its sisters in history—Switzerland, Holland— they produce medicines. And they need reliable test species, for which they will pay an immense price. No more dealers, no middlemen. They and any other pharmaceutical manufacturers will deal directly with me. This is my idea for a new market. You didn't think of it, did you? And, of course, Landcaster here, he never would have thought of it."

"Otto, you don't have to insult me like—"

"I already have sales arranged, just waiting for shipment. I demand all territorial rights of distribution, even to the country of trinket automobiles and all of Asia." Goethe glared at his competitor. "It's my idea, Mr. Yashimiro san. It's my reward," he said.

Yashimiro took another draw. He said nothing. He gazed at Landcaster, then blew smoke hard from his mouth, appearing as if he were waiting for Landcaster to make a decision.

"I can't make commitments yet, Otto," Landcaster said. "But shipping whole is risky, you know. Termination rate, you know, is highest during transit, even with the most scrupulous attention to incubator integrity."

"My purchasers will accept the financial risk," Goethe said, leaning back again, tapping his fingers together.

"We can't get insurance," Landcaster said.

"My purchasers don't care."

"I have to discuss it with—"

"Herr Doktor Goethe," Yashimiro asked, "do your purchasers intend to maintain the conceptuses in their own laboratories after the conceptuses are shipped to them?"

Yashimiro glanced at Landcaster.

"Of course," Goethe said. "They would die otherwise."

Landcaster looked at Yashimiro. He decided to let his Japanese broker keep talking.

"And how would your eager purchasers do that, Herr Doktor? Would they, for example, use Hegel's preparations? Hegel's techniques?"

Yashimiro's facial skin crinkled as he grinned broader than before. Smoke streamed out of his mouth, through the separations between his stained teeth. His tiny eyes, Landcaster was certain, were squinting. Landcaster turned his head to watch and listen to Goethe.

Goethe began calculating, forming a response. His face flushed red. Landcaster glanced at Yashimiro, whose cheeks were collapsed again behind his glowing cigarette. Landcaster almost heard Yashimiro think it when the tiny eyes caught his gaze: *Well, Richard, do you now get the point?*

Landcaster felt a pang of incompetence when Yashimiro set his gaze on him. Selling live conceptuses to Goethe would require also providing him the technology to keep the conceptuses alive. *Why couldn't I think of that?* After a quick review of what had happened since the meeting began, Landcaster concluded he had done just that. *Maybe I didn't do it outright, you know, plan to take on Goethe directly, but I led these two guys into the trap and cornered Goethe by cornering Yashimiro first.* He knew Yashimiro would protect his own exclusive rights to the Asian market. Landcaster felt pride enter him when those thoughts passed through his mind and eagerness to tell England how he had led the two brokers into a trap.

"I proposed a new market," Goethe had said in the last meeting in Tokyo, "extremities, arms, legs, it's only a matter of time with cloning."

"He is a sick, crazy Nazi," England had told Landcaster. "Forget it."

Goethe's calculations had ended. "Distrust and narrow-mindedness are characteristics of your culture, Yashimiro san," Goethe said.

Yashimiro bowed again. "That is a compliment coming from someone such as you, Herr Doktor," he said.

"Otto, we can't, you know, transfer our technology," Landcaster said.

"You must trust me!" Goethe said. The orange hue returned to his eyebrow follicles. "You run this business like a coward!"

"No, Herr Doktor," Yashimiro said. "He must not trust you. He must not trust me; he must honor his word."

"Guys," Landcaster said. "We have taken this matter as far as it can go. I will bring your requests to the equity owners. I'm sure, however, none of us has enough money to convince them to transfer Dr. Hegel's methods."

"I have another proposal," Goethe said to Landcaster.

"Come on, guys," Landcaster said.

"A customer of mine is willing to pay thirty million for this conceptus of yours called B/M0012," Goethe said.

Quiet fell on the room. Landcaster stared at Goethe for a moment, then glanced at Yashimiro.

Yashimiro set his gaze on Landcaster, smoke rising in front of his glasses.

"Thirty million?" Landcaster asked. The thought came to him that Jacqueline Reed had to be talking to the German. *That woman will be the first to get a pink slip when the business becomes legal.*

"And you can keep the technology and the Jew's preparations," Goethe said.

Landcaster was lost for words again.

"Don't you understand, Richard?" Yashimiro asked. "The future is approaching BioSysTech, and it doesn't look good."

"What?" Landcaster asked Yashimiro.

"Cloning, Landcaster," Goethe said. "You Americans, so caught up in your ethics, with all your commissions and committees. My customer has everything set up except one thing: a conceptus that tolerates the conditions well."

"I don't know," Landcaster said. "I'll have to take it up with the equity owners."

"You see, Richard," Yashimiro said, "the days of pretended pregnancy termination will come to an end in a few short years for what we sell. Didn't your female supervisors tell you that?"

Landcaster thought it better not to tell Yashimiro that he had brought up the subject of cloning to the equity owners when *Time* magazine reported that a sheep had been cloned. "Landcaster," England had said, "we're not in this for research. We get our inventory from healthy teenagers until we have to change. No sooner. Don't discuss cloning with the Nazi."

"Thirty million, Landcaster," Goethe said, "for one conceptus."

"I don't think we're interested," Landcaster said.

Yashimiro turned to Landcaster. "My customer will pay forty million for this little B/M0012," he said.

Landcaster paused. "Come on, guys," he said.

"There is always a price, isn't there, Richard?" Yashimiro asked.

"Always, Yashimiro san," Goethe said.

"Am I correct in assuming, then, Richard, that BioSysTech will continue business as it has done so well in the past?" Yashimiro asked.

"Yes, Sam, that is correct. Piece by piece, guaranteed fresh within a jet ride of termination."

Goethe stood up. Landcaster felt relief when he saw that Goethe appeared to be calm. "We shall discuss this again, soon," he said.

FRIDAY, JUNE 21

CHAPTER 6

$\int$heer exhaustion had caused Amanda to doze off a few minutes past 3:30 A.M. She remembered the time because she had opened her eyes in the dark morning hours more times than she cared to remember. She had seen 3:33 glow red on her clock radio as she felt the weight of her body sink into the mattress and her weary mind finally give in to the silence. Now the red numbers glowed 8:48.

Amanda's head ached just slightly, her muscles stiff to move. How nice of Dr. Hegel to give her today off. Fortunate, too. She would be little use in the lab with so little sleep, newly engaged, and worried to death.

She sat up in her bed, slid her feet close to her chest, and crossed her arms on top of her knees. Slide one. She recited the sentence in Dr. Hegel's seminar manuscript that cued it, then envisioned the slide itself. Even with her lack of rest, Amanda went through all nineteen of them: the slide number, the cue manuscript sentence, the image on the slide. If Dr. Hegel's last seminar as a research scientist didn't go well on Monday, it wouldn't be because she failed to rehearse.

But it wasn't Monday's task that had kept Amanda turning under the covers and glancing at the clock radio all night. Neither was it her new, deeper relationship with Geoffry. Thoughts of her father had kept her mind racing until it wore down.

From the day Amanda was born, even to the day he had given her a tennis player–style Rolex watch at college commencement, her father had doted on her. And not because she was his only child. He loved her. "Hello, princess," she had heard a million times as she sat on the sofa after school, doing what eight-, twelve-, sixteen-year-old daughters do as years pass.

Detective Dwayne Collins would come home from the station, take off his jacket, and sit in his overstuffed recliner, his shoulder holster and gun still strapped to him. Amanda's mother would bring him his first cold bottle of Budweiser and the day's issue of the *Boston Globe*. Soon her mother would have dinner on the table. But before then, he would ask Amanda how her day had gone. "When's your next ball game, my little ponytail princess?" The ball game could have been basketball, softball, track. Any sport. Amanda was the best.

"Saturday, Daddy," Amanda always answered. "You know that."

Of course he did. And he would be there in the stands, jumping and whooping at every effort Amanda made and jeering at every referee's, umpire's, or timer's adverse call, oblivious to the parents around him shaking their heads. On the Saturdays when no game had been scheduled, Amanda's father took her to the park and often to the police academy firing range.

"Ponytail, you handle that weapon better than a rookie," he had told her so many times.

"Honey, Mandy! Dinner!" Amanda's mother would shout while rushing between the kitchen and dining room with platters of the most delicious food imaginable.

Oh, Mother, I love you.

Detective Collins would push himself out of the recliner, saunter to his bedroom, and enter the kitchen in his undershirt and pants.

Warm nostalgia, perhaps a touch of homesickness, had run through Amanda when she nurtured those thoughts the night before, before other recollections of her father filtered in. Even after she turned off the light, she nurtured those memories about that little family living in one of several identical houses along a row on that narrow Boston street. But the smile left when the dark side of her father came to her mind. She tried to suppress visions of him, sounds from him. For hours she tried, glancing again and again at the red

LCD numbers that changed so painfully slowly.

I'll call Mother and tell her, after I straighten the apartment, before Geoffry comes over. Daddy will be in his squad car somewhere in downtown Boston, investigating another murder, enjoying his hatred as he always does.

⌐ ⌐

"Hegel can't speak tonight," England said, sitting on the sofa in the first lady's office in the Executive Wing of the White House. Her breakfast of fruit and vegetable juice had long since been digested. She glanced at her watch: 11:28. Hunger and Constance Frye made her irritable.

"I know," Constance said, tapping the eraser end of a pencil on her desk. She glanced at Madeline Gentcher, the first lady's chief of staff, standing at the side of the first lady's desk. "Madeline will meet Hegel at his hotel," she said. "She'll give him the new reception agenda. I'll do all the speaking."

Go figure. England made it a point to sit still and to avoid facial movements and to avoid looking up at Gentcher. *Even Dr. Hegel ought to shiver when "Constance's Enforcer" comes around.*

Becky Ingram sat on the sofa at the other end from England, gripping the armrest with her right hand as if she expected to be ejected through the ceiling. Except for an occasional glance at the pencil the first lady was toying with, Becky looked at England when she spoke, then shifted her gaze to Constance when she spoke.

"How are you going to stop Hegel from talking to the media?" England asked.

"Didn't you hear about the reports of anti-abortion terrorists hiding behind the columns in the East Room?" Constance asked with a smile. "I'll have an SS man on him."

"And if the press persists?" England asked Constance.

"Madeline will intrude," Constance said. "You say nothing to the press." Constance looked at Becky. "You, either." Constance returned her gaze to England. She dropped the pencil on her desk pad and interlocked her fingers. "Kristina, you stay next to Hegel, too."

England felt her pulse increase and her face flush warm with blood. "Okay, Constance," England said. "But something has to be done. I've told you over and over again, you're too far from the business to micromanage it. I'm doing a good job without your telling me what to do. I can move around. I can telephone Landcaster, or anyone else, anytime. You can't."

"I'm not going to go through this again, Kristina," Constance said. "My reform will be out of House committee any day now. I don't care what you think I can't do, but I'll tell you both what I can do." Constance picked up the pencil and began jabbing the eraser end directly at England. "I can end this right now, call a couple of people, and get you indicted." The first lady lowered the pencil and moved her gaze to Becky.

Becky shifted. She moved her hand off the armrest of the sofa onto her lap.

England stood. She looked down at the first lady. "Perhaps we will talk about this after your reform passes," she said.

Becky stood.

Constance rocked in her chair while holding the pencil with her thumb and index finger on both ends, spinning it toward England then away from her. "Hegel will be in the president's cabinet soon wearing that surgeon general uniform," Constance said. "What do you think about that, Kristina?"

England held her mouth shut tight and nodded slowly while staring at Constance. *I'll tell you what I think. I think you're building your coalition to eventually take over the entire business. I think the only reason you will appoint Hegel as surgeon general is to keep yourself in the front of the reform in the stupid minds of the rabble. You'll make sure he tells the press how brilliant you are, as if he needs to convince the press of that! I think you're a power monger.*

"That's just fine, Constance," England said. "Come on, Becky, it's time to eat."

By 11:30 Amanda had finished tidying her one-bedroom apartment, one of four in a converted old house on Cherry Street in Old Kingston. The wood floor, the old doors with the relic skeleton key locks, and the secondhand mismatched furniture made the cozy apartment look like a typical graduate student pad.

Amanda lounged on the sofa, the telephone receiver to her ear, listening to the ringing on the other end. *Come on, Mama. I know you're there. Where else could you be?* She stretched her legs over the old tin luggage chest with withered and torn leather straps that doubled as a coffee table. *I'll call back later.*

"Hello! Hello!" Amanda heard her mother just as she removed the receiver from her ear.

"Hello? Mama? It's me, Amanda."

"Mandy, baby. You all right, aren't you, baby?"

"Mama, I need to tell you something."

"What is it, baby? Did you go and lose that job?"

"No, Mama. Nothing like that. It's. . .well, Mama. . .I'm engaged."

"What?"

"I'm engaged, Mama."

"To that white boy you told me about?"

Amanda paused. "Please, Mama," she said.

Amanda knew better than what the movies showed about racism. In the movies, bigots are only white; they drive pickup trucks on the dirt back roads of Mississippi or Alabama. That notion angered Amanda; she knew racial bigotry didn't reside only in the South. Boston was as bad as any southern city, probably worse than most. And bigotry wasn't one way in Boston or anywhere else.

When Amanda came home from those Saturday high school games, always the star player, her father, exhausted and hoarse, while soothing his throat with his second or third cold Budweiser, would always manage to say, "There's not a white cracker girl out there as good as you, my ponytail princess."

Some of Amanda's dearest friends were "white cracker" girls, but she couldn't bring them home. Amanda and her mother lied to her father about what girl was giving the next slumber party and who would be there. "No daughter of mine ain't spending no night at some white's house!"

Twice, Amanda had heard her mother try to explain to her father the predicament his prejudice caused Amanda. "Do you know the white man killed two million slaves, our ancestors, every year before the Civil War? Fed them to the sharks! And the white man put AIDS in the projects, and drugs, too! The minister has proof."

Amanda had discovered long ago that her dad was the founder and head of the Black Boston Policemen Organization. She remembered reading her father's angry accusations of vicious bigotry against his brothers and sisters in the department in hiring and promotions.

The *Globe* quoted Detective Collins often, and he saved every article in his treasured scrapbook. Fueling racial strife sold newspapers, Amanda had learned; celebrity status—even if only local—blurred reasonable, objective thought. And living with obsessive hatred disturbed little black girls, too. Made them toss and turn in their sleep when they grew up; made them wonder if that kind of hate was directed at them, and if they were good enough to be somebody in a white man's world.

"Maybe you'll change your mind in a few days, baby," Amanda's mother said.

"No, Mama. I won't," Amanda said in a sharp tone. "Daddy has to change his."

"I'll call you after I talk to him," Amanda's mother said. "Maybe you shouldn't call here until you hear from me, unless you change your mind."

Amanda could hear the anxiety in her mother's voice. And she could hear her mother's unspoken question: *Why are you doing this to our family?*

Amanda hung up the phone. She brought her knees to her torso, then wrapped her arms around her legs. A recollection came to her mind, a time so long ago when she was deceiving her father, spending the night at one of her white friend's houses. She and her friend were playing on the floor by the television when she heard the song "Just as I Am" and watched all those people coming to the front when Billy Graham beckoned them.

Geoffry, I just don't know if it will work.

CHAPTER 7

Around the small legal community of Columbia, where the fame he enjoyed was concentrated, Griffin himself had heard that he was the most eligible bachelor lawyer in town. Griffin enjoyed the tributes; he enjoyed the attention the ladies gave him at the usual affairs: the state judge campaign fund-raisers, the Columbia Bar Association gatherings, and the appreciation dinners for attorneys who taught legal seminars.

But he always attended those gatherings alone, at least he had for the last two years or so. Way back when, Theresa Carpenter had accompanied him, not only to gatherings of lawyers, but to the movies, to everyday parties, to Columbia Cornerstone Baptist Church, and to Warren and Carolyn Jennings' house to play cards.

Theresa had incredible wit. A quick mind, much like Jennifer's. And she possessed an intangible something beyond physical beauty that lingered and grew in Griffin's mind from the first time he met her. They started dating. Griffin managed to put off marriage for the first year, but after that, it was he who began to bring up the subject. Griffin began to daydream of things he thought he would never even think about, like Pastor Grady marrying Theresa and him at Cornerstone, and not too long after that, Pastor Grady dedicating their children. *Babies, Griffin? You, a father?* Sure, with Theresa. It seemed natural.

Then Theresa had something difficult to tell him. She had run into an old boyfriend from college while she was in San Francisco, and old feelings had welled up in her. She was uncertain about things now. . .needed time with her old boyfriend to sort things out.

Theresa moved away from Columbia just a month or so later to San Francisco. Griffin heard that she had moved in with her old boyfriend. The guy was a loser, someone had told Griffin; he had a problem with cocaine. One of those charmers who didn't work. "What could Theresa have possibly seen in that creep?" Griffin heard in a poorly suppressed whisper at some judge's fund-raiser.

But Griffin dealt with it. He lost a lot of fat, jogging and working out at the gym. He read a lot, too. He was plodding through *Moby Dick* when Theresa telephoned him last year from San Francisco. He remembered feeling some relief when the telephone in his living room rang. A break from a seemingly unending ancient lesson on how the Nantucketers captured the Great Whale.

"Griffin, how are you?"

"I'm fine, Theresa," he had said. "How are you and Darryl?" *Time is a healer, but a slow one.*

"Oh, Griffin," Theresa said. "I'm so sorry. I've made such a mess of things. I love you, Griffin."

"Theresa. . ."

"He beats me. He. . ."

The sniffling brought images of tears flowing from Theresa's large brown eyes. But those eyes probably had lost their glisten.

"I need money, Griffin. Can you lend me a couple of thousand? He'll hurt me if I don't get some money."

"You're calling me to ask for a loan?" Griffin asked.

"I'll pay you back. I promise I will," Theresa said.

"Theresa, I don't think I can help you. You need to—"

"I'm not on drugs, Griffin. Only Darryl. I'm clean now. I swear. I'll come back right now if you send some money," Theresa wailed.

Griffin said nothing. Felt nothing, finally.

Theresa's voice lowered. Then she said softly, "Oh, Griffin. . . Griffin. I've made such a mess of things. Sometimes I remember Columbia, the church, you. I've got to go."

"Theresa."

Theresa died of a sudden heart attack four months after that call.

Now Griffin was cordial when a woman came up to him, and during the conversation when that familiar smile and gleam-in-the-eyes appeared, Griffin would study her, her diction, her tone, and her body language. Body language. The most often used form of communication, the easiest to discern come-on.

And there was some real irony in all of this women and relationship stuff Griffin dealt with. The one woman whom Griffin found himself attracted to, in a perverse sort of way, was, of all people, Constance Frye. Griffin wasn't sure why. Maybe the first lady's intellect attracted him, but any notion that the feeling was real was absurd. Still, he enjoyed watching her steer along the road to her goal, fueled by her ever-present ulterior motives for some ultra-secular, government-dominated utopia. Like Lennon's lyrics, the smooth words Constance spoke slipped into her listeners' psyches, guiding their thoughts around cleverly laid curves, changing, softening their principles, reversing their convictions.

Soon after the time when Governor Frye had retained him, Griffin had attended a party at the governor's mansion. Constance had begun maneuvering into domestic policy making, and Griffin felt she looked on him as an obstruction, one of those people who couldn't keep his religion out of his political beliefs.

Griffin remembered the little incident so vividly: He had drunk just a bit too much at the party. Not unusual for him back then. Constance stepped up to him. They weren't alone under the outside lights, but at that moment, everyone else had their attention on either something or someone else.

"You know, Griffin, we can be friends," Constance had said.

Griffin gazed into those green eyes. They almost turned him sober. An anecdote popped into his mind, and he had just enough alcohol in him to overrule the voice deep inside—*"Don't tell it, Griffin!"*

"Ever heard of the man who made friends with a snake, Constance?" Griffin asked, not moving his gaze off her eyes, feeling himself swaying a tad.

Constance said nothing. Griffin took another slug of twenty-five-year-old Wild Turkey, his favorite.

"A couple days later the man was walking down the street, the snake slithering on the road beside him." Griffin heard the voice warning him again, but decided to go for it. "The snake suddenly sunk his fangs into the man's ankle. The man stopped in his tracks. He looked down. Knowing he was going to die, he said to the snake, 'You said we would be friends. Why did you bite me?' The snake looked up, and with those green eyes with those black slits for pupils, he said, 'You knew I was a snake, didn't you?'" Griffin chuckled.

Constance fixed her gaze on his eyes. She grinned. "A day will come, Griffin, when Ashton is president. Then, when you least expect it, I'll sink my fangs into you. Perhaps you will remember I said that when the alcohol burns off."

That was the last time Griffin took a drink.

Now the whole nation was blessed with Constance Frye, and the first lady of the United States was Griffin's sworn enemy. *Good going, pal!*

On his way to Avraham Hegel's White House reception, sitting in the backseat of his limousine, Griffin had no idea what to expect from this fascinating woman, except that he should expect something.

What about this reception, anyway? This was a hot issue, this brain stem cell stuff. Even after reading letters for and against all of it on the op-ed pages in the *Columbia Picayune*—conservatives condemning it; liberals condemning the conservatives—Griffin still wasn't sure what the procedure was about. *How do they do it?* But today the debate continued, in a more confrontational manner, in front of the White House, with prayers and singing from one side, hissing and shouting from the other.

But Constance would find a way to get what she wanted. She would network, manipulate, threaten, bargain. And using the "for the good of the children" mantra for her reforms with the national press as her adoring, slobbering lap dog, what reasonable person would oppose her? Griffin chuckled.

And he, along with every other American who read the newspaper or listened to the evening news, was bombarded with implied or expressed criticism of men like Senator Jeremiah Gators, who dared to criticize the first lady's reform. Those religious, right-wing, backward myopics who questioned the motives of the most intelligent, well-meaning first lady since Eleanor Roosevelt, and, of course, her scholarly husband, too. What's his name again?

Men in dark suits, starched white shirts, and aviator-style sunglasses roamed the White House grounds. They panned the lawn, sidewalks, and streets, scanning the protestors and speaking into little black hissing radios.

About two hundred pro-life protestors had set up homestead outside the White House grounds, just beyond street barricades. Some protestors just stood; others swayed in groups, singing "Jesus Loves Me." Some carried handcrafted signs, "Hegel the Beast," and "King Avraham Herod." A few knelt and prayed. Toddlers stumbled on the concrete and grass, protest signs pinned to their backs, their eyes glazed with befuddlement.

Not far away, separated by about thirty feet of concrete and police barricades lined end-to-end, people from Anticipating Parenthood, perhaps fifty women and half that many men, marched and carried professionally made signs: "For the Living Children" and "Religious Terrorists Don't Belong in Government." White House police, twenty or thirty of them, wearing helmets and clear plastic face shields, paced between the two groups, twirling their night sticks on leather straps entwined on their wrists.

What do all these people do for a living? Griffin asked himself as he watched through the tinted rear window of the limousine, feeling the limousine roll to a stop.

A marine in full dress greeted Griffin as he stepped out of the limousine. The marine escorted him through Entrance Hall, down Cross Hall, then into the East Room of the White House. Griffin thought to himself that he was as husky and straight as this young marine. Not bad for his age, not bad at all.

Griffin's breath left him when he entered the East Room. The ceiling went up forever, and thousands of prisms glistened on huge chandeliers. Columns, some standing free, some half embedded in the walls, evoked the feeling that the room had no boundaries.

The East Room, more than any other room in the White House, except perhaps the Oval Office, radiated the power of the presidency. Griffin glanced at his watch: five minutes late. *Where are you, Constance?*

Griffin walked farther into the room. He had not met Dr. Hegel, but that had to be him, standing in the far corner, near the podium. Who was that woman standing next to him? A study of her tall, thin frame brought the answer. *Kristina England.* Griffin wasn't sure, but the blond standing next to her was— He couldn't think of the name. *Come on, Griffin—she's president of Anticipating Parenthood. You've seen her a hundred times on television—Rebecca Ingram, that's it.*

A marine corporal in full dress stood at ease on the other side of Hegel. Madeline Gentcher stood a few feet in front of Dr. Hegel with her back to him. Griffin hadn't seen Gentcher in awhile. She appeared the same, though—plain-looking and angry at anything that respired, except Constance Frye. No makeup. Hair brown, thin, and in a page-boy. Griffin chuckled, remembering his first encounter with Gentcher. Just to establish the fact that she was not intimidated that he was the president's private attorney, Gentcher had called him "Jackson."

Another marine in full dress stepped up to Griffin. He extended a silver tray of martinis and glasses of red and white wine.

"May I serve you, sir?" the marine said.

"No, thank you, Corporal." Griffin shook his head. Full-dress marine maids. Only in Constance Frye's White House. Ashton Frye, one of the smartest, shrewdest men Griffin had known, didn't have the courage to tell his wife, "No, not the marines as maids. Not tonight, not ever."

Griffin felt his pulse increase. Then he saw her, and the thought came to him right out of *Moby Dick: There she blows! Dead ahead, heading this way off starboard bow! Lower the boats! Ready the harpoons!*

She had gained a little weight after all this time. The supple black cloth didn't do much to hide her wide hips. That familiar green gaze stayed fixed on Griffin's eyes as she moved toward him. The snake story ran through Griffin's mind.

Constance Frye stopped suddenly just two feet in front of Griffin. At five-four she had to look up to speak to him.

"Well, hello, Griffin," the first lady said, extending her hand toward him.

"Hello, Mrs. Frye." He took her hand and squeezed it gently. Had she changed, after all?

With her eyes saying to anyone who caught them, "It's so nice to see you again," the first lady said just loud enough for Griffin to hear, "This is my night, not Ashton's. Don't talk about my investment with Ashton." Then she said in a normal voice, "I hear you're doing so well back home, Griffin."

"I like your new hair color," Griffin said. "Looks better shorter like that. What was it last time, auburn?"

Constance glanced to one side then the other, then moved her gaze back to Griffin. He couldn't keep his eyes off her. Her words ran through his mind: "A day will come, Griffin, when Ashton is president. Then, when you least expect it, I'll sink my fangs into you."

Constance resumed her near whisper, still smiling. "The young man to your left in the tux with the carnation pinned on the wrong lapel." She turned her head to her right just slightly and nodded. "He's Secret Service." Griffin followed the direction of her nod. A neat, barely thirty-year-old man smirked at him. Griffin returned his gaze to Constance.

"You never disappoint me, Constance," Griffin said.

"He'll join your conversation with Ashton, if I'm not able to prevent one." Constance's voice had risen a bit.

"I appreciate the special treatment," Griffin said. "You look, well. . .heavier."

Constance's head bobbed with her single chuckle. She walked away.

Warren Jennings returned to Griffin's thoughts, then Landcaster, as he watched the celebrity politicians. He decided to stay in spite of the encounter. He had to talk to Gordon Redden, who enjoyed demonstrating his significance in the Frye administration by offering off-the-record information.

Griffin approached another full-dress marine, who agreed to bring him a tall glass of soda water with a wedge of lime. "Serve it in a tea glass with ice, Corporal," Griffin said. "I'll be over there." Griffin pointed to a secluded spot toward the rear of the huge room where he would be able to see the privileged enter. He apologized to the marine for having to make a special trip for his drink. After the marine walked away, Griffin lifted his palm, turned to his Secret Service guard, and waved him along.

The nation's celebrity-politicians began filing in: Speaker Kareem Jukali, Vice President Courtney Packard, Attorney General Sheryl van Meter, then little Professor Wootan. Representatives and senators, too. All appearing in awe of the first lady, moving about in the line, waiting to greet the president's wife, turning toward each other, shaking hands, laughing. Griffin felt a change in the atmosphere of the East Room. Where was the confetti in this victory party? The balloons?

While the Secret Service fellow maintained his stare on Griffin, Griffin spanned the room to take in the sights. Kristina England, in a green pants suit, kept her eyes on Constance's every move, not looking too happy.

Get off the soap opera stuff, Griffin. Come on, Redden, you snitch. I want to talk about BioSysTech, then maybe walk around some. Watch Constance a little, too. And, Mr. President, about the investment Constance made—

"Hiding, Mr. Dowell?" a female voice asked.

Theresa! Griffin swung his head around in the direction of the voice, his heart feeling like it was pounding out of his chest.

She tilted her head with her blue eyes fixed on him. His heart settled.

"You found me, didn't you?" Griffin said to the woman, feeling sorry immediately for the tone.

She straightened, then looked as if she were going to apologize.

"I'm sorry," Griffin said. "Your voice just reminded me of someone."

"Whom were you looking for?" the lady asked. "I don't know many people here, but I'll help." She extended her free hand. "Ruth Hegel."

Griffin shook her hand.

"Ms. England over there by my husband told me you were the president's former private attorney."

"Former?" Griffin asked.

"She told me Mrs. Frye would be upset if I spoke to you," Mrs. Hegel said. "You're not a friend of the administration, it seems. Ms. Gentcher, who appears ready to box the ears off anyone who wants to talk to Avraham, told me the same thing. Tell me, Mr. Dowell—"

"Griffin."

"Well, it seemed to me, Griffin, that a person who wanted to interfere with Mrs. Frye's attempts to help America's children—their corpses lying in gutters everywhere, you know—would be interesting to meet." Ruth Hegel smiled.

And what a smile. Griffin looked closer at her. She was elegant, probably late forties, but her smooth skin and thin figure made her look years younger. "Thank you," Griffin said. "Mrs. Frye was nice enough to assign a Secret Service fellow to guard me. Sure you ought to be talking to me?"

"The first lady and I chatted before she started greeting the acceptable ones. She's obsessed with her government utopia. She believes Avraham is some sort of national hero for what he does. I had to excuse myself in the middle of her chatter." Ruth lifted her glass, then tilted it only enough that the wine wetted her lips.

Griffin looked at her hand holding the wine glass. Her hand was soft, perfect. *Griffin, behave yourself. Talk about her husband.* "I'm looking forward to hearing Dr. Avraham Hegel speak." *Really, Griffin?*

"Mrs. Frye has removed Avraham's speech from the agenda," Ruth said. "I couldn't be happier." Ruth turned away for a moment, then looked back at Griffin. The marine stepped up with Griffin's soda water, stood at attention, and extended the tray.

"Thanks, Corporal," Griffin said. "I wish I could do something about this assignment of yours."

"Thank you," Ruth said to the marine as she set her nearly full wine glass on the tray.

The marine nodded at Ruth, gave Griffin a slight tight-lipped smile, turned, and left with stiff steps.

"The young man," Ruth jerked her head with a mischievous smile, almost giddy, "over there, with the carnation on the wrong lapel, the one craning his neck?"

"That's him," Griffin said with a smile. "Skilled surveillance guy." They laughed. Griffin moved his head to the side, lifted his hand, and directed a baby-type wave at the agent. The young man's face flushed red. He took a deep breath and blew the air out of his nostrils.

Ruth and Griffin didn't speak for several moments. Griffin felt comfortable with her standing next to him. He felt he could say anything to this stranger and she would meet him at his level of wit. *Griffin, what are you thinking?*

In a new curiosity, he moved his gaze to Dr. Hegel, intending to put the couple together in his mind. Then something. . . Griffin couldn't explain it, couldn't think it through, but something was wrong. Then he realized what bothered him: Hegel was flanked by a marine and England. They hadn't budged. Hegel was being guarded, too, just like he was!

Time to do a little investigation. Just be careful, Griffin. Don't cross-examine her. "Can I ask you something, Mrs. Hegel?"

"Ruth."

"Would you like a fresh glass of Chardonnay, Ruth?" Griffin asked when he spotted another full-dress marine acting as though he had been ordered to beg the politicians to accept a drink off his tray.

"No," Ruth said, "but that's not what you wanted to ask me, is it?"

Griffin paused a moment. "You don't want your husband involved in this?" he asked.

Silence followed. Tension. Griffin could feel it. Not to the degree as that between him and a witness under cross-examination, but the same sort. *Okay, Griffin, just let this urge to question her pass. Chill out.*

More moments passed. Then Ruth broke the silence. No smile; no wit now.

"Avraham's first breakthrough was a mixture he formulated to ease pain suffered by research animals," Ruth said as if talking to no one. "He called it 'Alfa Alkaloid.' Except for those who believe animals are our half siblings, he received a lot of praise for that. It was important to him that the laboratory animals were free of pain, at least to the extent the experiments would allow."

Ruth's speech was soft, venting. Why was she doing this? It didn't matter. Griffin was going to learn something important. He knew it. *Concentrate, Griffin. Listen to every word.*

"Think about that," Ruth said. "What kind of researcher would recognize that animals should be used to save people's lives, but would then develop a formula to reduce their suffering?"

"I'm impressed," Griffin said.

"Then Avraham turned to fetal research. Not the cannibalism he does today, using brains from fetuses taken out of teenagers scared to tell their daddies they're pregnant or sophisticates too busy to give birth. He worked with fetal lung tissue. Avraham wouldn't accept the tissue unless he was satisfied the fetus had been aborted involuntarily."

Ruth gazed at her husband.

"About two years later, Avraham developed a preparation that accelerated growth of fetal lung tissue during gestation by injecting his preparation into the mother. The beneficial effect could be measured in a week and was fully effective in stabilizing the lungs in two weeks. If used properly in high-risk pregnancies when the mother has a history or is in danger of spontaneous loss of her baby, the mortality rate of babies born prematurely would be reduced significantly. It was a neonatal breakthrough. Avraham has always been famous for breakthroughs."

No laughter, no brightness in her blue eyes. No wit. Griffin watched her. He was sure Ruth didn't realize that she was glaring at her husband.

"You sound like a doctor yourself," Griffin said.

"Just a college English teacher and mom with two grown children. I used to help Avraham write manuscripts for publication and helped him rehearse his talks and seminars for national and international symposia. I was so proud of him."

"He still publishes?" Griffin asked.

"After he began working with the company he's involved with and began this work with fetal brains, I just couldn't. . ." Ruth glanced at Dr. Hegel and his guards.

"Constance Frye and her friends will destroy him," Griffin said. "They're vicious, agendized people."

Ruth looked up directly into Griffin's eyes. "He's my husband, but I don't know him anymore. He comes and goes, sometimes doesn't even tell me where. Now he wants to become involved in politics. He wants to move here, away from Kingston. The kids are gone, in college. I guess he thinks it would be easy—at least for him."

"If you prosper in this town," Griffin said, "unless you are one of them, a Constance, or one of those politicians that drool over her, they will persecute you. This city seethes with obsessed networkers who climb on the necks of friends." *Griffin, slow down.* He tried to review the past fleeting few minutes. *What happened in such a brief time to make us talk to each other like this, like old friends?*

"Do you know we used to celebrate the traditions? He read from the Old Testament before the meal. Avraham, our children—Joshua, Esther—and I. So long ago. So very long ago." Ruth crossed her arms and glanced at her husband again. She turned to Griffin. "It's nice to have someone to talk to. Kingston is a small, gossipy town. It's even smaller when your husband is the most famous man there." Ruth smiled, but it wasn't the same smile. She began rubbing the upper part of her arms with her hands when she forced that smile, and the smile left her as quickly as it had come.

She needed time to recover, to take a few breaths. Griffin wanted to hear her wit, her voice with laughter in it again. He decided to wait, not to speak for a few minutes. But he needed to know more. He couldn't immediately assimilate everything she had said, but he would later. He would sit back in his chair, staring out at the early morning Columbia skyline, before Jennifer or anyone else came to the office, and remember and think. He would jot down on legal pads every piece of the puzzle, every detail, every word and impression he could recall.

But he needed more pieces of this puzzle that stretched from Washington to Kingston to Columbia. He had to ask questions. *Be careful, Griffin. Don't treat her like a witness.*

"Ruth, the company your husband became involved with, was it Biological Systems Technologies. . .BioSysTech?" Griffin asked.

Ruth stared at him. "How did you know?" she asked.

"The fetal lung tissue compound, what happened to it?"

"BioSysTech bought the rights for a lump sum," Ruth said. "They said they could not promise royalties or other payments because of the Food and Drug Administration's testing requirements before human use. It's disappeared."

"The lump sum. How much?"

Ruth quieted. She went cold. "A lot, Mr. Dowell. A lot," she said. She took a deep breath and looked toward her husband. "I'm tired of all this. Please," she said.

"I'm sorry. I—"

"I'd better get back. Ms. Gentcher is stepping to the microphone." Ruth turned and walked away, her shoulders slumped. Griffin couldn't see her face as she walked away from him, turning her shoulders here and there to avoid a bump of a stranger's shoulder, but he could tell it was her eyes she wiped with the back of her hand when she lowered her head and returned to her husband.

Griffin, you're a jerk. Somehow, someday, you're going to apologize to her. His first thought was flowers; his second was *Don't be stupid.* Then another thought: *I have to talk to Warren Jennings again, to study every word, every mark on every page of the box of documents the courier is going to pick up at Jennings' office.*

He couldn't stay at this celebration of the death of the spirit of a once great man any longer. His interest in further studying Constance had gone. He surveyed the room, thinking the president might have come in without his knowing it. No, he hadn't. And no Redden, either. *What's the use?*

A marine stepped up to Griffin. Griffin set his glass of carbonated water on the marine's tray without saying anything to the marine. He headed for the huge doors of the East Room. He felt anger rising in him, at himself. He stopped toe-to-toe in front of his SS guard. Griffin had to look down to fix his gaze on the agent's widened eyes. Griffin felt as if he were about to ask that last question, the one under cross-examination that would expose a lying witness. He began poking the young man's chest as Madeline Gentcher was rattling off her introduction of the first lady, saying how much her mentor cared for America's suffering little children.

"You mental midget!" Griffin hollered in the tone of a marine drill sergeant. "Don't you know what lapel that flower is supposed to be on?"

Gentcher stopped speaking. The guard stiffened. He glared at Griffin, clamping his lips; his face flushed red again.

Griffin turned, then walked out of the East Room, sensing gazes following him. No doubt Constance's and Gentcher's. Probably England's. Maybe, just maybe, Ruth's.

Smile, Ruth. For heaven's sake, pick yourself up and smile again, then get out of this town.

MONDAY, JUNE 24

CHAPTER 8

According to the weatherman on WRXO News Radio in Kingston, a heavy rain driven by a hard southeast gale was due to begin at dawn. Amanda thought the weatherman must have been accurate in his forecast when the noise of wind whistling through the trees on Cherry Street caused her to open her eyes for a moment, though she wasn't fully awake. Large drops of rain thudded against the poorly insulated, one-hundred-plus-year-old building, a precarious barrier that separated Amanda from the storm.

By 7:15 the storm had diminished to a common rain, but it seemed to Amanda that the storm had blown through a long time ago. She'd had a night of deep sleep, no dreams, nothing but rest. Certainly her weekend with Geoffry had brought about the rest, not so much their time at the beach and the rented movies and pizza, but reassurances, just being with him in this new relationship. This was real; they could handle her father and forget their differences. She had even promised Geoffry that she would go to his little church with him on Wednesday night. *Daddy, will you ever understand?*

When Amanda floated out of her bed to begin her morning routine, she thought how fortunate for her the rain had held off until this morning. The weekend had been so wonderful, so sunny. Geoffry, of course, had everything to do with it, too. She and her fiancé had made plans—real, important plans—while sitting on towels at the beach under the bright sun. Yes, there would be babies. Two, maybe three.

"I wonder. . ." Geoffry had said.

"What do you wonder, honey?"

"I wonder what color they're going to be?"

Amanda slapped his shoulder gently, and they laughed.

I've got to hurry!

Dr. Hegel's seminar was today. *Finally!* Amanda had to be there for him in case he needed last-minute things done. Maybe she should get there even earlier than she'd planned. Something special was going to happen today; Dr. Hegel would be himself again. Amanda was certain of it.

Why am I so nervous about this seminar? He's not. That's for sure! He'll rivet them to their seats again.

Amanda felt proud of Dr. Hegel—proud to be a part of his work. Today she would be working with him in front of everyone, not merely an attendee, sitting in the front row of the Pit. Geoffry and Dr. Hegel were both supporting her, both loving her in their own special, re-spectful way.

You're a lucky girl, Amanda, she thought as she slipped an elastic band over her fistful of hair.

Hurry, hurry!

The toes of Amanda's left foot just wouldn't slip into her penny-loafer as she hopped on her right foot toward her apartment door.

⌞__⌟

Griffin squealed the tires of his BMW 740i into his parking slot on the fifth parking level of the Executive Plaza Building, almost smash-ing through the railing before he braked. He pulled the door latch and lifted the *Columbia Picayune* off the passenger seat. Even with his limp, he stomped across the narrow driveway to the elevator. He pushed the up button and waited.

It happened every time he became angry and lost control: His old leg wound throbbed. He had to calm down, not think anymore about what he had read on the front page of this morning's edition of the *Picayune,* what had sickened him at first, then caused Constance

Frye's green gaze to flash through his mind.

Don't think about it, yet, Griffin. Not while you're out of control.

"You'll be all right," the surgeon in the M.A.S.H. unit had told him after that intruder made his way into the perimeter and fired a round into Griffin's left thigh. "It'll do more damage to cut the thing out," the surgeon had said while cutting dead and torn tissue and packing antibiotic into the gaping hole. "You're lucky to keep that leg, Lieutenant. You might feel the bullet at times, rubbing against a tendon or ligament, but you'll be out there plucking off those geeks in no time."

When the elevator doors opened, Griffin limped to his office and stiffly lowered himself into his chair.

The tidal wave came, washing away any chance of peace, any justification, any excuse that he might conjure up. How could he have been so cavalier? How could he have missed it? Griffin opened the *Picayune* again to the article. He stared at the picture of his friend's body lying under a white sheet. Those newspaper people, they didn't have to show his body like that. Another lump formed in his throat; he felt numb. *You're so smart, aren't you, J. Griffin Dowell? You wouldn't listen to him, would you? Remember what you told him? "Warren, if someone's following you, Constance Frye has nothing to do with it, I'm sure."*

Griffin turned in his chair and looked down at the streets. Downtown Columbia was just waking up. Griffin dropped his face in his hands. *There will be one empty chair behind a desk today, Griffin. You could have prevented that.*

Griffin wasn't aware of passing time. He had managed to calm himself, though. His thigh no longer throbbed. He found himself praying. "Oh, God, forgive me. I'm sorry, Warren."

Remember, Griffin? Remember when you were a deacon, before Theresa—when prayer was a common part of your life?

Amanda drove into the parking lot of the Science and Agriculture Building at 8:11. The sun had come out; it shone particularly brightly through the drizzle. The brightness through the mist made it seem as if both were competing to control the day. It reminded Amanda of an eerie double-exposed photograph.

And, for a moment, as she pulled into the parking lot, Amanda lapsed into another battle with her mind about her father. Did Daddy know yet? Amanda had wanted to call again, but her mother was right. Her father might answer. What then? Hang up on Daddy? Mama would call when the time was right, after the hollering: "I don't have a daughter no more! I don't want no half-breed mulatto babies around here!" Amanda felt a deep sorrow for her mother having to live with that hate. But she was thankful for her mother, too. She had allowed Amanda to experience the joy in life that comes when blind, unreasonable hate is rejected.

Amanda turned into the parking lot. Her gaze caught the white Ford. The two men sat in it while it collected droplets on its windshield, obscuring her view of the passenger when she glanced his way.

She hadn't seen the Crown Victoria for days, and the image of the passenger had become as obscure in her mind as it appeared behind the beaded windshield. She didn't feel as frightened—as vulnerable today—as she had those other times. She was engaged now; she had Geoffry to protect her. Anyway, whatever the intentions of those two men, they didn't involve her. Amanda lowered her umbrella over her head and dashed to the building, up the outside concrete stairs, and through the door.

Once she arrived, she turned on the computer. During the computer's grinding and beeping, she realized she hadn't noticed Dr. Hegel's car in the lot. It had to be there. The rain, the umbrella, the running caused her to miss it, probably.

When the program's main menu appeared on the monitor, Amanda moved the arrow to "Notes and Reminders." Dr. Hegel might have left another message.

He had: "AFH—Amanda, you should probably come to my office immediately."

She was right. Dr. Hegel had some things for her to do before the seminar. It then occurred to Amanda that he might not want her to do tasks; that he might want to thank her for her eagerness to help him during these last few months and for her faithfulness and hard work. That would be just like the old Dr. Hegel.

You're yourself again, just like I knew you would be, Dr. Hegel. You don't have to do that. Look what you have done for me!

———

"It's not your fault," Jennifer said softly, as she set a cup of coffee in front of Griffin.

"Warren. . .overdose? He wouldn't know cocaine from Tide detergent," Griffin said.

"Griffin, please, you don't have to. . ."

"They put a gun to his head, maybe a knife to his throat. They told him to inject it, or Carolyn and his boys would die, too. I know how it works. It might be different tools, different reasons, but the method is the same." Griffin paused. "What am I supposed to tell Carolyn?" Griffin asked Jennifer, rubbing his hand through his hair. "She's like a sister. What do I say? 'Sorry, I could have saved him, but. . .' "

"Carolyn isn't going to blame you," Jennifer said.

It was good to hear a female voice with compassion for him. Jennifer was right. He had to quit the sniveling and look at what had happened. It had only been at Hegel's reception that he'd finally put the pieces together enough to know that something really was going on, something big and hidden by the power elite. It would take effort, but he would find out what it was. He would avenge his friend's death.

"When will that courier be here with those BioSysTech papers Warren was going to copy?" Griffin asked.

"He should be getting to Warren's office about now. Debbie's going to see to it that he gets the box. Mr. Schneider's like clockwork, Debbie told me. He walks into the office at ten every morning."

"Good ol' Walter Schneider," Griffin said. "He'll get Warren's interest in the firm without going to the trouble of suing. He must be overjoyed." Griffin paused a moment. "I want to wait awhile before calling Carolyn. I don't know what to tell her," he said.

"She's not going to blame you, Griffin."

The phone rang.

That's Carolyn. I know it is. Griffin felt a lump pass his throat.

Jennifer walked behind Griffin's desk to answer it. She pushed the hold button. "It's Walter Schneider," she said, holding the receiver toward Griffin. "He came in early this morning."

Griffin pondered a moment. "Coincidence, you think?" He took the telephone receiver from Jennifer's hand.

"Hello, Walter," Griffin said.

"Your courier is here, Dowell," Schneider said. "He wants a box of documents from our late friend. Any idea what documents he's talking about?"

"You don't know?" Griffin asked.

"No documents will leave this office," Schneider said. "I've spoken to Constance Frye. I'll be handling their business now."

"Wait, Walter, let me slip on my Captain Oatmeal ring and decode that."

"I understand you had a chat with Warren on Friday?"

"Come to think of it, we did," Griffin said. "Mind telling me who told you, Walter?"

"Anything about this firm's clients?" Schneider asked.

"You know Warren would never violate his clients' confidence. And I wouldn't disclose an attorney-client communication, either. It's privileged. Even you know that, don't you, Walter?"

"Your client is dead," Schneider said, then paused. Griffin knew why: to assess shock value. This was negotiation in a perverse sort of way. "You understand Warren's state of mind when he was in your office. All doped up. His professional competence suffering the usual results of addictions—imagining things. . .drug-induced hallucinations."

"Why, Walter, you sound like you're happy about it all," Griffin said. "Have you read Dickens lately? I can just imagine you slumped over a ledger, writing down your bank balances with your finger gloves on."

"You have room to speak, Dowell. The sleazy lawyer who represents sleazy politicians."

"I don't want to keep you," Griffin said. "I know you're in mourning. Why don't you pull your tattered shawl over your shoulders and resume your hunched position over your ledgers. And tell Constance hello for me."

Griffin hung up. He looked at Jennifer. Her arms were crossed over her blouse. She moved her hands as if she had a chill. Griffin realized his bantering insults with Schneider didn't have the therapeutic effect on her that it had on him.

"Find every document of any kind we have on the BioSysTech venture, on Richard Landcaster. . .on everything," Griffin said to Jennifer. "Go all the way back to the first day Ashton Frye told me to investigate the venture."

"That'll take some time," Jennifer said.

"Before you start, call Allan Cook. I need to talk to him."

"The FBI?" Jennifer asked.

As Amanda knocked on the dark wood framing the translucent rippled glass inset on the top half of Dr. Hegel's office door, the good feelings she had carried with her up the stairs about this meeting vanished. The sunlight beamed through the windows on the back wall behind Dr. Hegel's desk. The backlighting caused a jerky, surrealistic image through the rippled glass as Dr. Hegel stepped quickly from the bookcase on the side wall to his desk, carrying something. He plopped in his chair.

Amanda tried to focus on what he held in his hand. He had moved in such a hurry, and with the object's edges undulating through the rippled glass, she could only make out its general form, but it couldn't be what she thought she saw. *A fetus? Stiff with rigor mortis?*

"Come in, my dear," Dr. Hegel said without rising from his chair.

Amanda stepped into the office, something in his tone making her apprehensive. The notion that her mentor was going to pile appreciation on her dissipated. Then she felt relief. It was just an old doll that Dr. Hegel held. *An old doll?*

"Please close the door," Dr. Hegel said.

The morning sun shining through the windows behind Dr. Hegel illuminated the office. He lifted his silhouetted face and extended an open palm toward one of the two chairs in front of his desk. "Have a seat, my dear," Dr. Hegel said.

He set both hands on his desk. The old doll lay in front of him, almost equidistant between him and Amanda. Amanda glanced at the doll. She felt her brow furrow.

Dr. Hegel brought his hands together, interlocked his fingers, and after a few seconds that seemed to Amanda like several minutes, he asked, "And how are you and that nice young man doing?"

"Fine, Dr. Hegel."

"Did you two have a nice weekend?"

"Yes, thank you."

"I can tell you did," Dr. Hegel said. "I see your new ring and the brightness in your face." Dr. Hegel grinned, but it was a forced, emotionless grin.

Amanda felt no brightness. Her heart pounded. Something was wrong.

"I have a task for you before my performance this afternoon," Dr. Hegel said.

"Dr. Hegel, are you all right?"

"You do remember my seminar this afternoon?" Dr. Hegel asked, his gaze fixed on Amanda's eyes.

Can he hear my heart? Is this how his doctoral students feel when they defend their dissertations in front of him? And that doll!

"I rehearsed. . .like you asked." Amanda realized her voice cracked.

"You plan to attend then?" Dr. Hegel asked.

Dr. Hegel had not moved his head. His eyes did not move; they hadn't even blinked, Amanda was certain. They stared at her through those wire-rimmed glasses.

Dr. Hegel's left hand crawled to the old naked doll; his fingertips rested on its protruding belly. He began to tap the soft rubber skin with his pointing finger.

Amanda glanced at the doll, then returned her gaze to Dr. Hegel. She tried hard to ignore the *thump, thump, thump* his fingertip caused when it struck the rubber of the naked doll's belly.

Don't look at the doll, Amanda. He's lost it. He's trying to scare you. He is scaring you!

Dead silence, except for the thumping. Amanda's gaze passed over the doll. Its eyes were closed, but Amanda knew they would open suddenly if someone picked the doll up. Blue glass eyes, no doubt. The doll might even whine or say "Maaa-ma." Then Amanda noticed something else: two X marks on its forehead, made with a black marker, one just above each eyebrow, midway to the first row of nylon hair plugs.

"Her name is Millie," Dr. Hegel said.

Thump. . .thump. . .thump.

"Dr. Hegel. . .I'm supposed to help you this afternoon," Amanda said. "The slides. Remember?"

"Millie belongs to my daughter, Esther. It used to be my wife's," Dr. Hegel said. He stopped tapping the doll and put his hands on the desk in front of him. "I don't want to disappoint you, but the need for this new task has just come up, and it is very important, I assure you."

"Yes, but. . ."

"It is much more important than my little performance. Perhaps you mind?" Dr. Hegel spoke those words slowly, deliberately.

Amanda shook her head. "No. . .no, Dr. Hegel. I don't mind," she said.

"Thank you, my dear. I want you to return to the lab at three-forty this afternoon."

Amanda nodded.

"The rest of the morning and the afternoon, I'll be in the lab confirming growth of baby brain cells. . . ."

Baby brain cells? The words caused momentary confusion. "I've already done that, Dr.—"

"I will probably transfer more data to the log. It's important that you enter them in the program. You will do this, won't you?" Dr. Hegel asked.

"Yes, Dr. Hegel. Of course I will."

"And you will return to the lab at precisely three-forty?"

"Yes."

"Please do not disturb me today. Take the rest of the morning and early afternoon off. Have lunch with that nice fiancé of yours. You will need time with him."

What does he mean by that? Amanda wondered.

"Perhaps you should go now," Dr. Hegel said as he slid his hand and rested it on Millie's belly.

Amanda stood up. What had just happened?

In this very office they had discussed the lousy football record that had plagued URI for decades. Dr. Hegel had laughed about the folly of petty faculty politics. And then, the most important conversation with him of all, the one in which she had discussed her growing feelings for a fair-complexioned Irish boy. She had told Dr. Hegel her concerns about her father, how his bigotry would force her to cull either him or Geoffry from her life.

"Do you love the boy, my dear?" Dr. Hegel had asked Amanda softly, with his eyes the way they used to look. "Do you long for things good for him. . .to be with him?" Dr. Hegel's words, their tenor and inflection, unleashed joy within Amanda, causing her spirit to soar. *He understands! He understands!* she remembered thinking.

"Then, my dear, your differences are nothing. Your father must understand that. He must willfully and forever abandon his evil hatred. Hate destroys people, societies, and cultures. It destroyed my country and millions of my people throughout the centuries. The hate will callous his heart," Dr. Hegel had said.

But who was this Dr. Hegel today?

Amanda turned toward the door, hurt, her grip on the doorknob.

"You will be on time, won't you, Amanda. . .at three-forty, precisely?" Dr. Hegel asked. He stood, a tall silhouette. Amanda couldn't see his eyes. But she could feel his gaze. His shadow darkened the top of his desk and the old rubber doll.

"Yes, Dr. Hegel," Amanda said.

"Allan, I need to speak off the record." Griffin said into the phone as he gazed out the window over Columbia, recalling Allan's lanky build and Dick Tracy–chiseled face. *Bet he's still running fifteen miles a week.* "My prayer time," he had always told Griffin when they were in law school.

"What can I do for you—back off investigating some of your clients?"

"You might find this call a little bizarre," Griffin said. "But I need to know about your agency's criminal federal procedure."

"I'm supposed to tell you?" Cook asked.

"Come on, Allan," Griffin said. "You know I just do civil work, not your sort of federal criminal work. I wouldn't ask if it were not vital that I know."

"Okay, ask."

"Let's say the first lady is involved in a death," Griffin said.

"You think Warren Jennings was murdered?" Cook asked.

"How do you know I was thinking about him?" Cook's question caused Griffin's head to swim for a moment.

"Jennings was the president's CPA, and I'm FBI. That's how I know," Cook said.

Real smart, Griffin. "Okay, but hypothetically, Allan. Hypothetically."

"Go on."

"Let's just say she was involved in ordering the killing, and it was associated with some activity, an immensely profitable activity, immensely illegal, too."

"What's the question?" Cook asked.

"What kind of evidence would you need to order an investigative file opened?"

"Off the record?"

"This call never happened," Griffin said.

"Ideally, if you have probable cause to make an arrest, then opening a file would be the next logical step," Cook said. "Or I—well, the director in this case—might open a file just to investigate an allegation. There are other considerations, not the least of which is the identity of the target."

"And if it's the president's wife?" Griffin asked.

"Then you really have other considerations. Serious ones."

"Attorney General Sheryl van Meter. Is she one?" Griffin asked. He spun his chair to his desk and reached for a legal pad and pencil.

"The attorney general has a lot of power—more than you think," Cook said.

"Okay, just bare-boned, forget the intangibles. What evidence?" Griffin asked.

"Surveillance. Telephone tap, if possible. I'll tell you something you won't learn from the press. The day after the inauguration, the first lady set up office in the West Wing, the Executive Wing. She got the president to tell the entire staff that she was part of the Executive Team."

"The West Wing?" Griffin asked.

"First ladies traditionally have their offices in the East Wing to carry out their social agendas. But not Constance Frye. She also ordered a private phone line that was to be cleared electronically by the Secret Service every morning. Her line is untappable."

Griffin paused. "What about more evidence to compensate? What kind would you need to open a file?" he asked.

"In the face of an adoring press that would come against us with all they have, and an antagonistic attorney general and speaker to add to that mix, the other evidence would have to be enough to convict twice," Cook said.

"What kind of evidence?"

"Insider witnesses," Cook said. "Co-conspirators to testify maybe under immunity, maybe not. Probably witness protection. I would need power from the Hill. Certain congressmen would lash out against the Bureau, threaten reduced funding. And we need real evidence: photographs, documents. . . . Get enough of that, then a private meeting with the director. Then everything hits the fan. Unless. . ."

"Unless what?" Griffin asked.

"We could open a silent file, a secret investigation. But we need the same type of evidence to do that so we can justify doing it when the fact of the investigation leaks. And it will leak."

"Gordon Redden?" Griffin asked.

"Him and many others closer to the Bureau," Cook said.

Silence.

"If you get the evidence and succeed," Cook said, "you're a hero. Write a book, do television interviews. You're a millionaire."

"That's not my reason."

"But if you fail, that famous practice of yours goes down the drain; the famous J. Griffin Dowell will be no more. That is, of course, if you don't wind up indicted yourself, or disbarred."

"If Constance had anything to do with Warren, she wouldn't be satisfied stopping at that," Griffin said.

"I know you, Griffin," Cook said. "You're not going to let this go."

"How can I?"

"Still going to church?"

"Well. . ." *Why is everybody so worried about my spiritual condition?* Griffin remained quiet for a moment. "Thanks for your help, Allan," Griffin said.

"I must tell you one other thing," Cook said.

Cook's tone wasn't conversational. Griffin decided he should just listen.

"Before you do what you must, remember how David killed his giant. Do you remember, Griffin?"

Just listen, Griffin.

" 'You come with a sword, spear, and shield,' David said, 'but I come with the Lord of hosts; the battle is the Lord's.' Remember that, Griffin. It's not your battle, and if you make it your battle and don't go into it with the Lord of Hosts, then your giant will conquer you."

"Okay, Allan, okay—"

Jennifer stepped into the office and plopped a tall stack of BioSysTech files on Griffin's desk.

CHAPTER 9

Amanda had spent her free morning in her apartment. She had called Geoffry a little after noon to talk to him about the encounter with Dr. Hegel. Geoffry was sure Dr. Hegel was battling second thoughts about leaving research and the scientific community to join the Frye administration. "I told you," Geoffry had said, "he never should have agreed to it. Now he knows it."

Geoffry was wrong. Amanda just knew it. It was more than just a change of heart about his new position. Amanda considered how he had changed gradually, had gotten critical and intolerant of his colleagues. Now he mumbled nonsense to himself: soldier, generals, and evil impetuses. And today. Frightening. She was right; it was a metamorphosis, a transformation that had come to its conclusion. How could she help him? She had to try. She owed it to him.

Amanda drove around the parking lot, trying to find a space. Nothing, not even in the staff section where security was supposed to assure her a slot. She glanced at her watch: 3:30. She had to park. She had worked at the department long enough to know that except for Tuesdays and Thursdays, she could park next to the two Dumpsters at the back of the lot. She lifted her canvas satchel off the passenger's seat, got out of the car, and began walking toward the building. *I'm going to help him. Maybe when he sees how hard I practiced, then we'll have time to talk. I'll be glad when this all ends. But I have to help him.*

About midway through the parking lot, Amanda spotted Dr. Hegel. She stopped and stared. He was running, his lab coat billowing behind him. He kept his gaze on his car. He almost slammed into it, then jerked open the door, got in, started it up, and pulled away, tires squealing.

The white Ford pulled out of its parking slot just a few yards from Amanda. The Italian whirled the steering wheel, directing the big Ford toward Dr. Hegel's disappearing shiny black Lexus LS430. The passenger stared at Amanda, first through the passenger window, then through the rear window. He kept his head turned toward her, grinning with those gold teeth.

Dr. Hegel inserted *The Magic of Nan Mouskouri* in the CD player of his Lexus LS430. He glanced in his rearview mirror and then leaned back into the supple leather driver's seat. Ms. Mouskouri sang her rendition of "Yesterday." Dr. Hegel turned west on Rhode Island State Highway 138 and glanced in the rearview mirror again after he straightened the Lexus out of the turn.

"Man, how can he stand that music. He must have bought that CD last night at the mall," Fidel Ramos said. He reached down toward the signal receiver attached to the floor of the white Ford under the dash on the carpeted bell-housing hump.

"Let it alone," DiRosa said, holding his gaze ahead.

Ramos sat up in the passenger seat. "You better watch him, man," he said. "He never drove like this before, and his car is a lot faster than this one."

In the quiet of the Lexus, Nan Mouskouri's "Yesterday" took on new meaning to Avraham Hegel. He had changed. No, more than that; he had undergone a horrible transformation. He could have denied that until he saw B/M0012, that frail little thing with those two X-shaped surgical scars on its tender forehead where Jacqueline Reed had injected his Alfa Alkaloid following his procedure that had been intended for dogs and monkeys. And its empty, sunken eye socket, and the remaining little eye, moving slowly in its orbit, fixing its gaze on him, conveying to him its gratitude for taking its pain away.

Science must move forward, Avraham Frederick Hegel had always believed, resolving one hypothesis and then the next. Arguments of morality must be left to ethicists and the religious, to conservatives and liberals; the quest for knowledge could not be influenced by their obsessive fussing. The relentless march depended on men and women like him, the foot soldiers who apply the principle of moral neutrality for the sake of mankind. They take new ground, advance the front, generate new data that imply the next hypothesis that must be investigated, no matter how dark that next hypothesis might be. And, like a good soldier, he asked no questions.

But he had become a general in the scientific world, the leader of legions. He had convinced all of them in his publications, his seminars, and his classes to follow the principle of moral neutrality, to continue advancing the front. Who were they to question him? Avraham Frederick Hegel, the modern world's authority on fetal brain stem cells and creator of Hegel's Alfa Alkaloid, a vast improvement over Walter Freeman's abominable ice pick, his predecessor in neuro-murder, the newest dark medical discipline.

Ruth questioned him, though. *Darling, you always did. And you were right.* He hadn't thought of Ruth as "darling" for so long. He had become irredeemably evil; his soul languished beyond salvation.

Ms. Mouskouri began to sing "Amazing Grace."

Hegel hadn't prayed in a long time, but now he prayed until sweat beaded on his brow. He prayed that the sentences in his article in the *American Medical Research Journal,* the publication that began his association with BioSysTech—not his association, his bondage—would stop scrolling through his mind. But God would not answer. Why should He? The sentences kept coming: "Local pregnancy termination centers were asked to cooperate by furnishing fragments of human fetal nervous system tissue collected from routine human suction abortions. The appropriate severed parts of the conceptuses resulting from routine, elective second-trimester and, occasionally, third trimester abortions were identified as cephalic tissue."

"Tissue." That's what he had written. A meaningless word, like "conceptus." *No, Avraham, "conceptus" isn't a meaningless word, and you know it, don't you? It describes a living human being caught up in your and your conspirators' scheme that conceals not only its identity, but its very existence, so that anything can be done to it. Anything, Hegel.*

Oh, God, it was their little heads that I cracked on those blocks, as calmly as if I were cracking walnuts, and their brains that I dissected in those pans with no more emotion than it would take to slice butter.

"The physician collected the tissue in sterile dry-ice containers after rinsing in triple-distilled water. After reaching our lab, a portion of the cephalic tissue was separated and the remainder was cryopreserved. The separated tissue was carefully chopped and dissected and tested for viability. . ."

How could I have joined them? Where will they stop?

". . .by thawing fragments and seeding onto culture dishes with a gel-based medium composed of nutrients reported in an earlier article. After fourteen days of incubation at thirty-seven degrees Centigrade, presence and viability of human fetal brain stem cells were assessed using the technique reported previously."

They won't stop. And I showed them the way. Ruth, darling, you were right. Oh, God, you were so right!

The soft leather wrapping on the steering wheel compressed in Dr. Hegel's clenched grip.

Jesus. Are You the Messiah? Is it too late for You to help me? Are You real like those protesters who called me a "beast" hollered? Will You forgive me?

"That music is driving me crazy, man," Fidel Ramos said. He wanted to turn the volume down, but if he did, DiRosa would give him one of those looks. Ramos didn't want to be on the receiving end of that look again.

The device on the floor sounded steady beeps; the little red light flickered in short, consistent intervals. That woman's voice kept coming through the speaker singing those stupid songs. *Man, I wish he would turn her off.*

Dr. Hegel entered I-95 just before the Hope Valley town line and headed north. The Lexus accelerated into the middle lane of the interstate. Big tractor-trailers rumbled on the interstate, with a few cars zipping around them. Ramos saw an eighteen-wheeler in Dr. Hegel's lane about a half mile ahead. Dr. Hegel accelerated again.

"Better watch him," Ramos said. "I tell you, man. He never drove like this before."

After about a mile, Dr. Hegel moved from the middle lane into the left lane of the interstate. Ms. Mouskouri's rendition of "Power of Love" played on the CD player and through the speaker of the device that sat in the white Ford. The beeping that sounded at each flicker of the red light on the tracker weakened slightly.

"Catch up with him," Ramos said. "I think he knows we're back here, or he's going somewhere in a big hurry."

DiRosa merged into the left lane and accelerated. The beeping became louder, the red flickering brighter and increasing in frequency.

Ramos could see Dr. Hegel approach the left rear corner of the trailer. The hood of the Lexus edged up, next to the huge left front fender of the big tractor. Ahead, a sign read: "Rhode Island Highway 165 Exit: 1 mile."

"Catch up with him, man."

The operatic style of Ms. Mouskouri's rendition of "Bridge over Troubled Water" and Dr. Hegel's erratic driving unnerved the already anxious Ramos. DiRosa accelerated. Ramos listened. *Come on, beeps; get louder.*

The big, smooth, thirty-two-valve V-8 engine powering Hegel's Lexus pushed it quickly past the tractor-trailer. DiRosa accelerated.

The Ford approached the side of the trailer, still in the left lane.

Dr. Hegel pulled into the middle lane, in front of the big tractor. Hydraulic brakes spit huge, rapid breaths of air. Just then, light blue puffs of smoke spewed out of the dual exhausts of the Lexus; its rear end lowered as the shiny black car sped away. The Lexus swerved off the interstate onto the Highway 165 exit.

DiRosa tried to pass the truck. The sluggish Ford couldn't make the maneuver; DiRosa missed the exit.

Ramos looked at DiRosa. "Stop, man! Pull over!" he said loudly. "We're going to lose him, stupid!" DiRosa removed his left hand from the steering wheel and dropped it into his lap, clenching it into a white-knuckled fist. "Calm down, man. Calm down. No big deal," Ramos said. "You can just turn around, man."

At 3:42 Amanda lifted the log from the file cabinet drawer still wondering about what she'd just seen. Who were those men in the Ford? Were they government men? *Dr. Hegel, where are you going?* She walked to her desk. Dr. Hegel would surely be back in as much of a hurry as he had left.

Amanda had not forgotten this morning in Dr. Hegel's office. She still wanted to help him, but resentment had crept in. She didn't deserve to be treated like that, after all. She had come to believe she was more than an employee to him. Then she let out a breath. She couldn't hold anger, not against Dr. Hegel. Maybe she shouldn't be so hard on him. *He's nearing the end of his career; he's just uncertain about his future. Maybe Geoffry was right.*

Amanda decided to walk straight up to Dr. Hegel and give him a hug the next time she saw him. She would come right out and just say it: "Dr. Hegel, you're like a father to me. Whatever I can do, I will. Just ask."

If she hurried, she might be able to make the question-and-answer session—no gazing at that living photograph now. Anyway,

Dr. Hegel was bound to start the seminar late. Maybe the seminar would make him become himself again.

Before Amanda set the log beside the computer keyboard, she immediately realized something wasn't right. Something had been inserted between its pages. It was a URI business envelope with "Amanda Collins, Personal and Confidential" written on it in Dr. Hegel's scribble. She lifted the envelope and opened it. She pulled out two sheets of folded URI letterhead. The top sheet was a note. The second sheet had an outline of a key drawn on the top half and a real key taped on the lower half.

Amanda's heart started to thud as she read Dr. Hegel's words.

———

Dr. Hegel turned west on Highway 165. He accelerated after he made the turn. As he passed the turn for Millville, Ms. Mouskouri sang "Only Time Will Tell." He began to feel good about his performance.

This last task would be his atonement, if not with his God, then with himself. Soon Ruth, Joshua, and Esther would be safe and very rich. Dr. Hegel could actually feel a smile on his face, such a rare thing since the abduction and bondage of his soul. He loosened his grip on the steering wheel. *Amanda, you must follow my instructions. You must. To do so would be the beginning of the end of the evil I have created.*

Dr. Egas Moniz popped into Dr. Hegel's mind. He chuckled when the next thought came to him: *Well, my late colleague in neuro-murder, I have forfeited my Nobel Prize, haven't I?*

———

DiRosa braked. The truck passed them. He swerved to the right shoulder of the interstate about a half mile past the Highway 165 exit. "Hurry, man," Ramos said. He decided it was better to remember not to call the Italian "stupid" again.

The little red light flickered, but more faintly and at longer intervals now; the beeps were barely audible.

"If we lose him, Landcaster don't pay," Ramos said.

⌞ ⌊ ⌟

Oaks and maples lined Highway 165 between Millville, Rhode Island, and the Connecticut state line. As expected when he made his plans, except for the rare local driving from one small Rhode Island community like Millville to some small Connecticut town, Highway 165 was virtually abandoned on early weekday afternoons. Dr. Hegel felt alone now, but comfortable. Respite. That's what Dr. Hegel was feeling. It would all be over soon, all of it that he himself had caused to happen in a shameful moment of greed and the overpowering presence of Constance Frye. *It was your choice, Hegel. Oh, Ruth, what have I done?*

The sun flickered through the twisted branches and green leaves, and reflections of the branches and leaves raced up the tinted windshield of the Lexus as Dr. Hegel sped away from his pursuers. *What a wonderful gift from my co-conspirators—this vehicle with its impeccably finished wood and leather interior,* he mused. As Ms. Mouskouri ended her rendition of "Morning Has Broken," a thought floated into Dr. Hegel's mind: Coffins were finished in such detail and were just as quiet, too. He chuckled at the irony.

Then the next CD track began. "And I Loved You So" began to play.

Ruth. . .Ruth. He tightened his grip on the steering wheel and began to cry. "God—Ruth, forgive me," he said softly.

⌞ ⌊ ⌟

DiRosa turned east on Highway 165, away from Millville. After less than a quarter mile, the beeps became inaudible, the red flickers barely visible and seconds apart.

"Turn around, man! You turned the wrong way, stupid," Ramos said. Ramos's stomach clenched when he realized that he had blurted that word again. He kept his gaze on the road, choosing not to watch if DiRosa clenched his fist. Ramos knew all about this quiet Italian, even his real name. He considered apologizing. *I ain't afraid of him, man,* he told himself.

DiRosa stopped the white Ford and backed off the narrow highway onto the embankment. He spun the steering wheel while shoving the transmission lever into drive, then accelerated.

Ramos had been watching and listening to the device for weeks. He had learned to discern even the slightest change. He smiled when the frequency of the red flickers increased even slightly. As the beeps became audible again, he conceded that though they seemed to be a good distance away from Hegel, they were headed in the right direction.

"If we get to him, if he knows we're here, we're going to have to kill him, man," Ramos said.

"And I Loved You So" sounded louder from the speaker in the device between them. Ramos liked that song. He began reconsidering his harsh opinion of Ms. Mouskouri's talent. Then he remembered where he was. "Hurry, man," Ramos said. He made a conscious effort not to call DiRosa "stupid" a third time. He even thought again about apologizing for the last two times. *No way, man. I ain't afraid of nobody.*

⌞_⌟

Dr. Hegel had always insisted on the most effective equipment to perform a task in the lab. For this task, he did the same. He pulled over to the side of the highway and stopped. He put the Lexus in Park and reached under the driver's seat.

"And I Loved You So" ended. He pulled out a Smith & Wesson .44 magnum revolver. *Not a pretty or elegant weapon, like a Luger, but effective,* he remembered thinking when he first handled it. He raised the gun to his head. He held it so that the big muzzle was about an inch from his right temple. He cocked the hammer.

He leaned back. "I love you, Ruth," he said softly. *That song, darling, it is my tribute to you.*

Then, in the instant before he pulled the trigger, Avraham Frederick Hegel recalled the words of King Solomon: "What is crooked cannot be made straight, and what is lacking cannot be numbered. I communed with my heart, saying,"—what had been haunting his mind for a long time—" 'Look, I have attained greatness.'"

Amanda could tell Dr. Hegel had attempted to print as legibly as he could. He wrote like any other physician. Her hands trembled as she held the note in front of her eyes. It read:

"By the time you read this, Amanda, I will be dead. I see no reason why they would hurt Ruth or my children now."

What are you talking about, Dr. Hegel?

"I deserve this. You will find out why soon. If you are not one of them, you are in great peril, Amanda. They will come after you. They will kill you, but do precisely as I say, and you will be safe. It should be approximately 3:45 right now. You probably should check the time."

"Probably should?" Amanda asked softly. Amanda checked her watch: 3:47.

"No doubt everyone is waiting for me in the auditorium. The halls should be empty. The two men who have been watching me will soon be checking my car and my body now, if they have not done so already. You have less than an hour before they will return. You must use that time as I instruct you. You must not question. When they begin to follow you, they will eventually kill you, as they planned to kill me, but if you do precisely what I have written, you will be safe."

He's talking about those men in the white Ford!

"I have prepared a package for you to deliver to someone. You will learn who later. The package is in the top drawer of the file cabinet. Take this note, the sheet with the key, the envelope, and the package. Take them all. Leave the lab now. Go to your apartment. Say nothing. Don't make telephone calls, not even to that fiancé of yours. While you are driving to your apartment, read Note One on the package.

"Leave now, while you still have time. Follow my instructions in the Notes attached to the package precisely."

Amanda rushed to the file cabinet, unlocked the top drawer, and opened it. A box that used to hold a ream of paper and now wrapped in parcel paper and secured with packaging tape sat in the most visible place in the front of the drawer. Three envelopes marked "One," "Two," and "Three" were strapped to the package by a large rubber band.

Amanda clutched the package and stepped quickly back to her desk, her heart still throbbing. She could feel the beads of sweat rising, gathering on her forehead and her scalp, dampening her thick hair. She pulled her satchel from under her desk, lifted it, then turned it upside down and shook it. Her copy of Dr. Hegel's speech and the nineteen slides spilled over the computer keyboard, the URI envelope, her chair, and the floor.

Amanda stuffed the two sheets of URI letterhead into her jeans. She stuffed the log and package into the satchel. She lifted the strap onto her right shoulder. She began to run, but stopped. She turned again, stepped back to her desk, picked up the photograph of the couple on Narragansett Bay, and shoved it into the satchel. Then she ran out of the BioSysTech lab.

⌐__⌐

The beeps from the receiver on the floor of the white Ford sounded louder now. Ramos glanced at the small red light; it flashed brighter and more frequently. It occurred to him that this Dr. Hegel gringo must be parked somewhere. Ramos caught a glimpse of DiRosa lifting his shiny light brown Italian shoe off the accelerator and setting it gently on the brake pad.

Ramos looked ahead just in time to glimpse a yellow highway caution sign signaling a hard curve to the right.

"He has to have pulled over on the side of the road somewhere up ahead," Ramos said.

The Ford entered the curve.

Boom!

The sound suddenly blasted over the serene operatic voice of Ms. Mouskouri's "Ave Maria De Schubert," overloading the speaker's small paper cone. Nothing but static for an instant, then Ms. Mouskouri's voice returned.

"That's a gunshot, man. I know it!" Ramos hollered. "He might be waiting for us, man. Just go by like we're on a nice drive." Ramos turned to DiRosa. "That's got to be the longest religious song I ever heard," he said.

DiRosa said nothing. Ramos watched him squinting his eyes as the Ford rounded the curve.

Ramos looked toward DiRosa again. "You Catholic, man?" he asked.

"Shut up," DiRosa said softly, as he allowed the Ford to idle along.

So I called you stupid a couple of times, Ramos wanted to say. *People call me that all the time, man, and I don't get mad.*

Ramos saw the Lexus when he looked straight ahead, parked off the highway. Dr. Hegel was in the driver's seat. He appeared to be enjoying the balmy day and the music. It all appeared perfectly serene to Ramos, except that Dr. Hegel's head seemed to be gone.

DiRosa idled the Ford to a crawl alongside the Lexus. An I-knew-I-was-right feeling welled up and delighted Ramos. "I told you that was a gunshot, man. You didn't believe me, man. Whoa! He's really messed up, man!"

While DiRosa pulled in front of the Lexus, Ramos opened the dash compartment and lifted out a pair of thick yellow Playtex gloves. As he struggled to get them on his fat hands, he turned to DiRosa. "They say they can get prints off the inside of those surgeon operating gloves. You heard that? I quit using them. You can use these over and over," Ramos said. He reached back into the compartment, lifted out a small wrench, and slammed the compartment shut.

DiRosa stopped the Ford. Ramos walked quickly to the Lexus, gazing down both ways of the highway along the way. He opened the passenger door.

Man, I can't believe this!

Avraham Hegel's brilliant brains and blood had splattered on the beautiful tan leather driver's seat, on the matching leather and glossy burled walnut of the driver's door, and on the instrument panel. Red tributaries ran from a large red-and-gray blotch near the center of the shattered driver's side window. The driver's side air bag had inflated and then deflated, leaving Dr. Hegel's partial head and torso upright in the seat.

Ramos reached over the center console and turned off the engine. He saw the revolver on the floor in front of the passenger seat. He twisted and turned, grunting, to avoid touching the .44 magnum as he forced his body belly-up on the passenger seat. He reached under the dash and yanked the bug off the steering column. Then he struggled to get up. Ramos stared at what was left of Dr. Hegel's head. "Good shot, man," he said. "Bet you couldn't do that twice in a row." He laughed.

Ramos twisted his torso, shifting his gut and sucking in his belly to get out of the Lexus. After he ducked his head and pushed himself out of the front seat, he waddled quickly to the rear and lay on his back in the soft leaves. He scooted under the bumper, fumbled around, and located the transmitter. He found the nut that tightened the metal strap. He removed the nut with the wrench and jerked the transmitter from under the chassis. He would have to buy a new pair of gloves, Ramos thought; these were messed up with grease and grime. He gripped the bumper from underneath, sucked in his belly again, and scooted out from under the car. He lifted himself to his feet and wheezed to get his breath.

"Let's go, man. I got 'em!" Ramos hollered to DiRosa between his wheezes as he plopped on the passenger seat of the Ford and slammed the door.

DiRosa floored the accelerator.

"Man, now we can have some peace and quiet," Ramos said.

Amanda turned and slammed the door of laboratory 214 in the same motion. She ran down the hall and up the stairs to the third floor, holding the satchel tight on her shoulder. Dr. Hegel had to be in his office, ready to go to the Pit where everyone was waiting for him. She stopped in her tracks when she saw Professor Treadaway leaning against the rippled glass of Dr. Hegel's office door, peering through his tunneled palms. Amanda wasn't sure what to do. She decided to go to the Pit.

"Ms. Collins!" Professor Treadaway yelled. "Have you seen Dr. Hegel?"

Amanda shifted her satchel. "No," she said, feeling herself shaking her head too much. Professor Treadaway glared at her.

Amanda felt her heart pound. She had already violated one of Dr. Hegel's instructions—she had not gone directly to her apartment. *No reason to go to the Pit now, Amanda.*

"What's going on, young lady?" Treadaway said.

"Nothing! I don't know!"

"I saw him drive away at about three-thirty in that fancy car of his. A professor with a car like that. . ."

Amanda turned and ran.

"Where are you going, young lady?" Treadaway yelled.

"To find Dr. Hegel!" Amanda hollered without turning her head, holding on to the strap of her satchel with both hands. She ran around the corner of the hall and bounded down the stairs, two and three steps at a time, the satchel pounding against her back as she tugged on the strap. Now, finally, in the entrance area, she struck the aluminum door bar with her arm tight against her side as if she were knocking away an opponent on her way to a lay-up.

Oh, please, don't let them be out there waiting for me!

CHAPTER 10

The direct line of the telephone that sat on the oval partner's desk in Dr. Richard Landcaster's office rang. The former physician's office was as opulent as his ego was big. BioSysTech occupied half the thirty-ninth floor of the Chicago Towers Office Building.

"What is it?" Landcaster asked as soon as he brought the receiver to his mouth.

"Hegel shot himself," Vic Ricci said.

"Not in the lab!" Landcaster said.

"He stopped his car on a little road off the interstate. Nothing much left but his lower jaw."

"When?"

"Maybe ten minutes ago."

"The Lexus?"

"All the bugs are cleaned out."

"Scope the lab. . .his office, too," Landcaster said. "Do it yourself. Just make sure nothing's missing. Don't disturb anything unless you have to. I'll send our lawyer out there tomorrow. Got that?"

"Hey, I ain't Ramos," Vic said.

"And the lab assistant. Let Ramos take care of her."

"Dr. Landcaster, this is business," Vic said. "Things like this can be done with dignity. I swear on my mother's rosary, it will be done. But it don't have to be done like he does it," Vic said.

"You want your money, guy. You do what I say," Landcaster said, then hung up.

Amanda flung open her apartment door at 4:15. As Dr. Hegel's first note instructed her to do, she called Kingston Taxi Service. She turned on the lamp next to the sofa and rushed to her bedroom, where she gathered up a weekend of clothing for what Dr. Hegel described as an oven-hot climate with saturated air.

The telephone rang.

Amanda didn't want to answer it. It could be them checking on her. But it could be Geoffry, too. It could be her mother. She picked up the receiver. "Just checking, honey; we verify fares here. Have to. College kids and their pranks," the taxi dispatcher said.

After the dispatcher hung up, Amanda left the receiver on the old luggage trunk. She grabbed her things, rushed out the door, locked it, and ran down the stairs to the porch. She turned and dashed to the end of the porch, put a spare car key in the flowerpot next to the column, and whisked topsoil over it. Dr. Hegel would understand; he knew what love is. She ran to the street corner, praying the taxi would be there soon.

Will I ever come back? Of course I will. Dr. Hegel said so in his note. Oh, Geoffry.

The cab swerved to the curb. Amanda ran to the curbside rear door, threw all she had in the backseat, and climbed in.

"Hurry. To the airport," she said.

CHAPTER 11

The president's on line four," Jennifer said. Most secretaries in Columbia would have been awestruck by such a phone call. But Jennifer was used to it. Ashton Frye had telephoned often when he was governor. He even addressed Jennifer by her first name.

Griffin looked up from the BioSysTech documents blanketing the top of his desk and picked up the phone.

"Good afternoon, Mr. President."

"Hello, Griffin," the president said. "Missed you at the Hegel reception."

"I left early, but I had a nice chat with your wife."

"Redden told me," the president said.

Now, there's a surprise.

"After all the trouble you got me out of while I was governor down there, you'd think Constance would be more civil to you."

President Frye's voice had a low, reluctant tone to it. He sounded apologetic, or maybe distraught. Griffin wasn't sure.

"Are you all right, Mr. President?"

"I'm sorry about Warren. We all go back a long way, don't we?"

"Warren didn't overdose, not purposefully, not accidentally, Ashton," Griffin said. "Tell me about BioSysTech." *Slow down, Griffin.*

"That's Constance's business," the president said as if he felt he were being falsely accused of something.

"It's not that simple," Griffin said.

A pause.

"You used to be one of those 'Jesus' people, didn't you, Griffin?"

The "used to" caused a wave of guilt to rise up in Griffin's mind.

"We're called 'Christians.' You should know that, being a Baptist, Ashton." He paused. "What's happened?" he asked.

"Something that doesn't make sense," President Frye said. "I suppose death makes a man think about life and its meaning."

"Ashton, what are you talking about?" Griffin recognized that this was an invitation to talk to the president about faith, but then the thought came to him that he hadn't been to church and hadn't prayed in a long time. Who was he to talk about faith?

"I guess we get this way when some guy dies," the president said. "Just human nature."

Griffin had to shake the heat of anger that rose in him when he heard the president refer to Warren Jennings as "some guy." *Talk to him, Griffin. Forget the silly anger.*

"You feel the tug of God, Ashton," Griffin said. "That's why you called me, isn't it?" Griffin had forgotten how it felt, the voice of the Spirit speaking through him. He recalled the tingling deep inside and the words emanating with no thought of his own. As he spoke, he realized that God hadn't left him at all. He never would.

"At this moment, Ashton, you understand that our lives are not an unfolding of chance mysterious events that lead to personal spiritual expansion that no religion has ever clarified. Set aside that *Celestine Prophecy* notion. There is a real God, Ashton. He is real; He is the God of the Bible."

Silence.

"It's hard to accept the thought. . . . I just can't," the president said softly.

"Ashton. . ."

Nothing but silence on the other end of the line. Griffin didn't feel the urging of the Spirit. Anything more from him would be mere human soliloquy. Now the president was deliberating, debating with himself. If the president had the courage, he would ask for more understanding.

"Griffin, would you ever abandon me if I got into trouble? Would you refuse to represent me?"

"I don't think that would happen, Mr. President."

"You know the truth behind the photo-ops of me and Constance—getting off Air Force One, holding hands, smiling, don't you?"

"I've been your attorney for a long time," Griffin said.

"The media. They treat her like a queen. She saunters in front of the camera, and everybody drools. Maybe I should show some home movies, let them see how she can fling a plate across the room. It isn't the utopia she believes in."

"What do you believe in, Mr. President?"

A pause.

"Her reform has to pass, Griffin. It has to; if it doesn't, I'll have misery the rest of my life."

"She has the press, the nonprofits, the speaker, and Hegel. What could possibly stop her now?" Griffin asked.

"Well—"

"Ashton, why did you call me?"

"Are you sure you won't refuse to represent me if something happens? Do you promise?" the president asked.

"Talk to me, Ashton. This is me," Griffin said. "Tell me what's wrong so we can deal with it."

"Avraham Hegel drove down some back road in Rhode Island and blew his head off."

"What?" Griffin said, now realizing the president's "some guy" referred to Hegel, not Warren. Then Hegel's image at the reception and the three-point perimeter Constance had apparently ordered flashed through Griffin's mind. They didn't want him to talk. He remembered Ruth and his stupid cross-examination, pressuring her for more facts, more pieces, when she was pouring out to him because she had no one else to talk to.

Now Griffin worried about Ruth. He tried to sort what was going through his mind, to think rationally through his irrational feelings toward a just-widowed woman—a tragically widowed woman—whom he had met only once. *Griffin, get a grip!*

"Why are you telling me this?" Griffin asked the president.

"I want you to listen to what the people back home are saying about Warren and Hegel. Keep me informed. The rumors about Warren's death, they're getting ridiculous. It was suicide, Griffin."

"I'll never believe that," Griffin said.

"I need you, Griffin," President Frye said. "I don't know about all this baby tissue stuff. All of a sudden Constance tells me Hegel's dead and that I shouldn't say anything. She has a plan to use the suicide to help her reform pass. Help it! How? Hegel and that group have been into some—"

"Does Constance know you're calling me?" Griffin asked.

"Can't I even have a private talk with my attorney?"

Griffin could see Ashton Frye in his mind's eye, waving his free arm when he said that.

"You're the only friend I have, Griffin. Please don't ask me anymore questions. I just need to know what information is coming out about Warren and Hegel so I can send out early spins. I need to know I have someone down there on my side."

"Have someone fax me the police report," Griffin said. "I'll take it from there."

"I don't think the police know yet," the president said.

Griffin remained quiet as the president's words sank in. "Well, don't worry about that now, anyway." Griffin cleared his throat. "How's the terrorist hunt going?"

Come on, Ashton! Don't you realize what you just said? Don't you understand that you're there in Washington, D.C., and you know Hegel is dead on some Rhode Island back road even before the Rhode Island police know?

"Well. . .I. . .I don't. . .," the president said.

"The op-ed pages are giving you a hard time down here. And, anyway, when will you be coming down? We need to sit back with one of my frozen coffees."

"Yes, I could use—I could use one of those."

Good, Ashton! Good!

If things worked as they used to, the president's staff would make immediate arrangements for Griffin and the president to meet. The meeting would be at the Fryes' ranch about sixty miles northwest of Columbia during a "family reunion." No press.

But Griffin couldn't be sure whether a meeting would happen at all. Constance had gotten even more dominating as first lady at the White House than she had been at the governor's mansion. As governor, Ashton Frye hadn't had to deal with the religious fanatics who believe heaven rewards them for every American they slaughter, ethnic cleansing in obscure third world nations, and firecracker wars everywhere.

Anxiety saturated the president's voice. Griffin had heard the tone scores of times from county commissioners caught giving illegal contracts, state representatives paying a personal debt with campaign funds, and senators, like middle-aged Zellars, falling victim to passion with a twenty-something page.

"Redden will get back with you," the president said, then hung up.

CHAPTER 12

Ruth Hegel felt as if she were living life through another person after what the Rhode Island state trooper told her had finally sunk in.

When the telephone rang, Ruth was relaxing with a glass of iced tea and a rare letter from her daughter, Esther, in a wonderful world, all alone cuddled on one of the overstuffed sofas positioned perpendicularly to the huge stone fireplace in the Hegels' den. The call came at about 5:50 in the afternoon.

"Ruth Hegel?"

"Yes."

"Ma'am, this is Trooper Alphonse Palmisano, Rhode Island State Police—"

"Yes?"

"Well, ma'am. It's about your husband, Dr. Hegel."

"Yes?"

"Ma'am, there's been an. . . Well, ma'am, you have to come to the morgue. I'm real sorry, ma'am. Real sorry.

"He's—my husband—he's—"

"Ma'am, I can't say anything more over the phone. The Kingston police are at the morgue. They need you there."

On the way to the morgue, alone in her car, Ruth realized it would be her husband lying there; no one could tolerate a transformation like he went through, not even Avraham. Not after abandoning his God.

131

The suppressed truth grinding at his sanity had caused a slow, insidious change in him from a strong, wonderful husband and father to a frightening stranger, and the only person she had ever told was the president's lawyer, whom she would probably never see again. How else would Avraham, her husband of twenty-seven years, have reacted when he finally came to himself? And whom could he turn to? Constance Frye? Kristina England?

Ruth knew what had happened. He had finally seen himself through the beliefs he'd held to all his life.

It was really you, wasn't it, darling. It was you who took your life. There was another way. Oh, darling, I was here. I was always here. . . .

Ruth entered the morgue at 6:20. Detective Terrell Callahan stood by her as the coroner pulled the large stainless steel drawer from the refrigerated wall and unzipped the black bag to the corpse's navel. He grabbed both sides of the thick black plastic and pulled them back to expose the body within.

Ruth felt the blood leave her head. The floor swirled. Everything blurred. Her knees lost their strength. The coroner raised something to her nose. Ruth winced and jerked her head away from his hand and coughed. "I'll be all right," she said after the sting had left her sinuses.

She stared at her husband's jaw and the ring on his finger. The mangled gold wire-rimmed glasses in the small plastic bag lying on the familiar bare chest belonged to him, too. She turned, looked up at the coroner, and nodded.

It's just his body, Ruth, just a shell that he has left for a better place. She felt stronger. She shifted her eyes back to the body, placing her hand on her husband's chest.

"It's my husband; it's Avraham," she said softly. Even as her gaze rested on the nearly headless figure, she realized she had loved this body for a long time. She watched the coroner zip the body bag closed and push the front of the stainless steel drawer. She stared at the drawer as it rolled back into the wall.

"I have something I'd like you to sign," Detective Callahan said to Ruth.

"Detective," the coroner said, "I'd like to discuss some things with you—alone."

"No," Ruth said. "I want to hear. I want to know everything."

The coroner glanced at Detective Callahan. The detective shrugged his shoulders, then nodded.

"I'll take the photographs, measurements, and samples, but unless you produce compelling evidence to the contrary, this was suicide, pure and simple," the coroner said.

"There are a couple of things we're looking into, but just keep. . ." The detective glanced toward Ruth.

"Go ahead, Detective Callahan," Ruth said.

"We have tire marks from another car on the scene. We're taking prints."

"Doctor," Ruth said, "whatever tests you have to do, whatever photographs you must take, finish them by tomorrow. Avraham will be buried Wednesday."

"Mrs. Hegel, I haven't released the body," Detective Callahan said.

"The funeral will be Wednesday," Ruth said to Callahan.

"Can you do all the forensics in time?" Detective Callahan asked the coroner.

The coroner turned his gaze on Ruth. "I'll work overtime," he said. "It's the least I can do."

"I'll be at your office tomorrow morning," Ruth said to Callahan.

"Mrs. Hegel," the coroner said, "your husband's death is national news. You realize—"

"Oh, no," Ruth said. "I need to use a phone!" Joshua was in his second year at Johns Hopkins Medical School; Esther, a junior at Stanford University. She had to tell them before they heard it on the news. She had to tell them that their father loved them, that their father came to himself before he died. She had to call her children. Now!

"My telephone is in my office, right down the hall," the coroner said.

After Ruth made her calls, alone in the coroner's private office,

Detective Callahan led her through the halls of the morgue. The reporters had gathered by then with their microphones and camcorders, recording for tonight's nightly news, feeding to the national networks, some regular programs preempted for a "live-at-the-scene" report.

Detective Callahan ran interference as the camera people shoved their lenses in Ruth's face and the reporters jabbed their microphones toward Ruth's mouth. "Why did your husband do it, Mrs. Hegel?" one of the newsman asked. "Do you have anything to say?" another yelled. "How do you feel about your husband's suicide, Mrs. Hegel?" a newswoman hollered.

How can these people be so cavalier, so shallow? Ruth drew closer to Detective Callahan's back.

CHAPTER 13

As DiRosa sat in the car, Ramos stared at the windows of Amanda's apartment, trying to see movement. Nothing. But her gray Camry sat in the driveway and the living room light glowed through the curtains. Her telephone sounded a busy signal. Ramos racked his mind analyzing the circumstances surrounding "Sweetness," his new name for Amanda. The gringo doctor's suicide was all over the news, the television, radio, everywhere. She had to call that boyfriend of hers, Ramos reasoned. Maybe her mother, too.

By the time Ramos abandoned his musings, DiRosa had circled the block and had parked on the opposite side of Cherry Street across from Amanda's apartment building. Ramos would have preferred to rifle the files back at the BioSysTech lab rather than sit in this car with the tight-lipped Italian, just staring at a rickety old building.

"We gotta bug the girl's car," DiRosa said.

"Good, man," Ramos said. He felt a touch of excitement. He wasn't sure how it would happen, but in a few days, once Hegel's death had become old news in the community, Ramos would be alone with Sweetness. Landcaster owed this girl to him. *You promised her to me, Landcaster; break your promise, and I visit you at your nice penthouse.*

If it were not for his wearing tennis shoes, the empty halls of the Agriculture and Science Building would have echoed Vic Ricci's footsteps. Vic sensed the building wasn't merely empty; it felt like it had been abandoned. A few florescent lights were left on, dimly illuminating the interior stairs and second-floor hallway to the BioSysTech lab.

Vic moved his hand to his chest. He patted the crucifix under his tight black pullover shirt, the crucifix his mother had given him years ago at his confirmation. He tried to figure out why Hegel would kill himself. Vic worked so hard at staying fit. The image of his own body came to his mind, thirty-four and beautiful. *I ain't going to miss my workout again.* The only thing he hated about those sessions of sweat, pain, and gain was his toupee. He couldn't wear his toupee! Maybe he'd get some of that sewn-in hair. Maybe he was balding, but he was alive. Suicide was a terrible thing. Vic's priest had told him long ago that suicide was not an ordinary sin that might land you in purgatory so you could cash in on your indulgences. No! It was a mortal sin!

Vic crept down the hall to lab 214. He lifted the key from his pocket. It worked. Landcaster was on the ball. When he opened the door, the hospital smell made him gag. He held his breath, then began to breathe in gasps. He rushed to the file cabinet, pulled out the second, smaller key from his pocket, and unlocked the first drawer. When he pulled the drawer out, he spotted an empty section where he was told the records were kept. He pushed that drawer in and opened the next drawer, then the next. *The log they described is gone! Landcaster ain't gonna like this!*

Vic stepped over to the lab assistant's desk. Photographic slides lay all over the place—on the keyboard, the seat of the desk chair, and on the floor. He spotted a piece of paper on the floor next to the rollers on the chair base. He leaned over and lifted the paper to his eyes. Something about backbones and brains was written on it. He dropped the paper and wiped his hand on his pants. He pulled out a third key from his pocket and unlocked the top center drawer. Then he rifled through the desk. No log there, either. He closed the drawers and scanned the top of the desk. An opened, empty URI business envelope lay on the desktop partially covered by three photographic slides. He picked up the envelope and read the scribble: "Amanda Collins, Personal and Confidential." Vic nodded, smiling, feeling good about his investigative skills. A suicide note. *Do I earn my money, or what?*

Vic shoved the envelope in his pants pocket. He reached over and gripped Amanda's desk with both his hands at its corner. He jerked, just enough to move the desk so that he could fit his hand between it and the wall. He fumbled his fingers behind the desk, pulled the bug off the wall, and left the lab.

Vic climbed the stairs to the third floor. He lifted another key out of his front pocket and unlocked the door. Dr. Hegel's light was off, but the dim hall lights illumined his office, causing the desk and chairs to cast eerie shadows on the walls and floor. Vic wanted to turn on the light, but the window behind Dr. Hegel's desk would glow over the campus. Vic imagined the campus cops busting down the office door. "Hold it right there, mister!"

He stepped into Dr. Hegel's dark office slowly, stopping in front of the bookcase to his left, studying every spine of every book. None of them was the log Landcaster had described.

Vic walked behind Dr. Hegel's desk. He opened the middle drawer. Nothing. The top left drawer. Nothing. Nothing in the two drawers below that one, either. Then the top right drawer. . .the middle right drawer. Nothing! *Did this guy clear his desk before he blew himself away?*

Vic pulled opened the bottom right drawer. An old rubber doll lay belly-up, its eyes closed. Vic picked up the doll and moved its head closer to his eyes. The doll's eyelids opened, and it stared directly into Vic's eyes. Vic felt his eyes widen and his mouth drop open, then a rush of air entered his lungs with such force he could hear it. *Don't scream, Vic! Remember the campus cops!*

A chilling shiver raced up Vic's spine and ended as fast as it came, depositing a spiritual revelation into Vic's immortal soul: *A ritual idol! A demonic symbolic baby sacrifice to the devil! That's how he can take their brains out and the brains still live. The old man's one of those Satanic priests!*

Vic wanted to sling the little abomination to the floor, but another holy revelation sprang to his mind, no doubt because he had lit six candles just the other night. And now his faith was paying off, even in this, the devil's den. *Throw the desecration back down into its grave from whence it came, but first, bless it, or you will be cursed, my child!* the revelation said.

Vic glanced around the office, holding the cursed thing by one of its feet, away from his view, behind his back. *Where? Where is its grave? That's it! Put it back in its grave!* He slammed the horror of horrors back into the drawer. The thing whined, protesting that it could not possess him, no doubt. Vic watched it as it shut its eyelids. He moved his hand vertically once, then horizontally once in front of him. He shot a glance upward and repeated the gesture in the dim light of Satan's den. Vic was sure that his gestures had exorcized the poor baby now. He smiled at it, then gently slid its tomb closed. He felt very spiritual.

Vic hurried frantically now, deciding to set aside his priestly skills and resume investigating. He stepped to the bookcase again and reached behind it. He found the bug. But there was something taped to the wall. A piece of paper. A note. He brought the note close to his eyes.

"I AM DEAD, WAITING HERE IN THE LAKE OF FIRE FOR YOU. SMOLDERING. SATAN IS HERE. HE WANTS TO SEE YOUR SKIN BOIL OFF YOU, TOO."

Holy rosary!

Vic darted out of the office and down the hall. He dashed down the stairs and, with his knees kicking high, his arms pumping, ran out the building to his car. He jumped into the driver's seat, then reached his hand down the neck of his pullover and jerked out the old worn crucifix. He felt his toupee shift a bit to the front and slightly to the side as he jerked his head down to kiss the crucifix. No time to straighten his rug now! The rear tires squealed as one-time altar boy Vic Ricci sped away for his life, away from the Agriculture and Science Building at the University of Rhode Island, the den of Dr. Hegel, the evil baby brain transplanter, now smoldering in the fiery pit with his master, the devil himself.

The plane began its descent over the estuaries on the south shore of Lake Pontchartrain, near the twenty-six-mile toll bridge New Orleanians called "the Causeway." Between thoughts of Geoffry and worries about when she'd see him again, Amanda had tried to make sense of all that had happened. Even after several hours of thinking, she hadn't succeeded.

Dr. Hegel had to be dead. The key taped to the bottom half of the URI letterhead Dr. Hegel had placed in the binding of the log opened a locker in the Rhode Island Airport. Thirty-five thousand dollars in cash. *Why did he involve me in this? He's trying to save my life. I know he is.*

With the help of a Mideastern cab driver who gazed at Amanda in the interior rearview mirror more than he looked at the road, Amanda left the airport and registered at the Peacock Inn. Dr. Hegel described the motel perfectly in his first note: an obscure but clean little place near the airport on Airline Highway in Kenner, Louisiana.

Amanda felt like some kind of secret agent. After registering, she tossed her small suitcase and satchel on one of the twin beds and sat on the other with Dr. Hegel's second note in her hand. She moved to the telephone. No, she had better not call Geoffry now. Amanda considered reading the second note. She decided not to. She would wait until she got to Slidell, as Dr. Hegel had instructed in the first note.

Amanda lay down. It was nearly eleven o'clock. What a long, long day. She reached under the shade on the lamp sitting on the small table between the beds. She fought with the small black knob until she won the battle and the room went dark. The light just outside the door crept into the room where the draperies didn't quite reach the painted cinderblock wall and shone on the ceiling just above the draperies. *This is a dark, lonely, cold, cinderblock place.*

Tomorrow she would hear Geoffry's voice.

I don't think we'll be in the Wednesday service at your little church, Geoffry.

Vic Ricci had collected himself from the torments of Hegel's den and straightened his toupee by the time he pulled behind DiRosa and Ramos. He got out of his car and walked to the white Ford. DiRosa pushed the power-lock button. Vic climbed into the back. He scooted to the center of the seat and shot a quick glance into the rearview mirror to make sure his hair was on straight.

"Anything happening?" Vic asked.

"Nothing," DiRosa said. "Something ain't right. What about you?"

Vic fondled his crucifix. "I ain't saying nothing until I go to confession," Vic said. "I'm going to light some candles and pray that Landcaster don't send me there again."

"What happened, man? You look like you seen a boogie man," Ramos chuckled.

Vic shot a glare at Ramos. Then he said to DiRosa, "You guys been here for six hours, and she ain't showed?"

"She's here, man." Ramos jabbed his finger toward the windshield. "Look at her car, man. That light. And she's been on her phone calling everybody."

Vic turned his head to Ramos. He tightened his lips and said, "Ramos, you get up there. Don't do anything stupid. Just see if there's movement. You can't hit her. You got that?"

"Man, I ain't stupid," Ramos said. He opened the compartment in front of him. He lifted his new pair of yellow Playtex gloves from the compartment and left the car.

"He's a dead man if he knows," DiRosa said to Vic while watching Ramos step to the curb on the other side of Cherry Street.

"Luigi Vicarro, my good friend." Vic began moving his hands. "How can a stupid man such as this one, a reject of Castro, know anything about the FBI witness program? Anyway, it's bad for business to just kill him. Landcaster wouldn't pay us."

"If he knows, I won't kill him right then," DiRosa said. "I'll make a business agreement with him."

"Fair enough," Vic said, nodding his head. "Unlike that idiot, you, my friend, are an honorable man."

Ramos managed the four steps to the front porch of the apartment building but struggled up the flight of stairs to Sweetness's apartment. He hated to climb stairs, and doing that while struggling to get the gloves on made it worse, especially new gloves. He let out a deep breath when he lifted his body onto the last step.

Ramos could hear the television behind the door of the apartment across from Amanda's. He could see light under her door and even a faint glimmer through the skeleton keyhole when he moved his head just right.

He pushed his ear against her door. He had to concentrate; his wheezing made it difficult for him to pick up sounds. But he heard nothing. No stereo. No talking.

Ramos knelt on both knees and peered through the keyhole with one eye, closing the other. As he moved his head, he spotted clothes strewn on the sofa and floor. The telephone sat on the old trunk in front of the sofa. The receiver lay beside it, off its cradle. *Man, all this time I've been sitting out there watching your empty apartment, Sweetness? You smart little thing. You got away, didn't you?*

"What are you doing?"

Ramos jerked his head upward in the direction of the voice.

"Hello, sir," Ramos said. "I'm just trying to find out if my very good friend, Amanda Crowlins, is home." Ramos smiled, peering upward at a skinny young man, maybe in his mid-twenties.

"Don't move! I'm calling the police," the young man said.

"You don't have to call no police, man," Ramos said. Then he inhaled and said, "I told you I was just looking for my friend Amanda."

"I've known Amanda Collins since she moved here," the young

man said. "I know her friends. I see her every day at college." He pointed his finger at Ramos. "You stay right here, mister," he said.

The courage of the young man impressed Ramos. All the skinny kid wanted was to protect Sweetness.

Ramos let out a grunt as he stood. When he got to his feet, he shoved his three hundred plus pounds and Amanda's thin neighbor against the wall next to the young man's opened apartment door. As canned laughter blared from the young man's television, Ramos reached under his shirt and pulled his knife from its sheath. He waved the gleaming nine-inch blade slowly in front of the young man's eyes. Terror showed on the young man's contorted face, his body trembling and his breath coming in short gasps. Ramos grinned again. He stared into the young man's eyes, then nicked a bit of skin from his right cheek.

"Please—please. Don't kill me," the young man said, now crying, his face contorted, blood trickling from the nick on his cheek.

"Not so brave now," Ramos said with a grin.

Ramos moved the tip of the blade to the young man's chest and plunged it deep into his heart.

"You should have believed what I told you," Ramos said. "I might have let you live."

⌞ ⌟

"What happened?" Vic asked when Ramos opened the passenger door of the white Ford.

Ramos sat. "She's not there, man. She fooled us," he said to Vic.

"That's not what I mean," Vic said. He pointed to Ramos's shirt.

"Man, that's not a lot of blood," Ramos said. "You should have seen the wound. Anyway, I got another shirt in the trunk." Ramos started taking off the bloody yellow gloves.

DiRosa blew out a deep breath as he shook his head slowly.

"Tell me what happened!" Vic said through clenched jaws.

"A neighbor kid saw me, man," Ramos said. "I had to take care of him, man."

"Get out of here," Vic said to DiRosa. "Cops will be all over the place. I'll contact you later."

Vic jumped out of the Ford, slammed the door, and dashed to his car.

Ramos heard Vic mumble something about "holy rosary."

"He must be Catholic like you," Ramos said.

DiRosa shook his head slowly again, sighed, then pressed his foot on the accelerator.

TUESDAY, JUNE 25

CHAPTER 14

Amanda sat up and leaned against the headboard. She could see herself in the mirror above the Formica-topped dresser not more than three feet from the foot of the bed.

She decided to call Geoffry. He would tell her to come home, that he would protect her. *Please, let me hear him say that.* She reached for the telephone and dialed the number to the microbiology lab of Hope Valley Community Hospital.

Lisa, Geoffry's coworker, answered. Amanda heard her call out to Geoffry, "It's your sugar, Geoffry."

⌞__⌟

"Amanda, where are you? I've been calling and calling!"

"Geoffry, what are they saying about Dr. Hegel?"

"He pulled over on Highway 165 and shot himself. Something funny, though. There might have been another car with him at the scene."

"Another car? What kind of car?" Amanda asked.

"That's all they'd say. It's on the radio, television. . .in the papers. Where are you?"

"Just listen," Amanda said. "I'm going to call you at your apartment at four-thirty this afternoon. That's five-thirty your time."

"What! Honey, where are you?"

"Don't tell anyone I called. No one."

"Dr. Hegel's funeral is tomorrow," Geoffry said.

"I've got to go now."

"Amanda, honey, just tell me where you are!"

"I love you, Geoffry." Amanda hung up. She looked at the package and the note she was to read when she reached Anchorage Apartments in Slidell, Louisiana.

Dr. Hegel, you did something wrong, didn't you? Something really bad. That's why they were after you. Now that's why they're after me. They want the package you told me to take, don't they? What else could it be?

He stepped across the threshold of Professor Treadaway's open office door in the Agriculture and Science Building at 9:15 in the morning, extending a card in one hand. In his other hand he held a shiny snakeskin briefcase. Treadaway held his coffee cup steady in front of his lips.

"Professor Paul Treadaway?" the man asked, standing in the doorway in his light gray double-breasted suit, starched white shirt, and dark maroon patterned Italian silk tie with an amazingly tiny knot.

Treadaway lowered his cup. "May I help you?"

The man handed Treadaway his card. "Cantrell P. Dwyer with Banckroft, Rosenbloom, Martin, and Thurston in Providence. A custodian downstairs said you might be able to help me. Our firm represents Biological Systems Technologies. I have a rental truck outside with two men. We've come to retrieve the BioSysTech files and other property belonging to my client."

Treadaway stood up, grabbed the card, and shot a glance at it. Then he used it to gesture to the chair in front of his desk. "Please, sit down, Mr. Dwyer."

"The lab is 214?"

"Would you like a cup of coffee, Mr. Dwyer?"

"I would like to retrieve my client's property, Professor."

"Well, I don't think you have the right to just come in and take whatever you want. I need to call Dean Parks."

"It's not what I want to do; it's what I must do," Dwyer said. "There's a difference, Professor. Call the dean if you must, but show me the lab first."

"I don't—"

"If I leave without my client's property, based upon your refusal, the university will have breached the conditions of the grant with Dr. Hegel. Stipulated damages are in the millions. Would you like to be responsible for that, Professor?" Dwyer asked without raising his voice or moving his gaze from Paul Treadaway's eyes.

"I might have a problem finding a key for you," Professor Tread-away said.

"I have a key." Dwyer reached inside his suit jacket and pulled out a telephone, raised it to his ear, and pushed a button. "Come up," he said into the mouthpiece. "I will meet you there." He turned to Treadaway. "Thank you, Professor. If you have questions, I'll be in 214." He smiled, turned, and strutted out of the office.

Dean Parks stopped suddenly in front of laboratory 214. Professor Treadaway bumped against his back before he managed to stop his own momentum. Two men in coveralls in the lab moved here and there, obeying Dwyer's every command.

"Mr. Dwyer, I'm Dean John Parks. Would you please tell me what you're doing?"

Two campus policemen stood behind Treadaway, peering into the lab as best they could.

"Pleasure to meet you, Dean Parks," Dwyer said. "Do you have a copy of the grant BioSysTech entered into with Dr. Hegel, the one signed by the university president?"

"No, I don't," Dean Parks said. One of the campus cops managed to slip by the professors and attorney and into the lab. The two men in coveralls stood still and watched. The campus cop put his hand on the handle of his service revolver and glared at the men in coveralls.

Treadaway shook his head. "I knew no good would come of Hegel's experiments," he said softly. "Everything was so peaceful before the BioSysTech grant, before all this fetal tissue stuff."

Dwyer glanced at the campus policeman, then looked toward Dean Parks. "My client has exclusive proprietary interest in all data generated by Dr. Hegel. All the files belong to my client. I believe the file cabinet probably does also, but there may be some confusion with the wording there. So I will leave it."

"You aren't serious!" Treadaway said.

"Be quiet, Paul," Dean Parks said.

"The PC, the floppy disks and CDs, the information on the hard drive also belong to my client, as does the log and all papers on and in the lab assistant's desk. I'm not sure about the desk itself, though. You may have it," Dwyer said.

The other campus policeman made his way into the lab. Treadaway mustered the courage to stand side by side with Dean Parks.

"I have the right to search Dr. Hegel's office and to retrieve any document having anything to do with BioSysTech."

Dwyer turned to the men in coveralls. "Get back to work, gentlemen," he said to them.

"Dean, you can't let him do this!" Treadaway said.

"Stay with him, Paul," Dean Parks said. "Don't do or say anything." Dean Parks turned to the campus policemen. "You men, go outside and find the vehicles they came in. But just watch. Don't take any action until you get direct orders from me."

The policemen filed out of the lab. Dwyer's men resumed packing boxes.

"Wise counsel, Dean Parks," Dwyer said.

"Mr. Dwyer," Dean Parks said. "I'll not cause this university to be sued. I'll talk to you after I discuss this with the president and the university's general counsel."

"I would expect no less of you, Dean," Dwyer said.

Dean Parks shot a hard stare at Treadaway, who understood what the gesture meant: "Do just as I told you. No more, no less." Dean Parks hurried off.

Dwyer turned to his men. "Finish up here. Load the truck, then wait for my telephone call." Dwyer stared into Treadaway's eyes but continued to talk to his two men. "I'll be going to Dr. Hegel's office now. I will call if I need you."

Dwyer lifted the key ring and selected the key to Dr. Hegel's office door. He strolled behind Hegel's desk.

Treadaway stopped at the threshold and watched Dwyer for a moment, then stepped into the office and stood in front of Hegel's desk. Dwyer drew open the wide middle desk drawer.

"Did BioSysTech tell you anything about me?" Treadaway asked.

Dwyer said nothing. He pushed the wide drawer shut and opened another drawer on the right side of Hegel's desk. Then he pushed it shut. He reached for another drawer, then another, then another.

"I take it Dr. Hegel cleared his office before he killed himself, or did the university do it for him?" Dwyer asked Treadaway without looking up.

"He did. He was mad in the end, you know, insane." Treadaway said. "He mumbled fascist slogans. Stuff about generals and soldiers."

"That so, Professor?" Dwyer said, not looking at the professor, again opening another drawer, stooping, and shifting his head as if he were studying the rear corners. Then he pushed the drawer closed.

"I'm perfectly capable of continuing Dr. Hegel's work," Treadaway said. "Hegel often asked me for advice; he sort of depended on me."

"Really, Professor?" Dwyer asked, as he opened the last drawer to inspect. He leaned back on his heels, then bent sideways, gazing deep into the drawer.

"Oh, most certainly, that's so!" Treadaway said.

Dwyer reached into the drawer. He pulled out a doll and lifted it to his face. The doll whined, and its eyes popped open. "My mother used to have one of these," he said. "Too bad it's not on the list of my client's property. I would certainly take it home, but it would take some doing to remove those marks." Dwyer looked at Treadaway. "Tell me, Professor," he said, "why would a great scientist keep an old doll in his desk?"

"Did I not tell you he was mad?" Treadaway said.

Dwyer lowered the doll to his side. He looked at Treadaway. "Would Dr. Hegel's madness account for original research missing from the file cabinet in the lab, Professor? And the original data log?"

"I don't know anything about that. Hegel was sloppy. . .disorganized, too, particularly when he started his mumbling." Treadaway's voice cracked. He paused, then cleared his throat. "Well, what about it?" he asked.

"What about what, Professor?"

"What I said—you know." Treadaway cleared his throat again. "My taking Hegel's place on the grant."

"Perhaps you should discuss that when Dr. Richard Landcaster makes a formal demand that you return the missing property," Dwyer said. "You might consider asking your attorney to write a letter of recommendation after I seize your house and everything else you own to pay the damages."

"What have I done?" Treadaway asked, feeling as if he were talking to his mama. "Hegel did something with them, not me."

Dwyer raised his gaze to Treadaway's eyes and smiled. "Or perhaps I will have Dr. Landcaster telephone you this afternoon. Perhaps if you agree to assist him, you may be able to enter into a new grant with my client," he said.

A shot of excitement flew through Treadaway. He smiled back at Dwyer, feeling a plot developing in which he would be the main attraction. "I prefer that Dr. Landcaster call me at my home. Here, let me write down my number."

"I understand, Professor." Holding the doll by the head, he extended it to Treadaway. "Here," Dwyer said, "this might have sentimental value. Maybe you should give it to the widow." A soft whine came from the doll when Dwyer dropped it on the desk.

Dwyer walked out of the office. Treadaway grabbed the doll and hurried to follow him. "My number—here, my number," Treadaway said.

Dwyer walked down the steps, out the entrance door, to the steps outside. He held open the door for Treadaway, taking the small piece of paper with Treadaway's home number and slipping it into his suit pocket.

Dean Parks stood on the walkway, watching the men sitting in the rental truck parked in the loading zone of the Agriculture Building. Dwyer passed Dean Parks, saying nothing. He walked to the driver's side of the truck and spoke to the driver a moment, then glanced at the campus police who stood on the walkway near the rear of the truck.

The campus cops looked toward Dean Parks. He waved them away. The driver of the truck started the engine. Dwyer swaggered to his green Jaguar XJ8 convertible, swinging his glossy snakeskin briefcase. He stepped into his Jaguar, cranked it, then squealed his tires as he drove away. The engine of the rental truck roared, and the truck began to chug away, following the path the Jaguar had taken.

Dean Parks shrugged his shoulders as he watched the truck turn out of the lot. "Well, so much for BioSysTech and URI," he said.

"Hmm. . .," Treadaway said.

"Avraham. God bless him." Dean Parks shook his head. "He did so much for us, the university. My prayers are with Ruth and the children." Dean Parks paused. He glanced downward as if something had captured his attention. "What in the world is that?" he asked Treadaway.

Treadaway lowered his head and looked at the doll. "Must be Hegel's daughter's," he said. "I'll throw the filthy thing in the garbage where it belongs," Treadaway said.

"No, you won't, Paul!" Dean Parks said. "You'll take it to the funeral tomorrow. You'll not bother Ruth today. You will give it to Ruth. I have a feeling seeing it will bring her some happiness in this hard time. We owe Avraham that."

CHAPTER 15

Kristina England, Becky Ingram, and Madeline Gentcher waited for Constance in the Roosevelt Room, directly across the hall from the Oval Office. England was seething. She hated this tactic, the first lady's making them sit and wait so she could make her grand entrance. England would have said something about it if Gentcher weren't there. Gentcher, the spy.

England knew the press loved Constance Frye, and the reform had to pass. Soon. That was the only thing England couldn't do, get the press to push the reform like Constance could. But Hegel wasn't going to be the first lady's marionette in a surgeon general's costume now, was he? *One day Constance will be back in her home state. The business will be legal, too. Constance will fade into nothing, while I lecture, head up protests, and recapture the press's adoration. Just wait, Constance.*

England was preoccupied. Becky was considering leaving Washington. There'd be another Anticipating Parenthood president to find and dangle to the public and the wolves. *So much trouble, and Becky was perfect and even a friend. A rare thing for you, Kristina England.*

The first lady entered the Roosevelt Room twenty-five minutes late. She stomped directly to the head chair of the twelve-chair table. She slapped a notebook on the table, then sat, Gentcher to her immediate right, England to her immediate left, and Becky next to England.

They waited for the first lady to speak.

Constance glared at England, ignored Becky, and turned to Gentcher.

No, Constance, I'm not going to fuss about who should head up this venture. Not now. England said nothing.

Constance put her hands on the notebook and then opened it. She leaned forward and looked from England to Gentcher. She spoke slowly. "This is the most important meeting we've had to date," the first lady said. "We are not in a crisis; we can exploit this, but you must listen." Constance stared at England. "And there can be no dissension among us."

"What do you want us to do?" Gentcher asked.

Constance glanced at her notes, then looked up. "Avraham Hegel was frustrated because the children suffered unnecessarily." She pulled a sheet of paper from the notebook, turned to her right, and slipped the paper to Gentcher. "Study this for talking points to the press."

Gentcher scanned the page as a prideful smile crossed her face.

"Read it out loud, Madeline," Constance said, then looked at England, still ignoring Becky. "Listen to Madeline," she said. "Listen well."

Gentcher began to read the official White House spin on Dr. Hegel's suicide:

" 'Dr. Avraham Hegel was a wonderful man who, like the first lady, thought first of America's suffering children. He was a special man who understood so thoroughly the processes that make up living things. He knew how to use undeveloped life to help our precious living children. But he was caught up in a political world he did not understand. He received hate mail from the religious fundamentalists; columnists, who had not even spoken to Dr. Hegel, scolded him. They called him "Hegel the Beast" or "King Herod." They called him all kinds of dreadful names because they didn't understand.

" 'Politicians with special interests continued to hinder the first lady's efforts to bring healing to the children through her efforts with this great man, who himself wanted so desperately for Mrs. Frye's reform bill to become law.

" 'The first lady understands she must take some responsibility for the death of this great doctor—this great researcher, husband, and father. Constance Frye realizes now how fragile he was outside his laboratory world, where he was a general, a commander. She understands how the extremists and hate mongers made this deeply devoted man's life intolerable; they brought him to a place where he perceived himself stripped of personal dignity, just as the fascists had done with his forefathers.

" 'Dr. Hegel was an American hero. And like so many American heroes, he met a cruel death at the hands of America's philosophical enemies. The first lady's heart, and the heart of our nation, goes out to Ruth Hegel and her little children.' "

"Find out the names of the children," Constance said to Gentcher. "Say their names there."

Gentcher nodded.

"Hegel's children are grown," England said to Constance. "The daughter's in college; the son's in medical school."

"Folks out there don't know that!" Constance said, leaning into England, squinting her eyes.

Remarkable. England wanted to suppress that thought, but she couldn't. Then another: *This is deviousness at its best.*

Constance turned to her enforcer. "Go on, Madeline," she said.

Gentcher cleared her throat.

" 'The first lady asks that all Americans wear a red ribbon to show their appreciation for this man and this nation's commitment to its children, and to show solidarity behind her and her reform.

" 'Hereafter, her bill will be called the Hegel Bill, in honor of Dr. Hegel, and when the president signs the bill, it will be called the Hegel Act.' "

"Madeline," Constance said, "contact Rue, talk to your contacts at the Sunday talk shows. Try to get on the circuit. Push the red ribbon gimmick hard. Talk to your people at the *Times,* too. Telephone the friendly syndicated columnists. Fax a statement to party headquarters consistent with what you read. And I want the Department of Education on this one. I want to see a red ribbon on every child who takes a bite out of a school lunch that has one speck of federal subsidy attached to it."

Constance turned to England. "Kristina," she said, "I want you to do the same to all your nonprofits. Take this speech. Edit it to a news release for each nonprofit. Fax it today. See what wires will pick it up, the animal rights, environmental rights, all of them. They should be passing out ribbons by tomorrow morning. Remember: children and the red ribbons."

England wanted to say, "Do it yourself!"

"Where is the reform?" England asked, feeling subdued, ambushed. She hated to admit it, but this was a brilliant spin. *The rabble will lick it up like puppies.* No one was equal to Constance Frye at manipulating the public. She knew what she would see on the broadcast news and CPNN: all the national anchors and the reporters wearing red ribbons on their lapels. Larry King and the daytime television talk show hosts, too. England admitted it to herself for the first time. The first lady deserved to oversee the business. The "folks" would demand that Congress pass the reforms as a tribute to the man who killed himself to avoid being associated with it. Genius. Wonderful, morbid genius.

"Next week Representative Jukali will appear on black interest shows," Constance said. "He'll describe Hegel as a hero, too. He'll encourage all black Americans to wear the ribbons. The Caucus will use this opportunity to counter the growing notion that its members are anti-Semitic." Constance leaned back for the first time since she sat down. "It's all working out well," she said with a smile.

Reality hit England hard. No way was she in a position to maneuver this like Constance Frye had. *Concede, Kristina. Just concede. You'll all get along much better.* "I'll set up a conference call with the executive directors of my nonprofits," England said, intending a contrite tone. "I'll make sure they understand."

"No, you won't, Kristina," Constance said, suddenly leaning toward England again. "You will do just as I have said. The news release, that's all. If your people have questions, they are to contact Gentcher."

"What do you mean? Contact Gentcher?" England asked loudly. "What does Madeline have to do with my clients?"

"We're in the critical stage now," Constance said. "You have a lot of people in those nonprofits who think they're in some kind of religion. They're uncontrollable like any other religious fanatics."

"It'll do no good to start criticizing us now," Becky said. "They mean well, and they're loyal to your husband."

England couldn't believe Becky would risk confrontation with the first lady. Not Becky. Even Constance froze for a moment, apparently lost for words.

Constance glared at Becky, her green eyes squinting, her mouth tightly shut. Then the first lady appeared to calm down.

England didn't know what to do. The thought came to her that if she were to speak up now, she might not survive another confrontation with Constance. "And just who do you think the fanatics will vote for if not my husband?" Constance asked softly, glaring at Becky, who was hunched over her opened notepad. "Preacher Jeremiah Gators?"

Silence fell on the Roosevelt Room.

"And, my dear," Constance Fry said, still staring at Becky, "did you happen to read what that idiot Peterson wrote in his Brothers and Sisters in Fin, Feather, and Fur newsletter in last month's issue?"

Becky remained silent and stiff, except for her head, which she shook like a frightened little girl. Constance slammed her palm on the notebook and hollered, "Well, did you read Peterson's article, Becky?"

Becky shook her head faster, in short, rapid jerks. Her eyes widened; her lower lip quivered.

"Well, Peterson wrote that human fetal brain stem cells ought to be used in animals, too. And that the little creatures should be first on the list before us humans for using animals in laboratory tests all these years. What do you think about that, Becky?"

England had to help. "There's no need to. . ."

Constance glared at England. England quieted.

"That tripe is ammunition for the likes of Jeremiah Gators," Constance said to England. "Who, for your information, intends to read Peterson's stupid theory to the Senate before the vote on my reforms."

England said nothing.

"Well, Kristina, I'll tell you this," Constance said. "If you can't control your people, I will."

"I can control my nonprofits. You and Madeline just keep your hands off my clients," England said.

The first lady leaned toward England. "If Peterson wants legislation to treat animals with human embryo brain stem cells, that's fine with me after my husband signs my bill. They can inject them into their tofu burgers as far as I care, but none of your fanatics is going to jeopardize my reform bill before it passes with their stupid obsessions about animal rights and hugging trees. Understand?"

"Constance, I said I can control my clients," England said.

The first lady fell silent for a moment. "Okay, I'll back off, but it's too late for Peterson," she said. "Tell your people to consider him an example."

England glanced at Gentcher. Gentcher grinned at her.

Constance turned to Gentcher. "Make sure your staff knows what to tell them."

"Yes, ma'am."

"You can leave now," Constance said to Gentcher. "You have much to do."

"Yes, ma'am."

After Gentcher closed the door behind her, Constance turned to England. "Now, Kristina," she said. "Tell me what's going on."

CHAPTER 16

Amanda drove her rented Escort on Interstate 10 eastbound on what New Orleanians call the "Twin Span," another structure over Lake Pontchartrain comprised of twin seven-mile, two-lane bridges spanning the lake about fifty yards apart. She approached a rise in the bridge high enough to accommodate the masts of the sailboats that speckled the lake. From the top of the rise, she saw the blue roofs of the Anchorage Apartments. She felt relieved. She didn't know where she was, but she could see where she was going. Dr. Hegel had mentioned this very view in his note.

After crossing the Twin Span and veering off I-10 at an exit sign that read "Eden Isles," Amanda followed a newly paved road that wound through a subdivision. The backyard of each house ended in a cement bulkhead containing a canal in which a sailboat, party boat, or fishing boat sat still against the private wood docks.

The road led her out of Eden Isles Subdivision, past a sign that read:

ANCHORAGE APARTMENTS. MODERN.
FURNISHED AND UNFURNISHED. WEEKLY OR MONTHLY
RENTAL. MARINA DOCK RENTALS AVAILABLE.

Five three-story white-stucco buildings with maybe eighteen or twenty apartments each made up Anchorage Apartments. Three large swimming pools and, in the rear, a marina for boats, mostly sailboats, gave the complex a recreational atmosphere.

Dr. Hegel was right. This climate was oven hot with saturated air, but the tenants didn't seem to mind. Those who were out wore bathing suits, dark sunglasses, and sunblock on their noses. *Geoffry would love it here.* She parked in the slot in front of the rental office. *Dr. Hegel, you're with me. If it's that important to you that I deliver the package to whomever you say, I will.* Amanda felt safe here. She decided that she would buy a bathing suit. Who could find her here, anyway, in this hamlet named Slidell, Louisiana?

"Yes, Ms. Collins," the clerk said. "You're in apartment 105. The western end of the marina is at your back door. You'll love the view. No pets. Do you have a cat? They're so filthy."

"No, ma'am."

"Your rent is five hundred eighty-five per month," the clerk said. "Your father," the clerk cocked her head slightly and smiled, "has paid for the rest of the year."

"Yes, ma'am."

"This key is for the apartment; this one is for your mailbox. Please read this brochure. It has all our rules for the pool and apartment maintenance. No pets—especially cats. They claw our sofas and chairs and stench up the apartments with those filthy litter boxes. I just don't know how people live with them."

Chuckles. For the first time in decades, Amanda remembered the only pet she ever had. A big, white, furry cat.

"Where's Chuckles, Mama?" she had asked when she came home from fifth grade one day.

"Your father took him away, baby. He says you should have a darker colored cat. It's what the minister told the people."

Months went by before Amanda got used to bedtime without Chuckles and without crying.

"Ms. Collins—your keys and brochure—Ms. Collins?"

"Oh, I'm sorry. Thank you."

⌐ ⌐

Griffin had set some of the BioSysTech documents in stacks behind his desk against the window, but more documents cluttered his desk. He knew what Jennifer was going to say when she walked in.

"Griffin, you can't spend all your time with the BioSysTech file. It's two-fifteen. You haven't returned calls. Senator Zellars has called twice."

Jennifer was right. Griffin enjoyed a reputation of being accessible to his clients. Politicians didn't have a lot of time. If they needed him, he had to be there. And they paid. They had to if they wanted to stay in office. Politicians talked among themselves, too. Good advertisement. Griffin had been the subject of hundreds of conversations—he knew that. The only politicians who spoke ill of him were the ones not successful at destroying the reputation of a political opponent because of Griffin's skills, and even then, the criticisms implied compliments.

But now Constance might have gone too far. Could she have been involved in a murder? Arranged it herself? He wasn't sure what BioSysTech was selling, but he had ideas. And the ideas consumed him. He was on a hunt; he'd love to watch the first lady sweat for a change. Jennifer didn't seem to understand that feeling, the need to pursue. Relax and you lose the edge. In law, you lose the case; in combat, you come up lame or you die.

Griffin knew that. Eleven months and twenty-seven days into his tour in Vietnam, huddled against a tree in the darkness of the Vietnam forest, somewhere far north of Da Nang where his battalion had started their long, senseless march to Hill 689, at his watch on the edge of the perimeter, he had stood up when he heard movement out there. *Just a scout,* he thought. One of those captured, retrained VCs, he was sure, though a soft voice deep within cautioned him.

"Halt!" Griffin hollered, not bothering to get into position with his weapon.

The crack from the intruder's rifle sent a round into Griffin's left thigh, as he stood a stationary target.

Don't relax. Not in war. Not in this pursuit, either. Remember what Allan Cook said, Griffin? Remember what he told you David said to his giant? "You come with a sword, spear, and shield, but I come with the Lord of hosts; the battle is the Lord's."

"Did you find out when Hegel will be buried?" Griffin asked Jennifer.

"Tomorrow," Jennifer said softly. "Services will be held in a synagogue in West Kingston at ten o'clock. Maybe you can call Ruth Hegel tomorrow afternoon."

"Book a flight for tonight," Griffin said. "Get me a hotel."

"Griffin!" Jennifer said with her hands on her hips. "You have to call Senator Zellars! Call him right now."

"On second thought, charter a plane for the day."

"Charter a plane! Do you mean it?"

"I mean it."

"Call Zellars. Then I'll book. I mean charter."

Griffin lifted the telephone receiver. "Five, five, five," he began.

"Three, zero," Jennifer said.

"Three, zero."

"Six, nine."

"Six, nine," Griffin said. He turned to Jennifer, feeling a warm appreciation for her, and smiled.

Jennifer moved her lips, saying without sound: *Now I'll charter.* She stood and walked out of the office.

Griffin knew what Senator Zellars wanted to discuss. He wanted to settle. Not that he had done anything wrong, of course. Lawsuits like this happen all the time; people don't take them seriously anymore, anyway.

"Why pay all those attorney fees?" Zellars said to Griffin. "It's not like it was rape; just a little fun." Zellars chuckled. "And it was a great idea to have the wife along in public."

Griffin couldn't tell Zellars what he wanted to, that perhaps he should seek counseling, that maybe he should ask his wife to forgive him. Griffin said what was appropriate for a lawyer to say: "If you didn't do anything, then don't pay anything. If you did, then maybe settlement would be better before all the witnesses come out. More usually do in these types of cases. But you need to consider the implications with the subcommittee."

"That's taken care of, and the girl won't be around to talk. Just so happens she got a sudden academic scholarship to Colorado State. Got a good friend in the legislature there."

The telephone call with Zellars ended, and Griffin felt the weight of weariness settle on him.

"I got your plane," Jennifer said over the intercom.

"Would you come in here, please?" Griffin asked.

Jennifer walked into Griffin's office and sat in the same chair across from him. "Discussion session?" she asked.

"I'm looking for a place where medical procedures could be done," Griffin said.

"A hospital?" Jennifer said.

"No. It would have to be hidden somewhere. Things would have to be sold, too. Sent out for delivery."

"I'm lost," Jennifer said.

"Let's start with the owners," Griffin said, not so much directed at Jennifer, but more to himself. "Assume three people involve themselves in an illegal venture. One is an elitist New York lawyer. The second, a disgraced doctor, the apparent chief officer of the business. The third, a governor's wife who makes Rip Van Winkle's shrew look like the woman at Jacob's well."

Jennifer smiled. "You better watch out," she said. "You might not be going to church anymore, but He still hears you."

A pang of guilt passed though Griffin. "Where would the physical business—the real business of the venture—take place, assuming the physical business had to be kept secret?"

"An illegal medical business, like operations? Surgeries?" Jennifer asked.

"Any business—manufacturing overweight widgets, maybe."

"Where does the chief officer live?" Jennifer asked.

Griffin shook his head. "He lives in Chicago, in a penthouse. He probably plays hard in the evenings and on weekends. Can't be there."

"How's the ever-ogling Richard Landcaster doing nowadays?" Jennifer asked, in a tone that sounded like Mae West's "Why don't you come up and see me sometime?"

Griffin shot her a sideways glance. *Is Jennifer hiding something about Landcaster from me?* He continued, "The elitist lawyer, she's behind some podium, and she's either speaking herself or sitting behind the speaker at every official protest of the nonprofits she represents. When she isn't protesting or being the darling of the journalists' interviews, she's lobbying. She's not there, either."

"The state where the wife's husband is governor?" Jennifer asked.

"With the protections of the governor. . ." Griffin said.

"This state?" Jennifer asked.

"That's right. This state."

"But where in this state?" Griffin asked. He only now realized how carefully that information had been concealed. Everyone in the enterprise must have agreed never to write down the location of the business site. He would have seen it in all the documents he went through, most certainly.

"Somewhere around Ozark?" Jennifer said. The leg she had crossed over her knee began to swing a little harder. She grinned.

Griffin lifted his gaze from the clutter on his desk to Jennifer. "Why Ozark?" he asked.

"Landcaster called you from there last year, three times. I thought it was the cutest name. Ozark. Kinda hick, too, don't you think?"

Women.

"How do you know?" Griffin asked.

"Remember when I told you that Landcaster asked me to go out with him?"

"Yeah. Sure I do."

"Well, the last time. . ."

Come on, come on.

"Let's see. . ."

She's doing this on purpose, Griffin.

"That was the third time. . . . I kinda played with him, you know, led him on a little." Jennifer shrugged her shoulders and smiled a mischievous smile.

"Jennifer! The guy's a creep!"

"He said he was in Ozark, less than three hours away," Jennifer said. She uncrossed her legs and leaned toward Griffin's desk. She smiled and lifted her eyebrows. A gleam appeared in her eyes.

"Don't tell me you. . ." Griffin lost the courage to finish his question.

"Landcaster assured me the drive to Columbia would be very pleasant for him if he had someone like me to treat him really nice when he got here," Jennifer said, then winked.

"Creep," Griffin said. Then he paused. "Well?"

"Well what?"

"Did you go out with him?"

Jennifer stood up. "Now that I solved your problem, I'd better get back to my regular duties," she said, then sauntered toward the door.

"Well, did you?" Griffin asked, almost hollering.

Jennifer stopped and turned. "Your plane will be ready at six o'clock. I have your hotel reservations at my desk," she said, resuming her saunter to the door. She stopped at the door, turned, and put her right hand on the door frame. "I have to take my car to the shop again tomorrow. I'll need a ride here Thursday morning."

Griffin nodded, feeling himself smiling.

"I'll discuss the Landcaster affair with you then," Jennifer said. She put her left hand on her waist and tilted her head.

Lauren Bacall floated through Griffin's mind.

"See you Thursday at my place, say eightish. . .," Jennifer said. Then she continued her saunter out of Griffin's view.

Jennifer's wit reminded Griffin of Ruth—at least before his blunder. These feelings for Ruth Hegel made no sense. *All she needs is a faithful friend, Griffin. Remember that!*

┕╌╌┙

"Mama, is Daddy there?" Amanda asked.

"No, baby. He's at work. I haven't told him yet. It's not a good time. Where you calling from?"

"I can't tell you, Mama. You might not hear from me for a while. Don't worry, okay?"

"Ruth Hegel called me. She said you weren't in Kingston no more. She's worried. You married that boy, didn't you?"

"No, Mama." Amanda remained quiet for a moment. "Why didn't you tell Daddy?"

"Baby, there's been trouble at the station again. The association is saying the department is discriminating again. Your daddy's been in the paper every day. It's a bad time, and. . ."

"And what, Mama?"

"Your daddy says blacks who marry whites are trying to be white, denying their African heritage."

"Mama, I don't have an African heritage; I'm an American, and I'm just me."

"Your daddy loves you. He loves—"

"Mama, I love Geoffry just like you love Daddy. I can't live my life for Daddy like you did."

"I'm scared of losing you, baby. Scared I won't see my grandbabies. Scared I'll lose your father."

"Mama, I'll always be here for you, no matter what."

"Oh, baby."

"I've got to go now, Mama. Do me a favor. Call Mrs. Hegel back. Tell her you spoke to me, that I'm not scared or anything, that I'm just taking something to somebody. I love you, Mama."

Amanda sat on the edge of the bed. It was 4:10 P.M. central time when she ended the telephone call with her mother. She'd had to make that call. Her mother needed to know that her daughter would assume control of her own life, not allowing her father to control her, as he did everyone else. *Poor Mama, living with that hate and anger.*

Amanda decided to wait until exactly 4:30 to make her next call. She couldn't bear a busy signal; she didn't want to call Geoffry a minute early. She got up and began to pace, lost in thought and worry. The twenty minutes seemed like an hour, but finally the time came.

"Is that you, Amanda?" Geoffry asked after one ring.

"Yes. . .yes," Amanda said, feeling a wave of relief pass through her. "What's going—"

"Geoffry, listen to me. Dr. Hegel left a suicide note and a package I think I'm to deliver to somebody."

"A package?" Geoffry asked.

"Geoffry, two men in Kingston want to kill me. You've got to believe—"

"Amanda," Geoffry said softly. "I have to tell you something."

Amanda could tell by the tone of Geoffry's voice and the dead silence that followed it that she was going to be hurt. *Oh, please, Geoffry, don't tell me you've changed your mind about us. I need you now.*

"What is it, Geoffry?" she asked, twisting her engagement ring around her finger. *Brace yourself, Amanda. Be ready to be alone again.*

"Danny Barnwell was murdered in his apartment last night," Geoffry said. "No one's saying much. Rumors are it was a professional killer. There's a lot of talk about you missing. Amanda, they think the killer was after you."

"Oh, no." Amanda lowered the phone from her head, dizzy from the emotions welling up in her—grief, then terror. She held the receiver with both hands in her lap. She closed her eyes and bowed her head, sobbing.

"Amanda. . .Amanda!"

Amanda raised the handset back to her ear. "I'm still here," she said. "They were after me, Geoffry."

"Why?"

"What are the police saying?" Amanda asked.

"There's talk about you being abducted," Geoffry said.

"Geoffry, when you get home, leave your car at your apartment. Take a cab to my apartment. I left my car key in the flowerpot closest to the far-left porch column, just under the dirt. Drive my car to the Peacock Inn on Airline Highway, near the New Orleans Airport.

Can you remember that? The Peacock Inn. . .Airline Highway. Try to drive straight here. Check in. I'll see you there. Hurry, please."

"I'll be there," Geoffry said.

"Don't worry about me, Geoffry," Amanda said. "Dr. Hegel set everything up for me. I'm safe."

"We've been praying at the church, all of us, Aman—"

"Don't tell anybody you talked to me, Geoffry. Nobody should know, not even those at that little church you found."

After eight rings, a woman's voice muddled by chewing gum said, "Kingston Taxi Company."

"Send a taxi to 2140 Thornhill Road, Apartment B," the man said.

"Give me your name and telephone number. We verify calls, darlin'."

"Geoffry Reagan. Five-five-five-six-seven-five-six."

"Man, it's really a shame," Ramos said to DiRosa. "These kids waste good money on taxis when they could just walk." Ramos increased the volume on the listening device, hoping Sweetness's boyfriend would get another call from Amanda.

The phone rang again. "Geoffry Reagan?" the voice asked through the popping gum.

"Yes."

"Just checking. College pranks, you know," the dispatcher said.

Amanda calmed quickly after Geoffry hung up. His tone told her he missed her, too, and wanted to be with her just as much as she did with him. *Perhaps a day will come, Amanda, when you realize his feelings for you are real. You have to accept that. And you have to accept the fact that he is serious about his new-found faith.*

Amanda reached for the envelope marked "Note Three." Even before she read it, she knew it would describe, at least in part, the goal of this new game.

"AMANDA, YOU MUST HAND THE PACKAGE TO SENATOR JEREMIAH GATORS, PERSONALLY, AT HIS SLIDELL HEADQUARTERS. DO NOT FAIL IN THIS."

The goal: Get the package in Senator Gators' hands as soon as possible; the sooner you hand it to him, the sooner you win. Amanda already knew the other rules: Do not telephone anyone; do not tell anyone who you are or where you are from. Do not mention Dr. Hegel's name, except when you hand the package to the senator. Simple rules. *The only thing I did was to contact Geoffry; Dr. Hegel would understand that! And my mother, and—*

⌞　　⌟

Amanda looked up the number for Senator Gators' headquarters and quickly punched the buttons on the phone.

"Senator Gators' office." The voice belonged to a pleasant elderly woman with a definite southern drawl.

"May I speak to Senator Gators, please?"

"The senator is in Canada on a tour."

"Ma'am, I have an important package—"

"A package? We don't accept packages—not from strangers. This terrorist thing and germs, you know. Only from mailmen. We X-ray every package, just like they do at the airports."

"It's from Dr. Avraham Hegel, the research scientist. You know, fetal brains; the one who was killed." Amanda didn't want to say "suicide."

"Oh, dear me! Brains!" the woman said. "In the package? His brains are in the package!"

"No, no. You don't understand."

"Young lady, is this a prank call to a United States senator's office?"

"No, no. It's important, please!"

"Leave your name, and I'll—"

"I can't."

"Your phone number?"

"I can't. Please, ma'am," Amanda said. "I have to know when the senator will be back. I don't want to hurt anybody, but somebody could get hurt if I don't speak to the senator. I promise."

"We have security every day, all the time around here, young lady."

"Please, I've come all the way from—"

"From where?"

"I've got to get this package to the senator. Oh, please!" Amanda felt her voice crack.

A pause.

"Senator Gators will be back Saturday," the woman said. "He plans to be in the office with plenty of armed guards outside and inside from eight in the morning to about noon. We just had the metal detectors repaired; they work just fine. And the cameras work, too."

"Thank you," Amanda said.

"Just make sure you don't have any weapons on you, or you will be taken straight to jail."

"I won't." Amanda felt some relief when she hung up the phone.

Just four more days, Dr. Hegel, and I'll win this game. And I will begin my own life.

WEDNESDAY, JUNE 26

CHAPTER 17

The green dash lights glowed in the dark blue interior of the white Crown Victoria. In the darkness of 4:10 in the morning, the green glow highlighted the streaks of gray in DiRosa's black manicured mustache and soft thinning hair and illuminated his smooth olive facial skin. Ramos had stolen several glances at that face during the five hours they had followed Sweetness's boyfriend. An image of his own face came to Ramos's mind, not at all like the Italian's. Even in the little hamlet where he had been reared, where a man's appearance wasn't as important as here in America, they had laughed at him. "Why didn't your old man break the other side of your face, too?" they would say.

Ramos recalled his last day in that hamlet outside Ciego de Avila, Cuba. He'd gotten the woman drunk on that last night. Tequila, five shots. Or was it six? Then he'd half dragged, half carried her up the stairs while the mocking patrons of that little bar had toasted them through the haze of cigarette smoke. When he had stepped out the back door above the saloon at midmorning the next day, the woman had lain with a fatal knife wound to her body.

Ramos glanced at the flickering red light on the receiver, then at DiRosa, then smiled when the next thought came: They had laughed at him until they found her lifeless body. Ramos looked out the passenger window. The bright moon and stars shone on the trees whizzing by. Soon, man. Very soon. And he would find Sweetness.

"The young gringo's making good time," Ramos said.

DiRosa kept his gaze on the taillights of Amanda's Camry. He had not spoken three words to Ramos since Kingston. The beeps sounded loudly in the otherwise silent interior of the Ford; the red light flickered brightly at each beep.

A country song that Sweetness's boyfriend had just inserted into the Toyota's CD player came from the speaker of the device sitting on the floor of the Ford. Ramos hadn't heard the song before, but he liked country songs, especially the love songs.

"I gotta go, man."

"Not until he stops again," DiRosa said, his eyes focused ahead.

"We can catch up, man," Ramos said. "We know where he's going, man."

"We are not stopping," DiRosa said.

Ramos held his breath and tightened his abdomen. He felt better after a few moments. "You and Vic are from the same country," Ramos said.

"We are an endless family business, where the men are the head and we put our lives on the line, and nobody hurts the women and children," DiRosa said. "Something a pig like you can never understand."

"And what about traitors in the family?" Ramos asked.

DiRosa nodded his head. "You think you know a lot," he said. "But I tell you what, you don't know anything about us, who betrays who, and why things are done. It's best to be quiet about such things. You live longer not being in business with us."

"You don't think Cubans are as smart as you. But I am." Ramos looked at DiRosa. "I got famous in my country."

DiRosa said nothing.

"Castro was my personal friend," Ramos said. "I did favors for him. Like what you did for the CIA."

DiRosa said nothing. Ramos looked at him; DiRosa held his head stiff, staring out through the windshield, his lips tight, his jaw muscles working.

"One of Castro's generals thought maybe he could use organized crime in America to get rid of him. But Castro, he was already doing business with a lot of them. You know that, man, right? Organized crime in America and Castro, they were like that, man," Ramos said, raising his hand and holding his first two fingers close together.

DiRosa kept his gaze on the interstate and said nothing. Ramos thought DiRosa was either deep in thought or maybe listening to him. *Everybody likes stories about Fidel Castro,* Ramos thought. And it felt good talking to another man, like he would if he had a friend.

"I visited the general's house," Ramos said. "He had twin daughters, maybe fourteen or thirteen."

A roar. An eighteen-wheeler passing the Ford on DiRosa's side, its diesel engine in full throttle. Ramos stopped talking. He couldn't wait for the truck to pass. Finally, a conversation. Maybe they would become friends. The big rig rolled by. As its trailer passed the Ford, the roar faded away. The truck moved into the right lane in front of DiRosa, blocking the view of the Toyota. DiRosa didn't seem to mind.

"When the general got home, he found his wife and his daughters. I just stabbed the wife once. Like I did that kid back in Kingston. Quick. But I did scare her a little first. She was ugly. But the daughters, they were beautiful. I tied them up, so they had to stay with their mother while she lay on the floor."

Ramos turned and looked at DiRosa. "We do things different in Cuba," he said. "If a man does something, his family gets involved." Ramos moved his gaze to the rear of the tractor-trailer in front of them and quieted. The image of his mother lying on the dirt floor after his father slapped her down passed through his mind. "Don't hit her again!" the thirteen-year-old Ramos had hollered, just before his father's fist broke his jaw.

DiRosa turned the wheel, directing the Ford into the middle lane, and accelerated. "Only cowards and pigs do such things," DiRosa said softly. The Toyota taillights came into view.

"Everybody knew it was me. I was famous. Castro liked it, too. It made people listen to him. The general's family had friends. Powerful friends. They met with Castro."

DiRosa said nothing. He steered the Ford back into the left lane. The Toyota's taillights came into view. Then he steadied the Ford's speed. "I don't want to hear anymore," he said.

Ramos looked out the passenger window again. "What do you think about your friends turning on you?" he asked DiRosa.

DiRosa said nothing.

"Castro had me arrested," Ramos said. "Then he announced that he had rid Cuba of a serial killer. He sent me to the prison in Mariel. Guess who he put in prison with me?" Ramos chuckled. "The general! Castro knew I had to kill him, man!"

Silence.

"And then you know what Castro did, man? He ordered my execution! He told everybody he was so sorry the general had got killed like that. 'The general was a good man,' Castro said. And me? His friend? I was a deformed monster! Man, can you believe that? If the general was such a good man, why was he in prison with me?"

DiRosa turned his head and looked at Ramos. "I've heard enough," he said, then returned his gaze to the interstate.

"Castro really hurt my feelings, man," Ramos said. "He knew I would kill him if I could. So he was going to execute me. His friend. You just can't trust nobody no more, man."

Ramos waited for DiRosa to say something. But quiet fell.

"You understand politics, man? American politics?" he asked softly.

No answer.

"The American president. What was his name?" Ramos searched his mind. "Jimmy Colder, or something like that. He got me and a lot of my friends out of Castro's prison and gave us a boat ride to Miami. He saved our lives, man. He's my hero." Ramos looked out the window again.

DiRosa gazed ahead at Amanda's Camry.

Ramos looked toward DiRosa. "You're in that witness program thing, right? You're famous, too, man. I even know your real name."

DiRosa jerked his gaze away from the Toyota and directed it at Ramos. He glared. "We are not criminals, Fidel Ramos," he said. DiRosa returned his gaze to the road. "We are businessmen," he said in an angry tone. "We make fair deals. We expect men to be men. You understand?"

"Yeah, man. I understand."

DiRosa peered in the rearview mirror, then glanced at Ramos. He looked straight ahead. "Then I make this business arrangement with you, pig Fidel Ramos," DiRosa said. "You never mention to no one about me. You never say my real name to nobody. Not even aloud to yourself. You do that, I don't put a bullet through your ugly head."

Ramos turned his gaze away from DiRosa to Amanda's Toyota's taillights, several car lengths ahead. He decided he had talked enough for awhile.

I ain't scared of you, man.

CHAPTER 18

Somehow Griffin managed to twist his shoulders and wedge himself into the synagogue against the back wall. Griffin sensed they thought he was different. Perhaps it was his lawyerly attire, the perfectly cut black double-breasted suit with white starched shirt illuminating his gray patterned silk tie. *This is a funeral, for heaven's sake. I'm overdressed at a funeral?*

When Griffin looked around, he understood. The entire faculty of the University of Rhode Island must have been there. How differently academicians dressed. Casual. Rumpled. Even here in a synagogue, at a funeral.

Griffin stretched up on his toes and craned his head. She had to be in the front row. He moved his gaze down the middle aisle, to the casket, then to the left. *Looking for the widow at her husband's funeral with your heart thumping. What are you doing, Griffin?*

"He is with God now," the rabbi said. "One of Avraham Hegel's colleagues has asked if he could say a few words."

There she is. Front row, to the left, about five seats in. Those must be her two children next to her. Griffin felt his heart step up a beat.

Griffin could only get a glimpse of Ruth. He remembered her hair. Frustrating. He could just barely see the side of her face as she turned slightly and lowered her eyes into a black lace handkerchief. *What am I doing here? She probably won't even remember me.* Griffin let out a subdued, sarcastic chuckle. *If she does, she'll probably remember me badgering her. Jennifer, why didn't you talk me out of this!*

She tried. Remember, Griffin?

"Professor Paul Treadaway, would you please step up," the rabbi said.

A short, stout man in Dockers and an out-of-season corduroy jacket stood up just seven or eight rows in front of Griffin. He walked down the center aisle, carrying a paper bag. Ruth turned to watch him, then her gaze caught Griffin's. Griffin felt his heart flip. He even felt his wounded thigh throb just a little. *Griffin, get a grip, would you? You still haven't figured out a decent reason why you're even here.*

The man Griffin assumed to be Professor Treadaway set the paper bag on the podium and began talking. He wore a small red ribbon on his lapel. Griffin then realized nearly half the people he could see wore the same sort of little ribbon. He suddenly recalled that some newscast or radio talk show host had mentioned it: Constance's red ribbon campaign "for the children" was connected to Dr. Hegel's work. Symbolism and no substance. The essence of the Fryes' administration. Griffin shook his head and felt like sighing.

Emotional garble was what Treadaway's talk sounded like, with a strange hint of Shakespearean lingo. Griffin kept his gaze on Ruth.

A moment after Treadaway began his talk, she shot a glance at Griffin, moving her head around far enough to cause her shoulder to turn a bit. She almost smiled, Griffin was sure. Some relief came to Griffin. He felt certain Ruth would at least entertain an apology and his condolences. He relaxed and looked around the synagogue that seemed so different from the church buildings he was used to.

Griffin remembered the church he had attended so faithfully as a deacon before he just quit going. His law practice had become his purpose in life, studying files on Sundays, protecting the politicians, rising to celebrity status in his little community. In his church—that thought caused a feeling, guilt maybe—a six-foot wooden cross hung over the baptismal immediately behind the podium where Pastor Drew Grady preached every Sunday.

"Where have you been, Griffin? Did I say something to turn you away?" Drew had asked him the last time they talked.

"No, Drew, just trying to find myself," Griffin had said.

"Trying to find yourself? What kind of psychological gobbledy-gook is that?"

While this Treadaway guy bored the crowd stiff, Griffin remembered telling a young lady at a judge's fund-raiser—what was her name? It wouldn't come—how important it was to have faith in your life.

"I have to find out who I really am first," the young lady had said.

Same sort of nonsense. *Look at your driver's license if you need to know who you are,* he had thought. Drew probably thought the same silliness was coming from Griffin. A little grind in the stomach. *No wonder he didn't call back, Griffin.*

What happened to you, Griffin? What happened to the deacon who spoke so boldly about his faith, who had a passion for the souls of men? Theresa? Was it Theresa? Is that your excuse?

"Avraham Hegel created a new era in medical science," the professor said. "And I will remember him and be thankful for him." Professor Treadaway was winding up his obviously unrehearsed, self-indulgent speech from the podium he was using mostly to get a good view of the widow, Griffin was certain. "I was his good friend."

That's really original, Prof. Griffin didn't believe the professor suffered much because of Hegel's death.

Treadaway stepped away from the podium. He picked up the bag and stepped down the four carpeted steps. He glanced at Ruth, smiling as he passed her. No, this wasn't a nice guy. This was Professor Politician. Griffin could smell his kind like drug pushers could smell narcs, and now he was hitting on the beautiful rich widow.

The rabbi stepped up to the podium. He waited for Treadaway, who strolled proudly to his seat. The question popped into Griffin's mind: *What's in that brown bag the professor is toting around with him?*

Professor Treadaway settled in his seat and placed the bag in his lap. Then Griffin saw him, sitting directly behind Treadaway. Richard Landcaster! Landcaster leaned toward Treadaway and whispered something. Treadaway's shoulders lifted a couple of times as he chuckled silently. When Landcaster leaned back in his seat, the woman sitting next to him—it was Madeline Gentcher!—grabbed Landcaster's upper arm, leaned, and whispered to him. Landcaster immediately turned his head. His eyes widened when his gaze fell on Griffin. Landcaster glowered; Griffin looked toward the front. *It's reasonable, certainly, for Gentcher to be here. Constance might be expected to send a representative, even as high as chief of staff. But Landcaster? This man mourned nothing.*

Warren Jennings came to Griffin's mind. Warren, sitting there in that client chair, almost begging. "Have you heard rumors about Landcaster? Suicides. People who know too much suddenly disappearing." Could that happen to Ruth?

The rabbi raised his hands, palms up. He moved his fingers toward himself in three or four quick jerks. Six men, randomly seated in the congregation, one of them sitting at Ruth's side whom Griffin assumed was her son, stood and slowly began making their way to the coffin.

When the six reached the casket, they removed the flowers from the coffin and took their positions. The rabbi nodded. The men lifted the coffin. The congregation stood. The pallbearers turned and began to lumber up the aisle. Ruth—and it must be her daughter—followed immediately behind. Two of the pallbearers wore red ribbons.

Griffin, stop thinking about Ruth; don't stare at her. Just follow the procession. Keep an eye on Landcaster, Gentcher, and that Professor Politician in league with them. You'll say hello, give her your condolences at the right time, not now. What are you going to say when she asks you what you're doing here?

"Well. . .I just happened to be passing through Dodge, and I thought I would check out a funeral or two. . . ." Right!

Griffin watched the pallbearers struggle with the big coffin as they passed him, then Ruth. *She's coming.* Ruth stole another glance. Those blue eyes, did they appear pleased to see him? *Griffin, you're really losing it. Go to the funeral, say your good-byes, and fly back to Columbia where you belong. She's not in danger of anything. Professor Politician isn't carrying a bomb or her cat's head in that bag—you don't even know if she owns a cat!*

"What are you doing here, Jackson?" Gentcher asked.

Right question, wrong woman.

Landcaster stood next to Gentcher, almost leaning into her. Professor Treadaway stood behind Constance's Enforcer.

"Paying my respects," Griffin said.

Gentcher turned to Treadaway. "Go to the cemetery, Professor. Do what I said," she told him. Then she turned to Griffin as Treadaway walked away, still toting the paper bag.

"Don't get involved in this, Griffin," the Enforcer said.

"In what?" Griffin asked.

Landcaster stepped between Griffin and Gentcher. He lifted his hand. He was three, maybe four, inches shorter than Griffin. He looked upward, then began jabbing his finger in Griffin's face. Griffin spotted a gold diamond ring on his finger. It hadn't been there on the close-up exposures and videos his investigator had shot several years ago.

"Go back home, Dowell," Landcaster said in rhythm with his jabs. "I know about your investigators. Stay away from Ruth Hegel and forget about BioSysTech. Got that?"

Gentcher lifted a box of Marlboros and a lighter out of her purse. She quickly lit a cigarette. She bent her head back and blew a puff of smoke toward the ceiling of the synagogue. The few remaining mourners stared in disbelief.

Griffin shifted his gaze to Landcaster. He grabbed Landcaster's hand. He tightened his clutch until he could feel the strain in the muscles in his lower arm, then his upper arm. Griffin strained his pectorals to transfer more pressure. Landcaster's face contorted.

"Stop, Griffin," the Voice said.

Griffin pushed Landcaster's hand into the doctor's chest. Landcaster stumbled backward, almost falling, but caught his balance. He began massaging his injured hand with the other while he glared at Griffin, his face flushed red, his lips taut.

"You boys stop fighting now. We're in church," Gentcher said. She took another drag from her cigarette and blew the smoke in Griffin's face. "You shouldn't make enemies in high places, Jackson," she said.

"A threat, Madeline?" Griffin asked.

"Just a statement of general principle, Jackson," Gentcher said.

"Come on, Dick," she said, still holding her stare on Griffin. "Time to leave your playmate."

Landcaster shot another glare at Griffin, still massaging his hand. He turned and followed Gentcher out of the synagogue.

Do you know you're in trouble, Ruth? Do you have any idea what the likes of Constance Frye can do if she perceives you as a threat? No worse human enemy exists. Do you know they've recruited this man, this professor? Do you know that, Ruth? What's in that bag? I've got to know what's in that bag.

Griffin thought he might have to read the story of David and Goliath again. He limped quickly through the double open doors of the synagogue, convinced that he was supposed to be here, no matter what Ruth would think.

└───┴───┘

Amanda almost skipped out of her apartment at the Anchorage. Her ponytail bobbed, and her feet barely touched the ground. She wore khaki Bermuda shorts with a white sleeveless blouse. Louisiana had to be the hottest state, and the most humid, too, no doubt. Dr. Hegel was right about that! But it was still a beautiful day. Geoffry was more than halfway here by now, Amanda was sure. It was so sweet of him to drive all the way down here, to her little safe hideaway. She stretched her left hand in front of her, lifted her hand at the wrist, tilted her head to the side, and stared at her diamond engagement ring glistening under the summer sun.

After Saturday she would be free to do what she wanted. Geoffry would have to go back to Kingston, but she had enough money to get him down here by plane on weekends and to help him pay for a nice room at a Holiday Inn or somewhere while he was here. Certainly there was a Holiday Inn, even in Slidell.

Amanda spotted a young man waxing a boat that sat on a trailer next to her car. He wore only swimming trunks. He was nicely tanned with dark hair. He looked up when he noticed Amanda and stood straight, dropping his hand with the heavily stained cloth.

"Just moved in?" the young man asked. He leaned against his boat, causing his eyes to be level with Amanda's and allowing little room between him and the driver's door of Amanda's rental car. Amanda made an animated gesture with her left hand, reaching for the door. *See the ring?*

"Yesterday," Amanda said. She extended her right hand toward him.

"Better not." The young man lifted his free hand as if to take an oath. Green-white stuff caked the wrinkles of his palm and fingers. "Never learned how to wax my boat without getting the gook all over me," he said with a smile. "I'm Carl, Carl Hebert. Apartment 205."

"Amanda."

"Know how to water ski?" Carl asked.

"I. . .I have to meet my fiancé," Amanda said.

Amanda glanced at her car's driver's side door.

"Oh, sorry," Carl said. He straightened and stepped backward toward the stern of his boat. He watched Amanda, smiling at her, as she opened the door to her car. The passenger in the white Ford passed quickly through Amanda's mind when she looked into Carl's eyes.

As she started the car, she decided she would drive around the French Quarter this morning, maybe St. Charles Avenue, too, if she had the time. She would see the sights before Geoffry arrived. Tomorrow she would be Geoffry's personal tour guide, after he got a well-deserved long night's sleep.

Then, at about six o'clock, after her solo tour, Amanda thought she might return the rental car to the airport, take a taxi to the Peacock Inn, and wait. Maybe when she saw the gray Camry pull in, she would hide, and then surprise him. No, she wouldn't be able to do that. She saw herself grabbing the driver's side door handle even before Geoffry brought her Toyota to a stop.

The air conditioner in the rental car struggled. She rolled down the driver's side window to expel the oven-hot interior air as she approached the left turn onto the winding street leading through Eden Isles Subdivision and to the entrance onto I-10, on her way to the Vieux Carre.

"Wake up! Ramos, up!"

Ramos lifted his head off the passenger-side window and wiped the drool running from the right side of his mouth. He gazed out the windshield until the grogginess left him. He glanced at DiRosa. Better to sleep than to sit with this Italian whose business it was to streamline transactions by removing business partners.

He calls me a pig. What about those bullets everybody knows he uses, those little twenty-two magnum dum-dum bullets that gouge out the brain. Don't call him stupid again, man.

Ramos focused on the Toyota's right blinking taillight. DiRosa let the Ford coast without turning his turn signal on. The distance between the Ford and the Toyota increased. The Toyota veered off the interstate and onto the exit just outside Memphis, Tennessee. DiRosa waved at the driver of a pickup truck in the middle lane. The driver signaled that he wanted to ease over to take the exit. DiRosa slowed to give the pickup room. The pickup pulled in front of the Ford, then veered off the exit and stopped at the stop sign behind the Toyota.

Ramos was certain DiRosa was going to lose him, but he decided to say nothing.

The Toyota turned left on a Tennessee state highway that ran perpendicular to the interstate, under an overpass. The pickup turned right. DiRosa stopped at the stop sign. He waited and watched Sweetness's Toyota turn into the bright oasis of a Texaco Travel Center. DiRosa coasted into the station. Ramos watched the young gringo slow the Toyota to a stop next to the concrete gasoline pump island on the other side of the station, then step out of Sweetness's car.

"Use the bathroom. I'll fill up," DiRosa said, while watching Geoffry. "And get me a cup of coffee."

Griffin kept his distance from Ruth at the cemetery. Not so much because he didn't know what to say, although that had something to do with it. What were the enemies up to—Landcaster, Gentcher, and that professor? He pondered that question as he kept surveillance.

Landcaster leaned against the front fender of the black Lincoln stretch limousine he and Gentcher had come in. Apparently, the doctor had chosen not to join the mourners. Landcaster stared at Griffin, but then something caused Landcaster's head to turn toward the interior of the Lincoln. He hurried to open the door, sat down, and brought a car phone receiver to his ear. With a final glare at Griffin between the driver's door and its frame, Landcaster slammed the door shut. The Lincoln's dark tinted window rolled up.

Great! Now he's going to watch everything I do, and I can't see him, as he tells Constance, "Guess who's come to dinner?"

Griffin turned and spotted Gentcher trying to melt into the crowd. She, like most of the women, wore black, but she stood almost a head taller than the rest of them. This was Hegel's reception all over again. Guards all over the place. Odd, though. Gentcher made no movement toward Ruth, hadn't even talked to her yet and showed no sign of caring to. *What a smooth, calculating predator,* Griffin thought.

A flood of concern for Ruth flowed through Griffin suddenly when the thought came that it was only a matter of minutes before Constance's Enforcer would make her move. Gentcher wasn't leaving the cemetery any time soon. And now Griffin watched Gentcher study Ruth as a sly predator studies its prey, waiting to pounce.

Gentcher's advice about enemies in high places was as close to a threat being directed at him as he could remember. That was about as specific an ultimatum as one would find in a fortune cookie. But never having been a victim didn't mean Griffin didn't appreciate the zing of fear. Sometime today, at her husband's funeral, Ruth was going to suffer those words from the mouth of Constance's perfectly ruthless messenger. Griffin was sure of it.

And then there was Professor Treadaway, standing next to Ruth, still holding that bag. Griffin's imagination ran wild. Maybe they just wanted to warn her. Maybe the chubby little prof was really carrying Ruth's cat's severed head. *Griffin! Get a grip!*

Treadaway stood next to Ruth, extending his free hand to the men as they approached Ruth. He had hugged Ruth once. Griffin was sure she winced.

On the other side of Ruth stood her two blond children. The daughter had not stopped crying. Her son stood tall, his chin up. He scanned the crowd, and once his gaze caught Griffin's eyes. *Who are you?* the young man's eyes seemed to say.

And Ruth. She had glanced at Griffin twice, as far as he knew. *Do you want to tell me something, Ruth? Do you know you're being watched, just like that Secret Service guard watched me at the reception? Do you know you're in trouble? You're too smart not to know, aren't you?*

You can expect a call from me, Ashton Roosevelt Frye. You can expect me to call in chips, too; expect me to insist that you control that crazed, fanged wife of yours. You might hear me threaten to violate attorney-client confidences, Ashton. Write a book, maybe.

Amanda's wonderful day had taken a bad turn. She veered off at the Vieux Carre, Orleans Avenue ramp on the portion of I-10 that ran through New Orleans and wound around the Superdome on Poydras Street, then shot out over Martin Luther King Boulevard, where tourists dare not tread. *I must have turned left somewhere when I should have turned right, or maybe right when I should have turned left.*

She wasn't sure how she'd gotten here, on this choppy, broken asphalt lane barely wide enough for two cars to pass each other that ran between three-story brick apartment buildings. Porches protruded on the front of each floor of the buildings. A shallow patch of brown lawn blanketed with hamburger and French fry wrappers separated the building from the choppy lane. Young men were everywhere, thin, muscled, but bony shouldered, some without shirts, the rest with bright white undershirts. One young man seemed to talk more than the others, swinging a cell phone as he spoke. Elderly men and women leaned over the rails on the balconies on the second and third floors, their gaze following Amanda's car.

Children darted and dashed everywhere. *Get out of the way! Get out of the way!* Amanda wanted to yell, so that she could press down on the accelerator and speed away, but she could only idle along, watching, ready to brake in case one of the children darted in front of her rental car.

On the lawn to her right, a fourteen- or fifteen-year-old girl stood on the brown lawn, her gaze following Amanda, making her feel as if she were an uninvited stranger. Amanda looked ahead. She spotted another teenage girl, dressed like the first, in black leggings and a T-shirt with some sort of figure on the front made of sequins— a bird maybe?

Amanda couldn't understand why, but her heart hurt for these young people; she felt as if she were driving through some institution with invisible bars. *How can they get out?*

"Hey, baby," the talkative teenager said, pointing his cell phone toward Amanda as she idled by. He moved quicker, then stepped in front of the car. Amanda hit the brakes. As he walked toward the driver's side of the car, Amanda noticed a bulge in his right pocket. A small pistol, she was certain. *Be careful, Amanda.*

The boy leaned over and stared through the window at Amanda. "Don't just keep movin'," he said. "Stop, honey. Be nice. Talk to me."

Amanda glanced at him. Then at the bulge in his jean pocket. Yes, it was a pistol, she could make out the form weighing heavily in his pocket. *Oh, please. Leave me alone.*

Amanda lifted her foot off the brake; the rental car began to crawl away. Distance increased between the armed boy and the rental car. Amanda glanced in the rearview mirror. The boy's hands gripped his waist, the cell phone still in one hand, his eyes showing a look of frustration. Amanda tightened her grip on the steering wheel. She concentrated on keeping her gaze forward. There had to be an end to this choppy lane, a way to a real city street.

Ahead, maybe only four or five buildings down, cars drove by on what looked like a real street, but children still darted everywhere.

187

Some of them couldn't be more than four, maybe five, years old.

On Amanda's right, on a bottom porch, just a few yards away, two older teenage girls sat on a porch talking. Both girls wore tight black leggings and oversize aqua pullover shirts with sequins and rhinestones on the front. One of the girls set her eyes on Amanda, then the other. The tiny gold ball above the first girl's nostril glistened, as did the big gold circles dangling from her earlobes and the multiple gold necklaces adorning her neck. Amanda turned her head forward.

Now she could see the city street ahead. Yes, it was a real street! She was back in the real world now. Safe. She wanted to go home. She wanted to see Geoffry. She had lost her enthusiasm for driving through the French Quarter.

⌞__⌟

Ruth's two children walked away from her, the son with his arm around his sister's shoulder. Professor Treadaway stood next to Ruth, still extending his free hand whenever the opportunity arose, holding the paper bag with the other. He glowered at Griffin.

It's time, Griffin. You won't look out of place if you just walk up to her and offer your condolences. But what then? Leave? Fine, except for the fact that Ruth doesn't know the professor is Constance's newest agent.

Landcaster still watched him from behind the black tinted glass of the limousine. Gentcher walked to the limousine and stepped into it, then slammed the door. A strategy session, Griffin was certain, to decide when to make their move on Ruth.

"I'm so glad you're here," Ruth said to Griffin with a warm smile. "Paul, this is Griffin Dowell," she said. "He's President Frye's attorney, and he's a friend of mine."

Remember, Griffin. That's all you are, "a friend."

Treadaway extended his free hand, still holding the bag in the other. Griffin grabbed his hand. It was one of those handshakes that causes one to think of a soft, dead fish at room temperature. Griffin could feel the tension, though, emanating from the professor as he stiffened his neck and a slight flush rose in his chubby face. Now Griffin was sure the professor had been briefed by Constance's Enforcer.

"Good to meet you," the professor said. He shifted his gaze over Griffin's shoulder, toward the limousine.

The three remained quiet for a moment, Ruth and Griffin glancing at each other, Griffin trying to avoid looking at her for an unwarranted length of time and wondering what to do next but feeling certain he should not leave Ruth to the buzzards. Then an idea popped into his mind. He looked at Ruth. Her gaze caught his eyes. *Listen, Ruth. Listen closely.* Then Griffin turned toward Treadaway.

"Professor," Griffin said, "you and I have common friends, I've noticed."

"So you're the president's attorney?" Treadaway asked.

"I wasn't talking about the president. I was talking about Dr. Richard Landcaster and Constance Frye's chief of staff, Madeline Gentcher."

Griffin glanced at Ruth just as she turned her head toward Treadaway and furrowed her brow.

"Oh," the professor said with a chuckle. "I wouldn't call them friends, not exactly. I happened to meet them at the synagogue." The professor cleared his throat. "Do you read Shakespeare, Mr. Dowell?" he asked.

"What's the red ribbon for, Professor?" Griffin asked.

"Oh, it's. . .well, it's for the children, the reforms. . .you know."

Bingo! Griffin wasn't expecting to complete a line of dots so soon. *Want more, Ruth?*

"You mean the first lady's reforms?" Griffin asked.

"Have you read *Macbeth,* Mr. Dowell?"

"Weren't you sitting with them and standing with them when I passed you in the synagogue, Paul?" Ruth asked.

What a woman.

"Well, I. . .I don't see them now," Treadaway said to Ruth. "They must have gone."

"No, Professor," Griffin said, pointing to the limousine. "They're watching us from their limousine over there. Maybe even having a nice chat with the first lady herself by telephone."

"Paul, how do you know them?" Ruth asked.

Treadaway swallowed, then cleared his throat. "I have wonderful news, Ruth," Treadaway said. "BioSysTech is thinking about my continuing Avraham's work."

The nutty professor being manipulated by the best, Griffin mused.

Griffin was startled at the intensity of Ruth's glare at the professor. "I have some things I need to talk to Mr. Dowell about alone," she said to him.

Griffin fought back a triumphant smile.

"Ruth," Treadaway said in a tone as if begging. "I'll go back to using involuntary abor—"

"Please, Paul. Would you just leave us."

Treadaway turned and glared at Griffin, then turned toward Ruth again.

"Well. . .of course. But I have this." He opened the paper bag and reached in.

Griffin's eyes widened. Here it comes! The cat's—

Treadaway pulled out an old rubber doll.

"Millie!" Ruth said, bringing her hand to her blouse, as if to calm her heart.

"I found it in Avraham's office," Treadaway said. " 'Ruth would like to have it' was my first thought."

Ruth took the doll from the professor, tilted her head, and smiled at him. "That's so sweet of you, Paul," she said.

Can you believe this? A doll? After weeding this phony out, she smiles at him because of a doll? Griffin stopped himself from shaking his head.

"It's Esther's," Ruth said to the professor. "It used to be mine years ago. We had no idea what happened to her." Ruth clutched the doll to her chest. "Thank you, Paul," she said.

Treadaway grinned. He turned, shot a glance at Griffin, and walked away.

Ruth watched Treadaway stroll away until he was out of hearing distance. Then she turned to Griffin. "I've got to talk to you privately," she said. "Please follow me to my house when I leave." She moved her head to glance toward the limousine behind him. Her eyes widened.

Griffin moved his gaze in the direction Ruth was looking. Gentcher and Landcaster were marching side by side toward them, red ribbons fluttering on their lapels. Landcaster was carrying something in a leather sheath.

Ruth lowered her voice and said hurriedly, "Please don't leave me alone with these people. They want something from me, and I'm frightened."

"I'm not going anywhere," Griffin said softly.

"Hello, Mrs. Hegel," Gentcher said. "The first lady sends her condolences."

"Thank you." Ruth pressed Millie harder against her chest.

"And I do, too, Ruth. I'm Dr. Richard Landcaster. I don't believe we've met formerly." Landcaster extended his free hand, holding the leather sheath with the other.

Ruth ignored the offer.

"Mrs. Hegel, I've got some good news for you from Mrs. Frye. She's going to name her reform bill the 'Hegel Bill' in honor of your husband. This is what this red ribbon is all about. People all over the country will be wearing one. I have one for you, too."

"Red isn't my color," Ruth said.

"Can't Constance wait a few days?" Griffin said to Gentcher, making it a point to ignore Landcaster.

Gentcher turned to Landcaster. "Now," she said in a command-ing tone.

Landcaster unzipped the leather sheath. Griffin stared at what Landcaster would pull from it. *If it's a weapon, Doctor, you'll lose your nose!*

Landcaster pulled out a device with a gray plastic handle and a loop made out of what appeared to be aluminum tubing. He flipped a switch on the handle, and a small red dot glowed and a beep sounded.

"What—" Griffin started to say.

Gentcher smiled. "A metal detector, Griffin. Mrs. Frye has concerns about my safety," she said. "A lot of anti-abortion rights terrorists out here, you know, shooting doctors and all that. Got a gun, do you, Griffin?"

Griffin said nothing.

"Do you mind?" Gentcher asked.

"Tell your quack to be careful, or he'll be pulling that thing out of his throat," Griffin said.

Griffin heard Landcaster snarl.

"And you, Mrs. Hegel?" Gentcher asked.

"You are not going to search me with that thing," Ruth said to Gentcher.

Madeline looked at Landcaster. "Don't worry about her," she said to Landcaster.

Landcaster slipped the device back into the leather sheath. He lowered it to his side.

"I suppose the thing picks up tape recorders, too," Griffin said.

"You lawyers are famous for recording people secretly," Landcaster said. "It's time for you to leave, guy."

"How's that hand, Doctor?" Griffin said.

"I'll get you for that; I'll get you."

"Boys, boys," Gentcher said. She turned to Ruth. "They just never grow up, do they?"

"I don't want him to leave, Dr. Landcaster," Ruth said. She moved closer to Griffin. He could feel the cloth of her suit top brush against his jacket.

"Mrs. Hegel," Gentcher said, "I have to talk to you privately. I have a message from the first lady."

So here it comes. Griffin cleared his mind. He wanted to attempt to memorize the Enforcer's words.

"Mr. Dowell is my attorney," Ruth said. "Anything you have to say to me, you can say it in front of him."

Treadaway and the Hegel children walked up to them. "Mom, is everything all right?" Ruth's son asked. Griffin was impressed; this young man would make a great marine.

192

"Yes, Joshua," Ruth said. She turned to her daughter. "Esther, take Millie. You and Joshua go home now. I'll meet you there."

Joshua and Esther. . .Joshua and Esther. Remember those names, Griffin. Remember the Old Testament, Griffin. When was the last time—

Griffin glanced at Professor Treadaway. Now Griffin understood his first instincts concerning the professor when he had presented his halfhearted eulogy. Not that he had such intuition; it was just that he dealt with the political type on a daily basis defending them. Anybody could possess that political mentality: How do I keep what's mine and get somebody else's, too? *How could Constance have possibly gotten to Treadaway so quickly?*

"Paul, I want you to leave us now," Ruth said. "I don't want you to be part of this conversation. And please, don't call me for a while, and don't come to my house unannounced again."

"But, Ruth—"

"Please, Paul."

Treadaway's balding scalp flushed red. He stomped away, mumbling something Griffin thought sounded like a line from Shakespeare's *Othello*.

"Now, Ms. Gentcher," Ruth said. "If you have something that the first lady wants me to hear, say it, or go about your business."

Griffin loved Ruth's courage.

He loved her strength, her intelligence.

Griffin thought that he might love Ruth Hegel.

Griffin, Griffin. What in the world are you getting yourself into here? This is her husband's funeral! She needs you as a friend. Remember that.

"If Mr. Dowell's your attorney, maybe I should talk to him alone," Gentcher said.

"I don't want my name or my husband's name associated with that bill," Ruth said.

"That isn't for you to decide, Mrs. Hegel," Gentcher said. "Mrs. Frye is only thinking of the children."

"Where have I heard that before?" Griffin asked. He crossed his arms over his suit coat. He turned and scanned the area. Treadaway was just driving off. Ruth, Gentcher, Landcaster, and he were alone, fussing in the graveyard.

"Somehow I'll let people know the truth," Ruth said. "Avraham hated that bill in the end, and what it's really all about. It's what caused him to—"

"I'll help her let people know," Griffin said. He glanced at Landcaster, who remained silent but still glared at Griffin.

"I've something important to tell you, and we have documents," Gentcher said with her gaze fixed on Ruth, grinning. She pulled a Marlboro from its box and lit it.

Griffin and Ruth remained quiet, waiting for the words.

Ruth, can you handle the zing?

Griffin lowered his hand. He bumped it against Ruth's. The warmth of the skin on the back of her hand lingered on his as he moved his hand away. She moved her shoulder into his arm, just a slight lean was all it took.

What if I hadn't come?

Griffin believed Ruth could handle whatever was coming. But from whom would she have sought friendship and comfort? Professor Sleaze, that's who!

You did good, Griffin.

"We believe your husband was laundering drug money," Gentcher said. "Probably from cocaine."

"That's ridiculous," Ruth said.

"How else do you explain two million dollars in a Cayman bank account?" Gentcher asked, grinning again, and then taking another tote off the cigarette.

"I wonder if it's the same cocaine that killed Warren Jennings," Griffin said.

"I don't have to explain anything; it's a lie," Ruth said.

"There's other evidence, Mrs. Hegel." Another draw. "The first lady is doing all she can to keep this away from the press. The attorney general is cooperating. Laundering money out of the country is a federal felony, Mrs. Hegel."

"Come on, Madeline," Griffin said. "What does Constance want?"

Gentcher turned to Griffin. "Well, Jackson, there's evidence that your client here might have conspired with her husband. Attorney General van Meter was considering convening a grand jury before the first lady stepped in. Your widowed friend here is very fortunate."

Griffin lifted his hand. "Don't say anything, Ruth," he said, staring at Gentcher. "You and I know what is being played out here. Quit the threats, the innuendoes, the children nonsense. Tell us—"

"Don't like your clients being investigated, Dowell?" Landcaster asked.

Griffin felt his patience leaving him.

"Tell your little friend to go slither under his rock, or I'm going to send a fist into his face," Griffin said to Gentcher. Griffin's thigh started throbbing.

Gentcher took another draw from her cigarette, then blew the smoke up. "Dick, why don't you go sit in the limousine," she said. "You boys just can't seem to get along."

"You'll hear from me, Dowell," Landcaster said. "You'll rue the day you put your investigator on me or even heard my name."

Griffin stared at Gentcher, not acknowledging Landcaster.

Landcaster stomped away.

Gentcher dropped her cigarette on the ground, then set her black shoe on it and twisted her foot as she looked down. She looked up and stared into Griffin's eyes. "The first lady wants to protect the Hegel family's reputation," she said. "Any scandal now could jeopardize her reform bill. All for the children, you know."

"Madeline," Griffin said, "get off the script."

"Your client is to say nothing about the Hegel Bill. If the matter comes up in any context, she is to say something positive. Refer to children. Same with the Alfa Alkaloid and the lung tissue formula. She is to say nothing about BioSysTech or what it really does."

"What does BioSysTech really do?" Ruth asked.

Gentcher turned to Ruth. "For your own good, don't find out."

"Go on, Madeline," Griffin said. "Finish what you came here to say."

Open your mind, Griffin. Listen hard.

"Your client is to say nothing except supportive words about Mrs. Frye. The first lady can pretty much guarantee Hegel's and your client's reputations will stay intact as long as she follows these instructions. This is not a threat or anything like that, mind you. We're just trying to use our resources to avert a devastating crisis in your client's and her children's lives."

"I know what this is," Ruth said.

Gentcher looked at Ruth. She raised her voice. "The Hegel Bill is the centerpiece of the Frye administration right now. Your husband's drug dealing must remain secret. That's what this is about."

"Constance never fails to amaze me," Griffin said. "My client and I agree with your conditions. But send this message to Constance: I know a lot about her and her husband. Tell her a deal is a deal."

Gentcher wrinkled her brow for a moment. "Fine," she said. She looked toward Ruth. "You can keep the two million," she said. "Get in touch with me. I'll make the arrangements." Gentcher extended the card toward Ruth.

"I don't want your card," Ruth said to Gentcher.

"Take my word for it, Mrs. Hegel. One day you will," Gentcher said. "The number is my direct line. Your choice: Take the card, or I drop it on your husband's grave."

Ruth lifted the card from Gentcher's fingers and slipped it in her dress suit jacket pocket.

"I don't want any money from Constance Frye, Ms. Gentcher. I don't want to see or hear from her again," Ruth said.

Gentcher grinned. "That's fine with us, Mrs. Hegel," she said. "Just remember to keep those sentiments to yourself."

Constance's Enforcer reached into her purse and extended a small red ribbon to Ruth. "Here, wear this if the press interviews you. That would go a long way toward keeping you out of prison."

"I'd die first," Ruth said.

"We aren't considering that yet," Gentcher said. She grinned and put the ribbon back in her purse. "Remember the card, Mrs. Hegel.

You will use it. I promise." Gentcher walked away.

"Follow me to my house, Griffin, please," Ruth said. "There is so much you need to know."

CHAPTER 19

Amanda sat in a French café, LeMadelines, peering out the window at the Mississippi River end of St. Charles Avenue where it met with Carrollton, forming a peculiar intersection speckled with stop signs and entangled in winding streetcar tracks that only locals could maneuver without scratching their heads.

Steam rose from a cup of French roast coffee in front of her as she toyed with her fork, poking at her pasta salad with crabmeat and shrimp. She didn't think she would enjoy coffee on such a hot day, but New Orleanians didn't seem to mind. Anyway, it would be one of those things she and Geoffry would do tomorrow: sit with the tourists under the roof of Café Monde on Decatur Street, just off the sidewalk, in the humid ninety-plus-degree heat, drinking a mixture of hot, strong coffee and chicory with hot milk.

Just beyond the window were students, probably from Tulane and Loyola, chatting and studying. Whites, blacks, and Asians: Racial lines had become irrelevant among them.

Daddy, why can't you see that these young people of all kinds are so friendly? Why don't you help those people who live on broken back streets have lives like these?

Why don't you, Amanda? The impression came to Amanda so suddenly she halted her thinking, clearing her mind.

"What do you mean you're going to quit the firm, Bradley? Are you crazy?"

The young man's voice jerked Amanda out of her musings. She

shifted her gaze quickly to the table in front of the next window. She took another bite of shrimp and listened.

"You'll be chasing ambulances. Paying off tow truck drivers."

"I don't want to do insurance defense," the young man facing Amanda said, his voice softer, much more controlled than his partner's.

"Bradley, do you know what Windhurst got for zeroing those plaintiffs in the school bus case? A sailboat! Court reporters and paralegals crawl all over him out there on the lake. And you're twice as smart as he is. You're the best associate in the firm. And you want to quit?"

"I'm not doing what I'm supposed to be doing. People are out there. They need help, Craig. I think God—"

"Oh, come off it! You're a lawyer! That church has you brainwashed!"

The man named Bradley wore a starched blue button-down collar shirt with a yellow patterned tie. Clean shaven, square chin with neatly trimmed black hair.

He continued. "It doesn't make any difference to me what Windhurst has. I have enough money. There are multitudes of people out there, right here in New Orleans, suffering. And everyone at the firm I work with—they toil twelve, sixteen hours a day, for what?"

"A couple of million in their retirement fund and plenty of fun along the way, that's what!" the other young man said.

"Along the way is what I'm worried about," Bradley said. He lifted his large brown eyes. His gaze was suddenly fixed on Amanda. Amanda jerked trying to shift her stare. She dropped her fork. A feeling that she looked very stupid, that this stranger had realized she was eavesdropping, came over her. She slid out of her chair, still looking down. She picked up the plate and walked to the cashier.

"May I have this to go, please? I. . .I have to leave," Amanda said to the cashier softly. When the cashier returned with a small wrapped package of food, Amanda walked from the cashier station, through the dining area, and out the door. *Is that Bradley watching me?* She slid into the rental car and shot a glance into the restaurant. *Yes, he's staring at me through the window.*

She turned her car toward the parking lot exit on St. Charles and sped away. Relief came but didn't completely rid her of her feeling of stupidity.

Things weren't going too well. Amanda decided to go back to her apartment. Maybe call her mother again, make sure she was all right, make sure she had returned Ruth Hegel's call.

Remember the rules, Amanda.

CHAPTER 20

$\mathbb{W}$hat do you mean you have it all set up? How did you find out how to get something like that done?" Kristina England asked, trying with little success to ignore the noise in the background from wherever Landcaster had placed the call. "Who told you that you could?" she asked. "I can hardly hear you!" Swooshing air and car and truck engines roaring in the background muffled Landcaster's voice.

"Warren Jennings said he talked to him, remember?" Landcaster said. "And the documents—remember what Schneider said about those documents? The CPA had to tell Dowell everything he knew before he died. Even the donations and, you know. . .your attorney fees."

"You and I are the only ones who know how much attorney's fees are involved, aren't we?" England said.

"We have to work together, you know," Landcaster said.

"Why are you calling from a pay phone?" England asked.

"The point is the Frau isn't a problem anymore," Landcaster said. "Gentcher handled that very well at the funeral. Dowell is the problem. He'll always be; I know him. The guy has investigators. I can tell you that firsthand. And he's connected."

"The publicity," England said. "The feds will be involved. It's not just—"

"We're connected, too," Landcaster said. "Better than Dowell is. And he's controversial in his little community. A lot of enemies."

"She won't go for it."

"She won't go for your attorney's fees, either," Landcaster said.

"See what she did to that Peterson guy? All it takes is one phone call to van Meter. Look, I want this guy fried."

England felt she was losing ground in this argument. She just didn't have the energy. What Landcaster wanted to do was crazy! "Look, Richard, so far everything has happened unconnected," England said. "Jennings in Columbia, the suicide in Rhode Island, the lab assistant they think just took off. No one can tie anything together. There's no reason to worry."

"You should have been here today," Landcaster said. "What the widow knows happened in Kingston, Dowell will know now, too. You know that graduate student? If Dowell was interested before he found out what Ruth Hegel knows, he's going to be obsessed today. You should have seen him and Frau Hegel groping each other."

England shifted the handset to her other ear. The street noise in the background and Landcaster's persistent lobbying were giving her a headache. England brought her palm to her head.

"Just wait, Richard," she said. "Wait until he does something." England just couldn't muster the energy.

"Wait?" Landcaster asked. "Until when? Until the guy finds the facility? I'm involved here, too, Kristina. I want the guy mineralized, fried. I want them to bury nothing but charred bones."

"Don't do anything until I say—"

"Not this time," Landcaster said. "This guy wants to put us in prison."

"Landcaster, don't do anything!" England hollered, but she knew her words would go unheeded. She felt no power behind them.

Richard Landcaster slammed the receiver onto its cradle.

└─┴─┘

Dr. Jacqueline Reed and the nurse marched shoulder-to-shoulder down the hall leading to the conceptus growing room.

"These weekly rounds are a waste of time," Reed said. "I'm going to go over his head. Talk to England. I'm a physician, not his assistant. Discrimination. That's what it is!"

"Yes, Doctor," the nurse said.

"Landcaster's too demanding."

The white glossy cement walls reflected the light from the glowing fluorescent tubes running down the middle of the ceiling. Morning and midnight were indistinguishable twenty feet underground in Level 2.

The nurse stopped. Reed increased her pace toward the stainless steel elevator-type entrance doors to the growing room. She inserted a plastic card into the slot below a small flashing red light. A mechanism behind the slot hummed, grabbed the card, pulled it in, then beeped.

"Step back on the red line immediately," said a loud, high-frequency, synthesized feminine voice that resonated down the cement tunnel-like hall.

Reed stepped back behind the red line on the floor etched in the concrete precisely one and a half yards in front of the conceptus growing room entrance doors. She stood stiff, as a soldier would.

The red light continued flashing. "You are entering a restricted area. Failure to identify yourself properly upon request will trigger a silent alarm to security, who are instructed to place all intruders in custody or shoot if an escape is attempted. Do not move until cleared," the synthesized voice said.

A horizontal sliver of red light shone on Reed's hair and then moved slowly down across her body all the way to her shoes.

Reed knew what was being recorded on the computer's storage disk and faxed immediately to Landcaster: date, time, and—although the computer recorded them in metric, she thought in American measurements—five-six, 192 pounds. Embarrassing.

Why does Landcaster have to know my weight?

Reed had tried to convince Landcaster that the identification system was too elaborate. He wouldn't hear of it. *Just because he lost his license, he's punishing me,* Reed had thought a dozen times. *I'm going to talk to Kristina England about this, too!*

Reed liked Kristina England. If only she would stop all that lawyer-political stuff and get more involved in the business.

"Anybody could sneak in, anytime," Landcaster had snapped back at Reed. "Remember that hick kid that got by the guards? I want to know about every entry. Who, when, why? If a guy attempts to run, I want him shot. It takes too much time for the helicopters to get there."

Reed's mind ran on and on every time she stood there at attention, while the red sliver descended, while the computer recorded and faxed. *He's reading the printout, hot off the fax, right now, no doubt.*

"State your code name slowly," the computer chip sounded.

"Physician One Dash Harvest," Reed said.

"Your speech pattern is digitized and scanned. How many persons will enter?"

"Two."

"Identify," the chip said.

"Nurse Dash One," Reed said.

Reed stepped aside. The nurse stepped to the red line etched in the floor. The computer scanned him and ordered him to state his code name. The procedure was repeated.

"Thank you, Dr. Reed," the chip said.

The flashing red light blipped, then steadied to a continuous green glow; the two-inch stainless steel doors slid open from the middle. Reed and the nurse lifted the top hem of their surgical masks from under their chins to the mid-ridge of their noses and entered the conceptus growing room. The steel doors slammed shut behind them.

Their nurse's shoes made no noise on the gray cement floor that sloped toward the center to an eight-inch circular brass drain grate. Seventy-seven degree Fahrenheit, triple-filtered air circulated in the growing room through six vents near the ceiling, two vents each on the north, south, and west walls. The air flowed out of the growing room through two large vents near the floor on the north and south walls. The stainless steel–framed, tinted-glass incubators lining the east wall reflected the soft, dark purple bactericidal ultraviolet light emitted from the lighting inset in the ceiling.

Reed and the nurse walked directly to the south corner of the east wall where the stacked incubators began. Reed had to stand on her toes to see the LCD readout panel on the right side of the top incubator and to adequately assess the apparent condition of the conceptus that, except for its rising and falling belly, lay motionless, the bath of ultraviolet light causing its skin to glow purple-blue.

Reed spoke in a tone and manner as if speaking to herself, as she did, the nurse jotted down what Reed said on the Weekly Inspection Chart.

"W/F0902. Looks better. No signs of reinfection. Vital signs fine." Reed bent down just slightly. The red LCD numerals on the panel of the incubator immediately under W/F0902, in which thin eight-month-old B/F0213 lay, disturbed Reed.

"B/F0213 weight down twenty-eight grams. Prepare schedules for complete physical, including blood and chemistry."

"Yes, Doctor," the nurse said, not lifting his gaze from the chart, still writing.

Reed stooped to inspect the next incubator under B/F0213 and stooped even more to view the next conceptus while the nurse stood over her.

"W/F0421. Anal tube. Occluded. Replace it."

"Yes, Doctor."

So many incubators. So much time wasted. Landcaster, get another physician in here to do this. I'm the first commercial neonatologist! This is demeaning.

"W/M0323. Erythema noted in area of recent surgical wound. Antibiotic Schedule One.

"Yes, Doctor."

⌐　丄　⌐

After more than three hours, Reed had inspected nearly 250 conceptuses. *Only two more left.* She stooped.

"Landcaster needs to rearrange all of this. This is not at all comfortable for me," Reed said loudly to no one. "I've told him that a thousand times."

Reed turned to the nurse. "W/F0776 thirty-eight-point-four degrees Centigrade. Antibiotic Schedule Four. Code Two."

"Yes, Doctor."

"Potential loss of conceptus," Reed said. "Schedule it with B/M0012 for Final Harvest. We'll do them both."

"Yes, Doctor."

"Why did they ever pay for this little goop of trouble?" Reed asked herself, shaking her head as she gazed at W/F0776. "We can't have another loss of conceptus."

Loss of conceptus. Reed dreaded having to write that on the Weekly Chart. As soon as the chart inched out of Landcaster's fax machine, her telephone would ring.

"Explain, Reed! What happened?" Landcaster would shout.

As if it were her fault! Conceptuses like W/F0776 should never be sent here; they're like bad eggs—rotten to begin with.

And when Landcaster called her demanding an explanation, the argument would start all over again: "These conceptuses are under continuous stress, Landcaster! You think they can just relax on a leather penthouse sofa like you do all day? Hegel's preparation. . .the alkaloid—how many times do I have to tell you! Destruction of the lobes might reduce pain and eliminate awareness, but don't you understand? The physical bodies of these conceptuses aren't operating as intended, no exercise, no movement. That's stress. That's probably why they spontaneously terminate after seven or eight years, and some before then. Even if we had big enough incubators, there's nothing we can do about it! You're a doctor—well, you were, anyway. You should know it's not my fault!"

Reed understood why Landcaster reacted that way, though. Organs from prematurely terminated conceptuses simply couldn't meet the company's warranty requirements. Profit from them was a fraction of what it could be.

Although her training was in neonatology, Reed tried to convince Landcaster that she understood the business end of the venture, at least at the inventory level. Dr. Otto Goethe and Sam Yashimiro expected termination under controlled conditions, on the operating table. Their customers paid for fresh organs, virtually free of debilitated cells. That's what the brokers paid for; that's what they should get.

Who else should know better than me, the first commercial neonatologist!

Reed had her dreams, just like Dr. Hegel. When the business was legal, she would be the leader in her discipline. The first commercial neonatologist, ever. *Okay, Landcaster, reconsider my contract, maybe double my salary, or I'll take my experience elsewhere, maybe to Doktor Goethe, who is, unlike you, a visionary.*

Reed returned to her rounds. W/F0776 would certainly terminate without Schedule Four antibiotic treatment. Conceptuses reacted to antibiotic treatment differently than real human infants, Reed believed. Their sedentary existence, like she had tried to explain to Landcaster, certainly played a role in their slow response to the treatment. *Landcaster, what does he know?*

Maybe their damaged frontal lobes had something to do with it, too. Medical science would never know all the functions of that area of the brain. Maybe it was from that area of the brain that the conceptus's body got the final order after six or seven years, "Okay, shut down." And what were the effects of Hegel's alkaloid overall? Reed could see herself: the researcher finding answers to those difficult questions, publishing in journals like Avraham Hegel did before he went and killed himself. She would be the one giving seminars at the elite medical schools in the new discipline of commercial neonatology.

I'll show them my privileges at Mercy General never should have been revoked!

The harsher antibiotics such as those in Schedule Four caused almost immediate digestive problems, leading to occlusion of the anal tube. That led to bacterial infection. Even ordinary bacteria were pathogenic to those puny little things under that sort of added stress. Then the feeding fluid had to be reformulated, then the rate of flow readjusted. One thing after another.

Conceptuses like W/F0776 should be incinerated rather than cultivated. But Landcaster wouldn't hear of it. *Guess you can't blame him; he has to account for the company's finances to you know who. I'll be glad when I can sink my scalpel into W/F0776 and put an end to it; it's such a bother.*

"Make an additional entry. W/F0776 critical," Reed said to the nurse. "Poor initial quality. Poor prognosis. Garbage in. . .out. Circle that statement."

"Yes, Doctor."

Reed stood in front of the incubator containing the last conceptus she had to inspect. But for the rise and fall of its belly, all twenty-six pounds of B/M0012 lay motionless on its back in its three-foot-wide, eighteen-inch-deep, two-foot-high incubator.

A clear tube ran from its urethra through the back of the incubator; liquid that glowed a yellow-green under the ultraviolet light flowed through it, although at a rate only an expert in commercial neonatology like Reed could appreciate.

A one-inch tube ran from B/M0012's buttocks, between its legs, up and over its thigh, and, like the renal tube, out the back of the incubator. Another tube entered the back of the incubator near the top to a cup that covered B/M0012's mouth and nose.

Even with B/M0012's empty, sunken eye socket and the surgical scars, one running from its groin to its sternum, the other just below its navel, running from pelvic wing to pelvic wing, Reed regarded this conceptus as the most beautiful of them all. B/M0012 had survived so much, so well: removal of its right eye, its left lung, and its right kidney. Not one infection; and it had healed rapidly, too. And B/M0012 was the only conceptus to have moved anything after Hegel's Alfa Alkaloid treatment. This conceptus had actually moved its eye! It had actually fixed its gaze on Dr. Hegel! *I'd never believe it if I hadn't seen it with my own two eyes.*

Reed wondered how Hegel could act that way. Vomiting like that. Maybe he believed B/M0012 wasn't sedated enough, was feeling pain all this time. *Well, maybe so, but the way this wonderful conceptus takes it, maybe the alkaloid concentration should be reduced in all the new ones.*

Reed had thought many times that B/M0012 shouldn't even be

harvested; it should be maintained, studied, and, like the German told her, cloned for its superior genetic traits, whatever they were. She was sure this one wouldn't terminate spontaneously. It had adapted so wonderfully to the growing room environment.

Of course, B/M0012 was getting a bit large. That had to be taken into consideration. After all, its feet nearly touched the incubator glass now, and although its head didn't, the long mass of entangled black hair was actually flattened against the glass on the other end. A bigger incubator? No, that wouldn't work, at least not until the termination syndrome had been researched and figured out.

Anyway, the idea of growing conceptuses to adolescence concerned Reed. She was a neonatologist, after all. It was too late to go back to school to learn pediatrics. Maybe she shouldn't limit herself with the name "commercial neonatologist"; maybe she should name her new role. . .commercial harvester. . .no, commercial organist.

Good grief, one sounds like a tractor, the other like a musician. What can I call myself? No matter. Think of a name for this new discipline later, Jacqueline.

"Nurse, do you remember the name of B/M0012's mother?" Reed asked.

"It's right here." The nurse flipped through a chart, then nodded. " 'Keondra Johnson,' it says here."

"I wonder where Keondra Johnson is now?" Reed asked. "Maybe she has a sister."

With a continuous supply of trouble-free conceptuses like B/M0012 and the adjustment in Alfa Alkaloid concentration, the net profit would skyrocket. Landcaster wouldn't understand this new discipline, whatever it would be called, particularly not the inventory aspect or the implications involving human genetics. And with healthy conceptuses, these rounds could be done monthly, not every week. *That would be much better for me.*

"Says here Keondra Johnson died of gunshot wounds, Doctor," the nurse said.

"If I didn't have bad luck, I'd have no luck at all," Reed said.

"What about a sister?"

The nurse searched the chart. "No data," he said.

Reed peered closely at B/M0012's head. She thought she saw it move.

Like the others in the growing room, B/M0012 had two surgical scars in the shape of an X on its forehead, one above each brow, about midway to its scalp. Six years ago, Reed had cut the Xs, spread the flaps, and injected Hegel's Alfa Alkaloid into holes she had drilled through the bone.

On a statistical confidence level of 95 percent, as calculated by Dr. Hegel, 24 percent, plus or minus 3 percent, of B/M0012's frontal lobes were rendered meaningless living tissue by the reaction between the alkaloid and the DNA in the frontal lobe cells of B/M0012's brain. Reed agreed with Dr. Hegel's theory as to why the straight-line result occurred. And it was true: These conceptuses and so many other laboratory species benefited from the surgical injections of his alkaloid preparation.

It was good of Dr. Hegel to be so concerned about laboratory animals, but these conceptuses weren't mere laboratory animals that were watched as they progressed to death from injections or chemicals or microbes. These conceptuses were organ producers for live, functioning humans. So there were other considerations. Reed reached a firm conviction: She would reduce the Alfa Alkaloid concentration on new conceptuses. Sure, they might be able to feel a little more pain, but the risk-benefit profit analysis favored an increase in pain, as clearly demonstrated by B/M0012. *Anyway, that's a pure medical decision, a hypothesis based on observation of a qualified commercial neonatologist.*

Reed smiled at B/M0012. Another one like it would come along, maybe. She had scheduled B/M0012's Final Harvest for Saturday, June 29. *It's getting close.* A feeling something akin to motherhood passed quickly through Reed, warming her a little. *I did sort of rear the thing.*

"I want a complete workup, including blood work," the doctor ordered.

"Yes, Doctor."

"Begin the FH enriched mixture today."

"Yes, Doctor."

The right turn signal on Ruth Hegel's white Mercedes 600SEL blinked, and only moments later, the brake lights glowed. She came to a crawl, then turned off Rhode Island State Highway 14 onto a narrow dirt road that appeared to Griffin to be nothing more than a narrow opening into the woods.

The narrow road wound between oaks and maples and smaller trees beyond Griffin's botanical taxonomic skills. Bushes, vines, and underbrush appeared to have been thinned out. And Griffin saw how. Just beyond the second turn was a full-size green Ford tractor in front of a classic-style barn. Serious landscaping stuff in there, no doubt.

Into the third turn, between trees and shrubs, stood the three-story Hegel home, a stucco structure reminiscent of a small European mansion. Two huge red-brown Newfoundlands ran up to Ruth's car, their tails wagging. Ruth parked her car on the driveway. She could not enter the three-car garage. A canvas-topped jeep blocked one garage entrance. Two police cars, one marked, the other unmarked, blocked the other two. Joshua hurried to greet his mother. Griffin parked in back of the Mercedes just in time to hear Ruth say, "Joshua, why are the police here?"

"Mom, somebody broke into Dad's office," Joshua said, tension straining his voice. "A detective's inside waiting for you!"

Griffin stepped next to Ruth.

"Hello, Mr. Dowell. I'm glad you came," Joshua said, then turned to his mother. "Mom, I'm going back inside. Esther's not doing well with all this." Joshua glanced at Griffin, then jogged back into the house.

He remembered my name. Yeah, he would make a good marine. An officer.

"Go ahead," Griffin said to Ruth. "I want to talk to that forensic man." Griffin nodded toward a uniformed officer who held his nose

211

inches from a glass window, whisking a bottom corner near the frame.

"That's Avraham's home office," Ruth said.

———

"Find anything?" Griffin asked the forensic officer.

The officer pulled his head away from the glass and looked up. "Who are you?" he asked.

"Griffin Dowell. Ruth Hegel's attorney."

The officer turned back to his work. "I know just about all the attorneys around here," he said. "Never seen you before. But I can tell. You're a lawyer, all right."

"Any luck with prints?" Griffin asked.

"No. One guy, though. Used gloves. Probably the heavy rubber kind. Like the kind used to wash dishes."

"College kid?" Griffin asked.

The policeman looked up at Griffin again. "Not this perp," he said. "Professional tools—little damage, just a neat circle. See? Maybe would have never known the window was opened if it wasn't for those big dogs whining and carrying on, insisting the boy follow them to this window. Smart dogs. Smart boy."

"Anything you can guess about the burglar? Weight? Size?"

"Talk to Callahan inside," the officer said. "I do the forensic work; he does the guesswork."

Griffin turned and found his way to the front door, through the foyer, and into a room, thirty feet or so wide with a twelve- or fourteen-foot ceiling and a huge stone fireplace across from where he stood. Two uniformed policemen chatted in front of a small room off to the left. A detective sat on one of the two sofas placed parallel to each other in front of the stone fireplace. The detective jotted notes on a small spiral pad as Ruth talked to him. The detective glanced upward; Ruth suddenly quit talking and turned toward Griffin.

"Come in, Griffin. Please, come in," Ruth said. She turned to the detective. "Detective Callahan, this is my attorney, Griffin Dowell."

After the introductions, Griffin asked Detective Callahan what he thought had happened.

"Must have been about ten or ten-thirty this morning," Callahan said. "The perp disabled the alarm, broke the window. . ."

Broke the window? Something's up, Griffin.

". . .unlocked the inside lock, then lifted the window and gained access. That's the problem with these big houses set far in the woods. Easy pickings for any creep who reads the obits."

"Suspects?" Griffin asked.

"Had to be a small man, probably a kid. Athletic to get through the window."

"Detective," the forensic officer hollered from the threshold of the front door. "I need to see you for a minute." Callahan walked over to him. They huddled and whispered.

Ruth tapped Griffin's shoulder. "They're not going to admit it," Ruth whispered, "but this is related to some things I need to talk to you about."

"What?" Griffin whispered.

"This is a college town, Griffin," Ruth said, her voice slightly raised. "You—" She turned her head. "Wait."

Griffin looked up. Callahan was just a few steps away from them, walking, thinking. He stopped, then lifted his notebook.

"What do you know now, Detective?" Ruth asked.

"Not much." Callahan began flipping pages, up and down, down and up. "A perp burglarizes a rich family home built back in the woods when the family is at a funeral that everybody in the country knows is going on. He makes his way into the decedent's office through a window. Dogs scare him off. He doesn't have enough time to take anything and hightails it."

"Rubber gloves?" Ruth asked. "Did the burglar use rubber gloves?"

The question shifted Griffin into a state of confusion. *Rubber gloves?*

"Don't know yet, ma'am."

"Like the kind used in Danny Barnwell's murder?" Ruth asked.

Befuddled. That's the state of mind Griffin decided he was in as he remembered the forensic man mentioning rubber gloves.

Griffin could feel the air growing confrontational between Callahan and Ruth, and he watched Ruth nurturing the confrontation. Then it came to him: Ruth was doing what he had done with the political professor. She was educating him. *I'm with you, Ruth.* Then a little fear came to him: *Hope I can do as well as she's doing.*

"Ma'am, we can't be sure if the perpetrator wore any gloves."

Interesting, Griffin thought.

"The dogs didn't scare the burglar, Detective," Ruth said. "They bark and fuss but run up to everybody and lick. Certainly you have other ideas."

Listen to the words, Griffin.

Detective Callahan started flipping pages again. "Only one perpetrator. A male by the size of his hands. If the dogs didn't scare him away and he had time, it seems he didn't find anything he was interested in stealing."

"Nothing here in the den, like that five-thousand-dollar amplifier over there, Detective? Or that priceless antique microscope in my husband's office?" Ruth asked.

Way to go, Ruth!

"Well, the perp might have wanted something specific," Callahan said, appearing to Griffin to be a little nervous. "He concentrated his search on desk drawers, file drawers, areas that hold documents, papers—those sort of things." Callahan paused. "Ma'am," he said, "would you mind going through your husband's papers to help us find out if anything was taken?"

Griffin shifted his gaze to Ruth.

"I haven't been in that room for more than a year," Ruth said.

"Can I write that in my report?"

"You can write whatever you want in your report, Detective," Ruth said.

Callahan jotted down a note, a bit of relief in his appearance, Griffin thought.

"I don't think we can do anything else here, then," Callahan said, looking around and slipping his notepad in his shirt pocket, followed by his pen. "Probably just one of those dopeheads who lives on the other side, watching the obituaries. Lucky you got those dogs, ma'am," he said.

"It's related to Barnwell's murder and somehow to my husband's death, Detective. You know it."

"No evidence, ma'am. No evidence at all."

"And Amanda Collins missing, too," Ruth said.

"No evidence of that, either, ma'am."

"That's what you'll write in your report?" Griffin asked. " 'No evidence, ma'am'?"

Callahan looked at Griffin, squinting his eyes. "You get any better ideas, any more evidence, you call me, Counselor." He moved his hand to his shirt pocket. "Here's my card." Callahan dropped a card on the coffee table. "I'll put a uniform out on the driveway for a few days, just in case."

As Callahan closed the front door behind him, Joshua and Esther walked down the stairs. "Esther and I are going to pick up something to eat, Mom," Joshua said. "Would you like anything, Mr. Dowell?"

"Whatever you get, Joshua, thank you," Griffin said.

"Esther," Ruth said, "before you leave, would you go to my room? That gold-framed picture of your father and me, on the dresser. Bring it down to me, please."

"Sure," Esther said, then she and Joshua hurried out of the room.

"This graduate student, Barnwell, how was he killed?" Griffin asked Ruth.

"Stabbed in his apartment," Ruth said. "The evening Avraham. . . he. . ." Ruth looked down. "It's just so hard." She took a deep breath. "The police first reported Danny's death as a professional killing, but then they quit talking about it. You wouldn't think it ever happened now."

Griffin sat down, waiting for more. Ruth walked around the coffee table and sat on the sofa across from Griffin.

"Danny wasn't the person the murderer intended to kill," Ruth said. Griffin decided to be quiet.

"Danny's killer intended to murder my husband's lab assistant, Amanda Collins," Ruth said. "Don't ask me how I know. I just do."

"But why would a professional killer want anything to do with the lab assistant?" Griffin asked.

"My husband hired Amanda exclusively for the BioSysTech grant," Ruth said, staring into Griffin's eyes. "I believe she has unique information about what BioSysTech does."

"And Barnwell?"

"Danny was a master's student from Georgia. He lived across the hall from Amanda Collins in an old apartment house," Ruth said. "If you knew Danny, you would know he wouldn't involve himself in anything that would get him into trouble."

How could this fit into his puzzle? Griffin wondered. Then it occurred to him: Every person wanting to know has a different perspective, collecting different pieces of the same truth. Ruth had been collecting her pieces. Now they could share, but perhaps not all.

"Just so I can make sure," Griffin said slowly, wanting to collect Ruth's pieces of the puzzle, "everything appears to be going fine in this quaint college town. Dr. Hegel and his lab assistant are working on a BioSysTech grant. Then, within twenty-four hours, Dr. Hegel commits suicide, his lab assistant disappears, a graduate student is killed by a professional killer who really wanted to murder the lab assistant, and Dr. Hegel's home office is burglarized while we're at his funeral, right?"

Ruth nodded. "Quaint little town of Kingston; how still we see thee lie," she said softly.

Esther suddenly stepped up holding a framed photograph in one hand and Millie in the other. She handed Ruth the photograph. Ruth took it and gently set it facedown on the coffee table. Esther stood still holding Millie by her side the way a ten-year-old would. Griffin could tell she wanted to say something to her mother but wasn't sure how to begin.

Ruth looked up at her and set her hand on Esther's arm. "Are you all right, sweetheart?" Ruth asked her daughter.

"Mom. You and Mr. Dowell are talking about Daddy, aren't you?" Esther asked.

Griffin had no idea how to handle this. Esther sounded like a disturbed child in an Alfred Hitchcock thriller. She looked like it, too, holding the doll like that at her age.

"I can leave the room, go outside for a while," Griffin said.

"We're talking about a lot of things, including your father," Ruth said.

Esther shifted the doll. She held it with both hands by its feet and extended Millie's head faceup toward Ruth.

"Why would Daddy do that?" Esther asked.

"What, Sweetheart?"

Esther released one of her hands from Millie's foot and pointed to Millie's forehead. "That," she said.

Griffin leaned to see what Esther was pointing at: a black X written in what appeared to be permanent ink on the doll's forehead. No, two Xs—one above each eye.

"I tried to clean them off," Esther said, "but I think the ink is, like, absorbed into the rubber." A pause. "I don't want them on Millie, Mom."

Ruth studied the doll's head for a moment. "I'll take her to someone who can remove them, sweetheart. Give her to me."

"I love you, Mom. If it weren't for you—" Esther glanced at Griffin, then walked quickly away.

Ruth stared at the doll.

"Are you all right?" Griffin asked.

"Please keep asking me questions," Ruth said, staring at the doll. "They help me put things together."

"Tell me more about Amanda Collins," Griffin said, hoping Ruth would abandon her musings.

Ruth looked up and set the doll next to her on the sofa. "Amanda came here from Boston," she said. "I called her mother yesterday. Amanda called her but refused to tell her mother where she was. All her mother knew was that Amanda had something she had to do, something to give to somebody."

Griffin wished he had a notepad like Callahan so he could jot down Ruth's words. "You think Amanda's hiding because someone wants to kill her?" he asked.

"Yes. Amanda loved my husband like a father, and she has a boyfriend here, too. And she just runs away? I think she knows they're looking for her."

"And maybe because of whatever she has to give to somebody? Whatever it was they were looking for in your house?" Griffin asked.

Ruth took a deep breath. "Yes."

Griffin had to think, to assimilate.

"The police believe Amanda just left to get away from all this," Ruth said. "The BioSysTech grant expired formally on Monday—"

"Wait," Griffin said. "The BioSysTech grant expired on the day your husband com—"

Ruth nodded. "As far as the police are concerned, Amanda wasn't in the apartment building when Danny was killed, so she isn't a witness, but the killer's glove marks—"

"Rubber glove marks?"

"Yes, on her door. Danny was killed in the hall leading to Amanda's apartment. The news mentioned gloves before they stopped talking about the murder."

"And Danny Barnwell?" Griffin asked.

"Callahan has theories. . .some secret life Danny was living, drugs. All that. I knew Danny; he was a bookworm, proud of his knowledge about his field. Wanted to be a professor like Avraham. They were after Amanda. I just know it. Drugs—preposterous."

I know what you mean, Griffin thought when the image of Warren's covered corpse popped into his mind. "And the rubber gloves?" Griffin asked.

"Yes. The rubber glove marks." Ruth turned her head toward her husband's office. "Just like the ones used in there, in Avraham's office, I bet." She returned her gaze to Griffin. "There was another car, too.

It had stopped in front of Avraham's car after he. . .after he died."

Ruth lowered her head. Griffin waited for more.

"Callahan said there were tire prints and footprints to Avraham's car. The car. . .whomever it was left in a hurry."

"And they don't want to follow up on this?" Griffin asked.

" 'College pranks.' That's what Callahan said. Always 'college pranks' or 'dopeheads from the other side.' " Ruth quieted for a moment. She glanced at the doll again, then looked at Griffin. "This is a small university town, Griffin."

"But a murder. . .the police?"

"Remember the murders at the University of Florida several years ago? Do you know what that sort of thing does to enrollment? Big universities like Florida can absorb the financial setback, but not little commuter universities like URI. You should have heard our mayor when the reporters interviewed him on local news," Ruth said. "You'd think Danny's death and all of the things happening here were nothing more than a front of bad weather passing through."

"If there are no more murders and the intended victim is gone?" Griffin asked.

"Avraham's death, Danny, the lab assistant missing, Ms. Gentcher's threats, they're all related."

"Explain that," Griffin said.

"Someone broke in here, didn't they?" Ruth said.

"And BioSysTech is involved?" Griffin asked. "Richard Landcaster and Constance Frye. Madeline Gentcher. She just confirmed what I believed all along with her threats. Callahan's putting a policeman here for a few days because he knows, right?"

Ruth lowered her head. She remained silent, then glanced at Millie, then looked at Griffin. "Avraham tried to tell me he was going to do it," she said softly.

Griffin remained silent.

"During our stay at the hotel on the weekend of the reception, he told me that if he was awarded the Nobel Prize posthumously, to refuse it. He said he'll join the elite like the beast Egas Moniz in Sheol. I tried to talk to him, but he went back into his shell."

Griffin couldn't resist. "Who's Egas Moniz?" he asked.

"Some sadistic physician, I think."

"Ruth, I have to ask more questions," Griffin said. "If you would rather that I didn't, let me know, okay?"

"Go ahead," Ruth said, tearing. "It's just that maybe I could have prevented. . ."

"Ruth, what happened to Dr. Hegel's car?" Griffin asked.

"BioSysTech took it as soon as Callahan released it. It was supposed to have been a gift to Avraham, but BioSysTech actually leased it in their name and loaned it to him. They can have it."

"What else, Ruth? Think. Anything."

"Amanda's boyfriend. . .Geoffry. . .Geoffry something. I can't remember his last name. Maybe he can help. I'll try to locate him." Ruth paused. "One other thing," she said. "Avraham put a note in my black suit jacket pocket before he killed himself. He was a remarkably perceptive man. He knew what I would wear to the funeral." Ruth lifted the photograph off the coffee table. She slid the back out of it. A piece of paper dropped on the table.

"It's from Avraham. Read it," Ruth said.

Griffin picked up the note and unfolded it.

"CAYMAN FEDERAL BANK, PASSBOOK NO. 98320-1212-40. $2,000,000.00, PLUS INTEREST."

"That lump sum you were so curious about at the reception, Griffin," Ruth said. "Remember?"

Griffin nodded, feeling a bit sick.

"The lump sum was a half million. I have no idea what this two million is for, but I know where it had to have come from. They bought my husband. So now it's laundered drug money, isn't it?" Ruth asked. She crossed her arms over her blouse.

They just don't know who they're dealing with when they toy around with this woman. Griffin wondered if he could have collected the pieces of the puzzle Ruth had.

"Why is the first lady of the United States threatening me and my family?" Ruth asked. "What can I do? It's not just that reform bill; it can't be."

"They're selling something, something they can't sell openly," Griffin said. "And it has to have something to do with what your husband was doing for BioSysTech."

"The lung preparation?" Ruth asked.

"No. They could probably sell that. They just don't want to," Griffin said. Griffin paused to think. "The alkaloid," he said. "You said some companies have rights to it?"

Ruth nodded, then turned her head. She looked down at Millie. Her eyes widened.

"Oh, no!" Ruth said as she brought both hands to her face, covering her mouth.

"What? What is it?" Griffin said.

Ruth lowered her hands. She crossed her arms around her waist and rocked as if in pain.

"Avraham took Millie from Esther's room before he died. It had to be him," she said.

Ruth lifted Millie off the sofa and set her on the table in Griffin's view. "With monkeys, their foreheads are shaved. X's are cut into their foreheads, then they drill holes through the skull and inject the Alfa Alkaloid."

"Okay," Griffin said.

"The surgical wounds heal just like these black marks on Millie, and in about the same place." Ruth folded her arms against her stomach again.

"What are you thinking?" Griffin asked.

"My husband did nothing without a specific, focused reason. I don't know if I want to go further with this. I don't know if I can take it." Ruth moved her hands, intertwined her fingers, and set her hands on her knees. Her hands began to tremble.

"We have to," Griffin said. Whatever she had to say, she needed at least a moment before he began his examination. Another piece of the puzzle, one that revealed where a lot of others should be set, was about to be dropped. Griffin just knew it.

"Those marks on Millie's head, that's what you don't want to talk about, isn't it?" Griffin asked.

Ruth's hands trembled more as she spoke. "Avraham left nothing in his office at URI but a few binders and furniture. He cleared his desk, except for. . ."

"What?" Griffin asked.

"This can't be true," Ruth said. She looked at the doll's face. "But these marks—he couldn't have changed that much, couldn't have become that diabolical."

"Your husband cleared his desk except for Millie?" Griffin asked. "He wanted to make sure someone found this doll. He knew whoever found it would return it to you. Is that it?"

Ruth folded her arms against her stomach again. She began to rock. Her lower lip quivered.

"Dr. Hegel left this to tell you what BioSysTech is doing to babies with his preparation. That's it, isn't it?" Griffin said.

Ruth nodded while she rocked and trembled.

Griffin sat still. He decided to end the conversation there. "I'll have to take all this in slowly," he said. "Put all this with what I already know."

Griffin decided not to tell Ruth about Warren Jennings and accusations about drug overdoses. Not to tell her what he knew about BioSysTech and Constance Frye, or Madeline Gentcher, Kristina England, and all the other pieces of the puzzle he possessed. *Ruth has enough death around her. I won't shift the load.* He didn't want her to hurt anymore. *There comes a point when you take the pressure off, especially if you have feelings. . . . Griffin!*

Ruth appeared to have regained her strength, although she was much more restrained now. Griffin got the feeling she wouldn't say anything more about her husband, not now, not for a while, even if there was something else. Now she would have to deal with what she believed her husband had done.

"Call me if you need me," Griffin said.

"I don't know what I would have done without you today," Ruth said softly. "You were a godsend. Promise you'll call me sometime, when you find out more, anything more, no matter how insignificant."

Griffin paused a moment as he looked into Ruth's eyes. "I promise," he said.

Landcaster is out of control, England thought after the doctor hung up on her. She lifted herself from the chair behind her desk and strolled to her office window. She ran Landcaster's words through her mind as she gazed over New York's skyline. Nothing more than a typical male tantrum, fighting for posture, she thought. Every time Landcaster even talked about Dowell, he flew into a rage. It must have been something to have seen him at Hegel's funeral, forced to talk about Dowell, maybe even to talk to him. England chuckled at that thought. The chuckle ended as quickly as it began. She should call Constance, tell her about Landcaster's threats, about his growing illusion of machismo that had apparently taken him over. And about his new extreme plans concerning Dowell. But what then?

How much have you received in attorney fees from the venture, Kristina? Too much. Far, far too much. And that in addition to the equity payments. No way would Landcaster arrange it. A bomb? That's the only thing he could have been talking about. No way. He doesn't have the nerve.

No doubt now that Constance had taken hold of BioSysTech. All of England's efforts to wrest control had failed. England never would have believed it would happen. She had worked hard, networked frantically to become the attorney for the strongest nonprofits promoted through the media, board member on each one, usually the board member who took over every meeting. So here she was. A press release from her went directly to the AP and UPS wires, just as she'd written it, and the journalists she chose to contact treated her outrages against the pro-lifers and sexist males as if they were mainstream American feminine thought. She had become a regular commentator on CPNN, a speaker at the loud, rowdy protests in Washington, D.C., and policy advisor for the first lady's reform bill. The Hegel Bill. What a laugh! Constance Frye had not once asked her policy advisor for advice on anything, and Hegel the Squeamish would have night terrors in his grave if he knew that he was the namesake of Constance Frye's abortion products reforms.

In the end, after peeling away the thick skin of public perception, England realized she was nothing more than a successful attorney and lobbyist—parroting mantras, speaking and lobbying for clients with narrow, sometimes bizarre interests. It brought her notoriety, sure. But she was still only a representative of others, no matter how much they paid her. Not so with Constance Frye. England envied her. The first lady spoke directly to the people of America at her whim, the simpleminded rabble who forget yesterday before it ends. Rabble? Dry, mindless sponges more like it. All the first lady has to do is say "for the children," and the sponges get soggy.

Your fanatics at Fins and Feathers can make the rabble mourn over spotted owls and snail darters, Kristina, but they have to keep reminding them how important the stupid birds and bottom-of-the-food-chain line-minnows really are, and how vital they are to. . .whom? Constance Frye can perk the rabble's emotions with her "for the children" mantra, and the news anchors will parrot her daily. It's that federal government utopia she obsesses over, with the power to implement it if she had enough money. How can you compete with this woman? How could you have ever thought you could?

England had tried and had been sure she would win. But now she saw what Constance could do; even if Peterson didn't spend time in some federal pen, he was ruined for just writing what he believed.

Just one telephone call from Constance Frye to Attorney General Sheryl van Meter, and Constance's Enforcer will come tapping, tapping on your office door, with the press behind her, eager to feed on your bones, even if you're not convicted of anything.

England crossed her arms over her blouse and lowered her head. *Becky, why are you just throwing away all I gave you?* England looked up as her mind raced through the conversation with Becky this morning and the note Becky had slipped under England's door before she went to the airport on her way home, back to her little family, that little congregation of right-wing nuts in Tulsa, Oklahoma.

That conversation had occurred at 7:30 this morning, after England opened her door and saw Becky standing at the threshold.

"Becky?"

"We have to talk, Kristina," Becky said, then walked into the sunken penthouse living room and sat on the sofa.

After England sat down and silence fell, Becky said again, "We need to talk."

You knew this was coming, Kristina.

"Do you remember when I first came to New York? When we first met?" Becky asked.

"Why?" England asked.

"When I came here to work for the *Post*, I believed I would soon become a syndicated columnist. George Thompson promised to help me."

"Thompson promises all the pretty, young new reporters that he'll help them."

"You can't keep that out of your mind, can you?" Becky asked. "Mr. Thompson promised me because my work was good. I earned his respect, and he's been a senior editor for years."

"I didn't mean you didn't deserve Thompson's promises," England said. "It's just that men can't be trusted. How much was your salary at the *Post*? How much is it now as president of Anticipating Parenthood?"

"It doesn't matter," Becky said.

"Name me one man you can trust. Really trust," England said.

"Ian Apple," Becky said.

"Who?" England straightened her body without thinking. She felt herself waiting for Becky to answer her.

Becky paused a moment. She looked down, then raised her gaze to England's eyes. "Do you remember when you sent me to the airport to meet Jane Wellman from the Seattle chapter?" she asked.

"I remember," England said. She settled back in the sofa. A feeling that this was a different woman talking to her came over her.

Where is she getting her courage from?

"Jane's plane was delayed in Chicago. I sat in one of those molded chairs, waiting. I began reading the op-ed pages in the *Post*, and I remembered why I left Tulsa. I asked myself, Kristy. . .I asked myself how I came to be president of Anticipating Parenthood when all I wanted was to be a journalist, to have my own syndicated column."

"You earned the presidency," England said.

"I became president after you convinced me that I could make a difference in people's lives quicker than reporting or writing op-ed columns," Becky said. "I wasn't there at the board meeting, but I know how you did it. No one can stare you down, can they, Kristy? Except Constance Frye."

"Who is Ian Apple?" England asked.

"When I was reading the *Post*, I heard a man ask, 'Mind if I read the sports?' "

"Ian Apple?" England asked.

"He sat down in the chair one over from me. Ian asked that as if he were asking a great favor, intruding on my time and space. I realized I had forgotten what it felt like, my privacy being respected. Someone, a man, really caring if he's intruding in my life."

"I don't understand," England said.

"After a few minutes, Ian began a conversation. He had a raspy, deep voice. Masculine. I enjoyed hearing it. We talked and laughed. Ian is from Tulsa, Kristy. He teaches English at a small college there. Round, gold-rimmed glasses. Journalism! Would you believe he teaches journalism?" Becky's eyes glistened with her grin.

"And so girlish fantasies started bubbling up that will lead you to a life of slavery and abuse," England said.

England felt the heat of Becky's sudden glower.

"You see, Kristy," Becky said. "That's how you think. I didn't know what Ian's motives were; I distrusted him at first, thanks to you. But for the first time since I met you, I took a young man at his word." Becky paused. "Do you know I have a little brother? He hasn't called me since I became president of AP. My mother and father don't speak to me, either."

"The family as we know it is changing in structure; soon there will be no mothers and fathers at barbeques in the backyard. Soon there will be a daughter with two mommies," England said.

"I don't believe that," Becky said. "And I don't want to be a part of that movement."

"So what are you going to do?

"I don't want to judge AP, or you, but I now stand for things that my family and I once abhorred," Becky said. She quieted, then stared at England. "How did I earn the presidency of Anticipating Parenthood, Kristina?"

"You think you didn't?" England asked.

"Monday, when I crawled out of bed, I stood in front of my mirror. I thought about Ian and our conversation. I thought about my brother and my family and where I would be fifteen years from now."

"You're just going through a phase, Becky. Living in New York is a lot different than male-dominated Tulsa," England said.

"While I stood in front of the mirror, I remembered how I enjoyed talking with Ian, hearing that gentle, low voice, laughing. I missed him."

"Come on, Becky!"

"That afternoon I called Ian at the college where he teaches," Becky said. "He was in class, but he returned the call within an hour. Do you realize how important that was to me that he called me back so soon?"

England said nothing.

"Talking to him made me yearn for the respect and love of my family. I don't believe all of it was a coincidence," Becky said.

"A miracle, I suppose," England said with a chuckle.

"You have your views; they are hard and fast, your foundation. I finally understand that, and I understand that if I don't share them, you don't believe that I belong here."

"That's not so!" England said.

"And to Constance Frye and Landcaster, I'm your pet president," Becky said. "I have reconciled that; I allowed that to happen." Becky leaned forward and put her cup on the coffee table. "I told Ian who I really was. He told me he didn't care, that he was there for me. We've said wonderful things, Kristy. I've had wonderful feelings about him. I want to nourish those feelings."

"You think you can keep a relationship with this man and be president of AP, too?" England asked.

"You just don't understand, do you?" Becky said. "I don't want to be president of anything. I want to be a journalist. I want to be a mother, a wife," she continued.

England sat up. "You'll never get a job at a decent paper, Becky. I'll see to it," she said.

"Isn't that what it's all about? Power? Manipulation? You tell Landcaster you'll put him away if he doesn't do this; Constance tells Gentcher to put you away if you don't do that. Peterson gets indicted because he wrote a stupid article. Isn't that what it's all about in this town? Do this or you'll never get a job, or you'll be sorry, or. . .or you'll be dead?"

"If that's how you see it," England said.

"What I saw was the nothing Constance Frye reduced me to while I sat there in the Roosevelt Room of the White House, the monument I believed to be the symbol of freedom," Becky said. "Ian made me realize that freedom is something we have to fight for. And he made me remember who I used to be, and that my Creator made me so that I didn't have to feel like a nothing to anyone, not to you, not to Constance Frye, not to her mindless, militant slave, that Gentcher."

"You'll be nothing when you lose everything, Becky," England said.

"You're blinded by your greed for power and your prejudices, Kristy. By your agenda, too. Do you really think Constance Frye will allow you to come out of this free or alive?" Becky said.

"Go home, Becky!" England had yelled. "Get your man. You'll be back, whining, begging for another chance."

England stepped away from the window and the New York sky-line. She sat behind her desk. Regret welled up in her when she remembered she had actually told Becky to go home. She realized that she cared for Becky more than the previous presidents of AP whom she had arm-twisted the board of trustees to elect. Becky was sweet and pretty and presented a soft, believable perception of Anticipating Parenthood to the rabble. And she was a friend.

When England arrived at home that night, she found the note on the floor, just beyond the threshold of her door. The note read:

"I'm going home to be with my family. You have been good to me, and for that I'm grateful. I know you have trusted me with information you want few people to know. I understand that you and the people in the venture might consider killing me for that. If you do, all I ask is that you do it quickly and that you don't hurt my family. And please don't hurt Ian Apple."

England shook herself out of her self-pity. *I have to think about what to do. I'll have to do something.*

CHAPTER 21

Amanda sat on the edge of the pool at the Anchorage Apartments. The late afternoon Louisiana sun warmed her chlorine-scented, hot shoulders as she swished her feet just below the surface of the green water as if walking, while she waited for her chest to slow its heaving.

She'd begun swimming laps leisurely, but at some point the swim had turned into a full-blown aerobic workout, her blood pumping as she blew the stale air out of her lungs each time she punched her head above the surface. It all regenerated Amanda's mind.

She felt thankful that she was safe, thankful that Dr. Hegel had provided her sanctuary from her killers with his cunning. They were still driving around Kingston, looking for her, she was sure. And now she only needed to wait for Geoffry to join her.

Amanda's thoughts turned to her experiences earlier in the day. She recalled with embarrassment how the man named Bradley had stared at her in a way that showed he knew she'd been eavesdropping. And she remembered the faces and the glares of the young people as she idled on the choppy asphalt lane.

The government knows best for them; that's what we elected them for, Amanda.

"Really, Amanda?" a faint voice said. "Is that what you believe?"

I am really going nuts. She heard the thud of rubber thongs approaching her. She turned her head.

"Have a good swim?" Carl asked.

Amanda raised her head to meet Carl's eyes. "Hi," she said. She lifted her left hand to move the kelpish strands of hair clinging to her cheek.

"Still have a lot of daylight left for a boat ride," Carl said.

Amanda stood. "I really do have to meet my fiancé," she said, jiggling her engagement ring.

— | —

As Amanda drove to the airport to drop off the rental car, she didn't feel the overwhelming excitement about seeing Geoffry that had so permeated her emotions during the last two days.

It wasn't that she didn't want to see Geoffry. Rather, thoughts of the talkative teen with the gun and the teenage girls weighed heavily on her mind, and she felt unsettled, as if there were unfinished business to attend to. She didn't like that feeling now any more than she had when she worked in the BioSysTech lab or when her team was behind during intermission.

Amanda rolled the car to a stop at a red light. She read the big green sign ahead—"Long-term Parking and Rental Return"—as she sat, tapping the steering wheel, waiting for the light to turn green.

Amanda, your fiancé is coming. You're starting your new life. Safe from those killers. Remember them?

As Amanda pulled into the rental return area of the airport, she realized she hadn't thought about Dr. Hegel and his instructions for several hours. Even his image had become dim in her mind. Maybe because she didn't know which to conjure up—Dr. Hegel at the interview or Mr. Hyde in his office on the day he died. Perhaps she would just settle down here in Slidell, forget about everything, except Geoffry.

Amanda! You have to get that package to Senator Gators. That's why you're here! They'll find you. It might be a year or two, but they won't quit. Is that true, Amanda? Is that really true?

She glanced at the steel and gold tennis-style Rolex her daddy had given to her. Eight-twenty. It was getting darker. Geoffry had to be close now. Excitement arose in her now, finally. This would be the new beginning of a safe life.

Those killers will never find me.

⌞__⌟

Amanda's taxi pulled into the Peacock Inn parking lot, then rolled under the single-lane canopy leading to the registration office. Amanda searched the parking lot for her car. She knew Geoffry wouldn't be there yet, but she had to search the parking lot for her gray Camry anyway.

A small brass bell dinged when Amanda opened the glass and aluminum door to the registration office.

"Can I help you?" the clerk asked, lifting her eyes over the top of an *Enquirer* tabloid.

"Do you have a Geoffry Reagan registered here?"

The clerk lowered her head and sifted through some cards.

"He's reserved a room," the clerk said, then stared at Amanda. "You were here the other night, weren't you?" she asked.

"Thank you," Amanda said.

Twelve or fourteen worn plastic chairs sat along the interior half-brick, half-glass wall of the small lobby that resembled a waiting room for a department store complaint area. The wall to the left of the aluminum entrance door seemed almost to sit on the curb of Airline Highway. When Amanda turned to look behind her, she could see the entire unevenly lighted parking lot, surrounded on three sides by the two-story motel.

This was great! All Amanda had to do was sit in one of those chairs opposite the entrance, pick up one of those worn *People* magazines, read, and wait. A glance through the window out at the parking lot from time to time and she was sure to see Geoffry and her Toyota, a glance to the right and she could see him turn off Airline Highway at the red light. Perfect!

Amanda selected a seat, picked up a magazine, and opened it to a page she did not really care about. She lifted her gaze toward the red light and imagined her Toyota idling under it, its left turn signal blinking, Geoffry smiling behind the wheel. Excitement welled up in her now. She wasn't forcing it, she was certain.

The green LCD clock on the dash of the white Crown Victoria glowed 9:06. Ramos was excited when he saw the sign on the side of I-10 east that read "Louis Armstrong International Airport–Airline Highway." The boy in Sweetness's car would be turning off there, man. The young gringo would have to die; he would just get in the way.

"The girl. Vic tell you?" he asked.

DiRosa glared at Ramos. "You don't touch her until we get the package," he said.

Amanda's Toyota, the two cars behind it, and the Ford approached the red light on Airline Highway in front of the Peacock Inn. They slowed, edging closer together, with taillights glowing. The left turn signal on the Toyota began to flash; the Toyota veered into the turning lane and slowed.

The two cars between the Toyota and the white Ford continued eastward on Airline Highway. Ramos stared at the Toyota while he shut off the tracking device. DiRosa flipped on the turn signal. Ramos sat up. DiRosa turned into the turning lane. He stopped at the red light behind the Toyota. Ramos moved his gaze from the Toyota's rear lights and scanned the parking lot.

Amanda looked up from the *People* magazine just in time to see her Toyota roll to a stop in the turning lane. She squinted her eyes. She could just make out his profile. *Geoffry!* Her heart jumped, and so did she. She could feel her ponytail flop on the back of her neck. She threw the magazine on the seat and dashed to the entrance door.

Amanda shot one more glance at Geoffry while her hand was on the handle of the aluminum entrance door. She had her arm muscle tensed, ready to jerk open the door and sprint into the parking lot. Then. . .

"It's them! How did they—"

Dizziness from the sudden shift in emotions caused an instant mental blackout. She shook it off. She could see the passenger's eyes scanning the parking lot. Amanda stooped behind the brick half-wall. The clerk jerked her head and stared at Amanda. Amanda put her pointing finger to her mouth. "Shh!" she sounded. Her heart pounded; her stomach wrenched. She lifted herself slowly, peeking out over the brick.

"We don't want any trouble," the clerk said.

"It's okay," Amanda said softly.

Geoffry pulled into the parking lot, idled into a parking slot, then stopped inches from the concrete base of one of the poles, under a halogen lamp. The white Ford parked on the other side of her Toyota.

The Italian swung open the driver's door. He had something in his hand. He opened the door of the Toyota, then slipped quickly into the passenger's seat. The glow of the halogen lamp allowed Amanda to see not much more than the top of the dashboard, but she could make out Geoffry turning his head toward the Italian in the shadows of the interior. Amanda felt sick.

"Where's the ladies room?" Amanda asked the clerk in a whisper.

"That door there," the clerk said. "Just go around the counter."

"Please don't tell anyone I'm here. Please," Amanda said. She slumped and scooted quickly around the counter toward the ladies room door.

"We don't want trouble here," the clerk said.

"Then, please, don't let them know I'm here," Amanda said.

Amanda stepped into the rest room and closed and locked the door. How long should she wait? Should she call the police? Amanda remembered the warning in Dr. Hegel's note:

Under no conditions, Amanda, do you call the police. They cannot help you. The killers will only be let go. This is too much for mere policemen. You will lose control over the package. They will kill you, anyway, Amanda.

Mere police can't battle our enemies.

Now, standing there, wondering what was happening to Geoffry, everything came together in Amanda's mind. Dr. Hegel, Danny Barnwell, the passenger's frightful leer and crooked gold smile. Amanda lowered her head against the interior door frame of the bathroom. She wished her heart would slow down so she could think what to do. Geoffry was surely sitting in her Toyota now, probably with a gun or knife pointed at his side.

You broke the rules, Amanda. I'm so sorry, Dr. Hegel. Oh, Geoffry. I'll get you out of this, Geoffry. I'll get you out of this!

⌞　ㅣ　⌟

"May I help you?" the clerk asked.

"My name is Geoffry Riggins. I got a reservation."

"Riggin. . .Riggin," the clerk said, shifting through cards.

"We don't have a 'Riggin.' We have a 'Geoffry Reagan.' "

⌞　ㅣ　⌟

Amanda slowly turned the doorknob of the rest room and opened the door about a half inch. She leaned her ear toward the crack. *Concentrate, Amanda. Concentrate.*

"How stupid! That's me. Geoffry Reagan. This English language—" the man said, chuckling.

"Really?" the clerk asked. "How will you be paying, Mr. Reagan?"

"Cash."

"Fifty-four dollars for one night."

"Can you get me a bottom floor? I hate steps."

"Room 118," the clerk said. "It's right over there, directly across the parking lot."

"If a beautiful young lady comes looking for me, her name is Amanda; tell her I'm waiting for her in room 118."

Amanda listened for the ding of the brass bell. She waited a few more seconds after she heard it, then opened the rest room door. She gazed beyond the counter, out to the parking lot. She saw the passenger walking away, toward her Toyota. Amanda stepped to the entrance door and slumped in a chair next to it, keeping her head below the wall.

"You're Amanda, I'll bet," the clerk said.

Amanda nodded, then turned her head and craned her neck just enough to peek over the brick half-wall. The Italian and the passenger, with Geoffry in front of them, walked toward the line of motel rooms on the opposite side of the parking lot.

"We don't like you girls arranging things at this place. There's cheaper places down toward the New Orleans city limits."

Amanda nodded again. She felt stupid. Scared and stupid.

"You look like a nice girl," the clerk said. "How could you do this? And with that creep! Money might be tight, honey, but I'd die first."

Amanda lifted her head, craned her neck, and looked across the parking lot again. Nothing. Nobody.

"May I have change?" Amanda asked the clerk.

"Okay," the clerk said. "I don't want to see you back here again. I'm tired of telling you girls that."

The clerk gave Amanda change. She turned away and sat in her chair at the desk behind and to the side of the counter. She opened her *Enquirer* tabloid. Amanda looked out the aluminum-framed glass entrance door. She studied the doors of the motel rooms facing her. She couldn't read the numbers.

"Which door is one-eighteen?" she asked.

"Fourth one from the Airline Highway end of the building," the clerk said without lowering the *Enquirer*.

"Are there any pay phones I can use?" Amanda asked.

The clerk lowered the *Enquirer*. "You can come around and use this one if you want to. Just get your business done and get out."

"I need a pay phone," Amanda said.

"Private call, huh?" the clerk said. "There's a pay phone in every breezeway. Out the door, to the left, two doors down. I'm telling you. Don't make this place your office."

"The rooms, are they all the same?" Amanda asked.

"What you see in every cheap motel," the clerk said, her face showing irritation. "You open the door, you see two beds, a bathroom door in the back, on the side, a sink, a cheap chest of drawers with a television shackled to it, a cheap table with a couple of chairs. What can you do with rows of cinderblock caves?"

———

"I'm tired," DiRosa said to Geoffry sitting across the table, pointing the silencer-equipped muzzle of his pistol at him. "I could sleep easy right now. That pig over there. He wants to kill you and have his way with your girlfriend. If you do what I say, you'll live through this."

Ramos cut the electrical wires from the television set, looped the wire, and wrapped the last several inches of the cord around the middle, creating a bow tie-shaped coil. He shoved the coiled wire in his pocket and paced around the room, holding his nine-inch knife in his hand. He started for the window, on the left side of the door.

"Don't look out the window," DiRosa said loudly to Ramos. "The parking lot lights shine right in here. She sees your ugly face, she runs."

"Man, I ain't stupid."

"Sit down," DiRosa said. "She's going to call or knock. She has to."

Ramos plopped down on the edge of the bed closer to the door. He wanted to say something back to DiRosa. But after considering it, he decided not to. He would just sit and wait for Sweetness to knock or maybe telephone. He set his forearms on his knees and stared at the door.

———

Amanda's heart had settled. This was her against them now. Competition. She was used to this. And she was used to winning.

"If they come after you, they will kill you." That's what Dr. Hegel had written. And now he coached her from his grave. *They're waiting for me to call.* She wondered whether either of the killers was peering out the window. She had no choice. Better be careful. Run from cover to cover.

Amanda took off for the breezeway, running fast and low. She picked up the receiver, slipped the coins in, and leaned against the wall, her head behind the phone, out of the line of view from the window next to the door of room 118.

"Peacock Inn," the clerk said.

"Room one-eighteen, please," Amanda said.

A pause. "I can't believe this!" the clerk said. "Now I'm your secretary, honey?"

Ramos jumped up when the telephone rang. He drew his knife from its sheath, held it up, and stared at Geoffry.

Ring. . .ring. . .

"You walk over there, sit on the bed, and answer it," DiRosa said, pointing the pistol in Geoffry's face.

Ring. . .ring. . .

"He's got to answer it, man. . ."

"I'll have this gun pointed at the back of your head."

Ring. . .ring. . .

"She's going to hang up, man!"

"Get up," DiRosa said to Geoffry. "Walk slow. She doesn't come in here, you drop."

Ring. . .rin— "Hello?" Geoffry said.

"Geoffry," Amanda whispered, as she peered at the red door of room 118.

"Aman—"

"Don't say anything. Say, 'I love you. It was a hard drive.' "

"I love you. It was a hard drive," Geoffry said.

"I know they're in there. Ask, 'How long will it be before you get here, honey?' "

"How long will it take you to get here, hon?" Geoffry said.

"Move your head, like I'm trying to explain I have some sort of problem at the airport, having problems returning the rental car or something," Amanda said. "Say, 'What's with those car rental places?' "

"What's with those car rental places?"

"Listen, Geoffry. I'm going to ask you some questions. For 'yes' say a sentence with the word 'room' in it. For 'no' use the word 'love' when you answer. You understand, Geoffry?"

"I. . .I'm not going anywhere until you're in this room, Amanda."

"Look at your watch," Amanda said. "I'm looking at mine. Stare at it. Exactly ten minutes from now, do you think you can punch one of them and rush out of the room to my car?"

"I'll wait in this room until the rental car problem is solved," Geoffry said.

"I'm going to be in the Toyota," Amanda said, "slumped down in the driver's seat. Waiting."

"Okay," Geoffry said.

"Are you scared, Geoffry?"

"I'll be in this room."

"I'm so sorry, Geoffry."

∟ ⊥ ⌐

At the same time the receiver clunked on its cradle, Ramos yelled at Geoffry, "When, man? When will she be coming?"

"She's having trouble turning in the rental car," Geoffry said to DiRosa. "They're saying she scratched the car or something. She'll be here in ten or fifteen minutes."

"We don't know if she's got the documents with her," DiRosa said

239

to Ramos. "This is business. Don't do nothing until we know where the documents are. The girl will tell us for him."

"Okay, man," Ramos said. "She comes, I tie her up. Then we deal with the big gringo after we talk to her."

"We do what we have to do when we have to do it. That's what we do, pig," DiRosa said. He turned to Geoffry, pointing his gun, then waving it. "Come back over here away from the door and sit down."

Amanda stole her way back to the registration area. The clerk had finished with the *Enquirer*. Now she was on the phone at the desk, the parking lot and motel rooms out of her view.

"Do you have a pen or pencil?" Amanda asked.

"Just a minute, honey," the clerk said into the telephone, looking down toward her desk. Then she removed the receiver from her ear and turned to Amanda. "You know, you have a lot of nerve."

"Please."

Six and a half minutes left.

"Here, catch. Keep it," the clerk said. She lifted the receiver back against her ear and turned around. "You wouldn't believe this," she said to whomever she was talking to.

Amanda stared hard at room 118. No one appeared to be looking out the window, but she couldn't be sure. She had no choice but to walk with a normal gait to the parking lot. Maybe they weren't watching; maybe since they knew she was coming, they would just sit and wait for a knock.

She walked by the Ford, then slipped between it and her Toyota. She stooped, removed the cap from the air valve on the front tire of the passenger side of the Ford, and, using the pen, pushed down on the brass valve.

Sssssssss. . .

Four minutes left.

She opened the driver's door to her Camry and slipped into it.

She slid the key in the ignition. She slumped. *Please don't let them be watching me!* She stilled herself, then peered at her watch.

Three minutes.

⌞__⌟

"Man, why you keep looking at your watch?" Ramos said to the young gringo. "She's on her way, man."

⌞__⌟

Amanda glanced at her watch.

Two minutes.

She waited.

One minute, thirty seconds.

Amanda's heart pumped hard again. She could feel the sweat dampening her scalp. *Please, Geoffry, please.*

Thirty seconds.

⌞__⌟

Geoffry popped up from the chair and slapped the pistol from DiRosa's hands. He grabbed DiRosa's shirt and flung him on the floor. Ramos jumped up from the edge of the bed, moving his hand toward his side at the same time. Geoffry's fist flew into Ramos's nose. Blood spewed. Ramos flopped on the bed, then moaned. Geoffry ran to the door and jiggled the interior lock.

"No, don't!" DiRosa hollered.

The door opened wide.

⌞__⌟

The red door flew open. Amanda saw movement inside the motel room. She started the engine and revved it. "Come on, Geoffry. Come on!" Amanda said.

Ramos plunged his knife into Geoffry's back, between his fourth and fifth rib. "Don't ever punch me, gringo!" Ramos hollered.

"No, don't, you pig!" DiRosa hollered.

Amanda could see inside now, but she trembled and could not move as she watched Geoffry collapse to his knees in the glow of the inset light above the red door of room 118. As Geoffry fell and his head struck the carpet just inside the threshold, the handle of a knife sunk deep into his back came into Amanda's view.

The passenger stepped into the dim light. He leaned over, then pulled the knife out of Geoffry's back. He grabbed Geoffry's shirt collar, then jerked him up on his knees. He looked up. Amanda gasped at the sight.

The passenger stared at her. He pulled Geoffry's body inside, then yelled something and started running toward Amanda. The Italian ran out of the room, slamming the door shut.

Amanda regained her composure. She pressed down on the accelerator and the Camry jerked into motion. Tires squealed. The passenger tried to grab the car. Amanda raced toward the parking lot exit, increasing the distance between her and Geoffry's killer. In the rearview mirror, Amanda could see the passenger, his big belly heaving, waving his fist at her. Now she was at the exit, ready to turn onto Airline Highway. Another glance in the rearview mirror. The passenger started walking toward the registration desk. *Oh, no! The clerk.* She was going to die, too. The Italian stood at the front of the white Ford, shaking his head.

Amanda squealed the tires as she spun onto Airline Highway. Two, maybe three horns blew. The clerk came to her mind again; she would be dead soon, probably. *Oh, Geoffry!*

Amanda's vision blurred through her tears; still vivid was the image of Geoffry collapsing to his knees at the threshold of his cinderblock tomb, the light from the inset fixture above the door opening glowing over him.

No, no. I can't think about it! Not now. Hurry, Amanda. Hurry to the only place you know. Slidell, apartment 105, your home, what you thought was your sanctuary.

Amanda raced on the interstate, weaving between cars. She raced through the brightly lit strip of the interstate running through the business area of New Orleans, then the shopping malls and residential area of New Orleans East. Eighty, eighty-five miles an hour. Then the dark, less populated stretch running through the underdeveloped wooded area between New Orleans East and the Twin Span, still plenty of cars to weave around, plenty of cars to concentrate on so she didn't have to think, didn't have to remember.

A siren sounded behind her.

In a haze, Amanda pulled over.

A policeman appeared at her window. He tapped and pointed down. Amanda groped for the window button.

"Are you all right, young lady?" the policeman asked.

Tell him, Amanda! Tell him! Go ahead, break another rule. Kill somebody else.

"My fiancé is gone," Amanda said. She lowered her head on the steering wheel.

"What do you mean?" the officer asked.

Tell him, Amanda. "I saw him at a cheap motel. He. . ."

"You had anything to drink, ma'am?"

Amanda peered up at the officer. His eyes studied her.

"No," Amanda said. "I'm just tired."

"Where do you live, ma'am?"

Amanda ran her palm over her forehead, pushing back the strands that had fallen in her face. "Anchorage Apartments. Slidell," she said.

"You going straight home?" the policeman asked.

Amanda nodded.

"Get on your way," the policeman said. "You'll feel better about things in the morning. But slow down, because I'll be following you for a little ways to make sure you're all right."

———

The Twin Span looked like a dark seven-mile stretch over the black water of Lake Pontchartrain. Seven miles with nothing to do but think. Geoffry's image came to her mind again, on his knees, giving his life for her.

It's Wednesday night. He wanted us to be at church tonight! Why, God? Why?

Amanda's head collapsed on the steering wheel. She felt the Toyota swerve. She jerked her head up. She couldn't see. Tears, so many tears. She moved her hand over her forehead again. She wiped the dampness from under her nose with the back of her hand.

The sparkling lights of homes on the north shore reflecting on the black water came into view. If only her mind would fall into that dark pit and sink in it forever.

THURSDAY, JUNE 27

CHAPTER 22

You were supposed to be here at eight. It's ten before nine," Jennifer said as she settled into the buttery soft gray leather passenger seat of Griffin's 740i. "You shouldn't keep your date waiting."

"I couldn't sleep wondering about the Landcaster affair," Griffin said, glancing into the rearview mirror then turning the steering wheel.

"Affair?" Jennifer asked. "Presumptuous, don't you think? As a matter of fact, I invited him to church."

"Landcaster in church? Besides, 'affair' was your word, not mine." Griffin chuckled. Then he realized Jennifer would bring up church again sometime during the twenty-five-minute drive to the office. He had an excuse to hurry. Almost nine o'clock. He pressed the accelerator and began weaving through the traffic until he got to the West 6th Street and Ardenwood Boulevard intersection. Great. A parking lot.

"Pastor Grady asks me about you almost every Sunday," Jennifer said softly as they sat in the backed-up traffic. "He was hurt when you just stopped coming."

There it was. It seemed everyone wanted to talk to him about God, the church, or his soul. Jennifer wouldn't do this in the office, but in the quiet confines of his BMW, Griffin knew Jennifer couldn't resist. And now, here they were, stopped in two lanes of traffic waiting for the red light. *Change the subject, Griffin.*

"How many times has that car of yours been in the shop?" Griffin asked, feeling stupid and obvious. He glanced into the rearview mirror.

"What should I tell Pastor Grady on Sunday?"

"Tell him I'll be back," Griffin said. "I just need some more time."

Finally, the green arrow lighted. The brake lights on the cars in front of them began losing their glows, one after the other. The cars began to crawl. *Hurry, hurry.*

Jennifer put her elbow on the padded center console. She leaned toward Griffin. "You know what would have happened to us if at Gethsemane Jesus had told God, 'I just need more time'?" she asked.

Griffin shifted his foot from the brake pedal to the accelerator. "I used to be a deacon, remember?" He glanced into the rearview mirror again.

"God tells us not to forsake assembly, Griffin. You have so much to offer."

"You're preaching, Jennifer."

The BMW rolled into the next intersection. The green light turned yellow. Griffin accelerated and made the left-hand turn onto West 6th Street. He glanced into the rearview mirror again.

Jennifer straightened and resettled her shoulders in the seat. "That's the last time I'll preach to you, ever. I promise," she said.

"Okay," Griffin said, "back to Landcaster." Anything to do with Richard Landcaster intrigued Griffin now. Maybe Jennifer would say something else that could help.

Griffin peered at the green, dented '70ish Buick Skylark coupe he thought might be following them. As Griffin weaved through traffic, the Skylark kept two or three cars behind his BMW, weaving, too.

"When I suggested Landcaster meet me at church, he. . . Are you listening, Griffin?" Jennifer asked.

"Sorry—drifted off," Griffin said. The green Skylark made the turn behind him, running the red light. Now it was falling back again. "What county is Ozark in?" Griffin asked, shooting another glance in the rearview mirror.

"Colton, I think. Why do you keeping looking in the rearview mirror?" Jennifer asked.

"Find out about the county," he said, then glanced into the mirror again. A blue Taurus with a young woman driving tailgated him.

Frustrating. Griffin saw the passenger-side headlight of the Skylark creep out to the side from the rear of the Taurus. "I need maps of the adjacent counties, every state highway and county gravel road," Griffin said, now paying equal attention to the road and mirror.

"We have a CD with that information," Jennifer said. "What are you looking at?"

"Can you download the maps yourself?"

"It's so secret your investigator shouldn't even know?" Jennifer asked.

Griffin said nothing. He spotted the cabstand on the corner of Windgate and Sixth.

"Planning a trip?" Jennifer asked.

Griffin glanced at Jennifer.

"Stupid question," Jennifer said. "A mysterious facility some-where around Ozark selling or manufacturing something illegal. Constance Frye is involved, and so is Ruth Hegel, probably the president, too."

"A friend murdered, too," Griffin said softly.

"What are you looking at?" Jennifer asked. "You're scaring me, Griffin."

"Nothing," Griffin said as they passed Windgate Boulevard. Another glance. The Taurus turned right at the taxi stand on Windgate. The morning sun reflected off the Skylark's windshield. *If only I could see the driver.*

"Is someone following us?" Jennifer asked.

"Maybe," Griffin said. Griffin turned into the parking entrance of the Executive Plaza. He glanced into the rearview mirror again. The Skylark turned into the parking entrance and lagged behind. Griffin drove to the fifth level and pulled into his parking slot. The Skylark still cruised behind him. Griffin sat still and watched the Skylark creep past them in his rearview mirror.

"Are they following us?" Jennifer asked.

Griffin wanted to tell Jennifer what he really thought: *Yes, they are. I think they just want to let me know they know where I live.* "No, just somebody in the building showing off their old car," he said.

"Bet the telephone's been ringing off the hook," Jennifer said as she pulled on the door latch.

"Yeah," Griffin said, standing with the driver's door open, studying the license plate of the Buick Skylark as its brake lights glowed and it slowly turned and disappeared down the sloping parking lot exit. Griffin glanced at his watch: nearly 9:30.

——|——

By 10:30 the Louisiana June sun beamed down on the Anchorage Apartment's parking lot. The concrete radiated the heat, baking Amanda's Toyota. The windshield and black soft dashboard absorbed the hot rays; the interior temperature had soared to broiling. Amanda felt the heavy hot air entering her lungs while she rolled her head on the steering wheel and moaned. She coughed. Now she could feel the sweat streaming down the nape of her neck, down her back. She felt strands of her hair sticking to her face, her blouse clinging to her back.

Tap. Tap, tap. "Amanda. . .Amanda!"

Amanda lifted her head off the steering wheel. She tried to focus her eyes on the LCD clock on the dash, but the green numbers blurred into each other.

Tap, tap, tap. "Amanda!"

Amanda moved her palm over her forehead, pushing wet hairs up and out of her eyes. The LCD numbers came into focus: 10:31.

"Amanda. Open up, Amanda!"

She spotted knuckles tapping the window close to her head. The noise resonated in the interior of the Toyota and in her head. She lifted her left hand toward the tapping. She squinted, trying to push the pain from her head. Hard to breathe.

Tap, tap. "Amanda! Roll down the window."

Hairs fell back in her face. She ran her palm up her forehead again. Amanda turned her head. Carl's stare came into focus. She fumbled for the electric lock.

Carl swung open the door. "You all right?" he asked.

"I'm not sure how I. . ." Amanda was going to finish the sentence with "got here," but she felt the need to breathe when the fresh air hit her face.

"Come on," Carl said. He gently placed his hand under her arm.

"They murdered my fiancé," Amanda heard herself mumble as she staggered, leaning on Carl, her forehead resting in the palm of one hand, the other hand swaying by her side. "I saw them."

"Okay," Carl said. "Here's your apartment. Your key. I need your key."

Apartment 105. The numbers wobbled in front of her, then settled into focus. Amanda gazed at Carl. She put her head down, ran her palm over her forehead again. "I'll be all right now." She fumbled for her keys in the pocket of her Bermuda shorts. "I'm okay. Really," she said, feeling her body swaying a bit but not so much that she could not control it.

"Maybe I should call the police," Carl said.

"No. Please!" Amanda said. "I just had a bad night, just dreaming."

"Call me later," Carl said. "I have some stuff that will help."

"Okay. . .okay, thanks."

Amanda shut the apartment door behind her. As she walked into the apartment, the image of Geoffry falling dead to his knees just inside room 118 under the glow of the light popped into her mind again. The room began to spin. She gathered just enough strength to aim her body toward the sofa. She felt her head flop on the arm pillow.

Why Geoffry, God? Amanda felt her body sink into the cushions and her mind slowly shut down.

⎿   ⏐   ⏌

Griffin had kept himself busy the entire morning jotting down on legal pads every detail he could remember from the funeral and Ruth's house, then mulling over everything since Warren Jennings foretold his own death right there in that leather client chair. Hard to believe that was only a few days ago, Griffin thought as he pondered; so much had happened since—since he had ignored his friend.

Griffin kept revising and revising again. He jotted down questions and conclusions, accepting some, eliminating others. *Maybe I'll have another discussion session with Jennifer after lunch.*

"Hot off the CD-ROM," Jennifer said as she entered Griffin's office. "Colton County." Jennifer handed Griffin two maps. "Ozark's in the northeast corner of the state, about ten miles from the state line."

Griffin held a map in each hand, shifting his gaze from one to the other.

"The first one shows the interstate and paved roads," Jennifer said. "The other shows some of that but is taken from aerial shots. You can see every road big enough for a car, even private dirt roads on farmers' lands."

"Good," Griffin said.

"Bet there's a lover's lane, too," Jennifer said, smiling.

Griffin thought he might say something, but just couldn't think what to say.

"It's eleven-fifty," Jennifer said. "You're in your study mode. Chinese?"

"Shrimp with lobster sauce. . ."

". . .wonton soup with egg roll," Jennifer said, holding up her palm and extending it toward Griffin. "Your keys and twenty dollars, please. You're treating for scaring me like that this morning. Your voice mail will get the calls."

"Good."

"One other thing," Jennifer said. "You have other files, remember? I've done all that I can to keep up; everything else needs a lawyer. You know one around here?"

Amanda opened her eyes. Her blouse had dried; her hair clung to her cheeks. She pushed herself up to a sitting position. She wondered what time it was when her mind came around. She checked her watch: just past twelve noon. She had to call her mama. She went to the bedroom and sat on the bed. She glanced at the picture next to the phone of the couple on Narragansett Bay. She took a deep breath. Her first instinct was to hide the picture in the drawer. No. Not yet. She lifted the phone receiver and dialed.

"Hello, Mama."

"Baby, you all right?"

"Mama. I need to tell you about Geoffry, Mama. He's—"

"Your daddy and me have been talking about you and that white boy, Aman—"

"Mama?" Amanda had never heard her mother say "white" in the tone her father used.

"Your daddy's been good to you, Mandy. And he. . .the minister says they goin' to be a new Africa where only pure people like us can live."

"Mama? What are you talking about?"

"It's not right for us to spoil our bloodlines, Amanda. That's what your daddy and the minister say. They put AIDS in the projects."

"Oh, Mama," Amanda said softly.

Amanda's mother remained silent for a moment. Amanda heard her crying.

"Mama?"

"Baby, I can't lose your daddy. I got nowhere to go. I love you, baby. Ain't nothin' goin' to change that, but your daddy says he ain't got no daughter, and he won't have no wife if. . ."

"Good-bye, Mama," Amanda said. "I'll always love you." She hung up and then stared at the phone, realizing how devoid of feeling she was. Spiritual emptiness; emotional numbness. Alone, not caring whether she lived or died.

Amanda walked into the living room and began to pace. She crossed her arms, then uncrossed them, still pacing.

You knew the rules, Amanda. Remember that little intentional foul, the key in the flowerpot? Remember calling Geoffry?

Amanda paced faster, pushing back the stubborn wet strands clinging to her face, her mind racing. *Two-zip, Amanda. Geoffry,*

Danny. Three-zip, you're dead. Get prepared; get them. You can do it. "Execution," that's what your coaches always said.

Amanda stopped pacing. From the center of the living room where she stood, she saw Dr. Hegel's package on the bedside table.

Amanda hurried through the bedroom to the bathroom. She stood in front of the mirror. *How would I look in a rhinestone T-shirt and black leggings, with a gun? Would you show me that gold pocked-faced smile then, creep?* She slammed the bathroom door shut. Not moving her gaze off the angry reflection in front of her, she yanked each button on her blouse free. *You want to meet Amanda Collins? You will!*

She needed a shower before she traded in her Camry; that car would never do. What good would her new uniform be if her opponents could recognize her car? A new car would be part of her game paraphernalia.

Paraphernalia. Amanda realized that the last time she heard that word was when her high school basketball coach said it. She always said it, almost every day.

No time to reminisce now, Amanda. Got to get prepared to reenter the game.

⌞　⌟

Griffin had heard bombs before. Land mines that blew up equipment and artillery; trip mines that blasted feet and legs from his men's bodies. He learned the difference between bombs that just exploded, blowing everything to pieces in a single, violent burst, and the subtle jolt of incendiary devices. They shook just a bit, then spread flames as bits of sticky kindling flew everywhere, charring everything they stuck to.

The subtle jolt came from the parking lot, sending vibrations through the concrete and steel, through Griffin's socks. Fire alarms blasted.

Griffin lifted his gaze from the legal pad. It couldn't be—it just couldn't. Something moved behind him, something just outside the window, nine stories up. Griffin spun in his chair. He could almost touch the thick, black smoke billowing in front of him on the other side of the glass.

When Griffin tried to think, tried to deny, a wave of thoughts hit him: Who else in the building was trying to put an end to top-level crime being committed by persons who had the power to do anything they wanted?

Griffin bounded out of his office. He raced down the stairs. Sirens whined from the street below. He smelled smoke in the stairwell. He swung open the heavy metal door to the fifth-level parking lot. He opened it and rushed, pushing at the people who had already gathered. Then he saw Jennifer. Her blackened corpse sat in the driver's seat of his BMW, her head leaning on the melted steering wheel, yellow flames still licking at her. The passenger's side front tire popped, then the driver's side tire. Jennifer's charred form crumbled out of view with the clatter of the heavy steel frame of Griffin's 740i striking the concrete. Sirens, sirens. . .sirens.

Griffin turned and ran back up the stairs. His thigh throbbed. The building's fire alarm blasted intermittently from air horns hidden somewhere. He raced into his office, then to his desk. He grabbed the maps and his notes. He ran down the stairs, pushing people aside. "Get out of the way! Out of the way!" He ran out of the building, down West 6th Street, to Windgate Boulevard. He ran to the taxi stand and jumped in the rear seat of a Checker cab. Sirens. Sirens everywhere. Black smoke billowing from the Executive Plaza Building, obliterating most of the view of the sky behind it.

Griffin's thigh throbbed with pain. He could barely catch his breath when he spoke. "Two-forty-nine Wellington Court Condominiums. Quick!" He fumbled through his wallet, then tossed a hundred on the seat next to the driver. "This is your tip."

Griffin rubbed his thigh.

The driver turned his head back to Griffin. "You got it, pal," he said. He spun the steering wheel, squealed the tires, not bothering to jerk the meter arm down until the big yellow Checker was off to the races. "What happened to that BMW you drive?"

"How did you know that?" Griffin asked, watching the back of the driver's head and shoulders swaying in the direction he turned the cab.

The driver weaved through the traffic, chatting. "I been sitting on Windgate and West 6th for fourteen years from six to six. It's my spot. I can tell you every car that goes through that intersection on a regular time schedule. You go through it every morning between seven-thirty and eight, and then in the afternoon, usually after five. You're a lawyer, right?"

"That's right." Griffin wanted to tell him to just drive. But the driver was making good time. Griffin closed his eyes.

I'm sorry, Jennifer; they wanted me, not you.

Then he felt anger when Constance Frye's green eyes came to his mind. *How am I going to make you pay? I will. Somehow, I will.*

Griffin began massaging his thigh. *I don't know, but you will, Constance. You will!*

"Where's that BMW?"

"It burned up," Griffin said. That did it. The image of Jennifer's charred form, the flames licking at her, popped into Griffin's mind. The cab driver continued to chat, throwing his head back and sideways, leaning one way as he guided the cab into a turn, then the other.

Griffin gazed out the window. Downtown Columbia whizzed by. He had loved Jennifer. A brother's love. "I do miss the church, Jennifer," Griffin said softly. *Where will you set up the perimeter, Griffin? Where is the hill to take? Griffin. . .who's your Captain?*

The sudden stop jolted Griffin from his daze. The cab driver leaned his head over the seat. "Hey, pal," he said. "Want me to wait. Right? Keep the meter running. Right?"

"I'll be right back," Griffin said. He rushed out of the cab to his condominium.

Ten minutes later, Griffin ran out of his condominium lugging his stuffed duffel bag and a small suitcase. He threw the bag and case on the rear seat of the cab and jumped in. "Get me to the nearest place to rent a car," he said just after slamming the rear door shut.

The cab driver turned and looked at Griffin. "Don't look like a lawyer no more. Going golfing, right?"

"That's right," Griffin said.

"Budget's the closest, but it's in town. Going the other way. Right, pal?"

"That's right," Griffin said. "Hurry."

The driver pushed the accelerator to the floor. "Holiday Inn about eight miles out of town," he said. "They have a Hertz booth there."

"Fine," Griffin said, then dropped another hundred on the front seat.

"You're the boss, pal."

⌐ ┴ ┐

After passing the two exits into Slidell, in the opposite direction of New Orleans, the sign on I-10 east read "Gulfport, Mississippi." Amanda veered. A few miles farther a sign read "Waveland, 22 miles."

Waveland, Mississippi, seemed like a good place to buy a car. She lifted one of her hands from the steering wheel and pushed away the strands of hair that had fallen in her eyes. She pressed the accelerator down just a bit farther.

Antique shops and gift shops with piles of seashells in front of them welcomed traffic tooling along on the main street through Waveland, a boat dealership on the right, a seafood restaurant on the left. But no automobile dealer.

There, a mile later, a sign read "Waveland Ford."

Amanda had no sooner parked her Toyota Camry than a woman, perhaps in her late twenties, stepped out of the showroom and walked up to her, smiling, showing a pleasant, freckled face.

"Can I help you?" the lady asked with a definite Mississippi twang.

"I would like to look at some of your cars. Maybe used ones."

"Any preferences?" the lady asked.

"A convertible," Amanda said.

"I like a woman who knows what she likes." She extended her hand. "Ivy Ray," she said.

"Amanda Collins." Amanda shook Ivy's hand. She felt good about Ivy Ray. Perhaps it was the pants suit she wore, casual yet businesslike. "Maybe I should look around," Amanda said.

"Not much need for that," Ivy said. "We only have two, and I wouldn't sell you one of them for anything."

Amanda felt herself put on a doubtful countenance.

"So you're from Massachusetts," Ivy said.

"How did you know?" Amanda asked.

"Your license plate. We learn in our sales meetings to find out everything we can. I'm supposed to say something like, 'The weather's terrible down here. Back home in Massachusetts. . .' And then you say, 'Oh, you're from Massachusetts. So am I!' And then we chat. I gain your trust and sell you the chunkiest, most difficult-to-move junk at an outrageous price," Ivy said, looking into Amanda's eyes, smiling. "You out-of-towners always get our best deals." Amanda felt like smiling but didn't.

"Come on," Ivy said.

Amanda walked with her to the Reliable Waveland Certified Ford Pre-Owned Lot.

"This one looks nice," Amanda said.

"That's the one I won't sell to you," Ivy said. "The manager picked it up at auction in Tennessee. Thirty-two thousand miles. Yeah, right! Engine burns more oil than gas. Follow me."

Ivy walked to the driver's door of a forest green Mustang convertible with a tan top and matching tan interior.

"This one is a year older than the maroon one. But it's perfect," she said. Ivy opened the driver's door. "Go ahead," she said.

Amanda slipped into the driver's seat. Ivy went around to the other side and sat in the passenger seat.

"Now we can talk," she said. "The manager sneaks around. Sometimes joins in conversations." She popped open the dash compartment and lifted out a handful of papers. "See these records? The previous owner was a fanatic about maintenance, but not his finances. Lost everything in bankruptcy. The manager's asking sixteen-five;

he'll take thirteen-four. More than a thousand less than that bomb from Tennessee."

"This isn't the way I thought buying a used car would be," Amanda said.

"I'm starting graduate school at Ole Miss this fall. I promise." Ivy crossed her heart and smiled. "Let's go for a test drive," she said. "I'd buy this buggy in a minute if I could. . .rumble through campus and show off."

———

The Mustang didn't have the Camry's smooth ride. It rode rumbly, Amanda noticed. It kind of fought back when she drove it.

Amanda offered a firm, final offer of $13,400. Ivy came back with the news. "The manager fussed at me for not pushing harder," she said. "I told him you're the toughest out-of-towner I've ever dealt with."

"Right!" Amanda said.

"When will you pick it up?"

"I'm driving it off the lot."

"You're paying cash?" Ivy asked.

"Why not?"

"You're trading in your Camry you drove in here?"

"Is that a problem?" Amanda asked.

"Well, your car, it's not even two years old; that complicates things a little. Your car might be worth. . .but I guess you know what you're doing."

"I do," Amanda said.

"We have to appraise your Camry," Ivy said. "Check the title." Ivy's voice had changed. She sounded suspicious about something. "It'll take about an hour for our mechanic to look at it. Has it ever been wrecked?" she asked, looking squarely into Amanda's eyes.

"Never," Amanda said.

"We have to call your bank, too," Ivy said. "Let's go to my little cubbyhole and finish the deal. I need your keys."

Thirty minutes later a young man in blue work pants and shirt and with black under his fingernails stepped into Ivy's cubicle, interrupting their chatting. His shirt had a patch just above the front left pocket that read "Jerry." He glanced at Amanda with a puzzled look, she thought, but didn't say anything. He motioned Ivy out of the cubicle. Amanda could hear mumbling.

Ivy stepped back behind her cluttered desk. She sat down, then stared at Amanda with her eyes showing more suspicion than ever.

"The manager didn't want Jerry to tell me anything," she said, "but Jerry's a friend, and he thinks I should know. He left it up to me to tell you."

Here goes. Up goes the price.

"What?" Amanda asked, trying to produce a satirical tone. "The mysterious manager changed his mind about the deal, and you can't do anything about it, right?"

"No. It's a done deal," Ivy said. "I'll get fired for this because we probably should call the police," she said. "What the heck. I'm quitting anyway."

"What?" Amanda asked.

"Did you know your car is bugged?" Ivy asked.

"What?"

"It has a radio transmitter attached to the steering column under the dash."

Oh, Geoffry!

"A signaling device or receiver of some sort attached to the frame in the rear," Ivy said. "Jerry thinks it's one of those sounding devices used to locate people or maybe keep on their trail."

Amanda dropped her head in her hands. *Oh, Geoffry. . .Geoffry. I'm so sorry!*

"Are you okay?"

Amanda lifted her head then nodded.

"Jerry can take them off and give them to you if you want to call the police for evidence. The manager doesn't want any problems."

An idea came to Amanda. "Wait," she said. "I have a favor to ask."

Ivy furrowed her brow.

Amanda looked around to make sure no one could hear her. "How good is that mechanic?" Amanda asked Ivy softly.

"Our best," Ivy said.

"Will he do a little extra work on the Mustang for me if I pay?"

"He will if I ask and the work isn't that obvious," Ivy said. "The manager wants your trade-in. It'll sell tomorrow. You're getting the shaft on this deal big time, honey."

"Great," Amanda said.

⌐ ⌐ ⌐

The drive from Waveland to the Louisiana border only confirmed what Amanda first thought when she took the brief test drive with Ivy Ray. The Mustang wasn't anything like the Camry. Not nearly as smooth. The plastic on the dash appeared flimsier; things seemed looser, too. The V-8 engine had more roar than power, and the stereo didn't sound as good, either. But Amanda felt a deep peace about having left her Camry behind for good, that vestige of a quiet, orderly life in the Northeast that seemed so far away now.

Yes, it was good that the Camry was gone; they would believe she still drove it. They would be listening for her, but she would let them hear her only when she wanted them to. Part of the new strategy to match her ruthless opponents in this deadly game. Her newest on the list of her game paraphernalia.

Amanda glanced toward her left knee at the small square aluminum plate Jerry had attached to the dash on the side of the steering wheel. She reached down and snuggled her fingertip against the chrome toggle switch in the middle of the plate. She flipped the switch up. The small yellow bulb next to the toggle switch glowed. She flipped the switch down. Off went the little light.

That was the third test she had run on her most recently acquired piece of game paraphernalia—her controllable, bugged Mustang convertible.

When Amanda saw the first Slidell exit sign off I-10, she remembered the Wal-Mart on the service road where she had run in and out to buy her bathing suit. Wal-Mart was perfect. She could buy the fake fingernails, the clothes she needed; maybe they had jewelry, too. And hair dye. She couldn't forget the hair dye. Then she had to get a haircut after shopping and then visit Carl. *He's not going to believe what I'm going to ask him to do.* Then a nap. She would have to take a nap. Then makeup and then the game uniform. *Oh, Amanda, makeup. Don't forget the makeup.*

CHAPTER 23

Hello?"

"Kristina?" the first lady asked softly, then paused a moment.

Oh, what now? England thought.

"Van Meter called me a few minutes ago," Constance said. "Do you know what she told me?"

England knew the tone. Satirical, pregnant with restrained rage, a soft voice that would burst into a raging snarl at any moment.

"Sheryl told me the BAFT and the FBI called her a few minutes ago."

That envy-crazed peacock actually did it! England brought her hand to her forehead.

"Did you know about this, Kristina?" Constance asked.

England didn't answer. Her heart rate was bringing on one of those ice cream–cold headaches.

"Well, did you know?"

England had to move the receiver away from her ear.

"About what?" England asked.

"Somebody tried to kill Dowell," Constance said. "Not just tried to kill him. . .tried to burn him alive."

As England tried to push the pain from her head by squinting and furrowing her brow, Landcaster's words rushed through her mind: "I want the guy mineralized; I want them to bury nothing but charred bones." Then England realized what Constance had said. "Tried?" England asked.

"They charbroiled his secretary," Constance said. "Sheryl says whoever was paid to do it is probably out of the country by now with their fee. Probably illegal aliens, the entrepreneurish sort, hired by somebody." Quiet for a moment. "Any guesses, Kristina?" the first lady asked, her tone pregnant with accusation.

"Why do you think it was us?" England said, hoping her tone disguised her conscience telling her to just tell it like it was. "Dowell has a lot of enemies, or maybe it's another terrorist bombing."

Landcaster, you're going to pay for this, you fool.

"Don't insult me, Kristina," Constance said in a raised voice. "Why would terrorists just happen to want to kill Dowell?"

"I didn't say that, Constance. I said 'maybe.'" *Parsing words; what else can I do?* England asked herself.

"Did you and Landcaster set this up?" Constance asked. "Well, did you?"

"I don't know anything about it, Constance. I swear!" England said.

"That better be the truth, Kristina," Constance said. "The BAFT, FBI, and Homeland Security will be crawling all over this. Van Meter can only help us so much. I'm going low profile. You wouldn't be stupid enough to do this, but if Landcaster did, I can't be seen anywhere around him."

"Don't worry, Constance," England said. "I'll get to the bottom of this."

"If Landcaster is responsible, get rid of him," Constance said.

England wanted to remind Constance that she was the one who insisted Landcaster be CEO, but decided it was better not to make matters worse.

"What about Dowell? Where is he?" England asked.

"Gone," Constance said. "He knows he'll be a suspect. He's already a material witness to a bombing. They'll find him. But we have a problem. Too much happening at once."

"What do you mean?" England asked.

"The lab assistant or Dowell. We don't have the ability to deal with both of them right now. We know where the girl is; it's just a matter of time," Constance said.

"You're the head of the venture, Constance. Whatever you want to do, we'll do," England said.

"Schneider has gone over the books," Constance said.

A chill ran through England.

"I don't feel like getting into all that right now, Kristina. We need to get the girl now. We're sure she has the original studies. There's a reason she's tooling around down there in Louisiana," Constance said. "Can you guess?"

Think, Kristina. Think. . .

"I thought not," Constance said. "She happens to be in Jeremiah Gators' district. Coincidence, you think?"

England thought it better to remain quiet.

"You should have stopped Peterson from printing that article, Kristina," Constance's voice rose slightly again. "How did that get by you?"

"Constance—"

"Speaker Jukali says he has the votes in the House, easy. It's that preacher—Gators." Constance paused. "Madeline and I think that suicide note Hegel left the girl has some sort of instructions to get the papers to Gators," the first lady said. "If that happens, we have problems. Real problems."

"And Dowell?" England asked.

"Just keep watch on Landcaster. Don't mention anything about the bombing; let him bring it up. He's an idiot, Kristina. Don't think you can conspire with him against me."

"What are you talking about?" England said. Another chill.

"When he talks to you about the bombing, when he realizes Dowell's still alive, you make sure he doesn't try anything again. You make sure he leaves Dowell alone."

"Dowell's probably running scared anyway."

"Your every thought about men is tainted with ignorance and bigotry, Kristina. I know Griffin Dowell. He doesn't run from trouble; he gets into the mix, and if he's not dealt with, he's in your face."

England had no response.

"You say nothing to your nonprofits about it," Constance said. "I'll think of something to float about Dowell if this gets close to the White House."

I'm sure you will, Constance.

"I don't want Landcaster anywhere near Washington."

"All right."

"After Ashton signs the Hegel Bill, I want Landcaster. . ."

"I understand," England said.

Silence.

"That Becky. I heard she moved back to Tulsa," Constance said.

"She'll be back when she realizes what she left behind," England said.

"She knows too much, Kristina."

England said nothing.

"What are you going to do about her?" Constance asked. "You have to do something. I have enough with Griffin Dowell running loose out there."

Griffin took a room at the Holiday Inn outside of Columbia after he rented a brown Chrysler Concorde. He would need the room for five days, he had told the clerk, hoping that information would mislead the feds that were sure to come within the next twenty-four hours.

You're a material witness to a bombing, Griffin, first on the list of suspects. You might as well be the bomber until you can prove that you aren't. Hopefully the FBI will be after me, not BAFT agents. God, are You with me?

The prospect of BAFT agents hunting him didn't set well with Griffin. The BAFT didn't have a knack for bringing 'em back alive. Griffin knew the agency kept a low public profile, unlike the FBI. And worse, the last attorney general had set the pattern to use the agency as a military SWAT team against Americans. Griffin shuddered a bit when the realization came to him that he was now in all respects a federal fugitive, and who controlled the attorney general? Constance Frye.

Well, Griffin, now you're among the select of the first lady's targets, the religious separatists, the militiamen, outspoken tax evaders. But remember, Griffin, they have whatever protection groups afford. You are a lone target for Constance's hit team.

Griffin imagined what might be facing him as he drove the Concorde toward Ozark. In his mental movie, he was sneaking around in the dark in fatigues, maybe in the cotton or cornfields in some farming area, looking for the enemy. A few secretly briefed BATF men, also in fatigues, some behind him, some in front of him, were toting their laser-sighted rifles, scanning with their infrared glasses, looking for him, eager to carry out Constance's secret order to Attorney General van Meter: Shoot him on sight!

"One day I'll sink my fangs into you, Griffin," he remembered Constance saying.

And then Griffin imagined what Andrea Rue on CPNN would probably report: "Attorney J. Griffin Dowell, a former marine, was killed by federal agents this evening. Dowell was spotted wearing military clothing. He was hiding out in the rural areas of the state after having been implicated in arranging the bombing of his car and killing his secretary. It was feared he was searching the area for a remote farmhouse to take hostages."

And, let's see, Constance, Griffin mused as he drove, *there will be psychological profiles, too:* "As the psychiatrist who assessed him briefly during Vietnam, Mr. King, I can tell you that Jackson Griffin Dowell was a wounded marine who suffered undiagnosed posttraumatic stress disorder—we brilliant psychiatrists call it PTSD—that only now manifested itself."

"Why?" Larry King would ask through those nerdy glasses, hunched over that desk, his red suspenders sagging away from his sunken chest.

"We don't know," the brilliant psychiatrist would say after lowering his pipe from his lips. "We know he deeply resented the first lady, though we can't find any logical reason for it. He was a bachelor, you know. Couldn't get along with women. I think perhaps in the end he suffered from debilitating delusions. His law practice began to suffer, I understand. At least that's what his clients say. Probably blamed his secretary. He might have even seen her as the first lady somehow. Kill her, you get rid of the problem. Such extreme, sporadic, violent conduct isn't unusual with PTSD, Mr. King. We extremely brilliant psychiatrists have made up a wonderful sounding name for these episodes—'dissociative reactions.' Isn't that a brilliant-sounding term?"

Griffin gazed down the highway and increased his speed. *Griffin, you're getting as good as Constance with these spins. Amuse yourself. Jennifer's still dead. They meant it for you. They have so much power; they can do anything. Destroy anybody they want, whenever they want. And now you're on the top of their list.*

Remember what Allan Cook said, Griffin. Remember what David said before he reached in his bag for a stone—that he didn't come with only a weapon.

CHAPTER 24

Except for the dirty dishes piled in the sink and the power boating magazines stacked on the coffee table, Carl's apartment looked a lot like Amanda's. The same Herculon furniture, same patterns in the rayon draperies. Anchorage wasn't a summer resort; it was a place for people trying to adjust to transitions in their lives—divorce, financial setbacks, employment transfers, and the like. How many were running away from something or somebody? Most of them, Amanda was certain. She wondered what Carl's story was.

"Have a seat," Carl said. He lifted his can of Red Dog beer. "Beer?"

"No, thank you," Amanda said. She stepped to the sofa and sat on the center cushion. She placed the recorder on the coffee table in front of her. "I have a favor to ask," Amanda said.

"You cut your hair," Carl said. He sat down next to Amanda. "You look older." Carl blushed. "I mean. . .but it really looks good." He rested his forearms on his thighs and held his beer steady between his knees. "That looks like an expensive tape recorder," he said. He leaned a little, bumping Amanda's shoulder with his.

"It's the kind court reporters use," Amanda said.

"You a court reporter?"

Amanda shifted away from Carl, just enough so that if he bumped her shoulder again, he would have to make an obvious move. "Now, about the favor," Amanda said.

Carl set his beer on the coffee table, gazed at Amanda, then said, "Okay, but you have to promise you'll go for a boat ride sometime."

"We'll see," Amanda said. "But you can't ask why I ask you to do this, okay?"

Carl lifted his beer and took a swig, then belched. "Depends," he said.

Amanda pulled a sheet of paper from her pocket and handed it to Carl. "I want you to read this in your normal voice, not like you're acting," she said. "Here, read it to yourself first."

Carl set the beer on the coffee table. He took the paper from Amanda's hand and studied it for a moment. "Peacock Inn? Where's that?" he asked.

Amanda moved the thin black microphone attached to the recorder by a thin black cord toward Carl. "Just read it, okay?"

"Okay, but this is kinda dumb."

"Start now." Amanda pushed the red record button.

Carl started reading: "Look, baby, I don't want to get involved in all this. Why don't we go have some fun. I mean, I'm not scared, baby, but I'm not going to that Peacock Inn. Not after you told me what happened there. Drop me off first, then come back. We'll have some fun."

Click.

Amanda stood up. She lifted the microphone and recorder off the table. "Thanks. See you later," she said.

Carl gazed up at Amanda. "What about the boat ride?" he asked, reaching for his beer.

"We'll see," Amanda said. Then she left.

⌞　⌟

The cornfields along the 120-mile drive from Columbia to Ozark began about an hour outside Columbia's city limits. After about an hour and a half, the cornfields began to thin, and trailers with junk cars and rusty swing sets came into view on both sides of the highway. Then, a sign on the right: "Swifton, 2 miles; Ozark, 14 miles" Griffin decided to stop at Swifton to fuel up and maybe start asking questions.

The facility wouldn't be located within the city limits, Griffin was sure. The shaded area on the maps detailing Ozark, the largest town in Colton County, depicted its population center to be no more than two or three miles by two miles. Ozark sat in the northeast corner of the state. The facility could be either between Swifton and Ozark or between Ozark and the state line. In either case, Griffin believed, the activity of BioSysTech would be in or near a corn patch where it would go unnoticed or would perhaps be treated with indifference. Griffin surveyed the abandoned cars and neglected swing sets. The facility could be operating in these backyards and no one would care, he was sure.

Just before the Swifton city limits, on the left, a shack with four pickups in front of it came into view. A worn sign hanging on the front read "Dogpatch Lounge." Griffin noticed a gasoline island off to the side. His first thought was to pull over, but he changed his mind. The place didn't look at all friendly, and asking questions of the sort he had to ask could cause problems with the local barflies.

Highway 67 doubled as Swifton's main street. Griffin thought about stopping at one of the stores to ask questions. Then, just ahead, beyond the second red light, he spotted an E-Z Store sign raised high over the highway, on the right.

An old Chevrolet El Camino rumbled behind Griffin's rental as he pulled next to the gasoline island in front of the E-Z Store. The El Camino rolled to the opposite side of the concrete island between Griffin and the store. Two teenage boys sat in the El Camino, country music blaring from the open windows.

Griffin headed into the store.

"I'm going to fill up at pump two," he said to the clerk, extending his gas card.

"I need your license, too, mister," the clerk said, holding out her hand with her tooth-mauled fingernails. "You might be one of them drive-aways."

She was probably in her twenties, Griffin thought, but her thick, leather-like skin and missing teeth suggested a hard life during those few years. Not too promising, but Griffin thought he would question her. *Pump your gas first, Griffin.*

270

While Griffin walked back to the rental car, he watched the thin, muscular teenage driver pump gas into the El Camino. Griffin wondered whether all country boys wore caps and went shirtless. Scraggly, long blond hair moved on his shoulders when he nodded. "Nice day, huh, mister?" the teen said, smiling.

"Sure is," Griffin said. He decided he wouldn't ask the boy about a facility somewhere. He simply didn't look too smart. Griffin lifted the nozzle, flipped up its holder, and started pumping.

"You going to Ozark?" the teen asked.

Griffin nodded. "About the only town you can get to in this state from here," he said.

"You're right about that, mister," the teenager said. He stopped pumping and replaced the nozzle, then headed for the store. Griffin's pump jolted to a stop.

When Griffin stepped back into the store to pick up his credit card and license, the teenager was standing in the rear in front of the refrigerated shelving. Griffin stepped to the counter. The clerk handed Griffin his driver's license and ran his gas card through the slot and waited. *Now. Ask her now.* Two cans of beer slammed down on the counter just behind Griffin. Griffin turned. It was the teenager.

"Excuse me, miss," Griffin said.

She looked at Griffin just as the credit card machine began clattering out the receipt. Griffin tried to ignore the stale cigarette smoke mixed with the smell of stale beer and body odor that surrounded the boy. An idea came to Griffin.

"Is there a medical facility around here?" he asked the clerk. "Like a medical clinic?"

The clerk ripped the receipt slip from the machine. She dropped it on the counter and handed a pen to Griffin. "I don't know, mister," she said. She glanced at the teenager, then looked back at Griffin. "I only got here a couple weeks ago. Sign the white slip. You keep the yellow one."

"Any kind of big building?" Griffin asked. "Maybe in the country somewhere?"

271

"I said I just been around here a couple of weeks, mister," she said. She shot another glance at the teenager.

"Thanks," Griffin said. He signed the receipt, handed the original to the clerk, then turned to leave.

"Wait, mister," the teenager said. He turned to the clerk. "Darlene, why you lying to the man?" he asked.

"Ain't nobody's business, Wayno," the clerk said. "Comer said nobody was supposed to say nothing. He finds out I said something, I get beat up again."

"You tell Comer I talked about it," the teenager said. "Here, I pumped five dollars, and these beers."

"I'm goin' to get pink-slipped for selling you these, Wayno."

"Comer's goin' to pink-slip you out of your livin', anyway," the teenager said.

"Come on out to my truck, mister," Wayno said to Griffin.

"Johnny," Wayno hollered as he and Griffin walked to the El Camino. "This guy wants to know about the crematory."

Johnny opened the passenger door and walked around to the driver's side of the El Camino. Wayno tossed him a beer.

"Why you wanna know, mister?" Johnny asked Griffin, popping his beer.

"Why do you guys call it a crematory?" Griffin asked Johnny.

"That's a place where you burn people, ain't it?" Wayno asked. "Like the Nazis burnt Jews?" He took a swig and leaned against the front fender of the El Camino. He put his free hand in his jeans.

Wayno and Johnny were going to tell one of those small-town tales, Griffin thought. There's always a little truth in those tales.

"They do some weird stuff there, man. Local cops know about it but don't do nothin'," Johnny said.

"Military operation," Wayno said. "That's what everybody says. Army turned an old bomb shelter into a secret place for top-secret military operations."

Bomb shelter. *They're talking about a fallout shelter.* Griffin hadn't heard those words in decades. Images of himself ducking under desks in elementary school passed through his mind.

Johnny threw back his head, poured the last of the beer into his mouth, and swallowed. "Bunch of garbage," he said, then swiped his mouth with the back of his hand and belched. He tossed the can in the back of the El Camino. "Last year, Wayno dared me to sneak over that razor fence it's got. Said he would get me a date with. . .well. I dug under the fence and got caught. Got close to the building, though. The guards are stupid. Real stupid."

"Especially Comer!" Wayno laughed. "Dresses like Rambo in those soldier clothes." Wayno finished off his beer and tossed the can in the back of the truck.

"They didn't turn me in for trespassin'," Johnny said. "They kept askin' what I seen. Comer said they'd beat it outta me. I didn't see nothin'. But the air smelled awful. Ever burn your hair? That's what it smelt like."

"They burnin' people all right," Wayno said. "We think they burnin' homeless people who don't pay taxes or something."

Johnny crossed his arms. "Jason, the guardhouse guard, told Comer to let me go. But Comer likes to hurt kids and women. He took a punch at me. Broke my nose. See?"

Johnny moved his head closer to Griffin and rubbed a knot on the bridge of his nose.

"Just tell me where the place is," Griffin said, trying to calm the eagerness rising in him.

"No problem," Wayno said, "but you ain't going to remember if we just tell you, not with all these back roads around here."

"Wait. Just a minute," Griffin said. He hurried to the Concorde and lifted the maps from the passenger seat. He looked toward the store while he closed the passenger door.

Darlene stood behind the counter staring at him through the glass storefront with her arms folded across her blue E-Z Store smock. Griffin hurried back to the teenagers. He handed Johnny the detailed road maps. "Show me where, son," he said to Johnny.

"You sure are anxious, mister," Wayno said.

Johnny stared at the map. "I ain't never seen maps like this," he said as if to himself.

Griffin craned his neck gazing at the map, partially holding his breath.

"It ain't easy to find," Wayno said, leaning toward Johnny. "It's off 228 in the middle of the corn patches."

"There's 228," Johnny said. "And there's the first turn."

"Let me look, Johnny," Wayno said. "You need to start with Tractor Road."

"I know, I know—there, right there," Johnny said. He poked his finger at the upper corner of the map and turned to Griffin. "This here's Tractor Road," he said.

"Okay, mister," Johnny said as he tilted the map toward Griffin. "See here? We're here now. Keep goin' on 67, toward Ozark. Right here is Highway 228. Go right. Ya gotta be careful now, 'cause the next turn, right here, is easy to miss. See this road?" he asked Griffin.

Griffin nodded, concentrating.

"Turn right, there," Johnny said. "That's north. Don't know what that road is called, but about a mile up, you'll see an intersection, an old rusty sign, leaning. That's Tractor Road. About a mile and a half more along the corn patch, the crematory is on the right." Johnny poked the map with his pointer finger. "Right there," he said.

"They made a big hill around it, except for the front. People say it has an elevator goes all the way down to hell," Wayno said.

"Nobody believes that bunk, Wayno," Johnny said.

"Well, maybe that ain't so, but you better watch out, mister. Comer beat up Johnny real good. He was crying like a baby when they let him outta there with a broken nose."

"That ain't so!" Johnny yelled at Wayno. "Anyway, Comer won't pick a fight with him; he's as big as Comer is."

"Where's the nearest motel?" Griffin asked.

"About four miles down the highway," Wayno said. "Called the Bell Motel. Ain't the kind you probably used to, though, with a TV and all. You gotta go all the way to Ozark if you want that."

"Better take some air freshener!" Johnny said with a chuckle. "That old lady, she's like the one in that old Hitchcock *Psycho* show, and just about as crazy, too."

"Thanks, boys," Griffin said. He slipped into his rented Concorde, dropped the maps on the passenger seat, and sped away.

It had to be the place, Griffin thought. Griffin felt his pulse increase. He needed surveillance. Most of all, he needed help. Not another person, just help. Griffin couldn't think it through, couldn't understand why he felt that way. He wanted orders. A Captain.

But how am I to get that?

Griffin felt it was more than the marine in him, more than retribution or revenge for Warren and Jennifer. This was the beginning of a fight for something much greater. If only Jennifer were here to help him, even preach to him. If only he had not abandoned his faith. Griffin remembered what Allan Cook had told him. He felt guilt, and now fear.

You stop now, Griffin, you spend the rest of your life in federal prison.

⌐⌐

Ahead on the left was the Bell Motel, a dozen small sun-blistered cabins that all leaned slightly. Weeds covered everything.

Griffin pulled in front of the largest cabin with a sign on its door that read "Registration Office."

As Griffin stepped inside, an elderly woman came out of a small room behind a wood counter. Her neck appeared to have grown out of her hunched shoulders, reminding Griffin of a turtle's neck—a turtle with thinning gray hair.

The old woman looked at Griffin with a puzzled stare through her thick glasses. "Who are you?" she asked.

She peered over Griffin's shoulder, out the window, then returned her gaze to Griffin, still appearing puzzled. "You alone?" she asked.

"How much for a room?" Griffin asked.

"Staying overnight?" the old lady asked.

"Two days," Griffin said, trying to control the images of *Psycho* running through his mind in black and white.

"Cabin number eight," the woman said. "Forty dollars." She reached under the counter, produced a key, then dropped the key on the countertop. "We don't have television, just that pay phone there. We don't have a pool, either. And we don't have room service or a restaurant."

"Fine," Griffin said.

She glanced out the window again, then looked at Griffin. "Sure you're alone?" she asked.

"Yes, ma'am," Griffin said. He paused for a moment, then asked, "Ma'am, do you know anything about a building built into a hill on a road off Highway 228, just past Tractor Road?"

The old lady straightened her head as much as her tired neck and shoulder bones would permit. Griffin could see her scalp redden through her thin gray hair. Her eyes widened behind her glasses. She shot another glance out the window and turned back to Griffin.

"Mister," she said, with a look that urged Griffin to heed her warning, "you shouldn't be asking people around here about that place."

"How much did you say the room was? Fifty dollars?" Griffin slapped a fifty on the counter.

The old lady opened the drawer. The bill disappeared. She leaned toward Griffin. "That used to be a fallout shelter for the governor and the mayors, all those people who thought they shouldn't be blown up by the Russians, but it isn't a shelter anymore."

"What is it?" Griffin asked while he slipped another twenty on the counter.

The old lady shoved the twenty back toward Griffin. "Sir," she said, "unless you are willing to buy this place from me at my price, that's all you'll get from me."

Griffin drove to the cabin, an 8 marked on the door with what looked like black finger paint. He grabbed the maps, got out of the car, lifted the duffel bag and suitcase from the backseat, and walked to the cabin. He unlocked the door and swung it open. A mixture of stale cigarette smoke, cheap perfume, and sour liquor aggravated his sinuses. Griffin stepped inside.

Cigarette burns stained the Formica dresser top. Yellow-brown stains speckled the mattress where the dirty sheets didn't cover it. Griffin had seen worse. Mud trenches in the forest during the driving rain with the smell of blood in the water running under him.

Griffin set the suitcase and duffel bag on the floor next to the bed. He needed sleep now. He glanced at his watch: 4:22. He checked the map again. About thirty-five minutes to get there, maybe give himself twice that time. He had to be on watch at 7:00 when the shift changed. The more activity he could see, the better.

One hour, Griffin. Ignore the stench and get one hour of shuteye. You remember how that used to be, sleeping in mud and stench, but grab a shirt from the suitcase and wrap that pillow with it before you put your head on it.

CHAPTER 25

Ramos flipped the switch on the tracking device from "city" to "rural" then back again as DiRosa drove on Airline Highway. No beeps, no flickers of light. "She ain't around here, man," Ramos said. He felt sick in his disappointment. He wanted to call this guy "stupid" again, but decided not to.

"We will find her," DiRosa said. "I'm going to pull in here, use the phone."

"Who you calling, man?" Ramos asked.

"Just stay put," DiRosa said.

Ramos watched DiRosa at the pay phone in front of one of the used car lots that lined Tulane Highway at the edge of Orleans Parish. *Bet he's talking to that England woman.* DiRosa hung up and dialed another number. *Who is he calling now, man?*

"We gotta watch some senator's office back toward Kenner," DiRosa said to Ramos after he slid behind the steering wheel.

"The girl ain't gonna be there, man," Ramos said.

"Listen, pig, we have to be careful with that body in the trunk. Those blankets can't hold the smell too long."

"I ain't stupid, man."

"She's somewhere around Gators' offices in Kenner or across the lake," DiRosa said. "We cruise and watch all afternoon, most of the night. All day tomorrow. No way she can resist coming back to Peacock Inn. It's a natural thing for her to do. We'll hide the car. Stay there tonight."

"I don't know, man," Ramos said, feeling Sweetness slipping away from him.

"You listen to that receiver and watch."

"Where we gonna dump the kid's body?" Ramos asked.

"We dump the car with him in it. I fly away and disappear," DiRosa said. "You go back to Chicago and see to it that Landcaster pays us, or you both get a visit from me. Then I never see you again unless you break our business agreement." DiRosa paused. Fixing his gaze on Ramos's eyes, he said, "If you do that, I come back out of nowhere and blow your stupid brains out of you."

"I can keep a secret, man," Ramos said. *I ain't afraid of you, man,* Ramos wanted to say.

"You don't talk to me," DiRosa said. "Don't say nothing about Cuba, Castro, or the way you slice up women. I don't want to hear it. Understand?"

"I get the girl when we find her, just like Landcaster said."

DiRosa sighed. "Gators' office is around here somewhere, on a street called Clearview," he said. "Help me look for it."

"Sure, man. Sure." Ramos felt good that DiRosa asked him to help. "Who else you called, man? I'm your partner. I ought to know," he said.

DiRosa said nothing as he made a U-turn and headed back toward Kenner.

"You can trust me about your name, man. I keep secrets good."

"Just remember our agreement," DiRosa said.

Silence.

"When I met Landcaster, he was on vacation in Miami," Ramos said softly. "Maybe twelve years ago. He paid my way to Los Angeles. I collected rent from apartments he owned. Collected loans, too. Stuff like that." Ramos paused. "I liked it in L.A. Everybody was so friendly. They don't care how people look."

"Just watch and listen to the tracker," DiRosa said.

"He was doing abortions. He got into trouble with one of the teenagers. I saw her, man. She was a beautiful Hispanic. They have gangs out there. The cops, they ain't so bad—just get a good lawyer.

But the gangs, man, that's something else. The DA told him to leave town, but he was going to do that anyway. Those gangs, man, they don't fool around when they get mad at you, like Castro's secret police, man."

DiRosa turned his head away from Ramos. Ramos was sure DiRosa was looking for street names. Maybe listening to his story, too. *Now I know he's going to be my friend.* "I promised Landcaster I'd never tell nobody about that teenager. See, you can trust me, man. I keep secrets good."

DiRosa shook his head again.

Griffin lifted himself from his office floor. The documents that covered him fell away, all of them with BioSysTech letterhead, each with different writing on them in varying colors, red mostly. When he reached a standing position, he extended one arm in front of him and brushed his suit jacket sleeve with the other. Then he brushed the front of his suit with the palms of both hands. He straightened his tie and looked down, ready to pick up the BioSysTech papers. *Thank you, Warren,* the thought came to him. *They really helped.* But the documents disappeared when his gaze fell on the carpet again. Was that Walter Schneider snarling in the background?

Warren Jennings stood at the threshold, not quite in the office. "You wouldn't believe me."

"Warren, I. . ." Griffin reached out his hand.

While Jennings faded away, Carolyn Jennings rose up from the carpet, replacing her husband's image, wearing a black dress, a black veil covering her face. "Griffin, I have to know the truth," Carolyn said. "Why don't you tell me the truth? My family is ruined; my children's souls are dying. Can you do something for my boys, Griffin?"

As she faded, Griffin cried out to her, "I'm sorry, Carolyn. I will help your boys. . .somehow." Then she was gone.

"Griffin," a charred figure called to him softly, standing at the threshold of the office door. "I died in your place, Griffin," Jennifer said. Griffin started to cry. "I'm all right, Griffin. This is the old body I left behind," Jennifer said, then faded away.

"Excuse me, Griffin, may I come in?" Constance Frye asked. Griffin looked up. Constance was gone. Then in front of him, sitting in the one of the client chairs. . .was Ruth. Constance materialized in the other client chair. /

"Ruth. . .Ruth!" Griffin yelled. She couldn't hear him.

"Where's my husband! Where's my Avraham!" Ruth cried out to Constance.

"Which Avraham?" Constance asked, laughing hard, her green eyes gleaming. "Yours or mine?" she asked.

As Ruth lowered her head crying and Constance bobbed her head laughing, they faded away.

Griffin was now sitting in his chair, Columbia's skyline behind him. "Why do you think your Captain is not with you, Griffin?" The voice came from a glowing form of a man standing at his office door. A mist that accentuated the glow rose in his office.

"I. . .I. . ."

"Your Captain has never left you," the apparition said. "It was you who left Me, Griffin. You deserted the good fight."

"Can I come back?" Griffin asked.

"What are you wearing, Griffin?"

Now Griffin stood in the middle of his office, in fatigues, holding a rock in his right hand. *Do you remember, Griffin? Do you remember whose battle it really is?*

The form dissipated. Jennifer stepped out of the mist wearing a flowing white robe. She glistened and gleamed. She glided up to Griffin. "Remember discussion time, Griffin?" Griffin felt a lump form in his throat and perhaps a pang of fear.

"Maybe you should lead this one, Jennifer," Griffin said. "And you can preach, too, if you want."

"They're stealing His little temples, Griffin," Jennifer said. "Defiling them. You must listen to Him; He's your Captain. He's the

281

Captain of the host. He has selected you. He will speak to you through your heart. Listen. Prepare yourself as Allan told you."

"Jennifer. . ."

"I have to go now," Jennifer said. "Do not despair for me, for I was ready. I return to gold streets and a mansion, and to songs and praise."

Jennifer began to fade in the mist.

"Jennifer!" Griffin called.

"They're praying for you, Griffin," Jennifer said as she vaporized, her voice sounding as though it resonated from a distance. "Pastor Grady, the congregation, Allan. We feel their prayers. It is up to you. . . ."

Gone.

Griffin jumped out of the bed. The dream was so real he had to regain his thoughts. Jennifer. She was real, and so was the Captain in the mist, Griffin was certain. Ruth and Constance, Warren and Carol were creations of his own mind, but not Jennifer and that man. And he was sure Jennifer had come to give him an important piece of the puzzle: "They're stealing His little temples, Griffin." *No, not buildings, Griffin. Remember? Temples? In Scripture, our bodies are referred to as "temples."*

Griffin fell on his knees. He set his elbows on the bed and rested his forehead on his clasped hands. He closed his eyes. "Lord, my Captain," he said softly, "my enemies come with swords, but I go into this battle with You, and with You, I can do all things. Faith I must have, but this battle is Yours."

"I am your Captain, Griffin," the Voice said. "I am with you always."

Griffin remained still and silent in the warmth. He stood. He glanced at his watch: less than an hour of sleep. No matter, not now. He had to get into his fatigues and sort out his equipment. Then it occurred to him that he had reenlisted in the army of soldiers fighting the good fight. Should he fail, should he die or prevail, was not a consideration. Just fight.

"You paid a quarter of a million dollars out of the business's operating account?" England yelled.

"The guy doesn't get the other half until he gets it right," Landcaster said.

"Forget it! How do you think we're going to explain it? Capital expenditure?" England asked.

England had told DiRosa when he called her from a pay phone in New Orleans that Landcaster was reckless and dangerous. "After you get the documents and the girl," England had told DiRosa, "do Landcaster."

"Okay, okay," Landcaster said, "the guy's probably on the run, anyway. He's probably hiding in Canada or somewhere, shaking in his drawers."

"That's what Constance and I think, too, Richard," England said. "You really scared him. You just keep doing the good job you're doing there in Chicago. Just leave Dowell alone until the Hegel Bill makes it through the Senate, okay?"

With the background noise of trucks rumbling down Airline Highway, England had told DiRosa when he called her from the pay phone that the hit should look like the result of an argument between Landcaster and Ramos, not one of DiRosa's signature two-shot killings, one in the forehead and the second, the insurance shot, behind an ear.

"Yeah, that's going to settle things down," Landcaster said. "When the law is passed, we can operate like a real business."

"And you're an important part of the business, Richard," England said. "We need you to keep it going."

England had suggested to DiRosa that Landcaster probably should be stabbed with Ramos's knife—make it look like an argument about money between old business friends.

"That's nice of you to say, Kristina," Landcaster said. "I owe you. I really do."

The hit should be far away from Chicago, England had instructed DiRosa. Somehow she would get Landcaster and Ramos to go to the Caymans. "It should happen there," England had said to DiRosa. "Don't tell Vic. After the hits, disappear."

————

A forest of cornstalks planted in orderly rows, green and tall, lined Highway 67 and Highway 228. Griffin made the turn, thinking only a farmer would be on this road or perhaps someone working at the facility. But a guy in a rental car, wearing fatigues? Right. Why don't you just yell to them, "Hey, I'm coming after you!"

A dirt road barely wide enough for two cars came into view. A wood post, with a white, rusted metal sign, leaned in the narrow grassy area between the road and the cornfield. Through rust stains, Griffin made out the words "Tractor Road." Griffin turned left. He steadied the front tires as they wriggled in and out of the furrows that had been gouged by big tractor tires. After about a quarter mile, Griffin got out of his car. He strapped on his equipment belt, smudged green gook on his face and hands, and entered the cornstalk forest.

Griffin checked his watch. He began maneuvering parallel to the unnamed highway, trying to avoid bumping into the cornstalks so the tops would not move. At the end of each row, he could see the highway; there was no reason why he would not have heard vehicles if any drove by. None had. He maneuvered through the field for twenty-two minutes.

A few more rows. No facility on the other side. More rows. Nothing. Griffin checked his watch: twenty-six minutes. The facility had to be there. The teenagers might have been lying, but the old woman wasn't. That warning through those squinting eyes wasn't an act. A few more rows. Then an odor—faint, very faint. Johnny was right. That's flesh or hair. Jennifer's charred body popped into his mind's eye. His heart sank.

No, Griffin, remember what she looks like now and where she is. Keep crawling.

On the other side of the highway, the corner of a hurricane fence came into view, maybe twelve or fourteen feet high with three-foot razor coils running along the top. After the next row of cornstalks, Griffin crawled closer to the highway, about twenty-five feet in. Then another three rows. The building had to be close. He glanced at his watch: 6:10. Good. Forty, maybe fifty yards of fence. Griffin moved forward slowly, row by row. It had to be. . . . *There it is!*

Griffin crawled on the plowed dirt, now about ten feet inside the corn patch from the edge of the highway. A cement-faced fallout shelter stood right there, right across the highway, embedded in a hill, just like Wayno and Johnny had described. Griffin had believed that all of these monuments to the Cold War had long since been razed, but here one stood, like a temple, and in his own state. *How could a governor not know, Ashton? Of course you knew, didn't you? And Constance. The green-eyed goddess of the temple.*

Griffin pulled his binoculars out of their case. He pushed his elbows in the soft dirt and brought the lenses to his eyes. He concentrated as he watched. A guard sat in a guardhouse positioned directly in front of the facility. He could just see the guard's head. He was sitting, reading. Griffin scanned the area. There were two lanes, one on each side of the guardhouse, the left an exit, the right an entrance. The right lane had a lift gate.

Movement on the outside of the guardhouse! Griffin quickly shifted the binoculars. Another soldier. No, not a soldier. Those weren't regulation fatigues. Close, but not regulation. The guard strode along the walkway in front of the concrete facility and stepped into the parking lot. A white Lexus, two pickup trucks, one with ridiculously big wheels and jacked up at least three feet off the ground, a big Bronco, and a Mazda were parked in the lot. The guard climbed into a military-style Jeep. These men, or whomever they worked for, were attempting to convince the locals they were army. It wouldn't take too much, after all.

Preliminary assessment: two outside guards, one inside guard, an executive of some sort inside, with a secretary or some type of worker.

The guard drove the Jeep to the exit lane, stopped for a moment at the guardhouse, and yelled something. He turned onto the highway, toward the Tractor Road intersection. He drove slowly. Looking to one side, then. . .Griffin rolled over and lay still on his back. The Jeep kept going. Griffin studied the sound of the engine. A tightly geared four-cylinder. He had ridden in many of them himself in Vietnam, had even gotten used to the characteristic grinding whine at its top speed of fifty.

Griffin resumed his surveillance position and glanced at his watch: 6:30. The guard was probably going on a scheduled patrol.

Keep that in mind, Griffin. Thirty-minute scheduled patrols. He'll be coming back the other direction soon.

Griffin decided to crawl backward a few yards and snuggle up to the cornstalks just a bit more. He could still see the parking lot beyond the guardhouse and the dull gray steel door, maybe eight feet high and ten feet wide. That had to be the entrance to the concrete facility. It had to be an electronically opened door; it was too large to be opened by a human. A ramp led up to the door to accommodate vehicles.

The door jolted, then began to slide back. Griffin jerked back slightly. The door slid open about four feet and stopped. A heavyset black woman stepped out. The door slammed shut behind her. The lady walked toward a white Lexus. He watched as she opened the driver's door of the Lexus and slid behind the driver's seat.

Griffin heard the jeep's engine whining hard. He turned on his back and lay flat, holding the binoculars close to his stomach. The Jeep passed. Griffin resumed his surveillance position.

The Lexus pulled out of the facility and turned toward Tractor Road.

The steel door opened again. A white male, maybe in his thirties, got into the Mazda. He wore scrubs. A doctor, nurse? He backed out and drove out the exit, the guard in the guardhouse standing outside now, waving the little sedan through the exit.

A tattered Ford Thunderbird built in the '70s, the kind with a long front end and a body that outlasted its paint, pulled up to the entrance. The guard in the guardhouse stood and moved his arm. The lift gate rose. Another pickup, with six lights racked over its cab and two men in it, pulled behind the Thunderbird. The seven o'clock shift was here.

The pickup and Thunderbird parked. The two men who jumped out of the pickup wore the same army-like gear as the guards. Griffin shifted to view the Thunderbird driver's door. It looked like the driver was dressing. The door opened. The driver climbed out of the Thunderbird. He wore a green beret and matching ascot with his green and brown camouflage–patterned shirt. He bent down, reached into the Thunderbird, and lifted out a carbine and cartridge belt. As he walked toward the Jeep, he slipped the cartridge belt over his shoulder so that it angled across his chest. His shoulders dipped and lifted as he strutted. His holstered .45 swung on his side. Rambo.

That's got to be Comer.

Comer tossed the carbine into the Jeep and climbed in. Griffin shifted again. One of the guards from the pickup stepped to the steel entrance door and reached into his top pocket—*Watch him, Griffin; watch closely*—and lifted out a card. Fat—pudgy, even. One good one in that soft belly would do him in. Griffin felt better about this one. *Got to get Rambo first.*

The chubby guard inserted the card into a slot just to the left of the door. The door slid open about four feet. The guard entered the facility. The door slid shut behind him. Comer strutted from the Jeep to the guardhouse. The guard beginning his shift in the guardhouse was about five-nine. Thin. Easy.

You'll have do deal with three guards at about three or so this morning, Griffin. One in the guardhouse, one inside the facility, Comer on patrol. Griffin figured he would have to contend with Comer first, clearly the strong arm of the graveyard shift, its first line of defense. The element of offensive surprise was the essence of Griffin's battle plan. It had to be; if Comer weren't caught off guard, Griffin believed he himself would be too injured if he managed to overtake him to get into the facility. Sneak and hide, then pounce on Comer? Sure! Right out here by the open highway and chain-link fence.

Better get ready to do a little play acting, Griffin.

Griffin needed some bourbon. What did he used to drink? Wild Turkey? Too smooth. Something else. Something a little harsher. Old Granddad. That will do, but just a half pint!

⌐ ┴ ┐

Amanda stood in front of the bathroom mirror to assess her success in mimicking the young females standing along the choppy asphalt lane. She stretched toward the mirror. She puckered her glossy red lips and gently rubbed her blue eye shadow. She straightened and pulled on the bottom hem of her powder-blue shirt. Wal-Mart didn't have one with a rhinestone bird figure, but the red sequin double heart with two chubby cupids flying over it looked just as appropriate. Black leggings and a lot of gold costume jewelry completed her new look. Amanda put her hands on her waist as she gazed in the mirror. She twisted from one side to the other with her feet planted on the carpet. Not a bad-looking game uniform, she thought.

Ten o'clock. Time to leave. Amanda decided to keep the package in the trunk of the Mustang; she felt more comfortable having it with her at all times. More game strategy. She picked up the package and left the apartment, then got into the bugged Mustang, lowered the top, and headed for the choppy lane in search of the talkative teen with a gun in his pocket.

⌐ ┴ ┐

Griffin stepped into the E-Z Store. Darlene stared at him with her arms crossed over her blue smock. He walked to the refrigerated shelves at the back of the store and lifted out two ready-made liver cheese sandwiches and a quart bottle of orange juice. He stepped to the counter.

"Don't tell me you got a job with that place, too," Darlene said.

"What?" Griffin asked.

"Why you wearin' soldier clothes?" she asked. "Never mind. Don't say nothin'." She started punching the cash register's keys, shooting glances at Griffin's face.

"I looked for the place," he said. "Nothing but cornstalks. I don't believe a word Wayno and Johnny said."

"That's good, mister," Darlene said. "Real good."

"Give me a half pint of Old Granddad for the ride home. Going to mind my own business; so you don't have to worry about your boyfriend."

"I ain't telling Comer nothin'," Darlene said as she stuffed the sandwiches in a plastic bag. "He'd break Johnny's nose again if he knew they go around talking like that." She lowered the juice and whiskey into another plastic bag. "Ain't nothin' out there, anyway. I told you that, mister."

———

After Griffin returned to cabin 8, he pulled out a casual shirt and jeans from the duffel bag. He sprinkled some Old Granddad on them and then took off his dirty fatigues. He thought how nice a hot shower would feel when the odor of his armpits rose as he lifted his elbows to slip on the cheap bourbon-scented shirt. Then he realized he had to remove the green gook off his face if he was going to pull this off. *Drunks don't wear military camouflage, Griffin.*

He ate the sandwiches, washing them down with the orange juice. He moved his tongue along his teeth. A good tooth brushing would be nice, too. He poured whiskey in his mouth and gargled it. That taste. The last time it had been in his mouth was the day he told Constance the story of the man and the snake. "Someday I'll sink my fangs into you, Griffin."

Griffin set his wristwatch alarm for 2:30 A.M. He lay on his stomach on the floor and began doing push-ups. He kept going until he was out of breath. Two hundred? Griffin hadn't kept count. Then he turned and lay on his back. When his breath slowed to normal, as new sweat began to bead on his forehead, he began doing sit-ups, crunching hard until his abdominal muscles sent him the message,

"That's it, marine!" Sweat saturated the front of his shirt; he felt the cloth clinging to his back. Griffin got up off the floor and lay on the bed. He lay on his back on the stained sheet and mattress. He crossed his arms over his chest. "I know you are with me, Captain," he said softly. He felt himself drift into sleep.

———

Looking for the brick buildings on the choppy asphalt lane and finding them wasn't as easy as getting lost and suddenly being there, but Amanda knew she had to take the Orleans Avenue–Vieux Carre exit on I-10, then veer right, away from the city. When she exited, she craned her neck as she drove; cars behind her tailgated then passed her as the drivers tossed up their hands in a huff. Then she saw the it—the lane and the red brick sixplexes with their brown patches for lawns. *How could I have—well, I did.* Amanda turned.

As soon as she turned onto the lane, she saw the glowing street lamps creating oases of dimly lighted areas along the lane. Kids darted about on the side of the alley in the light. No babies, but small kids who should have been sleeping.

Amanda continued to cruise toward the lights, her left arm on the driver's door, the entire night sky above her in the convertible Mustang. That young lawyer at LeMadelines, that Bradley, he had to be talking about this. He had to be.

She slowed to an idle. No one stared at her; she wasn't an uninvited stranger now, not in her uniform. Suddenly, there he stood, the talkative teen, standing at the front edge of the court, swinging the cell phone in his hand.

One of the young men with the teen turned his head, looked Amanda's way, and tapped his friend on the shoulder. The teen stopped talking and turned. He smiled and began to walk toward Amanda. Two young men followed him. Amanda stopped.

He stopped. He rested his left elbow on top of the Mustang's windshield frame.

Amanda smiled. She waited for him to say something.

"Honey, you are the most beautiful thing I ever seen," he said with a bright smile. "You gotta tell me your name."

"I need something," Amanda said. "I think you might be able to get it for me."

"Whatever you want, I can get."

"I need a gun," Amanda said, staring hard at him, feeling an air of negotiations moving in on them. "At least a thirty-two caliber, with cartridges."

The teen jumped back from the Mustang. "Hey, there's laws out there about them things," he said.

Amanda glanced downward. She set her stare on the teen. "What about the piece in your pocket?" she asked.

The teen stood up and stiffened. "You can get your pretty self hurt, girl. Hurt bad," he said. He seemed to calm down, then rested his arm on the windshield frame again and leaned toward Amanda. He smiled. "What if I pull you outta this fine machine, take out my piece, and do whatever I please?" he asked.

"Listen, boy," Amanda said, scared to death but staring as she remembered her father had in his rages, with eyes glaring and brow furrowed. "Go ahead and try."

The teen jumped back. "Wow!" he said. "Don't worry, baby, I don't want no trouble! Just playing."

"Stop playing marbles like a kid," Amanda said. "How much for the gun?" Amanda felt sweat forming under her arms.

"Sit pretty," the teen said.

Amanda watched as the teen and the other two strutted away. Then fear shot through her when she realized where they seemed to be headed—toward a policeman standing in a dark area. *Speed away, now!*

The three boys stopped in front of the policeman. The talkative teen was throwing his hands around as if negotiating or explaining. He pointed his cell phone at Amanda. The policeman glared at her. *Start the car, Amanda; get out of here.*

The policeman said something to the teen and whisked him

away. The teen turned and strutted back to Amanda. He stood next to the driver's door and scanned the area quickly. "Two hundred dollars for me; a hundred for the man," he said in a firm tone. "He wants you to show me what bills you have first."

"What?" Amanda asked.

"I need to see the money," he said. "I don't see big bills, you don't get your gun."

Amanda opened her purse. She fumbled to find her wallet. She lifted six one-hundred dollar bills partially from her wallet's fold. "Good enough?" she asked.

"This gun business is gettin' better every day," the teen said. He lifted his hand with the cell phone and waved it.

Amanda glanced at the policeman. He was going to come at any time. *He's just waiting for transfer of money, for a completed illegal transaction.* She glanced at her watch: 11:40. In a few minutes she would be either armed to kill or on her way to jail. What would Daddy say?

One of the two teens who had been following the talkative one came running out the front door of the building swinging a McDonald's paper bag. He stopped at the Mustang and handed the bag to his leader. The teen opened the bag, glanced inside, and handed the bag to Amanda.

The paper bag didn't have a spot without a dirty crinkle. Amanda gazed into it. She saw a pistol and a box. Amanda lifted the pistol out of the bag. A three-inch barrel, .38 revolver. She held it under the dash. She released the mechanism holding the chamber in place. She flipped the chamber to the side and spun it, then slapped the chamber back in its place. She cocked the hammer and studied the form of it. She put her thumb on it. She squeezed the trigger slowly until the hammer released in the grip of her thumb. She pulled the trigger. A double-action revolver, the spring mechanism in good shape. She raised the gun to her nose and sniffed. Well oiled. She lowered the gun into the bag. She checked the box. The cartridges were there, all of them.

"You handle that real good," the teen said. "With my customers, if I give them a bad product, they would use it on me."

Amanda lowered the bag to the floor on the passenger side. She glanced at the policeman. He was watching.

"Here." Amanda handed the teen three bills and started the Mustang. Its engine rumbled. "Good doing business with you," she said.

I'll be back. Somehow.

The teen smiled while he stuffed the bills in his pocket. Amanda shot another glance at the policeman. He was looking away now. Amanda turned her head and put the Mustang into gear.

As she lifted her foot slowly off the clutch and the Mustang began to move, the talkative teen yelled, "You need to do any more business, you come right back and ask for me—the man with the plan!"

CHAPTER 26

To B/M0012, six years wasn't a long time. Nothing was a long time. Time didn't exist. But while he lay in the incubator, he had developed a modicum of thought power. And sometime during his life the thought had actually come to him: *Why I know my mother do?* His mother was named "Doctor," B/M0012 had come to believe. She came around with his father, the one that made fewer words. Or was his father the other that a voice in him said to look at with his one eye?

B/M0012 felt pain every day, especially when things were put inside him. *All feel pain like that, but Mother have no things in her.*

"Well, my precious B/M0012," Reed said, "it's Final Harvest for you. Disconnect, Nurse."

"Yes, Doctor."

Mother, take me out. The light come hurt eye.

The nurse disconnected B/M0012's incubator. He pulled on it; it slid from its mounting. He reached into the incubator and disconnected the tubes at their harnesses about three inches from B/M0012's torso. Then he disconnected the tube leading to B/M0012's mouth, the harness for it about two inches from B/M0012's face. The nurse lifted B/M0012 and laid him on a gurney.

"Hello, my precious," Reed said, stroking B/M0012's long, entangled black hair.

Can't open eye like did once; want to see you, Mama.

When the nurse pushed the gurney out of the softly UV-lighted conceptus growing room into the hallway, the illumination from the fluorescent ceiling lights penetrated B/M0012's closed eyelid. Pain shot through the eye and into his skull. B/M0012 let out a soft moan. *Eye hurt make noise this time!*

"I knew it! I just knew it!" Reed yelled. "It moaned! This conceptus didn't get enough alkaloid! That's why it managed to move that eye!"

B/M0012 moaned softly again.

"Don't worry, baby," Reed said. "It'll all be over with soon."

B/M0012 began moving its head from side to side. Reed couldn't believe it.

The nurse stopped the gurney.

Here before.

The nurse lifted B/M0012, then laid him on the operating table.

Been here before; will hurt eye big more.

The nurse strapped B/M0012's arms to the table and then its legs, then laid a strap across its forehead. He switched on the operating light over the table.

"Ohhh." B/M0012 tried to roll its head to the side.

"This won't hurt a bit, my precious," Reed said.

B/M0012 moaned again as something pierced its fatless arm at the bend inside its elbow.

"There now," Reed said. "In just a minute or two all the pain will go away." Silence for a moment. "Nurse," Reed said, "make a note: I want to review B/M0012's chart." Reed recounted her observations to reconsider the current methods and to develop a new hypothesis: "The reason B/M0012 responded so well to the incubator protocol had to be because of the lesser amount of alkaloid. There has to be a middle ground on this. Maybe a little more than what this conceptus received, but we have room to move downward on the alkaloid concentrations in the new conceptuses."

Feel. . .feel like. . .can't talk to me no more, can't hear Mother no. . .

The rise and fall of B/M0012's belly stopped.

"Termination," Reed said. "Let's get to work."

"Yes, Doctor."

"Look this way," the Voice said to B/M0012. "My light does not hurt."

It was the Voice that had told B/M0012 to look at that other man. B/M0012 had obeyed, ready to endure the sharp pain sure to come.

Nothing was above him but bright light, and there was no pain. Something different. B/M0012 gazed at his arms. They were larger, much larger. His hands were strong; he felt new strength in his fists. And his legs. He saw muscles pushing on the smooth, shiny, dark brown skin. He moved his hands on his chest and belly. Smooth. No scars.

Eyes open! Both of them! And B/M0012 realized it now: He could think clearly; he felt his mind swelling with memories.

B/M0012 looked down. He saw two people leaning over his corpse, straps across his forehead and thighs, working frantically, removing parts from the corpse's small cavity. The one B/M0012 thought might be his mother spoke as they removed parts, putting them into white buckets.

"That is not your mother," the Voice said. "You shall never see them again. But soon a day will come when they both shall stand before Me, and on that day I shall remind them of you, of your life, of this day, and of My other little temples they raised as they did you."

"My mama?" B/M0012 asked.

"She waits for you beyond My light."

"Is the other down there my father?"

"He is not," the Voice said.

"The other who visited, upon whom you commanded me to look with my one eye, is he my father?"

"No, but he is with Me, too," the Voice said. "He asked that I forgive him, and it is My promise to all that I will forgive when asked. Now he will ask your forgiveness. What will you say?"

"What did he do that I would need to forgive him? And if he did something, how can I not forgive him if You have? I should ask that You forgive me. I have done nothing in my life here."

"You obeyed My command," the Voice said.

The Voice fell silent for a moment, then said: "Your name is not 'B/M0012'; you shall never be called that again. Your name is 'Michael.' Your mother named you. But I knew your name when you were in her womb."

Little Michael felt a warm wind blowing on him.

Reed straightened from her hunch. "There," she said. "The harvest is complete. It's ready for the incinerator."

"Yes, Doctor."

The nurse unstrapped the small empty corpse and tossed it in a stainless steel cart.

"Now for rotten little W/F0776," Reed said as the nurse rolled the cart to the side of the operating room.

The wind increased and turned Michael upward.

"Who is my father?"

"I Am," the Voice said. "It is time for your true harvest. Now come."
Swoosh!

Michael felt himself flying up into the light. An image beyond the light was coming into focus. Michael moved faster. He could make out the image now: a beautiful young girl with her arms opened for him.

"Hurry, Michael!" the young girl called.

And Michael threw himself into her arms.

"Oh, thank You," Keondra yelled in joyful laughter that rang like small bells throughout the brilliant light.

FRIDAY, JUNE 28

CHAPTER 27

The high-pitched beeps from Griffin's watch alarm woke him. His first semiconscious breath, filled with the stench of sour whisky mixed with fermenting liver cheese and the fetid perspiration from his skin and clothes, yanked him through what otherwise would have been the slowly dissipating haze of an inordinately early awakening. Griffin pushed the button on the side of his watch and lifted himself out of the bed. He groped in the dark until his hand felt the light switch next to the cabin door. What he would do for a shower and a good tooth brushing! He slipped his bare feet into his tennis shoes, pushed his miniature camera down into his jeans, then lifted the car keys, the whisky bottle, and his infrared night-vision glasses off the dresser.

Under the bright stars and full moon of the June night, while the country folk slept, Griffin hurried to his rental car and headed for the intersection of that unnamed highway and Tractor Road. Along the way, twice he gargled swigs of whisky, swallowing just a little, allowing some to roll down his chin. The rest he used to muss his hair, while glancing in the rearview mirror.

Griffin stopped and turned out his lights about three miles before he reached the Tractor Road intersection. He strapped on his night vision glasses and glanced at his watch: 3:14. He gazed down the highway. No Jeep. Just as he expected.

Comer would be pulling out of the gate on his scheduled round in sixteen minutes, not much time to get into position. He accelerated down the highway and backed his car onto Tractor Road, parking it in the same area he had yesterday afternoon.

"Okay, Captain," Griffin said softly, "let's roll." He began his crawl through the stalks wearing his night-vision glasses, turning and twisting to keep from hitting the stalks. A pleasant romp considering what he had endured in the dark, critter-infested forests of southeast Asia.

After he spotted the beginning of the razor fence, Griffin scuttled about eight rows of cornstalks farther. He crawled to the edge of the cornfield, near the side of the unnamed highway, and watched for the Jeep. Not yet. He jerked the night-vision glasses off his face, dropped them in the dirt, and raced across the highway. When he felt the crunch of the rocks that lay between the highway and the strip of grass in front of the razor fence, he dove to the ground. He rolled until his hand hit the fence. He lay on the ground, on his stomach.

After what Griffin thought was perhaps twenty minutes, he heard the distant whine of a Jeep engine grinding through its gears. The sound came closer; his heart began to beat harder. He could perceive headlights. He pulled the bottle of whisky from his pocket. The sound of the Jeep's engine was right near him now. Its headlights shone on him. Griffin moaned. He heard the squeal of brakes. The door opened and shut. Griffin rolled his head and groaned. He lifted the bottle of whisky as if he were trying to take a swig. The bourbon trickled down the sides of his cheeks.

Footsteps crunched the gravel beside the highway, coming toward him. One man. *Is that you, Comer?*

"Now, just what do we got here?" the man said.

Griffin squinted his eyes as he looked up. He moved his forearm across his mouth, thinking it better not to try to slur words. He wasn't sure he could pull that off. Better to remain quiet.

"Ahhh!" Griffin heard himself say when the butt of the carbine hit a rib. Griffin kept his eyes shut. He rolled his head toward the fence and groaned. He knew the butt of the carbine would leave a deep bruise; bruises and contusions on the body are fine with marines in combat. *Pick me up, Comer. Are you Comer?*

"You filthy drunk dog. Wake up! I want you to feel the beating

I'm gonna give you."

Griffin's chest ached, but the anger that rose in him quenched the pain. This wasn't a Viet Cong fighting a military enemy; this was an American reveling in beating another American to death, a drunk unable to defend himself. Wayno was right. He would probably kill Darlene one day. Now Griffin's thigh throbbed. *Not if I can help it.*

"Maybe this will bring you around."

"Uhhh!" A steel boot toe landed in Griffin's side at the base of his rib cage.

Pick me up.

Griffin opened his eyes in a squint. He caught a glimpse of the ascot and the beret. He moaned again and rolled onto his back, away from Comer. If another kick was coming, better that it be on the side not already aching. *Pick me up, Comer. Pick me up.*

Comer set the toe of his boot on the nape of Griffin's neck. Griffin felt the hard, damp leather pressing against him, then pressing harder.

"Wastin' my time on you, drunk," Comer said, then poked the carbine's muzzle twice between Griffin's shoulders, as if he was checking for life. "I ought to shoot you right here."

Griffin groaned. Comer stepped away. Griffin felt Comer's hands pat his rear pockets. Then he lifted Griffin's pelvis and moved his hands over the front pockets. Griffin could feel the miniature camera in his briefs pressing against his groin.

Comer moved away again. Griffin groaned and opened his eyes in a squint. He saw Comer's boots walking toward his head. Comer set the toe of his boot on Griffin's neck again and exerted pressure on Griffin's windpipe.

Griffin heard the hiss of the two-way radio and the clicks of the mike button. "Jason. . .Comer. Come back."

"What you got?" the scratchy voice said.

"A drunk laying off the highway," Comer said. "Somebody beat him up real bad. Come back." He pressed his boot harder against Griffin's neck.

"Is he dead? Come back."

"Not sure," Comer said. "Somebody crushed his head in with a bat or something. Looks to me like half his head is caved in."

Griffin moved his head and lifted his right forearm. He moaned, then dropped his hand on the ground. *Pick me up, Comer, before you kill me.*

"Can't bring him here, Comer," Griffin heard the man say through the scratching. "Take him down toward Tractor Road away from the facility. Dump him there. Can't be no murder found nowhere near these grounds."

"That's a ten-four," Comer said.

"Don't get no blood on the grass there. Out."

"Ten-four."

"Well, scumbag," Comer said. "You and me goin' for a ride, and I'm gonna do a free killin'." Comer skidded the sole of his shoe on the skin, causing Griffin's neck to feel as though someone had laid a torch on his skin. Then Comer began to shift, to change positions.

Griffin felt Comer's breath as he lifted Griffin's upper torso. Griffin let out a groan, forcing a breath of air out of his lungs, then fell limp.

"Aw, man!" Comer said. "You gonna make me vomit. You're dead meat."

Comer heaved with his arms under Griffin's armpits and around Griffin's chest. He began stepping backward, toward the Jeep, dragging Griffin along. Griffin opened his eyes just enough to see the carbine strapped on Comer's shoulder. He flopped his head and dragged his feet. His thigh throbbed. He suddenly lifted his head. "You helping me, good buddy," he said to Comer, forcing as much air as he could into Comer's face.

"Aw, man!" Comer said. He stopped, then lifted Griffin straight on his feet. "Stay up," he said. "I'm going to turn you around."

Griffin stood straight. "Thanks, good buddy," he said in his normal voice.

Comer's eyes widened; his mouth dropped. Griffin sent his right fist squarely against Comer's jaw. He felt the bone break; he heard the crack. Comer's head snapped backward. His arms flailed on his way to the ground, his mouth spewing blood. Griffin watched Comer's face swell, then change to black and blue.

Comer groped for his carbine while lying there. Griffin watched, assessing the damage the blow caused. *Go out, Comer. Go out while you aren't hurt so bad.*

Comer used his carbine like a cane to lift himself from the ground. Grunting, groaning. He staggered and winced, trying to figure out which end of the carbine he was supposed to point, the pain of his jaw apparently overtaking him.

Griffin stepped up to him. *This is for Johnny.* He sent another right slam to Comer's nose. Blood spewed from Comer's nostrils as his body followed his head, flying backward. Comer landed in a sitting position against the fence, his legs spread open. His head dropped. The carbine toppled across Comer's lap.

Griffin's thigh throbbed; his chest ached. He felt his blood heat his face as he looked at Comer, sitting against the fence. *Cool down, Griffin.* Griffin lifted the carbine off Comer's lap.

Shoot him!

Don't do it, Griffin!

Griffin thought he ought to send a kick hard between the legs for Darlene. He started to position himself.

"No," the Voice said.

Calm down, Griffin.

Comer's head lifted; his eyes opened wide and then shut. He fell over on his side, moaning. Then he quieted and appeared to pass out.

Griffin lifted Comer and threw him over his shoulder. He carried him across the highway about ten feet into the corn patch. He laid Comer on his back. *Where's the beret? The radio? The keys? The carbine?*

Comer heaved for air through his open mouth. The red mess that was his nose appeared to be too cluttered to let air in. Griffin peeled off Comer's shirt and then turned him around, stomach down.

Okay, Rambo, now you won't suffocate on your own blood. You'll be all right when you wake up this morning. Maybe a few munching, sting-ing critters will have a good time, but you'll live. I have a Captain. If He didn't speak to me, you would have a hole in the center of your forehead.

Griffin searched Comer's pockets. Keys. A ring of them. Then the top pockets of Comer's shirt. Yes! The card key. He ran across the highway. The beret, carbine, and radio lay in plain view where Comer had hit the ground and the fence. Griffin picked them up, put on the beret, ran to the Jeep, and cranked it.

Griffin assessed the situation. The only common physical trait between him and Rambo was thick brown hair, although Griffin had considerably more gray. Comer was almost as tall, but leaner, with a longer torso. Comer's shirt fit Griffin like a brother's hand-me-down given a little too late.

The guard at the gate would know. Griffin had to think of something. He turned on the Jeep's A.M. radio and moved the dial just off a broadcast channel. He leaned toward the dash.

"Jason. Comer. Come back."

"That you, Comer?"

"That's a ten-four, Jason."

"Can't hear you good."

"That drunk made me throw up. Throat burns. Dropped the radio, too."

"Fill me in," Jason said. "Come back."

"Dumped him." *Remember your Ozarkese, Griffin.* "But got a lot of blood on the seat. I'll be comin' in through the exit lane, drivin' straight through to clean the Jeep."

"Use the spigot on the west side," Jason said. "Don't want the old lady to pull in suddenly like she does sometimes and see you cleanin' blood. Nobody needs to know nothin' about that guy. Afterwards, come get another two-way."

"Ten-four."

Griffin waited five minutes. Long enough, he hoped, for the guard in the guardhouse to settle down in his chair. He shifted the beret, covering as much of the right side of his head as he could. He checked the ascot as he drove down the unnamed highway.

The exit lane of the facility came into Griffin's view. *Fast? Should I drive fast through the gate?* He decided he wouldn't race through it, just turn hard, slow, then accelerate out of the turn onto the exit lane.

As he made the right-hand turn onto the exit lane of the facility, Griffin cocked his head slightly to the right and downward, as if looking on the passenger seat for something. He drove to the parking area and turned toward the west side. He studied the wall for a spigot. He decided to give up the idea and stopped the Jeep where the walkway met the building.

The two-way radio crackled. "Comer, you all right?"

Griffin leaned toward the dash.

"Ten-four. Just fixin' to throw up again."

Griffin could hear Jason's laughter.

Griffin looked in his rearview mirror. He watched Jason settle down. He climbed out of the Jeep and stepped along the walkway to the entrance door of the facility. He reached into Comer's top shirt pocket and lifted out the card and. . .there! The slot. He slipped the card in the slot; the door slid open. Griffin pulled the card out and slipped into the facility. The door slid shut behind him.

By 3:05 in the morning, Kristina England had managed some sleep, thirty minutes here, forty there, maybe one full hour, once. *"What are you going to do about Becky, Kristina?"* Constance's question lingered in her mind as she lay in the king-size bed of the penthouse master suite. From the first day Becky began talking about Ian Apple, England realized it would come to this: killing Becky.

England rolled under the covers.

Becky deserved it; she had made the decision to leave everything, to forfeit the presidency of the best-known politically active nonprofit in the country, to be on national news as a symbol of women's rights. *You stupid, stupid girl! What do you think you're going to amount to with that Ian Apple? Baking cookies while he hones his skills and then leaves you for some curvy trophy secretary? And you! What will you be? Some bush-league small-town newspaper reporter.* The thought of having to find another presentable lemming president—with the Landcaster problem looming, too. It was all too much.

England sat up and then got out of bed. She walked to the kitchen and put a cup of water in the microwave. A cup of Sleepy Time tea would do well right now. She popped two Percodans and then strode in the dim light to the living room while the tea bag steeped. *What will I do about Becky? What choice do I have?*

But it wouldn't be that easy. Heartland of the religious right-wingers. Churches of all sorts crowded Tulsa, Oklahoma. Large ones, small ones. The heart of the right-wing conspiracy, England believed. She had been to Tulsa once, three years ago. She went there to speak to a group who wanted to organize a local chapter of Anticipating Parenthood and open an Anticipating Parenthood abortion clinic. Oh, no. . .not an abortion clinic, a family planning clinic—a pregnancy termination center. Whatever.

For reasons she could not understand, her stupid secretary made arrangements for her to stay at a motel across a boulevard from Oral Roberts University. England couldn't stand it. The people at the motel, staff and guests, prayed. At breakfast, lunch, and dinner they prayed. "Praise the Lord," they said constantly. And every one of them was pro-life. Stupid, shallow-minded pro-life. What was she doing there?

The local press showed up. But they weren't friendly like they were in Atlanta, Seattle, and everywhere else. They referred to conceptuses as "babies" and "unborn children." Jargon to cause trouble. Why would anyone want to start an AP and clinic here? It would just cause trouble.

England had telephoned the head of the local group from the holier-than-thou hotel. "Sorry, I have a sudden emergency in New York. I have to leave," she told the organizer. There *was* an emergency: She had to discuss matters with the secretary who had made the Tulsa accommodations. The secretary was the first person England said a full sentence to after she stepped out of the cab in front of her office. "You're fired, you idiot." That sentence had ended the discussion.

England sipped her tea. The steam bathed her face. A professional hit there? A chill. It wouldn't work. It just wouldn't work. DiRosa would stick out like a sore thumb; that hideous Ramos would be worse. *Better not, England. It'll fall apart and come back on you, just like it did on Landcaster with Dowell. He's a dead man, and you would be a dead woman if it was botched or found to be a professional killing.*

England felt the Percodans and hot tea making her float a bit. Give Becky time. She'll come back when she begins to crave the life she had here. No way she'll settle down with a man named Ian Apple. *I just don't have the time to find another president.*

Another sip of steamy Sleepy Time tea. The fluid warmed her; drowsiness and a slight dizziness fell on her. A firmer assurance that Becky would come back floated to her mind. Becky wouldn't have to die. At least not yet.

England set the teacup down. She lifted herself off the sofa and ambled to her bedroom. She flopped down. While the room spun, she drifted off to sleep.

Griffin surveyed the interior walls of the facility, then the ceiling, perhaps twenty feet up. Four surveillance cameras mounted on the walls oscillated, each with a dot glowing red. Unless the fat guard, wherever he was, had been sleeping or on rounds, he was watching, recording, too. *Constance is going to see the tape. Probably no later than tomorrow. You'll either be dead or hiding, Griffin. Hiding? Where?*

Griffin's heart began to pump harder; his thigh began to throb. He scanned the interior. The elevators were to his left, maybe twenty feet away. He ran to them, pressed the single button. Maybe the inside guard was busy on rounds. Maybe the guard was sneaking around looking for him, maybe radioing Jason. Too late to turn back now.

The elevator doors spread open. Griffin stepped in. Two choices:

Level 1 or Level 2. Griffin pushed the L-2 button. The elevator doors shut, and the descent began. Griffin prepared himself to bolt out. He concentrated on the elevator door. The elevator stopped with a jerk. The doors began to open. *Get ready, Griffin. Get ready to attack.*

Just a white concrete wall appeared when the elevator doors slid open. The inside guard station had to be on Level 1. Made sense. It was centrally located and had the quickest access to the two other levels.

Griffin tried to develop a probable scenario while he crept down the hall of Level 2: The inside guard sees him on a monitor, decides he needs assistance; he calls Jason; Jason calls Rambo. "Comer! Comer! We have an intruder. Where are you, Comer?" Precious time while Jason tries to find their strong guy. Jason's probably on his way. Maybe they'll keep trying to find Rambo.

Griffin crept to the end of the hall. A door, and a red mark on the floor. He saw a slot for a card to the right of the door. He inserted the card in the slot. A mechanism drew it in with a whine.

A siren blasted. A mechanical feminine voice resonated from everywhere. "INTRUDER! INTRUDER!" the voice yelled.

So much for the probable scenario.

Griffin ran the other way, toward the elevators. One was coming down. He dashed to the other end of the hall. There he saw a metal catwalk four steps up. He ran to it.

The smell of burning flesh was stronger here.

He reached in the crotch of his briefs as he ran toward the end of the catwalk, toward a crimson-stained furnace door. A stainless steel cart sat in front of the furnace door.

Griffin yanked the miniature camera from his briefs and pointed it at the furnace when something in the cart caught his eye. He looked into the cart. He retched at what he saw. At the bottom of the cart a little boy and a baby lay with emptied chests, entangled in each other's arms, legs, and entrails, the surgical "Y" autopsy cut on the torsos.

Lord, how could they? He felt the heat of his blood in his face.

"INTRUDER! INTRUDER!"

Griffin retched again. Jennifer's words rang in his ears: "They're desecrating your Captain's little temples, Griffin. You must stop them!"

"INTRUDER! INTRUDER!"

They can shoot me, but I will kill them before I die. I will kill them!

Griffin pointed the miniature camera into the cart. He snapped several photos. Griffin swallowed to fight the nausea that began to climb up from his gut.

Footsteps in the hall, running toward him. Griffin shoved the camera in his front pocket.

I'll kill them!

No, you'll listen to your Captain's voice, Griffin.

"INTRUDER! INTRUDER!"

Griffin grabbed the rail of the catwalk with both hands and threw himself over it. He raced toward the sound of the footsteps coming from the hall. The fat guard in his counterfeit army gear appeared, lifting his black 9mm Glock pistol toward Griffin with both hands. Griffin dove at him. The guard's eyes widened; he jerked his head back and bent his elbows up as Griffin landed on him. A deafening blast from the Glock echoed in the hall. The guard fell to the ground on his back. Griffin found himself sitting on the guard, straddling him, and punching him in the nose, the mouth, the eyes, pounding him with both fists. Blood spewed from the guard's nose and mouth. The skin along his eyebrows split. More blood.

"INTRUDER! INTRUDER!"

"Stop, Griffin," the Voice commanded.

The sight of the entangled eviscerated babies clung in Griffin's mind. He raised his fist, ready to strike another blow.

"No, Griffin!" the Voice said in the same command tone.

Griffin lowered his fist. He rested his hands on his thighs, rubbing his throbbing thigh. He lowered his head and sobbed. "How could you!" Griffin yelled at the blood-saturated guard.

The guard groaned, his sounds mingling with the feminine computer voice still resonating in the hall. *Where is the gun? There!* Griffin got off the guard. The guard's moans echoed down the hall. Griffin grabbed the guard's gun. The elevator sounded—the other guard was coming.

Griffin froze in a standing position, holding the Glock with both hands aimed down the hall at the elevator. The elevator stopped; the doors spread open. The muzzle of another black Glock pistol appeared first, then the two hands holding it, then the arms. *Come on, Jason. Come on, boy.* Then a foot. Then the guard popped out.

"Lower your weapon!" Griffin yelled.

The guard turned his head slowly. His gaze fell on Griffin's eyes.

"Don't turn your weapon toward me!" Griffin said, aiming the muzzle of the gun at the guard's head. Griffin assessed the guard: small framed. Easy for any marine to take on hand to hand.

The guard held his pistol, but out of aim of Griffin. The guard looked at the gun pointed at his head. Griffin watched as the guard looked at him, then to the side, where the other guard lay on the floor, moaning. The guard's eyes widened; his mouth opened. "Okay, okay," the guard said. He lowered his gun to his side.

"Drop it and kick it toward me," Griffin said, "then put your hands behind your head."

Griffin watched the gun slide toward him and stop not more than a foot in front of his tennis shoes.

"I just guard the place, mister," the guard said.

"You're Jason?" Griffin asked.

"Yeah. You the drunk?"

"I'm the drunk."

"Some drunk!" Jason said.

"You want to live, Jason?" Griffin asked. "You want to leave this place with your face in one piece?"

A groan came from the other guard's blood-caked face.

"That's a ten-four," Jason said.

"Keep your hands on the back of your head." Griffin waited a moment. "What's your last name, Jason? Where do you live?"

"Rivers, Jason Rivers, Jr. I live in Pleasure Land Trailer Park, trailer 14. Just on this side of Ozark, but if I get out of this, I'm movin'."

"You know what's in that cart on the catwalk, Jason?" Griffin asked.

"Guess so," Jason said.

"You got any babies of your own, Jason?"

"Guess so."

"Everybody here's going to federal prison, Jason," Griffin said. "You know that?"

"Guess so."

"You don't want to go to prison, do you, Jason?"

"That's another ten-four," Jason said.

"I want to see what's in that room on the other end of the hall."

"That's where they grow 'em," Jason said.

"Your card fit that slot?"

"Nope," Jason said. "Only the doctor's card does. You put a card in that slot that don't belong. . .well, you hear it. A silent alarm goes off in Chicago, too. Men in helicopters will be on their way to shoot first and then ask questions. You take me hostage, they kill me, too. I ain't nothin' to them."

Griffin hurried his speaking now. "Where are the records?"

"I'm just a guard, mister. They pay us good, but they don't tell us nothin'."

Get out, Griffin! It's time to leave!

"Where are the surveillance tapes?" Griffin asked.

"In the guard station, one floor up."

Griffin jerked the muzzle of the sidearm. "Come on," he said.

Griffin followed Jason into one of the elevators and then to a small room fronted with glass on Level 1, off the main hall. Four CD-ROM recorders sat on the long counter in the room, each with a monitor sitting on it. Griffin removed the CDs. "Come with me," he said to Jason, swinging the muzzle of the gun at him.

"I told you," Jason said as they walked, "you take me hostage, they'll just shoot me first, then you."

"You know what immunity is, Jason?"

You need witnesses, Griffin. Insiders, Allan Cook had said. *As many as you can get. Anybody you can get.*

"Like, when you agree to help the cops," Jason said.

"The FBI. . ."

"The FBI. And they won't put me in jail?" Jason asked.

"I think I can arrange that for you," Griffin said. "Get into the Jeep. Drive with the lights on."

⌞___⌟___⌟

Griffin heard the swoosh and whirl of helicopter blades in the distance. He gazed up. Two helicopters fluttered in the sky, their spotlights panning the cornfield and highway in front of them. No time!

"Don't describe me," Griffin said to Jason. "Tell them I had a mask. Tell them you don't know what happened to the CDs. Tell them the intruder was short and skinny, that you were driving alone trying to chase me, but you don't know which way I went. Can you remember that?"

"I'll remember," Jason said, "but if they find out I'm lying, they'll shove me in that oven with them babies."

Griffin jumped out of the Jeep and darted into the corn patch. Jason took off.

The helicopter noise grew louder, near deafening, the spotlights maybe only a quarter mile away, Griffin estimated.

"Stop the vehicle," Griffin heard.

The helicopters flew closer, panning the fields, the highway.

Jason hit the brakes. Turbulent, swirling air now accompanied the whirling and swooshing. Griffin scurried deeper into the corn patch. After five, maybe six strides, he hit the plowed ground, landing on his stomach, facing the highway. He lay still.

"Stop where you are! Move and we shoot!" The voice came from a loudspeaker.

Griffin lay still. He watched as Jason hunched next to the Jeep in the middle of the jerking spotlight. Jason held one hand up. He crossed one of his arms over his eyes; the front of his uniform flapped against his torso.

Both helicopters hovered to the north where Griffin had left Comer. One helicopter began a descent near the highway in front of the Jeep, its lights washing out everything in front of it. The other raced away, fluttering down the unnamed highway, on the way to the facility.

Griffin crawled toward the next row of stalks, toward Tractor Road. The air swirled and swashed above Griffin as he crawled. Another row. He kept crawling through the fluttering and swaying stalks. Griffin could make good time now, at least for the next several rows.

The flutter became increasingly distant; the fanning and swaying stalks calmed. The air stilled. Griffin kept crawling, slower now, more cautiously. He was close to Tractor Road; he could feel it. He could hear nothing, though glances backward and upward revealed faint lights glowing from the highway in the distance behind him.

He kept crawling until he came to the end of the patch where the rows of stalks abruptly stopped and the dirt of Tractor Road began. Only with the feeling of relief that followed did he remember hearing the voice—"Stop, Griffin. Stop"—that had kept him from beating that guard to death. And there, on the edge of Tractor Road, he realized his Captain had been with him. Then, though his adrenaline pumped, though he had crawled this distance pounding his knees into the dirt, his thigh did not throb. It should have been killing him with pain.

And there was the rental car, unseen. Brown like the dirt. No doubt the helicopters didn't turn on their searchlights until after they flew over it. *It's true, isn't it, God,* Griffin thought when he remembered young David's words.

CHAPTER 28

When Amanda had stepped into her apartment at 1:10 in the morning, she had set the McDonald's bag on the coffee table next to her new recorder. After nearly an hour of shampooing and scrubbing, after she had become herself in the mirror again, she had fallen across the bed in exhaustion.

At 7:10 she lifted herself from her bed and shuffled to the bathroom. She gazed into the mirror. Her mussed blond hair looked horrible. Another shower in the morning light cleared her mind. Now, in her robe, Amanda walked to the kitchen and made herself a cup of instant coffee. She sat on the sofa and braced her toes on the edge of the coffee table. She sipped again. A different uniform today, she mused. Not as much makeup, no rhinestone T-shirt. A regular blouse would do.

Sunglasses, her brown-framed, dark-lensed Ray Bans, would do well. Yes, sunglasses were a must; the gold-grinned passenger knew her eyes. And she would drive with the Mustang's top up today, not like last night, when she had wanted the talkative teen to see as much of her as possible. Today the game plan was for her to be hidden, as she toyed with her killers in her controllable bugged Mustang.

Amanda took another sip and gazed at the recorder. *Okay, Carl, let's see how you sound.* She rewound the tape and reset the tape counter to 000. She pushed the play button. Carl's voice was clear without a hiss in the background.

Amanda lifted the revolver out of the McDonald's bag. She remembered the Saturdays with her dad at the Boston Police Firing

315

Range. She decided the gun should be near her at all times. Better keep it between the driver's seat and the Mustang's center console with the handle exposed just enough to grab it quickly.

I'll stay in the car until I hunt them down and find them and then blow them away.

Amanda set the handgun by her side and sipped coffee again. Something deep inside came upon her, like the feeling she got when she charged an opponent on the basketball court without the referee seeing the foul, knocking her opponent to the hard wood floor, then running for an easy lay-up.

Wrong? Sure. But it's all in the game.

Amanda slumped on the sofa. She lifted the cup to her lips. She remembered Dr. Hegel the day of her interview, how sensitive he was, and then how he brought her into his confidence and helped her with her feelings about Geoffry. They made Dr. Hegel kill himself. They destroyed her mentor, and they killed her fiancé.

The end does justify the means, sometimes. Right, Amanda?

Amanda jumped up. No more debating. No time to get soft now.

If you don't do it, who will?

It was time to get into her new uniform.

Amanda decided to drive over the Twin Span and cruise around the Peacock Inn. She had to know whether the clerk was dead. She longed to see where Geoffry had died, too, to view calmly the last place where he'd been alive. She might even ask if she could step into room 118. Anyway, she had to go back to the Peacock Inn where her new imaginary boyfriend refused to go.

England sat alone on the leather sofa in her penthouse apartment, her mind floating, wondering what this day would bring. She felt she had lost control of everything. The phone rang. She dreaded having to

316

answer it; she knew of no one now who she wanted to speak to.

"Hello," England said.

"Someone broke into the facility," Landcaster said.

England thought she was going to black out when the dizziness abandoned her in one breath. Two words popped into her mind: Griffin Dowell. "How could anyone get in there? Who was it? Talk to me, Landcaster!"

"We don't know who the guy was," Landcaster said.

"I want to know the damage, understand?" England said. "You don't have to explain this to Constance; I do. Tell me everything." England's sudden crispness of mind and her new-found energy surprised her.

"The surveillance CDs are missing, two guards beat up."

"And?" England said.

"Both guys are in the hospital; one's in ICU."

"Which one, Landcaster?" England asked.

"The guy who thinks he's Rambo."

England drew in a deep breath. It had to be Dowell.

"The guard they found by the incinerator says the guy was like seven feet tall and drunk and stunk," Landcaster said, then said nothing.

"And?" England asked.

"He said. . ."

"He said what?" England asked.

"The guard said that Big Foot attacked him."

"Big Foot?" England asked softly, then sighed.

"The doctor said the guy had at least four blows to his head hard enough to crack bone," Landcaster said. "As a physician mysel—"

"As a physician?" England said, feeling her teeth grind. "Get off the medical jargon."

"The Rambo guy," Landcaster said, then paused. "I forget the guy's name. . . . They found him unconscious in the corn patch across from the facility."

"Has he come around? Did they debrief him?"

Silence.

"Landcaster?" England asked. "Did they debrief Rambo?"

"The intruder left him in the corn patch in his underwear," Landcaster said.

"I can't believe this," England said softly, feeling a touch of nausea rise in her.

He was pretty chewed up. Swollen up with, you know, beetles, mites, flies, red ants. . .," Landcaster said. "Lots of toxins, probably major polymicrobial infection problems as secondary scenarios, too."

"Come on, Landcaster, get off it!"

Silence.

"They think he's in toxic shock, but he'll be able to tell us what happened in a week or two, I guess."

England ran her hand through her short hair. She sighed. "It was Dowell," she said softly, intending the words to be to herself.

"Maybe not," Landcaster said. "The third guard said he chased the guy. Nearly caught him. He said the guy was short and skinny, dressed in black. Looked like a teenager. Remember when one of the local kids tried to break in a few months ago? That's all it was, I'll bet."

England felt like Constance must feel when anger rises from her gut, then explodes in words. "Somebody beats up this Rambo guy enough to undress him, drags him into the corn patch—"

"Kris—"

"Then he gets inside, pounds another guard into never-never land where Big Foot lives. He steals the surveillance recordings so we couldn't see him, and you think it was a hick teenager?" It occurred to England for the umpteenth time that Landcaster was a perfect specimen of male incompetence.

"Well—you know—yeah. I think that's what happened," Landcaster said.

"I'll tell you what's happening," England said, gritting her teeth, feeling her veins rising on her neck. "You tried to burn up Dowell because he hurt your feelings. Now he's causing big damage. No telling where he is or who he's talking to."

"You don't know that it was Dowell!" Landcaster yelled.

"Constance was right," England said. "Dowell's not going to run away and hide like you would."

"Come on, Kristina—"

"We have to close down for a while, move the conceptuses out."

"I've got orders to fill."

"You just don't understand it unless it wears a miniskirt, do you?" England asked. "If this thing comes apart because of your stupid attempt at bombing Dowell, you'll pay for it. I don't intend to go to prison because of you. And if I do, you're a dead man."

"Give me twenty-four hours," Landcaster said. "I'll show you. I'll have the kid picked up by then," Landcaster said. "We have intelligence that that last kid had a friend. Bet you the two of them crawled to the facility with tire irons."

"You've got until tomorrow. Close of business day," England said, then hung up.

CHAPTER 29

What must they be thinking of me? Griffin couldn't imagine.

They certainly weren't thinking that the man they were crinkling their noses at was a high-priced lawyer, famous for getting crooked politicians out of the trouble they deserve. And they certainly wouldn't think he was the personal lawyer of the president of the United States.

Griffin stood looking at his reflection in the mirror hanging on the wall of the men's room at the Ozark National Airport. The scent of sour whiskey and rotten liver cheese on his breath didn't dominate now; the smell of his perspiration had long since taken over, he was certain. Splashing water on his face from the faucet didn't help much, either. *When I reach Atlanta, there has to be a shower somewhere.*

Only eighty or so unfortunate passengers boarded the 727 with Dowell at the Ozark Airport, and they scurried off the jet as soon as the attendant permitted. Griffin managed to clean up some in Atlanta, but he still needed a good soaking, scrubbing, and shampooing.

Now Griffin snuggled his shoulder between the seat and wall of the 727 and gazed out the window as the jet evened its attitude above the clouds. Griffin mused over when he would call Ruth and how he would call her. They had her line tapped, most certainly. The Enforcer would not overlook that.

As Griffin took in the mountains of clouds under him, he inventoried the evidence he had gathered to show Cook, all neatly packed in the bag under the seat in front of him. The photographs of those entangled, empty little bodies, the surveillance CDs. Jason would testify, too, if he was still alive. And Comer and the fat guard would be placed under cross-examination after they healed from their plastic surgery. Griffin couldn't wait to tell Allan Cook all he could, reading from his legal pads from the day it all started, the day Warren begged him for help. Hurt came to Griffin when he thought about that.

Lord, I just know it isn't enough. Constance would shut down the facility, move the babies out of—what did Jason call it?—the "baby growing room"?

If you don't get them put away, if you don't stop them, Griffin, hundreds more babies will die.

Griffin lifted his head, then settled back in the seat. *Where do they get the babies? Why aren't there reports of missing babies, crying young mothers? Where is that lab assistant Ruth mentioned? How much does she know?*

There are always missing pieces, aren't there, Griffin?

"Look at the sailboats, man!" Ramos said, gazing out the Ford's passenger window. "This is so much better than riding around the motel and that office. Bet there's a lot of beautiful women on those boats, man."

About three miles onto the seven-mile Twin Span, DiRosa lifted a road map with his right hand while steering with his left. He glanced at the map. "The third Slidell exit," he said. "That's where England said we have to turn off. Gause Boulevard, Highway 190." DiRosa set the map down next to him. "Gators' office is close to the exit somewhere. Pay attention to the tracker."

"She's not around here, man," Ramos said, staring out the window. "She's not around here for sure."

Amanda entered I-10 westbound at the Eden Isles entrance, the last entrance before the Twin Span toward New Orleans. She flipped the toggle switch up. The yellow light glowed. She decided she would leave the switch on for a while. It had been off except for the few tests she had made on the way from Waveland.

She glanced at the tape recorder sitting on the passenger seat. The tape was rewound and ready to play. Press the on button, hit play, and Carl would be sitting right next to her as far as the two killers knew. She slid her hand into the niche between her seat and the center console. Her hand fit perfectly around the handle of the .38, snuggled deep in the niche. She envisioned herself jerking it out in a flash. All the paraphernalia checked out.

Amanda took a deep breath and settled back in the leather seat. Seven miles of water, then about thirty-five or forty minutes to the Peacock Inn. She began a strategy session with herself again, debating with herself whether she should leave the system on or turn it on when she got into the vicinity of the Peacock Inn.

No, it would be better if I saw them before I turned it on. She reached down to flip the switch off.

⌐ ⌐ ⌐

Beep! Beep! Beep! The little light flickered bright with each beep.

"She's here! She's here, man!" Ramos said. "Sweetness!" Ramos felt a surge of joy run through him. He instinctively reached for the bone of his knife handle. "Hurry, man. Hurry!"

"Shut up and listen," DiRosa said.

⌐ ⌐ ⌐

Beep. . .beep. . . .beep. . . . . . .beep. . . . . .beep.

The beeps stopped. So did the flickering.

DiRosa gazed into the rearview mirror. "She's headed toward New Orleans," he said.

"Hurry, man. Step on it. You going to lose her, stu—"

"There's a cop back there," DiRosa said. "Three cars behind us in the right lane. You remember what we got in the trunk? You want me to speed, you pig?"

"Sorry, man," Ramos said. He realized that he might have gotten a little too excited, that he should trust DiRosa's judgment better than his own. Anyway, stalking people had been DiRosa's profession for forty years, man. He did it in New York City, Detroit, Chicago. And he was all business.

Ramos knew all about this quiet Italian who had hit three family bosses for the feds and then disappeared, this Luigi Vicarro. And now Ramos was in partnership with him. *Don't forget your part in the deal, Ramos!*

"We'll find her," DiRosa said. "You just sit back and shut up."

———

Amanda flipped the toggle switch down and resumed her strategy session. She decided she would keep the system off at first, then cruise around the Peacock Inn, down Airline Highway, around the airport, and into town. If she didn't see them, she'd follow the same route with it on. If she saw them, she'd turn the switch off to confuse them and then turn it on and play Carl. Amanda felt good about her plan as it passed through her mind.

Okay, Geoffry, Dr. Hegel, and Danny, I'm going to get them for you.

———

DiRosa looped onto I-10 east at the Eden Isle exit. He was concentrating. It occurred to Ramos that he wouldn't like this Italian hunting him down as a "business" matter. The force of the Ford accelerating pushed Ramos into the seat and his musings out of his mind. DiRosa glanced into the rearview mirror. Checking for cops, probably.

"They ain't going to bother us as long as you don't go crazy and we look like respectable businessmen," Ramos said.

"Shut up, pig."

—⌞——⌟—

"It's the first lady on line two," England's secretary said.

How does Constance find these things out so quickly? England dreaded this conversation. And only when her secretary said those words did she realize how desperately she wanted Landcaster to be right, that it was just a couple of local teenagers with tire irons getting revenge.

England picked up the receiver.

"So you thought Griffin Dowell would run and hide, did you?" Constance asked softly. England knew what was coming. The first lady's rage. She didn't want to answer, but she had to. This could have her indicted, just like Peterson.

"Constance," England said in a voice she knew was weak and not at all credible. "Landcaster thinks it was—"

"One of those kids down there? You believe that, Kristina?" Constance asked.

England felt her restraint evaporate; she just didn't have the energy to hold back.

"You're the one who got that fool Landcaster involved in this, Constance! Not me!" she yelled into the phone. "I've had it with your blaming everyone but yourself. You want me to take care of Becky? I will, somehow. Landcaster's your blunder, your lemming, remember? You deal with him."

"I can put you away with—"

"Well, do your Peterson trick," England said, surprising herself. "I know a lot more than he does. Do you think I'm going to fall on the sword for you like Madeline? I have records, Constance. I have records hidden. They'll find them."

A quick, clever lie. England felt justified.

Not a sound on either end.

"Now, can we try to sort through this?" England asked softly.

Still no sound from Constance. England felt like herself again. She had quieted the queen.

"What do you suggest?" the first lady asked.

"When will the Hegel Bill be voted on?"

"Jukali's got all the support needed in the House," Constance said. "The Senate is close. We have the votes now, but Gators is gaining support." Constance paused for a moment, then said, "No matter what you think, the Peterson article really hurt us. You have to feed this stuff slowly; the notion to give human fetal stem cells to puppies is just too much of a bite for most people to swallow, at least right now."

"Okay," England said. "I agree, but—"

"Peterson's article has been mentioned on every radio talk show," Constance said. "Redden was right. Gators is going to read it in the Senate Chambers."

Peterson's article. Peterson's article. The sound of it was getting England sick.

"Your spin has taken care of Peterson, Constance," England said, trying to put some force behind her words. "Andrea Rue shovels it out with every news show. Peterson is an animal rights whacko embezzler. But that was my point," England said. "The indictment just highlighted the article."

Silence.

"The senators want to go home," Constance said. "The Whip has agreed to keep them there until they vote. That will help. The press has done well. Folks have been e-mailing, calling, and faxing, mostly in favor. The red ribbons on the public school teachers and children have helped, but it's not going to be a slam dunk. We have to hurry."

"So we have a week," England said.

"If that," Constance said.

"We quit all sales," England said. She felt good after she said that. "Then I'll take care of Landcaster."

"How?" Constance asked.

"Don't worry about that." Then a quick, silent plan: *The next time DiRosa telephones me, I'll tell him to fly to Chicago and do Landcaster, and that Ramos, too.* A fresh start, then. She'd start up the facility and run it herself when it was legal, then select a person loyal to her to operate it. Probably some abortionist who was weary of his work. *Aren't they all, Kristina?*

"Make sure van Meter stays on our side," England said.

"What?" Constance said.

England perceived a puzzled tone. "Dowell's out there," England said. "He's a good lawyer. If he's not running, he's trying to gather evidence to take to the authorities, probably the FBI. He has the CDs showing the inside of the facility. But they don't show much. Nothing with conceptuses or the growing room. Just himself. Landcaster assured me of that. But you have to keep van Meter and the press on our side and after Dowell."

"That's easy," Constance said.

"We just have to let Dowell do what he's doing, not go after him, concentrate on getting the Hegel Bill into law," England said.

"I'll take care of Dowell," Constance said. "It's only a matter of time. You make sure we get the girl and the package."

"DiRosa will get it done."

"I'll push the legislation harder and keep the press with us," Constance said.

"That's what we need from you," England said to Constance, "Dowell's head and the press."

A pause.

"Maybe you and I can work closer together from now on, Kristina," Constance said.

"Good-bye, Constance. I'll keep in touch. We'll get through this."

"I'll pay you back for this, I promise," Constance said.

England hung up. She felt much better now. More than a part of the team, she was the leader. A few more maneuvers and maybe she could take over.

See, Becky. You were wrong.

⌞__⌟

It's them! Amanda couldn't believe it. As she drove in the far right lane on I-10, the white Ford passed her in the far left lane. The passenger gazed straight ahead. Amanda's heart felt like it jumped to her throat; her stomach twisted. *This is it!* Amanda decided to move to the center lane, then carefully to the left lane behind them, then follow them. It was like in any game: There has to be flexibility in the strategy in case the unexpected happens, as it usually does.

Take your time. Concentrate, Amanda.

Ramos still sat back in the passenger seat of the Ford. His reward was coming soon; he could feel it. He looked at DiRosa just as DiRosa glanced into the rearview mirror again and formed a puzzled look on his face.

"Another cop, man?" Ramos asked.

"No," DiRosa said. "Just keep still. Don't turn around."

DiRosa slowed. He merged into the middle lane and then into the far right lane. He slowed again.

"What's going on, man?"

"Don't turn around," DiRosa said.

"What are they doing?" Amanda asked in a soft voice. She slowed, dropped back, and pulled into the right lane, several cars behind the Ford.

Fifty miles an hour now. Two miles later, the Ford picked up speed, sixty, then sixty-five. It merged into the middle lane. A car passed it on the left. Then the Ford merged into the far left lane, putting distance between it and Amanda's convertible. *Amanda, you have to do something.*

"What's happening, man? What's happening?" Ramos asked. He could see DiRosa was concentrating, glancing in the mirror continually.

"Just look straight ahead," DiRosa said. "There might be undercover cops or somebody following us in one of those fancy, fast cars."

"We can take care of them, man."

"This ain't Cuba. They got radios. You understand that? You kill a cop, and you got trouble," DiRosa said. "If they're following us, they're running our plate. They won't find nothing suspicious. I'm going to slow down again, get in the right lane. Give him a chance to pull me over. You do what I say. If we get pulled over and you do something stupid here—"

"Okay. . .okay, man."

Amanda's hands began to sweat on the steering wheel. She decided to pass them, merge into the right lane a few cars in front of them, and then. . .then figure out what to do next.

Ramos divided his time between looking straight ahead and glancing at DiRosa. DiRosa continued shooting glimpses in the rearview mirror as he slowed again to fifty.

"What they doing, man?" Ramos asked.

"Coming up in the middle lane, but it ain't 'they'; it's a girl, I think. Yeah, it's a girl," DiRosa said. "She's coming up now. Don't turn your head. Wait until she passes. She's in the middle lane. Green convertible with brown top. Don't look around. . . . ."

The green convertible passed them.

"I couldn't see her clear through the tinted window," DiRosa said, "but she ain't no cop."

"No, she ain't, man."

"She's about the same age as the lab girl," DiRosa said.

"Come on, man," Ramos said. "Let's get going. Let's find that Toyota. It's up there some—"

Beep. . .beep. . .beep. The little red light flickered brightly with each sound.

"Hey! I told you, man! She's up there, close!"

"Listen to me, pig. Trackers don't work like that. They don't just blast on unless they're broke. Something ain't right."

"What do you mean?" Ramos asked.

Beep. . .beep. . .beep. . . .

"It ain't bro—"

Then through the speakers a voice sounded clearly. "Look, baby, I don't want to get involved in all this. Why don't we go have some fun. I mean, I'm not scared, baby, but I'm not going to that Peacock Inn. Not after you told me what happened there. Drop me off first, then come back. We'll have some fun."

"See. I told you, man!" Ramos said. "I told you it ain't broke!" Then he calmed down until the next thought crossed his mind: "Man, she got another boyfriend real quick!"

"She ain't the type," DiRosa said.

"What do you mean, man?" Ramos said. "She can have any boy she wants."

Ramos watched DiRosa take a big breath and shake his head. Ramos smirked. *See, I'm smart. I won that argument.*

DiRosa accelerated out of the right lane, into the middle lane, then into the left. "Look straight ahead," he said to Ramos. "We're going to pass the convertible."

Ramos shot a glance at DiRosa then shifted his gaze directly ahead.

"Hard to tell with the window tint. She might be black. Her size, that's right, though," DiRosa said softly.

Amanda blew out a deep breath. They didn't recognize her, she was certain, and she was certain they were heading to the Peacock Inn. *Your plan's working perfectly.* Amanda flipped off the system, then decided she would be the invisible stalker for a while. She felt that same thrill that saturated her when the momentum of a losing game shifted suddenly to her side, when the score was close and the coach would say with her sweaty, heaving teammates around her, "Okay, Collins, you get the last shot before the buzzer."

———

"This is what I want you to do," DiRosa said, keeping his eyes on the road. "You're going to listen, and you're going to do it."

"Okay. . .okay, man."

"We go to the motel, find a place to park and watch, but off the street. If I'm right in what I think, I get out of the car and walk to the motel. You understand," DiRosa said.

"Landcaster. He said I get the girl, man."

"Just make sure you stay out of sight and listen close to the tracker."

"What, man?" Ramos asked.

"I'll speak to you from the girl's car. If you don't hear from me in an hour after you drop me off, come back to the motel. You understand?"

"Yeah. But you remember. The girl. Don't hit her yet."

DiRosa lowered his head, shook it slowly, and sighed.

———

Griffin pressed his forehead against the window and closed his eyes. Air hissed above him over the steady humming of the jet engines. In his pondering, he rotated mental jigsaw puzzle pieces, disjointed facts he had gathered, and tried to make them fit. Dr. Hegel's preparation that accelerated lung growth in fetuses, a breakthrough in neonatology, Ruth had said that. BioSysTech was using it. No wonder Ruth was sickened. Somehow they were acquiring children with no birth records.

Prematurely born? Hegel's lung preparation was for babies at risk of premature births, Ruth had said. Selling the organs of the prematurely born. No matter how he spun that piece, no matter how he angled it, it wouldn't fit. How did they get that little girl, that little boy, and nobody complains?

And those marks on Millie. The Alfa Alkaloid that lobotomized the children. Could even Constance Frye be so cruel? Hegel had meant it for monkeys. . .dogs. . . . She could if she didn't think the children were people—humans who are not registered, no social security numbers, no parents to complain—and if, like so many, she believed that the unborn, even partially born, had no constitutional right to live.

Where did the children come from? Griffin felt a headache coming, he was thinking so hard.

Griffin lifted his head off the window. Growing room? The preparations. Alfa Alkaloid. The piece fell into place. "I know!" Griffin shouted. He sensed the people sitting in his area staring at him. He slumped, smiled, and gazed forward, directly at the rear of the seat in front of him.

Griffin's heart sank suddenly when the excitement wore off, when the image in the stainless steel cart hit him, the open cavities, the X marks. *Is that it, Constance? Of course it is. They don't always perform abortions at those Anticipating Parenthood clinics, do they? Sometimes they birth the fetuses after treatment with Hegel's lung preparation. The feds give AP tax money; AP gets inventory for the secret business of BioSysTech.* The throbbing pain in his thigh—it would come as anger rose in him, Griffin was sure. Griffin moved his hand on his thigh, ready to massage. But the pain did not come.

"It will not come again, Griffin," the Voice said.

Washington, D.C., couldn't be more than thirty or so minutes away now. *Cook is never going to believe this. If only I could've gotten into that growing room.*

———

When Amanda turned right off Williams Boulevard onto Airline Highway toward the airport, the Peacock Inn's sign came into her view four blocks down on the left. She merged into the left lane. She glanced at the dark bulb above the toggle switch. If her game plan was going like it should, the Ford should be in the parking lot with them sitting in it, waiting for whatever sound the thing makes. She stopped at the red light.

The green arrow came on. She turned and pulled into the lot. She cruised passed the registration office, gazing in the window and through the glass of the aluminum door, hoping to see the clerk alive. No one in view. She cruised between the strip of rooms to her left and the parking slots to her right, turning her head to study the parking lot. No Ford. She turned right and slowly cruised along the strip of rooms that faced Airline Highway and then turned right again.

Amanda, the Ford isn't here. The lot is nearly empty. This is overkill.

Her game plan wasn't working. They should have been here by now, waiting for her. Did they hear the recording? Amanda wondered.

Their not being here yet gave her a little time, maybe. She needed to know. She drove to the registration office and parked under the canopy in front of the aluminum door. This would only take a second, she thought. She hurried to the registration desk.

———

"That's your girl," DiRosa said softly. "Getting out of that green convertible."

Ramos moved his head closer to the windshield. He squinted, trying to make out the girl's face. But the sunglasses covered her eyes, and the hair, coarse blond, stuck up all over the place like one of those stupid rock stars. Then a quick scan of her body. "You're right, man! That's her!"

"She's smart," DiRosa said. "Real smart. We'll watch. She's going to park. She'll wait for us. When she does, I get out and walk."

"Landcaster said I get her."

"Not until we get the papers, pig."

———

"Excuse me," Amanda said.

The clerk lowered the *Enquirer* tabloid and looked up at Amanda. Amanda's heart soared. "You're alive!"

"What?" the clerk asked.

Amanda felt so much joy, as if she had made a go-ahead lay-up at halftime. She had to bop up and down a little. "Have the two men left who were in room one-eighteen yesterday?" Amanda asked.

"What?" The clerk remained seated. "Look, you want a room?"

Amanda cleared her throat. "How often do you clean the rooms?" she asked.

"Every day beginning about nine," the clerk said. "Why?"

Amanda turned and walked to her car, the thought repeating in her: *Where did they put Geoffry?*

She got in her car and drove to the strip of rooms facing Airline Highway, then spotted a parking slot in about the middle of the strip. She backed into a slot until her rear tires bumped against the edge of the concrete walkway between the lot and the strip of rooms. She cut the engine, sat back, and watched Airline Highway, where the Ford would pull into the parking lot sooner or later.

As Amanda sat, she debated a change in strategy, whether she should just shoot the passenger, the real killer, and speed away, then get the package to the senator. Sometimes you can't win them all. So many coaches had told her that, after a tie, while she and her team-mates moped in the locker room.

—————

"Griffin?" Special Agent Allan Cook said.

"I'm in D.C.," Griffin said. "You recording this?"

"Beginning this very moment," Cook said.

"Right, Allan."

"Turn yourself in," Cook said. "I can help you then."

"Where can I talk to you?" Griffin asked.

"Attorney General van Meter ordered a special BAFT team on the case. You know what that means?"

"I can guess," Griffin said.

"Armed and dangerous. News will break anytime now."

"You give me a chance to talk to you alone, and I'll turn myself in. You don't, I run until they get me," Griffin said.

Cook paused. "I could get busted for this," he said.

"They're getting away with something you'd never believe humans would do," Griffin said.

"Get a cab," Cook said. "Get away from there. No one would believe you have the nerve to come to D.C. There's a Wellsley Inn in Fairfax. You have to hurry. When the news breaks out, some airplane employee will report your whereabouts; they're on high alert for anybody and anything now."

"I know."

"Take a cab to Wellsley," Cook said. "You got cash?"

"Plenty."

"I'll be there sometime this afternoon," Cook said. "I'll listen. It better be good."

"It's not good, Allan, it's diabolical," Griffin said.

"If it's worth it, I'll arrange a meeting with the director for tomorrow. You stay there tonight. Nobody works here on Saturday."

"Thanks," Griffin said, relief finally going through his body.

"If what you have to show me isn't worth the risk, I take you into custody as a material witness. We'll try to protect you, but van Meter will do everything she can to turn you over to BAFT, and she can do a lot. That a deal?" Cook asked.

"Do I have a choice?" Griffin asked, then a shallow chuckle came out of him that he regretted.

"As far as I know, you fried Jennifer Taylor," Cook said. "You better be there this afternoon or this telephone call never happened."

"I'll be there," Griffin said.

Ten, maybe fifteen minutes had passed. No Ford. What went wrong?

Maybe the mechanic didn't wire the toggle switch right. Amanda glanced in the interior rearview mirror. She felt her eyes widen when she spotted someone behind the Mustang.

Go in your room, please. Just go in your room. I don't want witnesses!

Amanda realized the Mustang was easily identifiable, not like her Camry. She had to know if the man who had walked past the rear would be outside when she pulled the trigger. She looked toward the exterior rearview mirror. Amanda's heart leaped. Somebody was there! Standing by the door!

She slapped her hands on her chest in a startled instant.

She turned her head. The man pointed a gun at her. It was tipped with a silencer and covered with a newspaper. Amanda looked up. It was the Italian. She dared not move her hand to her .38, not yet. He nudged the muzzle up and down. Amanda rolled down the window.

"Give me the keys," the Italian said.

Amanda pulled the keys from the ignition and handed them over.

"Stay in the car. I'm coming around," the Italian said. Despite her heart pounding, Amanda thought out an emergency plan as she had done so many times dribbling the ball in high school. The Italian had to find out where the package was before he would shoot her. She slid her hand onto the handle of the .38 revolver. She tightened her finger around the trigger. *Wait. Wait until you hear the door latch. When he gets in, his body will depend on gravity for an instant. Watch for the right time; he's vulnerable in that instant. Be ready, Amanda. Be quick. Concentrate. Watch the ball. Execute, Amanda. It's not all talent; it's execution.*

But she wouldn't be able to get the passenger. He was the one she really wanted to kill. She would have to shove the Italian's body out of the Mustang and speed away.

The muzzle entered first. The Italian kept it pointed toward Amanda, even though his head wasn't in the car. *He can't see me. Get ready.* Amanda tightened her grip on the .38. His knees bent; he looked into the interior. He stared at Amanda for an instant. He reached down, lifted the recorder from the passenger seat. His head disappeared upward, then his leg bent into the interior again. Then his shoulder bent into the Mustang.

Now, Amanda!

Just as the Italian gave way to his weight to sit in the low passenger seat of the Mustang, Amanda grabbed the muzzle of his pistol with her left hand and shoved it downward. With her right hand, she jerked the .38 from its niche. The Italian flopped down in the seat, the muzzle of the .38 barrel in front of his nose. With his own pistol pointed to the passenger seat floor, he shifted the gaze of his deepset, dark brown eyes to Amanda's, and then he smiled.

"I knew you were smart," DiRosa said. "But I still underestimated you."

"Sit still!" Amanda hollered. She scooted back against the driver's door as far away from the killer as she could. She held the gun aimed at the Italian's chest with both hands. He glanced down at his pistol.

"Drop it and close the door." Amanda's heart was off to the races.

Oh, God. How do I end a man's life?

The Italian sat straight up in the passenger seat, his hands in his lap, his pistol on the floor in front of the passenger seat. He looked out through the front window. He said nothing. He sat there and smiled, showing Amanda the profile of a middle-aged, handsome, classic Italian man: deep eyes, neat gray-black hair, trimmed mustache.

Amanda raised the gun. She took aim at the side of his head just above his ear. *Pull the trigger, Amanda!*

"Who are you?" Amanda asked. "Why did you kill my fiancé?" Amanda felt the sweat beading on her brow.

The Italian turned his head and fixed his gaze on Amanda's eyes again. He lifted his right hand and moved it as if chopping; then he hunched his shoulders. "It's my business, young lady. It's what I do," he said. He lowered his hand. "Shoot," he said softly. "I understand. If you don't, it will be you who will die. Such a shame, a young girl like you."

It's not supposed to be like this.

The weight of the revolver began to strain the muscles of Amanda's upper arms. Sweat wet her palms, lubricating the handle of the gun.

Amanda tried to keep the muzzle steady and her hands from shaking. But no use. The muzzle bobbed and waved.

"Get out of my car. Give me my keys. Let me go!" Amanda hollered, trying not to cry, trying to push back the wave of hysteria that beat against her sanity.

The Italian tilted his head and smiled. "Amanda? That's your name?" he asked, keeping his smile. "My name is DiRosa."

Amanda's biceps hurt; the pain crawled into her shoulders. Sweat drenched her palms. The perspiration beading on her brow and on her scalp would soon begin to drip, Amanda thought. She would have to wipe her brow. *He knows, Amanda. He knows. You'll have to wipe the sweat off.* Amanda's arms ached.

The muzzle swayed and bobbed. Amanda set her hands with the pistol in them on the console, still trying to keep the muzzle steady and aimed at DiRosa.

"You really going to kill me, Amanda?" DiRosa asked.

Stop smiling like that! Please stop smiling.

"When you kill a man," DiRosa said, "a part of your soul dies, and a new part is born. The new part likes the feeling, the power of taking a life."

Amanda wept. She tried to hold the weapon steady. "Please, Mr. DiRosa, let me go," she said, crying.

"You will be a new person," DiRosa said, "like the religious people say, 'born again,' when you shoot me. A human life will mean nothing to you then. Watch what I tell you if it's not so."

Amanda couldn't hold her hands and the gun steady anymore; she couldn't shoot. She didn't want to keep her eyes open. She stopped crying, just sniffled. She felt herself relax as DiRosa's warm, soft hands lifted the .38 from her wet hands.

"Where are the papers Hegel gave to you, Amanda?" DiRosa asked.

Amanda lowered her hands to her lap. "I don't have any papers." Amanda wasn't afraid of him. She realized that wasn't the reason she cried. She had failed, dropped the ball. The Italian had his pistol pointed at her now. *It's okay. Shoot.* She had lost, not only this game, but everything, everybody. *Oh, Mama.*

"Only if you try to run away will I kill you, Amanda. You're a very smart girl. You have a chance to live if you tell me where the papers are."

Amanda shook her head slowly, her lips shut tight, her gaze fixed on DiRosa.

DiRosa leaned down. He turned his head toward the dash where it met the driver's door. "That switch," he said, "that's how you turn the tracker on and off?"

Amanda said nothing.

"It's only the second time it has been done to me," DiRosa said. "But a girl such as you. I'm impressed. Now turn it on."

Amanda glanced at DiRosa, then shook her head. "No," she said.

DiRosa lifted the muzzle to Amanda's face. He leaned forward and with his free hand reached over Amanda's thighs and flipped the toggle switch up.

"I like you, Amanda," DiRosa said. "It would be nice to have a daughter like you. Maybe if you tell me where the papers are—"

"I'm not going to tell you, Mr. DiRosa, no matter what you do," Amanda said softly.

"It won't be me," DiRosa said.

Amanda turned her head away from DiRosa. If she attempted to open the door, she would be shot. Three, maybe four rounds in her side and back. She didn't want to die, but she wasn't just going to hand over the papers, either. Maybe she could get away somehow. Maybe she could still get the package to Senator Gators. *It's going to be three-zip, Amanda, and you won't even be around to see the end of the game.*

The Italian was in control now. All she could do was wait for a mistake, an opportunity, an error by the other side.

But Amanda's heart sank when she saw the white Ford pull into the parking lot. Her heart began to pound when she spotted the driver's beady eyes gleaming at her. She began to tremble when she saw that gold grin.

"There are things much worse than death, Amanda," DiRosa said softly.

Amanda didn't look; she couldn't bring herself to. *Think escape, Amanda.* She had to get away, and she had to get away alive, with or without the Mustang, but with the package.

She heard the Ford's door slam shut. Then she sensed him standing by the Mustang's driver's door. She refused to look. Her heart pounded harder now. This man's hideous leer invoked terror in her—heart-pounding, trembling terror.

He opened Amanda's door. Amanda shrugged and looked away. "Sweetness!" the man yelled, smiling.

He gripped Amanda's upper arm with his fat, dank hand. Fear paralyzed Amanda. She couldn't look; she couldn't find the will to fight now; she could do nothing but what she was told. She couldn't think. Couldn't plan like she could with the Italian. *Don't look at him!*

DiRosa climbed out of the Mustang. He walked around the trunk and stood by the driver's door as the passenger opened it. Amanda lifted herself out of the car. DiRosa grabbed her other arm, holding his pistol tucked close to his side, pointed at Amanda's ribs.

Amanda kept her head down, toward DiRosa. She felt the pain of their grip on her upper arms.

Thoughts were clearer now. She couldn't just let this happen. *Do something, Amanda.* She would scream, just begin screaming. *Do that, Amanda, and DiRosa will put a bullet in your liver or maybe strike you on your head and wait until you come to, somewhere. Keep them moving. Don't let them think about searching the trunk. But don't look at him, Amanda. Keep your eyes anywhere else, the walls, the walkway, DiRosa, but not on him!*

Four doors down, Ramos tugged Amanda to a stop. DiRosa jabbed the muzzle in her ribs. Ramos reached in his pocket with his free hand and jiggled the contents. He pulled out a key and slipped it in the door lock. Numbness came to Amanda; light-headedness came when the daylight flooded over the poorly cleaned bloodstain just inside the threshold. "He never should have punched me," the passenger said with a sneer that caused a chill to race through Amanda.

He moved behind Amanda. With his grotesque bulk, he shoved Amanda into room 118. "Big boy, your boyfriend," the passenger said, showing his gold teeth in his grin, "hardly fit in the trunk."

"Shut up, pig," DiRosa said.

CHAPTER 30

In our final segment, we have a CPNN exclusive report, a bizarre story," Andrea Rue said into the camera. She was wearing a navy suit with a little red ribbon on the right lapel. "Sheryl Hastings reports from Washington."

Hastings stood in front of the camera with the White House as a backdrop. "Andrea," she said into the microphone, "unidentified sources have told me that the president's former private attorney, Griffin Dowell, is being sought for the firebombing of his own car, which killed his secretary. The bizarre story seems to have started when Dowell and his secretary allegedly became romantically involved. Dowell, who is a wounded Vietnam veteran and might be suffering from posttraumatic stress disorder, allegedly ordered his secretary to take his car to pick up lunch. He allegedly planted the bomb in the car sometime before then. His secretary, Jennifer Taylor, burned to death in the car.

"The source disclosed that Dowell fled the scene and is still on the run. Attorney General van Meter has assigned a special task force from the Bureau of Alcohol, Tobacco, and Firearms to search nationwide for Dowell with orders from the White House to take him alive. Dowell is considered armed and dangerous. The BAFT has issued a warning not to attempt to apprehend him. He might be homicidal and is probably delusional."

Hastings faded away, then a picture of Griffin appeared on the screen. "Here's a photograph of Griffin Dowell," Hastings said in the background. "Authorities believe he might be headed for the

Rhode Island area. If you see this man, call the BAFT immediately at one-eight-hundred-five-five-five-B-A-F-T. The number is there on the screen."

Hastings reappeared. "Remember," she said, "Dowell is the prime suspect in a brutal murder. He is considered armed and very dangerous. Back to you, Andrea."

"Thank you, Sheryl," Rue said. "I see you have your red ribbon on, too."

"It's for the children, Andrea," Hastings said with a broad smile.

Andrea smiled, then turned to the man who appeared next to her as the camera widened its field of view. "What's in sports, Barton?" she said.

Barton gazed into the camera and grinned. "Well, Andrea," he said. "The only way the Mets will beat anybody is if they get that lawyer to bomb their opponents' locker room—"

Ruth Hegel lifted the remote and pushed the off button. She felt sick to her stomach when the thought came that she was somehow to blame for Griffin's impending death. Then she remembered the card that Madeline Gentcher gave her at the funeral. *You have no choice, Ruth.*

Ruth hurried up the stairs to her bedroom and searched through the suit jacket she had worn to her husband's funeral. When she found it, Gentcher's words raced through her mind: "Remember the card, Mrs. Hegel," she had said. "You'll use it. I promise."

Ruth dialed the direct line.

"Madeline Gentcher," the voice said, interrupting the third ring.

Ruth shivered when she heard that voice.

"Miss Gentcher. This is Ruth Hegel."

"Well, hello, Ms. Hegel," Gentcher said. "So nice to hear from you."

"I want to help with the Hegel Bill," Ruth said. "I'll go on camera, wear the first lady's ribbon, if you want me to."

"Looks like Jackson's two-timing you, doesn't it? Men, they're all alike," Gentcher said with a chuckle.

"I'll do anything the first lady wants; just don't hurt him."

"He's a ruthless killer, Ms. Hegel," Gentcher said.

Ruth wanted to scream at her, insult her, but decided it would do no good.

"He burned his secretary to a crisp. He's armed and dangerous. Even so, the first lady has assured everyone that he is to be taken alive and given all the care and treatment possible—"

"Miss Gentcher, please," Ruth said. "Don't hurt him."

"I wonder what he's going to do when he sees those BAFT men in their military clothes coming after him. Think he'll try to escape?" Gentcher asked. "Maybe go into one of those posttraumatic episodes? Who knows what delusional homicidal crazies like Jackson Dowell will do? Wonder what'll happen when he fires on those agents?"

"I'll go on television here," Ruth said. "I won't tell the truth, I promise."

"The truth is your boyfriend is an armed fugitive who barbequed his secretary; the truth is I warned him about making enemies in high places; the truth is your dead husband was a drug dealer, and you conspired with him. The truth is you can be indicted anytime, and it's only out of the first lady's kindness and her concern for the children of America that she doesn't put you away. Whatever the rabble out there can be made to believe is the truth, Ruth Hegel."

Ruth found herself getting dizzy, sick, wondering how these people had entered her world.

"You can do anything you want," Gentcher said. "But what you do will have consequences. Dire consequences. It's too late for Griffin Dowell; he's as good as dead. That's the truth."

Ruth lowered her head into her free hand. She rubbed her fingers on her forehead. She could feel her lip quivering, her body crumpling.

"Thanks for the offer, Ms. Hegel, but the Hegel Bill has all the votes it needs without you."

Click.

A dial tone.

Oh, Avraham! How could you have gotten involved with this evil?

CHAPTER 31

The electrical cord from the television and lamp sliced into Amanda's wrists and ankles. Water from the wet hand towel the passenger had shoved in her mouth dripped down her throat. Amanda coughed as best she could. She could hardly breathe. She stared at the ceiling, still trying to avoid looking at the passenger, but she knew where he stood. She couldn't help but glance. He leered at her, standing at the foot of the bed, his gleaming eyes focused on her, his gold grin glistening, as she lay tied to each corner of the bed.

Amanda struggled, trying to free her hands and feet from the bed frame.

The Italian sat on the other bed, his pistol next to him. Amanda had glanced at him a few times, trying to show the torture in her eyes. That was her only chance now. Maybe he would sympathize with her. His words about wanting a daughter like her passed through Amanda's mind.

"Where are the papers, Amanda?" the Italian asked.

Amanda shook her head; she tugged on the electrical cords again. The cords cut deeper. She felt blood trickle from her wrists.

"His name is Fidel Ramos," DiRosa said. "The fat pig is going to have his way with you. Didn't I tell you there are some things worse than death?"

Amanda shot a glance at Ramos. He grinned at her and began tugging off his shirt. She could smell him. His large, soft pectorals sat on his huge belly. He panted as he grinned, his belly moving in and out. Amanda saw the knife handle, too, his roll of fat pushing the handle off to the side, the same knife that had killed Geoffry and Danny. How many more?

The game is over, Amanda. You've lost. But you can't let it end this way—oh, Mama. . .Mama!

Amanda turned her head toward DiRosa and nodded. DiRosa moved over her and pulled the hand cloth from her mouth.

"It's in the car. In the trunk," Amanda said.

DiRosa walked to the door.

Amanda hollered, "You said. . .!"

"He didn't tell you the truth," Ramos said. He lowered his hands under the roll of fat that covered his belt buckle. He lifted his shoulders and sucked in his belly. "We have an agreement. He gets the papers. I get you. These Italians, they always keep their agreements." He jerked on the end of his belt.

Amanda turned her head to the side. Her desperate gaze caught DiRosa's eyes as he stood watching at the door, his hand on the knob. Amanda was certain she saw sadness in his brown eyes.

Ramos looked toward the Italian. "You can stay and watch if you want, Vicarro, but turn off the light there next to you, man. I like it romantic," Ramos said through his widening gold grin.

Amanda could hear her heart pounding. Sweat. Fear. She couldn't scream. She tugged, squirmed. *Oh, God. Oh, no!* She closed her eyes. She rolled her head. "But you said, you said, Mr. DiRosa!" she hollered in DiRosa's direction.

Ramos shoved the rag hard into Amanda's mouth.

DiRosa left the room, slamming the door shut.

Amanda's blouse clung to her. Her chest heaved. She couldn't keep her eyes off the terror in front of her.

Ramos reeked of old perspiration. Amanda tugged at the cords with her arms and legs. He lifted the knife and moved it slowly side to side in front of Amanda's eyes.

"Women, they don't like me so much," Ramos said. "It ain't my fault I ain't pretty."

Amanda couldn't make a loud noise. She couldn't slow her chest, couldn't keep it from heaving. She kept struggling, hoping one of the cords would loosen, just a chance to kick him or slap him. Anything!

Ramos lowered the knife.

Amanda shook her head, jerked her arms, heaving. She could feel more blood trickling from her wrist. She didn't care. If only one hand would pop loose, she could slap! If one foot, she could kick!

"I am going to make you squirm some, first," Ramos said.

The door lock sounded. The door opened. Ramos turned his head toward DiRosa, who stepped into the room holding the package and shut the door behind him. Amanda lifted her head. She shook her head to move strands of hair out of her eyes, then as best she could, stared at DiRosa. *Look at me! Help me! Shoot me!*

Ramos looked at DiRosa. "You come back to watch, my friend? Look how beautiful," he said.

One big blow of her lungs. The cloth popped out of her mouth. "Shoot me, Mr. DiRosa. Please, kill me!" Amanda watched as DiRosa tossed the package on the other bed. He pulled his pistol from his waist.

"I get her first!" Ramos yelled.

"It's business, pig," DiRosa said. "It's just business. I told you that."

Amanda's chest heaved as DiRosa pointed the muzzle of the silencer at her face. She turned her head and closed her eyes shut tight. She clenched all her muscles, straining, waiting.

"Landcaster said. . ."

Phhhht.

A thud on the floor.

"Open your eyes, Amanda," DiRosa said.

Amanda opened her eyes when she heard the voice. DiRosa stood over her. Ramos lay on the floor, groaning. His legs and head jerked in spasms. DiRosa moved over Amanda with Ramos's knife in his hand.

"Me and him, we had a business agreement," DiRosa said. "He did not keep his part of the bargain." DiRosa looked down at Ramos and shook his head slowly. "I knew he couldn't. Such a stupid pig," he said.

Ramos groaned again; his body jerked in spasms.

With the knife in one hand and his gun in the other, DiRosa

stood over Ramos. He lowered the muzzle to an inch or so from the back of Ramos's left ear.

Phhht.

Ramos's body jerked once with a groan, then lay still. Blood trickled out the back of his head onto the carpet.

DiRosa turned his gaze on Amanda. "See, Amanda. See how easy it is?" he said. He raised the muzzle to Amanda's head, then paused. "What is my name, Amanda? Do you know my name?"

"It's Mr. DiRosa. Please, Mr. DiRosa, please!"

"Did you hear the pig say my name?"

"No, no. . ." Amanda hoped her lie was convincing.

DiRosa lowered his pistol. He cut the electrical cord that bound Amanda's left hand to the bed frame. Then he laid the knife on her blouse.

DiRosa leaned over. He placed a quick kiss on her forehead. "I like you, Amanda," he said. "Stay here for an hour; you call nobody."

Amanda nodded.

"We're even now," DiRosa said to Amanda. He lifted the package off the other bed and walked out of the room.

Amanda waited until the door shut, then she cut herself free. She jumped from the bed and ran to the bathroom, slamming the door and locking it. She sat on the floor in the corner and drew her knees up tight to her torso. Her chest was heaving. She realized it was over. The passenger's corpse lay in the room, in its blood. Just what it deserved, Amanda thought.

No more killers would chase her now.

Then sadness. Regret. Guilt. *I'm so sorry, Geoffry. So sorry, Dr. Hegel and Danny. I failed you all. If only I had followed the rules!* Amanda lowered her head to her forearms and began to cry as she sat there in a tight coil.

⌞　⌟

"Okay, Griffin. Let's hear it," Allan Cook said as he plopped down in a chair.

Griffin paced as he spoke.

"When I spoke to you a few days ago, I didn't know what Constance was doing. I know now. They're growing fetuses, selling their organs." Griffin tossed the two photographs on the table. He stared at Cook. He wanted to watch his response when Cook studied the entangled eviscerated children.

Cook maintained a cool demeanor, but Griffin saw the blood leave his face. "Sit down," Cook said. "Tell me everything you know." Griffin heard anger in Cook's voice.

An hour later, Cook stood. "I'm going to get you a radio to stay in touch, but you can't stay here."

"Where am I going to go?" Griffin asked.

"My place," Cook said. "Too many people have seen you, and you're a dead man if you're found."

"Allan—"

"I'll call the director," Cook said. "Somehow we have to meet tomorrow. It's Saturday; there won't be many people at the office."

Cook was formulating a strategy in front of Griffin, talking to himself in a determined voice.

"You'll have to shave your hair," Cook said. "Maybe I can get you a wig or beard or something. Anything to get you into the director's office."

"DiRosa found the girl," England said. "He has the package, too. I'll have it before six in the morning."

"Good," Constance said. "BAFT is briefing me every thirty minutes. Dowell's somewhere here in D.C. It's probably a matter of hours, if not minutes, now. What about the girl?"

"Done, and Landcaster's hideous friend, too."

"That's wonderful!" Constance said.

"DiRosa's on his way to Chicago," England said. "He's going to contact me before he does anything with Landcaster."

"Things are working out, Kristina," Constance said. "We work well together."

"When I get the package, I'll call you," England said. "But no need to worry now."

———

While Amanda drove to her apartment, she kept the radio and CD silent. Quiet. She needed as much quiet as the Mustang's rumbling motor and interstate traffic would allow. She needed to think, to ponder what went wrong, as she always did when she lost a game. She had come to grips with the loss while coiled on the floor of the bathroom of room 118. As the high twin bridges of the Twin Span came into view, a numbness set in.

Where do you go from here, Amanda?

Kingston had never been home, and Boston—maybe later, but not now, not back to the bigotry. She had no one. *DiRosa might as well have pulled the trigger.* Amanda pulled into the Anchorage Apartments parking lot. *Who would have cared?*

When Amanda stepped into her apartment, the first thing that entered her mind was a hot shower. She needed to be cleansed, to wash away everything and see it swirl down the drain. Then, in a few days, maybe she'd apply for a position at the University of New Orleans, or maybe Tulane.

When the thought came, it jolted her.

Do you really think you can use Dr. Hegel as a reference, Amanda?

Amanda tried to imagine an interview with a prospective employer. No way, not for some time, anyway.

You not only have no one, you have nowhere to go. A lump came into her throat.

Then the choppy asphalt lane passed through her mind, the talkative teen and the teenage girls. She wanted to do something.

Amanda the social worker. Right! *Why don't you just find a job waitressing. It'd be a miracle if you could do anything about all of that now.*

349

Amanda slowed her thoughts for a moment. She realized the game wasn't over, that she was walking off the court with time left on the clock. Now Geoffry's death came to her mind, then Dr. Hegel's last moments racing away from the building, and the image of Danny the last time she saw him in the old Cherry Street building. So long ago, so very long ago, it seemed.

Amanda decided she would go to Senator Gators' office tomorrow morning and take everything she had brought with her from Rhode Island, even the picture of her and Geoffry. Without the package, the senator would probably laugh her out of the office. But no other option existed for Amanda if she were to have peace in her life. No way she could just quit a game.

"Play it through," the coaches told her, even when the team was far behind and the opponents smirked as the minutes ticked away.

SATURDAY, JUNE 29

CHAPTER 32

Last night, after DiRosa told England the good news, England had telephoned the special delivery courier. She threatened a lawsuit if the package wasn't delivered to her penthouse by six in the morning. The package came at 5:54. England ran to the door when the delivery boy knocked. She snatched the package from his hand. "Ten more minutes and your job would have been history," she said to him, then slammed the door in his face.

She hurried to the sofa, sat, and with the package on her lap, ripped at the tape.

You thought you were so smart, didn't you, Hegel? Thought you could undo everything you did for us? Cowards blow themselves away like that. Cowards get little girls to do their dirty work for them. Hegel the Squeamish Coward.

England lifted the top off the box. A letter in a University of Rhode Island envelope addressed to Senator Jeremiah Gators lay on a stack of papers. She lifted the envelope. With her other hand, she fanned through the stack of papers. Original patient studies, two hundred or maybe three hundred pages. Wait. . .something else under the papers. A notebook. *What have we here, Dr. Hegel? The log? Thank you, Doctor.* England opened the log to its first page.

"BioSysTech log. Private and confidential. Property of Biological Systems Technolgies, Inc. Not to be viewed by unauthorized personnel."

Delight ran through Kristina England as she set the log on the sofa and opened the envelope. *Now, Hegel the Coward, just what did you have to say to Senator Jeremiah Gators, our favorite right-wing religious nut?* She unfolded the letter and read:

"Dear Senator Gators,

"I am Avraham Frederick Hegel. You know me as the late science advisor for the first lady's reform bill, also known affectionately by your supporters as 'Hegel the Beast.' I could not live with that title, with doing what I did for her. Eventually they would have killed me, my wife, probably my children, too. That is why I am dead.

"The studies you see in the box show original data for Parkinson's disorder patients after I transplanted the preborn babies' stem cells in the patients' brains. God forgive me. These data show no benefit of the procedure whatsoever. The same is true for the Alzheimer's patients.

"Also you will find my log for the Parkinson's patients, in which I was to transfer the original data so that my lab assistant could enter them into a computer program. Under the instruction of the first lady, and for payment by Biological Systems Technologies, Inc., a company owned partially by Mrs. Frye, I did not transfer the actual data. I skewed the data so that statistically significant differences would result upon analysis. My lab assistant did not know. She, along with every-one else, believed I was revolutionizing medical science. In fact, I was a fraud.

"Such fraud could not go unnoticed. My reported and published results are now being shown incorrect even as I write this. I have received a letter from one researcher who accused me of criminal fraud. Of course he was right. But what of it? I was soon to become one of the first lady's protected marionettes, assured of the respect of the press and all her people, as I dangled on her strings for the sake of the children.

"BioSysTech was never interested in fetal brain stem cell trans-plantation; it desired only to make a profit in an industry whose inven-tory consists of baby organs, and whose existence is kept silent by those who have the power to eliminate or ruin those who would make it public. And I helped them.

"They needed a scientific facade to hide what the company really did with my help, with my fetal lung preparation, which could have been available by now to save thousands of premature babies. But we used it to keep fetuses alive, fetuses that were not aborted at Anticipating Parenthood clinics but birthed without the knowledge of the young mothers.

"BioSysTech grew the babies in incubators, like exotic plants, and harvested the fruits of their abdominal cavities. The babies couldn't feel the pain, though, thanks to my Alfa Alkaloid lobotomies that chemically destroyed the frontal lobes of their brains.

"You see, Senator Gators, BioSysTech's real business is harvesting organs from these babies, even though they may be as old as six years. The facility where this is done is in the president's home state, outside a small town called Ozark, on Highway 228, in an old, forgotten fallout shelter.

"And why does the first lady want to pass her bill? You know, don't you, Senator. I've heard you speak. You're among the few in Congress who really know. She and her colleagues have the blood of infants on their hands. The bill she proposes provides that fetuses of any sort, even those that survive abortions, are not given constitutional protections to life until their cardiac and respiratory functions perform independently and without medical intervention. Do you understand the implications of that, Senator? Perhaps I should explain it to you.

"You must tell them, Senator. You must tell them that the first lady's bill is a mere extension of the killing of the partially born. Tell them that her reforms provide that constitutional protections to life apply only to those babies born who function independently and that they cut off those protections to fully born babies who depend on any sort of medical support, either mechanical or medicinal, to live for more than five days. Horrible? Unbelievable? Was it unbelievable when the Supreme Court permitted the murder of a baby born but for the crown of its head still in the mother?

"Tell them, Senator. Most of your colleagues don't know or care;

and the people, they go about their lives ignorant of the evil that governs them and that moves science forward. We are entering a new, profitable millennium for the new industry. And the first lady will be its first magnate. Her reforms will supply her inventory and, in her twisted mind, rid her secular utopian world of the weak among us at the same time.

"You see, Senator, such laws creep into society in increments, unnoticeable to people in their everyday lives, as the evil agenda slithers in. I read what you said. Even though the reporter quoted you in a mocking tone, you were right, Senator. 'Evil never rests.'

"Don't you see the next increment? Why just let the organs go to waste? Use them for the sake of the live children. I provided the preparations for the new industry. The great Avraham Hegel.

"The first lady's business in blood sells baby organs to two brokers, one out of Germany, the other out of Japan. I do not know the one from Japan. The name of the one from Germany is Otto Goethe. I know Goethe. He is a brutal, neo-Nazi physician blinded by greed and hate.

"Before the senators vote, take these studies to Dr. Wilma Kileen-Suitor. She is a professor of biomedical engineering at Johns Hopkins, a true leader in her field, not a fraud as I was. Ask her to compare the original studies to those in the log I published. Have her testify after she reads this letter.

"God forgive me for the babies I let grow and be slaughtered in that evil facility.

"I was evil, Senator. I was hideously, irredeemably evil. I asked the Messiah to forgive me. I don't believe even He is capable of it.

"Avraham F. Hegel, M.D., Ph.D.,

"Late Science Advisor to the First Lady."

⌞ ⌞ ⌟

Well, well, dead science advisor to the first lady, it appears that old Senator Gators won't be getting his mail. England chuckled as the thought passed through her mind. *You were right; even your Messiah couldn't help you.*

England jumped up, refreshed and relieved. No need to call Constance about this. The best place for the whole package was in the river, with a rock. Dowell was a dead man; Landcaster would soon be out of the way. She was gradually taking over control of BioSysTech. Things were finally going well!

England expected a call from DiRosa sometime today. She decided she would tell DiRosa to wait until the Hegel Bill passed to deal with Landcaster. Why should she risk running the business until then? After all, Hegel was right; some people would believe they were actually murdering those little globs of profit. Landcaster wouldn't do anything now. Not after that major blunder, not while believing he was alive only because of her.

Nothing could go wrong now. Except Becky. What was she going to do about Becky? She decided to give Becky more time.

It was a wonderful summer Saturday morning. Maybe she'd do five miles this morning. The route along the river seemed best for today.

———

Griffin still had not gotten used to the feeling of air on his shaved scalp, and the glue holding the beard on him made his skin itch. *Deal with it, Griffin.* He sat back in his chair in front of FBI Director Jacob Martin's desk.

Martin rocked in his chair behind the desk. For two and a half hours he had listened to Griffin. He had mulled over the photographs and played the four security CDs. As Griffin spoke, Director Martin had jotted down every name he mentioned, the first lady, Kristina England, Becky "somebody," Richard Landcaster, even Wayno, Johnny, Darlene, Comer, and Jason. Griffin's dead friends, Warren and Jennifer, too.

Director Martin leaned forward. He gazed over his black horned-rimmed reading glasses. "Her name is Rebecca Ingram, Mr. Dowell," Martin said. "My knowledge of this bizarre matter precedes you, although at that time I thought I was dealing with—well—another one of those conspiracy theorists that manage to get to me."

You always pave the way, don't You, God? So many aren't willing to trust enough to take the path. And I was one of them.

"Ms. Ingram is willing to testify, even if that means going to jail, if it will stop the Hegel Bill from passing in the Senate."

Griffin glared at Allan Cook, sitting next to him.

"I didn't know about her, Griffin!" Cook said. "The director doesn't tell agents everything that's going on."

"She said she's getting married soon and has recommitted to her faith," the director said.

A jolt of guilt hit Griffin.

"Her fiancé is active in his church," the director continued. "She says he told her that confessing our sins isn't enough, that we must do all we can to undo the hurt we've caused."

· Director Martin lifted one of the photos of the eviscerated babies from his desk. "What Miss Ingram tells me meshes with this abomination," he said as he studied the photo again.

"What do we do now?" Griffin asked the director.

The director lowered the photograph and peered at Griffin over his glasses again. "I call a news conference," he said. "Announce that you've been captured. Attorney General van Meter orders us to turn you over to the BAFT so they can shoot you. I refuse. I get called down by the White House; Constance Frye tells the president to threaten me with insubordination."

"How do you want me to handle the media?" Cook asked.

"Deny everything. No investigation is underway," the director said.

"Sir," Cook said, "the media. . ."

"Right," Martin said with a chuckle, "I'm protecting a delusional, woman-murdering maniac." Martin chuckled. "I hate women, native Americans, and bowlegged tall people with blue eyes."

"We open a file?" Cook asked.

"We open a silent file," the director said. "You head it up. Use Porter. She's loyal and knows how to keep her mouth shut."

"Right, sir," Cook said.

Director Martin pointed to Griffin. "I want him out of the country," he said to Cook. Then he turned to Griffin. "Your name. Change it. Rodriguez, Carlos. You don't look like that, but the name disappears off the page if someone searches logs or documents in Mexico City."

Griffin felt his brow furrow.

"That's where you'll be staying," the director said. "We'll get you there today."

"Yes, sir," Dowell said.

Director Martin quieted for a moment, staring at Griffin. "You go to church, Mr. Dowell," he said. "Believe in prayer?"

"Yes, sir," Dowell said.

"Well, I'd pray if I were you," the director said.

Allan and Griffin glanced at each other, smiled slightly, and got up from their chairs.

"Hold on, Mr. Dowell," Director Martin said the moment Griffin set his foot on the threshold of the office door. "I have a couple more questions." He motioned for Griffin and Cook to sit back down.

"This Amanda, Hegel's lab assistant. Mr. Dowell, you said she's missing? And Ruth Hegel told you her mother called her?"

"There's some confusion there, sir," Griffin said.

"Disabuse me, Mr. Dowell," the director said, his brow furrowed. "What did Amanda's mother tell Ruth Hegel?"

Griffin paused to think. He wanted to get it right. Every piece of the puzzle was important, even the smallest, and the director had now made it known that this particular piece of the puzzle might have some special meaning to him if it was rotated and angled properly.

See, Griffin, you're not as smart as you think you are.

Griffin wanted to make sure he made no misrepresentations. He decided to speak slowly, purposefully: "Amanda's mother. . .told Ruth Hegel. . .that her daughter, Amanda, said. . .she—Amanda—had something important that had to be done. . .that there was something that she—Amanda—had to give to somebody, and Amanda told her mother that she was all right." Griffin paused. "That's what the lab assistant's mother said to Ruth Hegel."

Director Martin leaned over his desk and stared over his reading glasses at Griffin again. "Somebody?" he asked.

"Yes, sir. I wish I knew who," Griffin said.

Director Martin started stroking his beard again. "Don't leave yet," he said to Griffin. "I want to think this completely through."

"Yes, sir," Griffin said.

Director Martin sat quietly, musing.

"Director," Griffin said, "while you're going over your thoughts, there's something I want to ask you."

"Go ahead," Martin said.

"Well, I need you to sign an award certificate, maybe even write a letter declaring someone a hero," Griffin said.

"This is a bureaucracy, Mr. Dowell," Director Martin said. "I'm not supposed to sign any certificate or awards without going through the proper channels, but tell me more, anyway."

Amanda rummaged through her dirty clothes, through the drawers in the night table next to her bed, and through her canvas satchel. She gathered everything Dr. Hegel had given her: the locker key, the letter she had found with the two sheets of paper in the URI envelope.

The envelope! Amanda's stomach churned. She saw the envelope in her mind's eye, on the keyboard, right where she had dropped it, face up: "To Amanda Collins, Personal and Confidential." *That's what started them after me!* Then she remembered again what her coaches had always told her, "It's not only talent; it's execution. You have to execute."

Angry at herself, Amanda shoved her collection of evidence into her satchel, then raced out of apartment 105.

A short while later, Amanda swung open the entrance door of Senator Gators' small Slidell office suite. She stomped to the desk where the elderly woman sat. The lady's eyes opened wide. Amanda moved her thumb under the satchel strap, shifted her head, and glared at the elderly lady.

"I want to see the senator," she said.

"Young lady, we have security here!" the lady said.

Amanda quickly scanned the reception area. She saw only one door. Then she returned her gaze to the lady. "Are you going to announce me, or do I barge in?" Amanda asked.

"I'm going to call the police!"

Amanda spun around and continued her stomp to the door. She flung it open. "I nearly got killed to see you!" Amanda yelled.

A pleasant-looking black gentleman sitting behind a large desk jerked his head up from papers sitting in front of him, his eyes wide and white with surprise. Amanda stood at the threshold, about to say something else, when the elderly woman ran into the office, pushing Amanda aside.

"She might be a terrorist!" the lady hollered.

Amanda felt herself glaring at the lady. "I'm not a terrorist," she said. She turned to the senator. "Dr. Avraham Hegel told me to bring something to you," she said.

"Avraham Hegel? The first lady's science advisor, the one who—"

"Yes. I'm Amanda Collins, his—well, his former lab assistant, and I have to speak with you, Senator." Amanda turned and glared at the elderly woman. "Alone," she said.

Senator Gators looked at the lady. "Gladys," he said, "you can go now. I'll be all right."

Gladys stomped out of the room.

"Sit down, child," the senator said.

Amanda sat. She moved the satchel from her lap and began lifting the contents out, placing them on the senator's desk. She was going to take her time, tell him everything she could, using everything she had in front of her to help her remember what seemed to have begun a long, long time ago. Maybe she would learn some things, too. Maybe she would come to understand what this was really all about, why her life had come apart, why she was now alone with no future.

Director Martin suddenly stopped stroking his beard. He pulled out a thick paperback book. Griffin read the cover: *Directory of Elected and Appointed Officials of the United States of America. United States Government Printing Office.*

The director licked his finger. Griffin could barely hear what the director was saying, like a mantra, under his breath while he fingered the pages of the book. Was it "Gators. . .Gators. . .Gators"? Director Martin mumbled numbers. He picked up the telephone receiver and poked the buttons on the phone, then leaned back.

"Hello, Alma. This is Jacob Martin. Alma, where's that old coot preacher husband of yours?"

The director rocked in his chair as he listened to the woman's response.

"Okay. I'll call him there. I've got the number. Save me some of that crawfish pie, now." The director hung up, smiling. He peered over his reading glasses at Cook. "I have a hunch," he said while he dialed the phone.

"Gators?" Cook asked.

"If I'm wrong, he can help us, anyway," Martin said. "We need every senator we can get."

"Yes, sir," Cook said.

The director peered at Dowell while waiting for the senator to answer. "Let me know if you want to talk to him," he said to Griffin.

"Yes, sir," Griffin said.

The phone on Senator Gators' desk rang.

"Well, hello, Jacob," Senator Gators said. "How's the Bureau?"

Amanda ran her hand over her hair. *This is not the time for a friendly chat,* she wanted to say. She shifted in her seat.

"I do have time for a long story," the senator said. "I've been listening to one myself. Put those big feet up on your desk and tell it."

Senator Gators glanced at Amanda, then motioned with his finger for her to stay put.

Amanda settled back in her chair and looked at the senator as he listened. It must be an interesting story. Senator Gators' forehead wrinkled; then his eyes widened and his mouth opened. An uncomfortable feeling came over Amanda, as if she were eavesdropping. The senator raised his head and stared at Amanda, as if she had done something wrong and they were talking about it. The senator kept staring at Amanda, nodding, listening.

"You have him there?" Gators asked, staring at Amanda. "Put him on."

For the next five or ten minutes, it seemed to Amanda, the senator sat frozen except for the nodding of his head. Then he returned his stare to Amanda. Amanda wanted to say, "I didn't do anything wrong!"

"She's right here," the senator said. "Right in front of me. Wait. I'll put this on conference."

Senator Gators punched a button. "You've been a busy young lady," he said with a smile that brought relief to Amanda. He looked up and hollered, "Gladys, come put this call on my loudspeaker!" He looked at Amanda again. "Every time I do it, I lose the connection." He chuckled.

The chuckle brought relief to Amanda. Something radiated from this man. Something wonderful.

What would it be like to have a father like him?

Gladys stomped into the office. "Senator, you have an intercom, you know!" Gladys said. Amanda watched her poke three buttons on the phone pad. "There!" she said and stomped out of the office.

"Can you hear me, Jacob?" the senator said.

"Fine," the director said. "I have one of my agents, Agent Cook, here, too, with Dowell."

"Amanda, this is Griffin Dowell. Do you know who I am?"

"Everybody knows who you are, Mr. Dowell." Amanda recalled the photograph she had seen of him somewhere. Here she was, talking to a guy they say burned his secretary alive, talking to him with a senator and the FBI!

"Amanda," Dowell said in an urgent tone, "did Dr. Hegel give you a package?"

Guilt. "Yes, but—"

"Where is it?" Dowell asked.

"They took it away from me," Amanda said.

"Who?" another man asked.

"A man named. . ." Amanda remembered Ramos inviting "Vicarro" to watch; she remembered the Italian talking about the arrangement after he had saved her life, asking her if she had heard his real name. Her heart thumped when the Italian's large brown eyes came to her mind, how they showed an odd sort of fatherly fondness for her. Maybe she would tell them one day, but not now. "DiRosa," Amanda said, "I don't know his first name. The name of the other man, I'll never forget. It's Fidel Ramos. His body is at the Peacock Inn in Kenner. My fiancé's body is in the trunk of their car; Ramos killed him."

"Make a note; check that out, Cook," another man said.

"She has a few papers here, Martin," the senator said.

"Can you fax them to us, Jeremiah?"

"Sure." The senator cupped the receiver again and hollered, "Gladys!"

Gladys stepped into the office again. She didn't glare at Amanda this time. Amanda even thought she saw the beginnings of a smile. Gladys took the sheets from the senator. "Sometimes you're just like a bad little boy," she said to the senator.

Senator Gators kept the phone mouthpiece cupped and looked directly at Amanda. "She's been listening," he said, showing that warm smile again.

No voices came from the loudspeaker for a moment. Then a man said, "Amanda, this is FBI Director Jacob Martin. I'm going to talk to you more about this, but you must not discuss any of this with anyone except the senator. It is a matter of national security. You understand?"

"Yes, sir," Amanda said, not believing what was happening.

Gladys came in, dropped the papers on the senator's desk, patted Amanda on her shoulder, then rushed out.

"I'm worried about the girl, Jeremiah," the director said. He paused, then said, "We got the papers."

———— | ————

Amanda could hear the director, Dowell, and the agent mumbling over the papers. Then a voice: "Amanda, this is Griffin Dowell. Do you still have the key to the airport locker Hegel mentions in his instructions?"

"I have it right here." Amanda reached for the key that sat in front of her on the senator's desk.

"See where Dr. Hegel drew an outline of a key on one of the pages of his suicide note?" Dowell asked.

Amanda looked at the outline. "Yes," she said, then leaned toward the speaker.

"Lay the key you have in your hand on the outline that Dr. Hegel drew, Amanda." It was the FBI agent's voice now.

Amanda laid the key on the paper. She held the edge of the paper with one hand, then slid the key slowly in the outline.

"Do they match?" Dowell asked.

"They are the same size, the same kind of key," Amanda said. "But. . ."

"The teeth, Amanda," Dowell said. "Do they match?"

"No. . .no. They don't," Amanda said. She felt frustrated, as if she had an easy lay-up but the ball circled the rim and fell into an opponent's grasp.

"There's another locker key somewhere," Amanda heard the FBI agent say. "Hegel hid something in another airport locker."

A pause.

The director, agent, and lawyer spoke to each other for a few minutes. Amanda couldn't understand what they were saying.

"Ms. Collins, this is Director Martin."

"Yes, sir?"

"We think Dr. Hegel hid another airport locker key somewhere," the director said.

"Yes, sir," Amanda said.

"Now, from what we know, Amanda," the director said, "Dr. Hegel was a brilliant, thoughtful man, and you worked closely with him for almost two years."

"Yes, sir," Amanda said, on the verge of tears. "He was like a father to me."

"I want you to think, Amanda. You are all we have," the director said. "I want you to tell me where you think Dr. Hegel might have hidden a key like the one you have in your hand."

Think, Amanda. Think!

"I don't know!" Amanda wanted to cry. She threw up her hands.

"Amanda," Dowell said, "would Dr. Hegel hide the key in the lab?"

"They owned everything in there," Amanda said.

"Okay," Dowell said, "he hid it either in his house or in his office."

"Was he close to any of the other professors?" the agent asked Amanda.

"He wasn't like any of the other professors," Amanda said.

"It has to be somewhere in his house," Cook said.

"No," Dowell said. "He doesn't think like that. Hegel hid it where we would find it when he wanted us to find it."

Pause.

When Amanda heard Dowell say that, she started to rock in her chair. She felt herself squinting as she pushed her brain.

He hid it where I would find it when he wanted me to. Think, Amanda, think!

Thump. . .thump. . .thump. The sound passed through her mind. Amanda felt her eyes widen. She drew in a deep breath.

"I know!" came out of her mouth. "He was showing me!" Amanda leaned toward the speaker and shouted. "In his office! The day he died! He was showing me!"

"What, child? What?" Senator Gators said.

"In the old doll! That has to be it!" A thrill ran through Amanda when she realized that Dr. Hegel was himself that morning, not a Mr. Hyde! *He didn't mean to treat me like that! He was just acting, making sure the image of that horrid old doll burned into my mind. He was doing it just in case they got the package.*

"Amanda," Dowell said. "The old doll you're talking about. Was it an old blond-haired baby doll named Millie?"

"Yes, yes!" Amanda said. "With X marks on its head!"

Another pause.

"The key's in Millie. I know it is!" Amanda's body began to quiver with excitement.

"What do you think is in the locker, Mr. Dowell?" the senator asked.

"That's speculation, sir," Cook said, "but we have an idea."

"I'll keep you posted, Jeremiah," Director Martin said. "Are you safe where you are down there, Amanda?"

"I guess so."

"Don't you worry, Jacob," the senator said. "Nobody's going to hurt this child. She's going to be eating some good down-home fixin's and playing around with Lukandee for as long as it takes."

Amanda felt relief, then confusion. *Lukandee?*

"I'll send a few agents down there to pick up a quart or two of Alma's gumbo," Martin said.

"Amanda, I'll be talking to you soon," the FBI agent said.

EIGHT DAYS LATER

CHAPTER 33

Amanda strolled into Senator Gators' front yard. He lived in the country, eleven miles down Highway 90 from Slidell. Pine and oak trees stood tall in his yard; birds flew and disappeared in the green foliage. Squirrels leaped from one branch to another. A pond, stocked with perch and green trout and a four-foot alligator named "Lukandee," glistened between the house and the main road.

Two FBI agents sat in a plain-looking black car where the shell driveway met the highway. Another agent stayed inside. He slept during the daytime, stalked the grounds at night. Another agent shared shifts with another, lying on the roof of Senator Gators' home, with scoped sniper rifles ready. And another sometimes sat on the front porch, sometimes the back porch, depending on where Amanda wandered on the property.

The senator told Amanda that he had heard talk from Washington, D.C., that she was dead. And that was fine, too. Senator Gators had left for Washington two days ago. Amanda had already given a long statement to Agent Porter. Things seemed to be happening so rapidly now. But in the safety Amanda enjoyed now, in the warmth of Senator and Alma Gators caring for her, she didn't mind the rumors, not even if her mama heard them. She would fix all that later.

Amanda had watched the senator prepare his speech to the Senate in opposition to the Hegel Bill. He didn't rehearse in front of her. He said it would be better that she not hear it. Strange. And she noticed something else. He prayed more than he studied the documents that

Agent Cook had sent to him. She recognized those documents, too. Amanda's heart jumped when she saw them; she had almost died trying to keep the originals from the killers. In a way, Geoffry had died for them. Amanda spotted a letter from Dr. Hegel addressed to Senator Gators that must have been wrapped inside the package she had, because she had not seen it, but the senator refused to allow her to read it.

It was the night before Senator Gators left for Washington that they had their first real talk, alone at the kitchen table. That talk would change her life, Amanda just knew it.

"Amanda, I need an assistant I can trust," the senator had said. "The pay is good, but you'll have to spend some time in Washington and live here in St. Tammany Parish."

Should I? Should I get into politics? Like Doctor Hegel?

Amanda wished there were someone to tell her what to do.

During that talk, Amanda told the senator how much she had loved Geoffry, adding that she felt empty now, that she had no one.

"That will change, child," the senator told her as he cupped his huge hand over hers. "Someone has been with you always," the senator said in his soft, powerful voice.

But he wouldn't explain. She told him she was confused.

"I got lost in New Orleans, and I can't get out of my mind what I saw and heard there."

"You only believed you were lost," Senator Gators told her. Then he said something about how the heart knows its ministry, but he wouldn't explain that, either. "All in God's timing," he had told Amanda.

The senator's frequent mention of God puzzled Amanda. During her childhood, Amanda hadn't heard much about the God everyone talked about and prayed to. She certainly had not heard about God from her father at home.

She had decided to accept the senator's job offer. And she found herself doing something she had never done before with a potential employer: bargain!

"If I do, will you let me try to help the young people trapped in the welfare cycle?" she had asked the senator in the best ultimatum tone she could muster.

"We'll see," the senator had said. "A federal program has never changed a heart, my child."

What is he talking about?

"Tell you what, child. You come to church, and I'll introduce you to somebody who might be able to help you."

Sure, sure.

CHAPTER 34

Y ou'll see why I had to make an example of Peterson, Kristina," Constance said, sitting behind her desk. She spoke over the voices coming from the closed-circuit television that sat in a mahogany cabinet. "In a few minutes, Gators will read Peterson's article."

England had noticed that Constance spoke more softly to her lately, since the problem of the girl and the package had been taken care of. They were truly working together for the venture now. And soon the venture could start up again, England thought. This time as a legal business. Of course there would be an uproar by the right-wingers. But CPNN, with the rest of the mainstream broadcast and op-ed print journalists, would begin a new worship and praise week for Constance. The rabble would forget about the debate on the morality of harvesting organs from conceptuses, those federally created subhumans.

The rabble always forget. Remember all the commotion about partial-birth abortions? Now just as routine as a haircut. All of the hoopla will die down. Only the religious right-wingers will keep fussing, and the more they do, the more they're ignored. See Becky. I have to do something about Becky.

Of course, Constance was right again. Peterson's article could have been a major setback. How clever it was of the first lady to take every opportunity to renounce the thought of fetal brain stem cells being transplanted into animals for retribution and to publicly call for Peterson's head. And, of course, with the press bringing out all sorts of new revelations about Mr. Peterson's hypocrisy and thieving ways. . .well.

CPNN had learned that Peterson wasn't really a vegetarian at all

371

and that he even wore real leather shoes! Reliable sources said he might have misused the funds people had donated to Brothers and Sisters in Fin, Feathers, and Fur and stated that he should resign his position because of the indictment. And, of course, Peterson did resign. England herself had issued a news release, insisting that he do just that, for the good of all the other politically aggressive nonprofits and, of course, the children of America.

So what did Senator Gators have at the cost of Peterson's career? An article from a disgraced animal rights whacko embezzler? An article that the folks perceived the first lady believed to be just as reprehensible as Gators did?

Constance took the wind right out of your sails, Preacher Gators, England thought.

"Madeline, what's wrong?" England asked. Gentcher looked nervous, sitting next to England and squirming in her chair. Gentcher glanced at the first lady. England followed her eyes. The first lady nodded. Gentcher turned to England.

"Redden is talking off the record again," Gentcher said. "I'm afraid there might be fire where there's smoke this time." Gentcher pulled out one of her Marlboros. She shifted her gaze to Constance.

"Go ahead," Constance said softly to Gentcher.

Gentcher lit the cigarette and continued, "I spoke to Redden personally. I told him he would be mopping floors if he kept up his rumor mongering." Gentcher took a drag on her cigarette, turned her head to the side, then blew the smoke away from England and the first lady.

"What's he saying?" England asked.

"That the FBI is secretly investigating BioSysTech. Maybe looking to indict somebody. Probably Landcaster."

England felt cold fear run down her spine.

"That's why this bill has to pass today," Constance said. "That's why I'm so proud of you, Kristina, for getting the girl out of the way and the package, too."

Another chill.

"The press? Redden?" England asked.

Gentcher blew another breath of smoke to the side. "I told the key people that Redden was lying, as usual, that he dislikes the first lady, and that to repeat his nonsense would do nothing but hurt her efforts to help the children. Redden has pretty much been ignored. Just the usual right-wingers' radio and cable news flap."

"What about Dowell?" England asked.

"Ashton met with Director Martin about that," Constance said. "Ashton tells me Martin believes Dowell is suffering from posttraumatic stress disorder relating to his being wounded in Vietnam. He thinks Dowell should be kept in protective custody until the press lets up. Then maybe a quick plea bargain. Maybe insanity, life in prison. It's not as good as we hoped, but it'll do."

"Do you believe him?" England asked Constance. Something didn't sound right to England. Dowell wasn't the sort to give in to this posttraumatic stress slop.

"Who?" Constance asked England.

"Your husband," England said.

A red flush came to the first lady's face. Not the intensity of one of her rages, but an indication to England that she should have said "the director" instead.

"Are you suggesting my husband would lie to me?"

"No. No," England said.

"And there's more good news," Gentcher said. "Gators isn't going to filibuster. Talk is he's just going to read Peterson's article and then preach a little. We have the votes, maybe three or four more than we need."

Thank you, Madeline, for interrupting. England was certain that if the subject had not been changed, Constance would have pounced on her. It was just plain stupidity to have to endure all of this just to get a business going.

"What about Becky, Kristina?" Constance asked.

Constance Frye's words entered England like a knife. Her relief gave way to a fear that numbed her spine. That tone. It was the soft question before the rage.

"I. . .I. . ."

"You didn't do anything, did you?" Constance paused. "Did you, Kristina!" she yelled, slapping the top of her desk. "Redden says your little Becky's been talking to the FBI. Why didn't you do something?"

"I thought—"

"You thought!" Constance yelled. "I'll do the thinking." She leaned toward England, her face beet red. "It's a good thing I pushed this legislation through on time! I always have to salvage your lousy work."

England clammed up. She slumped in her chair. Maybe Gentcher would lend her some support again: another interruption, a friendly gesture—anything. She looked toward Gentcher, who was just removing her Marlboro from her mouth. She stared into England's eyes and then blew smoke in England's face. Not moving her gaze from England's eyes, Gentcher grinned.

"Don't think you and Landcaster are going to do what you think you're going to do," Constance said to England. "You had no intention of getting him out of the way until it was convenient for you. He knows you took all that money, and I know it, too."

"Constance."

"I'll deal with you," the first lady said. "I'm not sure how. You're lucky you have some value to me, Kristina."

"Ms. Frye," Gentcher said, pointing to the television.

Senator Jeremiah Gators stepped up to the podium of the Senate Chambers. England, the first lady, and Gentcher turned their attention to the television. Constance reached for the remote and raised the volume. The senator began to speak.

"My colleagues, my fellow senators," Senator Gators said. "I ask that you listen to me with great care, for I will be reading to you something that will chill your souls. And then I have an announcement, one that will turn this wonderful country upside down. But with God's help, we'll survive."

" 'Announcement'?" Constance said softly, "Peterson's probably spilling his guts for immunity." She chuckled. "Let him!"

The Senate Chambers quieted. England noticed it immediately.

Senator Gators continued, "I open with a prayer. My prayer is that you listen to what I read to you and have faith that it is the truth, as I know in my heart it is, as I have confirmed it."

A pang of fear shot through England. Senator Gators was too

confident. Something didn't fit. Something was wrong, England kept thinking.

"Great drama, Gators," Constance said through a smirk, directing her comments to the television. "By the time you read Peterson's first paragraph, they'll be mumbling and shuffling papers like they always do, waiting for your hot air to dissipate."

England's heart pounded. Peterson's silly article could not generate the emotion she saw in this powerful man.

"And, my fellow senators, I know God answers my prayers," Senator Gators said. He lowered his gaze to the sheet he had placed on the podium. Not a sound came from the Senate Chambers, as most of the senators were leaning toward him, waiting for him to speak. The senator still waited, maybe for half a minute. England felt sure she was going to explode. Then, in his rich, deep voice, Senator Jeremiah Gators began to read to his entranced colleagues:

" 'Dear Senator Gators, I am Avraham Frederick Hegel. You know me as the late science advisor for the first lady's reform bill, also known affectionately by your supporters as "Hegel the Beast." I could not live with that title, with doing what I did for her. Eventually they would have killed me, my wife, probably my children, too. That is why I am dead. . . .' "

The first lady jumped up. "What is he reading?" she shouted. "Kristina! What is he reading?" She pointed the remote at the television and raised the volume.

"Oh, no!" England said softly, unable to keep her eyes off the television set.

"Kristina?" Constance said.

"It's the letter. The letter that was in the package," England said.

"What letter?" Constance asked.

" '—Under the instruction of the first lady, and for payment by Biological Systems Technology, Inc., a company owned partially. . .' "

"I thought I had gotten rid of it," England said, "tossed it into the river. I did! How did they—"

"Tell me what it is! What will he say?" the first lady screamed at England. For the first time ever, England saw fear in the first lady's eyes.

"I guess they found a copy somewhere," England said.

None of the three women spoke as Senator Gators continued to read. England glanced at the first lady, then at Gentcher. She didn't know what else to do but to monitor their response as they watched Senator Gators and listened.

" 'BioSysTech grew the babies in incubators, like exotic plants, and harvested the fruits of their abdominal cavities. The babies couldn't feel the pain, though, thanks to my Alfa Alkaloid lobotomies. . .' "

Constance plopped in her chair. She lowered her head and took a deep breath. England heard Gentcher mumble something. She didn't want to glance at Gentcher, not now.

"You better listen," Gentcher said, directing the comment to the first lady. "You will need a spin, quick!"

England got up from her chair. She wanted to leave, but that would be impossible. Where would she go? She walked to the sofa that sat farther away from the first lady's desk than the chairs. She drifted a moment, but when her mind cleared she heard this mighty man from some small Louisiana town reading the words Hegel the Coward spoke from his grave, stripping the facade of "for the children" from the first lady's mantra.

" 'God forgive me for the hundreds of babies I let grow and be slaughtered. . .' "

England had to watch now. Not only listen. She had to see what was sure to cause her eventually to be indicted, or worse.

" 'I was evil, Senator. I was hideously, irredeemably evil. I asked the Messiah to forgive me. I don't believe even He is capable of it.' "

The television camera brought Senator Gators close in. With tears rolling down his cheeks, the senator said softly: "You are watching us from Glory, Dr. Avraham Hegel," the senator said. "My soul knows it."

Senator Gators surveyed his silent colleagues. Without looking at the note, he said, "Dr. Hegel signed the letter 'Avraham F. Hegel, M.D., Ph.D., late science advisor to the first lady.' "

England dropped her head in her hands. This isn't happening! It isn't being announced to the public, being broadcast over the whole country. *Yes, it is, Kristina. Yes, it is.*

England had to see what the first lady was doing. She looked toward Constance.

Constance moved her head slowly, then looked into England's eyes. She said nothing. She didn't have to. Her beet-red face, her grim frown, and her squinted green eyes said it all: *You're going to pay for this, Kristina! You're going to pay for this with your career, maybe your life!*

Constance reached for the remote. "I can't stand any more of this!" She screamed.

"No, wait," Gentcher said. "He said he had an announcement."

A knock sounded at the door.

"Get that, Madeline," Constance said, staring at England. "Tell whoever it is that I can't be seen right now."

Gentcher stood and strode to the door.

"My fellow senators, I was told just this morning that. . ."

England watched the door open.

"Mrs. Frye, may I talk to you for a moment, ma'am?" a man said, with a woman by his side.

England knew what FBI agents looked like.

"I'm Special Agent Allan Cook; this is Agent Sandra Porter. FBI." They flashed their identification. Porter stared at England, then moved close to her, between England and the door.

"Ma'am, we have a warrant to arrest Ms. Kristina England," Cook said.

Agent Porter looked down at England. "Would you please stand up and turn around," Agent Porter said to England.

England stood. The instant she turned, she felt cold handcuffs clamp on her wrists. "Turn around, ma'am," England heard Porter say softly.

Porter met England's stare. She lifted a card and began to read: "You are under arrest. You have the right to remain silent. Anything you say. . ."

England couldn't think as she heard the words. Her heart pounded.

"Are you armed?" Agent Porter asked.

England shook her head. She stared at Constance. Constance stood, staring back with an expression of uncertainty.

Agent Porter tugged gently on England's arm. England stiffened and looked at the first lady. "Don't think you're going to get off scot-free, Constance," she said.

Agent Porter tugged a little harder. England began to walk with her toward the door. Agent Cook walked behind them. As they escorted England out of the office and down the hall of the White House, each gripping an arm, England heard Agent Cook say to Agent Porter: "Remind me to call Carlos. The director says it's time he came home."

———

Richard Landcaster stared at his television in disbelief, as Andrea Rue, without her red ribbon, announced the latest breaking news on the Dowell bombing investigation:

"CPNN has learned that Kristina England, the well-known New York attorney and policy advisor to the first lady on her reform bill, better known as the Hegel Bill, has been arrested by the FBI.

"Senator Jeremiah Gators, in his stunning speech in opposition to the first lady's reforms, announced that more arrest warrants will be issued. Several indictments are expected.

"The FBI will not give details on what England has been charged with but did say mail fraud and embezzlement are among the charges. We have one report from a reliable source that even murder charges will be brought.

"And now, another exclusive update from Sheryl Hastings on what might be a related story, the fugitive-lawyer, Griffin Dowell."

Hastings appeared on the television, standing in front of the J. Edgar Hoover Building. "Andrea," she said into the microphone, "although the FBI will tell us nothing about Kristina England, we have learned that attorney Griffin Dowell has been cleared of all charges relating to the death of his secretary and the firebombing of his car.

"Director Jacob Martin did tell us, however, that Attorney General van Meter has ordered the director to relinquish jurisdiction to the BAFT. According to Director Martin, the White House has asked van Meter to arrange for a special force of BAFT agents to take Dowell into protective custody as a material witness. The director refused.

"It's likely the White House will review the director's conduct to consider appropriate sanctions, perhaps dismissal. If you recall, Director Martin has been accused of racial and sexual discrimination several times over his career. Back to you, Andrea."

Andrea turned to her left. "Well, Barton, things are moving quickly," she said.

"That's right. Too bad the Mets don't have a player who can swat a ball that quickly, Andrea," Barton said into the camera with a stern look on his face.

Landcaster began to pace in his pajama bottoms on the posh carpet of his Chicago penthouse, his heavy gold chain lying on his bare gray-haired chest.

"What's wrong, honey?" the young brunette said, sitting on the sofa in Landcaster's purple robe, resting her bare feet on the coffee table, filing her nails.

"Shut up!" Landcaster yelled at her. He hadn't yet stiffened his hair with spray, so his hand ran easily through his hair. He now stood still in the middle of the living room, images of men in prison uniforms grinning at him running through his mind.

"Sorry, Barton," Andrea Rue said. "This just breaking: CPNN has just learned that the Hegel Bill failed to pass the Senate. The vote was 148 to 52. Speaker of the House Jukali said the Senate has no courage, that Gators has single-handedly condemned millions of critically sick children to their deaths."

"We go back to Sheryl Hastings in D.C. at the FBI," Rue said.

"Andrea, everything is moving so quickly now," Hastings said, looking into the camera appearing as if she were trying to catch her breath. "Attorney Griffin Dowell is a free man; all authorities have cleared him of any wrongdoing, and he will not be held by the BAFT as a material witness—"

"What happened?" Andrea asked.

"Not sure, but I heard that the president's policy advisor, Gordon Redden, says that President Frye ordered the immediate release and freedom of Dowell after the president spoke to him in a private telephone call."

The telephone rang. Landcaster lifted the receiver, anxiety rising up in him as he brought the receiver to his ear, trying to guess who was calling now.

"You see that on TV, Dr. Landcaster?" Vic Ricci said.

"I saw it."

"England was going to tell DiRosa to hit you," Vic said. "But you don't have to worry. DiRosa's gone. He killed Ramos. He let the girl go; she's probably singing her guts out. He's going back into the program. So you don't have to worry."

"Sure, guy. Sure," Landcaster said.

"I think that other warrant is for me," Vic said. "I'm leaving the country; got some family members who can get me back to the old country."

"Good for you, Vic," Landcaster said. "But you're a nobody to these guys. You get immunity easy. They want me, and they know where I live."

A knock sounded at the door.

"And I'm not going to prison—not ever."

Landcaster dropped the receiver on the sofa.

"Dr. Landcaster? Dr. Land—"

"Get the door, will you, baby?" Landcaster asked the young woman as he passed her on his way toward the back wall and the balcony doors. He heard the penthouse apartment door unlatch and a man say, "Dr. Richard Landcaster, please."

Landcaster opened the dual balcony doors and stepped onto the balcony. He braced his hand on the railing, lifted his leg, and swung his weight over the top, into the air.

Somewhere in the middle of Landcaster's descent, approximately forty-four stories from the street, Dr. Richard Landcaster drifted into unconsciousness as he felt his body accelerating toward the automobile tops and concrete below.

ONE WEEK LATER

CHAPTER 35

Griffin lifted his hands from the keyboard and turned his gaze from the monitor to Bonnie Sibley. Bonnie stood in front of his desk, trembling.

"What's wrong?" Griffin asked.

"I'm so sorry, Mr. Dowell. I meant to tell you." Bonnie lowered her head, then lifted it again. "To let you know I put her on your calendar for this morning, but I forgot."

"It's all right, Bonnie," Griffin said. "I'm not going to fire you, even if that's what you heard I would do. I flog my secretaries now."

Bonnie's eyes widened.

"I'm kidding, Bonnie. Just kidding."

Bonnie looked like she wasn't sure.

She'll come around. Give her time. She'll be bossing me around in no time. Griffin leaned in his chair. "Now, what is it?"

"Carolyn Jennings is here," Bonnie said.

Carolyn Jennings' image from the dream he'd had in cabin 8 ran through Griffin's mind.

You should have called Carolyn, Griffin, should have gone to her house and talked to her.

Griffin couldn't recall exactly what FBI Director Jacob Martin had said when he asked him about a certificate for heroism. Something like, "I'm a bureaucrat. If it's not procedure, I can't do it." Somehow, even after Martin said that, Griffin knew Martin would give in after he explained everything. The director, Griffin had thought, looking at Martin in all his rugged intellect, had that soft spot that men who know the Truth can't hide.

"All right, Dowell," the director had said. "I'll do it. Frye is going to find some way to get rid of me, anyway."

Griffin jerked himself out of his musings to face what he had to.

"You're not alone, Griffin," the Voice said.

"I'll see Carolyn in myself, Bonnie," Griffin said. He got up from his chair and walked to the reception area.

Carolyn stood when she saw Griffin at the door. Griffin's heart sank when he saw her. In her black dress, she looked as though she had just come from her husband's funeral.

"I have to talk to you," Carolyn said.

"Let's go in my office," Griffin said. He felt anger at himself.

Why didn't you talk to her before this, Griffin? How could you have made her come to you? Now explain to Carolyn how you sent her husband out of your office. . .how you refused to believe him.

Carolyn slumped in Griffin's client chair. He could see she wanted to speak, but she appeared not to know how to begin. Griffin decided to start the conversation.

"Carolyn, I'm sorry I haven't talked to you since Warren died. Maybe if I tell you what happened, you'll understand why."

"No one talks to me now," Carolyn said. "It's like I have some disease. The boys, too. They've changed. They don't play anymore. They don't laugh. They've lost their friends. The psychiatrist wants to put them on some medicine; I don't know if that's good for them. I just don't know." Carolyn lowered her head. "Everything's so dark," she said, gazing down but appearing to look at nothing. Then she raised her head and looked into Griffin's eyes. "My poor little Tommy," she said. "He still cries himself to sleep."

"Carolyn, I'm sor—"

"I didn't come here to make you feel guilty, Griffin," Carolyn said softly. "I know Warren came here before. . ."

"How could you know?"

"Jennifer told me before she died."

"I'm sorry," Griffin said, finding no other words.

"I just need to know. So I can tell my boys," Carolyn said. "Warren didn't commit suicide, did he? Please tell me. I want to see my sons run and play again, laugh again. But what I tell them has to be the truth."

"Warren didn't kill himself," Griffin said.

"Are the rumors true, then?" Carolyn asked. "Did the White House have something to do with it?"

"Two thugs killed Warren. They've probably been killed themselves by now. They made Warren inject himself with that overdose of cocaine, probably threatened that you and the boys would be killed if he didn't."

Carolyn folded in the chair. Griffin waited until she recovered.

"The first lady and others had Warren killed," Griffin said. "It'll take some time, but I'll tell you why."

For the next hour, Griffin told Carolyn the events beginning Wednesday, June 19, the day Warren entered his office, to the day the FBI arrested Kristina England. Carolyn didn't move in her seat; she didn't take her gaze off Griffin as he spoke.

"I drove by the facility a few days ago," Griffin said. "I needed to go back, to make sure that guard survived and to thank Jason Rivers. Thank God I didn't kill that guard. The National Guard had bulldozers and backhoes at the facility. It was about leveled when I drove by."

"What about the babies?" Carolyn asked.

Griffin felt his countenance sink. "God help them," he said. "Jacqueline Reed knew what she was doing. They all survived, if that's what you call it. They're spread out in children's hospitals in seven or eight states." Griffin shook his head. "Sometimes I just don't understand."

"Dr. Reed," Carolyn said. "What happened to her?"

"Agent Cook told me they made a deal with her. She surrendered her medical license for life and agreed to testify according to her sworn statement. For that, she gets immunity. That testimony would be devastating to the defense, maybe to the country, if they ever used it."

"Will they use it, Griffin?" Carolyn asked. "Will the truth about my husband come out?"

"Probably not now that Kristina England has plea bargained. One count of violation of wire fraud. The New York State Bar Association will disbar her, no doubt. But she'll be back. Senator Gators and some House members are calling for an investigation of Anticipating Parenthood, too. But don't look for any of that in the media. Speaker Jukali's fighting it. The president certainly won't push it."

"And the stroke the first lady suffered?"

"Spin at its best," Griffin said. "No way a first lady is going to jail. What's the use? Her husband could pardon her if he wanted. No law against that. In lieu of the embarrassment of an indictment, she consented to informal house arrest at her home here outside Columbia for the rest of the time her husband's in office. It doesn't make much difference; civil actions are coming, lawsuits brought by the mothers of the babies. The Fryes are headed for bankruptcy with all the judgments coming against them. Madeline Gentcher disappeared the day the FBI arrested England. Not sure what they'll do with her."

Carolyn settled back in her chair. "I feel better, Griffin," she said. "One day my sons will be old enough to understand all this. I know one day I can make them feel better about their father."

"Warren was a hero," Griffin said. "Your boys need to know that. He started the collapse of the whole enterprise." Griffin pulled open a side drawer of his desk.

"I just wish the other children. . . . This is destroying my boys," Carolyn said.

"Give them this," Griffin said as he handed Carolyn an envelope.

Carolyn opened the envelope and pulled out a gold-colored medallion attached to a red, white, and blue ribbon. Engraved on the medallion were these words:

"FBI DECLARATION OF HEROISM TO WARREN JENNINGS FROM THE DIRECTOR OF THE FEDERAL BUREAU OF INVESTIGATION OF THE UNITED STATES OF AMERICA."

Carolyn let out a whimper; her free hand flew to her mouth.

"Read the letter," Griffin said.

Carolyn unfolded the letter and read as Griffin recalled what he had persuaded FBI Director Jacob Martin to write and personally sign:

"This is to declare that Secret Agent Warren Jennings is officially a hero of the Federal Bureau of Investigation for giving his life in defeating an enemy of the United States of America and its citizens."

Carolyn breathed heavily as she read the words. She dropped the letter in her lap when she finished. Color returned to her face. Griffin watched the real Carolyn Jennings resurrecting in front of him.

She stared at the letter as she refolded it. She sniffled. She pressed the letter and the medal against her chest, her eyes filling with tears.

"Do you know what you have done for my boys? Do you know you have given them back their faith in their father?" she said.

Griffin couldn't find words right then, and if he did, he wouldn't be able to speak them; the lump in his throat just wouldn't let the words pass. He took a deep breath. Time for him to try to speak.

"Carolyn, do you remember when you and Warren used to go to church?" he asked.

Carolyn nodded.

"You've got to go back," Griffin said. "You've got to get the boys involved. They'll find peace there."

"Now they will, Griffin," Carolyn said. "Now they will."

It was after Carolyn stepped back from Griffin and smiled, after she hugged him, that the thought came to him. *You have to call him now, Griffin. No getting around it. Yeah, yeah.*

"Hello, Amanda," Gladys said when Amanda greeted her on the telephone. "Some things I need, dear. Your Social Security number. . .number of dependents. Maybe you should stop by the office today so we can get you started. I need your signature on a bunch of things, anyway."

"Yes, ma'am," Amanda said.

"You'll have to go to Washington for a training program. I think it's next month sometime while the senators are still on vacation. But we can talk about that when you get here."

"Yes, ma'am."

"And stop calling me 'ma'am.' "

"Yes, ma—. . .okay."

"We have a special Wednesday night service at church tonight. The choir is performing, and the senator will say a few words, too. He would like to see you there, Amanda. You're very special to him and Alma."

Amanda held the receiver to her ear though her mind briefly wandered to other things. Her gaze fell on the photograph of her and Geoffry. Maybe she would send it to his parents, but she had better call first and see how they would respond. Funny, she thought, Geoffry mentioned them but never introduced her to them by telephone or any other way. *Did they know about me?* Amanda slipped the photograph in the drawer.

And she wanted a cat, a big Persian, one of those giant white ones, maybe. "Chuckles" would be his name.

Amanda had spoken to the senator three or four times since that night in the kitchen when he offered her the job. And Alma had kept her company since the senator's return to Washington. Amanda envied her, having a family and a home. Admired her, too, for keeping up with all of it, maintaining it in the love that flowed from her for her husband. She wondered why they had no children, just that alligator.

"I know you wonder," Alma Gators had said. "We can't have children. God works in mysterious ways. Jeremiah would have been a wonderful father."

Oh, he would have been, Amanda thought. The talkative teen on the choppy lane slipped into her mind. What kind of family does he have? All those children, those babies? What kind of families do they have? Every time Amanda spoke to the senator, she felt compelled to talk about those young people and the future they were condemned to live.

"Why does the government perpetuate their condition, Senator? Can't you do something?" Amanda had asked him.

"The federal government cannot change hearts," the senator had told her over and over again. "It takes a ministry to do that. Is that your ministry, Amanda?"

"Me? What can I do?" Amanda had asked.

"In time—in time, my child," Senator Gators always said. "Have you called your mother?"

Why? What does my mother have to do with it? In spite of his wisdom and power, Amanda thought the senator spoke in riddles sometimes. She had to know what he was talking about.

"What time does the service begin?" Amanda wanted to end the conversation with Gladys. She wasn't ready yet to be so familiar.

In the little time she had had the opportunity to come to know her, Amanda discovered Gladys wasn't the hysterical elderly woman of her first impression.

"Gladys works hard to keep my husband organized," Alma Gators had told Amanda. "I don't know what Jeremiah would do without her." Alma paused a moment. "There's something that might help you understand," she had said. "It was Gladys's father who led those robed men to burn down the senator's grandfather's church; it was her father who swung the rope over the tree limb."

Oh, God. Daddy. Can't you see the wonderful forgiveness?

Amanda, can you?

"Seven o'clock," Gladys said. "You don't have to dress fancy."

"I'll be there. . .Gladys. Promise," Amanda said.

└──┴──┘

"Griffin Dowell. I can't believe it! Finally found yourself, did you?" Pastor Drew Grady said.

"Okay. So that was stupid," Griffin said. Griffin hated to deal with men or women as smart as he when he was on the wrong side of the facts. "I just called to tell you I'll be coming back to church."

"This Sunday?" the pastor asked.

"Well, no. I've planned a trip to Narragansett, Rhode Island. Sort of a working vacation by the beach. I have a good friend in Kingston."

"Ruth Hegel?"

"You're still the same, Drew. Nosy," Griffin said with a chuckle. "We're just friends. I filled about a dozen legal pads during my adventure. Ruth is an extraordinary writer. That makes a great beginning for a good book."

"Hey, I didn't say anything." Pastor Grady's voice had a ring of childish denial. But then his tone changed. "Jennifer and I talked about you every Sunday, Griffin," the pastor said. "You were the big brother she never had. I miss her; I miss you, too. It's a blessing to hear from you."

Should I tell him I talked to Jennifer a few days ago? That she was sparkling and beautiful. . .that she floats around in a mansion on golden streets?

"I'll see you in a couple of weeks." Griffin felt good when he said that. He should have known Pastor Grady would have responded this way.

"I have something else to say, Griffin."

Now he's stretching this reconciliation stuff just a bit.

"What?" Griffin asked.

"Tithing is a retroactive proposition," the pastor said.

"You take promissory notes?" Griffin asked.

⌐   ⌐   ⌐

Amanda couldn't believe what she saw after the opening prayer when the choir sang "I'll Fly Away." The men, women, and teens in the choir and all over the sanctuary clapped and swayed. Gladys played the piano, kicking up her knees and swinging her hands high as she hit the keys. She made Amanda think about those old black-and-white films of Jerry Lee Lewis.

And there was Alma, in the front row with a group of older ladies, all of them clapping, swaying. Amanda shook her head. *This isn't what I thought it would be like.* Everybody seemed so free.

The air was alive. But even here, the talkative teen and the teenage girls came to her mind. *If only they could be here!*

At first Amanda chose not to clap. But the urge was too great. She clapped, but she still felt as though she should not clap as freely as all those other people; she let herself sway with the music a little.

The choir sang "What a Friend We Have in Jesus." A longing welled up in Amanda when she heard that song. What was happening to her? She felt her spirit surge. The rest of the people sat, and Amanda did, too, but she wanted the choir to keep going.

Senator Gators stepped up to the podium. That wonderful smile that Amanda loved to see emerged. Amanda knew now. This was where this great fighter got his power; it didn't come from himself.

The senator preached about ministries and gifts and the parable of the talents, how every one of God's children is an essential part of the body of the church. Amanda felt as if the senator were preaching to her.

At the end of his sermon, Senator Gators said, "Everyone bow your head. Search your heart. Ask yourself if you are a child of the living God. Ask Him to help you to forgive."

Forgive?

The choir stood and began singing a hymn softly. Amanda wasn't sure at first; then she realized the song was the hymn that Billy Graham always ended his public sermons with, the song she had heard at one of her secret nights at her forbidden friend's house.

"Just as I Am"? That's it. Amanda started singing what words she knew of the hymn to herself. As she stood with her eyes closed, her head bowed, a living peace enshrouded her. *Oh, Mama, I love you. You, too, Daddy.* Then she asked herself, *Are you a child of God, Amanda? Are you?* Her answer to herself was no. *Oh, I want to be. I want to be!*

A warm feeling ran through her. Her heart increased its rate gently as she felt a weight suddenly lift from her. She had never felt this way; she was different now. She wanted the choir to sing again; she wanted to clap and sway.

"All of you who could not answer that question with a 'yes,' I want

390

you to come down to me," the senator said.

I understand now. She felt a tug from somewhere.

As Amanda walked down the aisle, she saw Senator Gators waiting for her with that smile. Tears were coming; Amanda could feel them on her cheeks. She glanced at Gladys sitting at the piano at the edge of the stage. Gladys had the look of a proud grandmother on her face.

As the senator smiled at Amanda, his precious love for her spilled all over her. He stretched out his hands and placed them on Amanda's shoulders. "It's God's time now, Amanda," he said softly.

Amanda stood still for a moment after the senator hugged her. She felt power welling up inside her. She turned. As she walked back to her seat, she felt a gaze on her. She glanced to her right. *What is he doing here?* It was Bradley, that young lawyer from LeMadelines. He was staring at her, smiling. Amanda lowered her head quickly and hurried to her seat.

Not long after she sat, Senator Gators dismissed the service. Amanda wanted to hug him. Tell him she understood now. She stood, walked down the aisle, and waited behind the crowd that had gathered in front of him. She could see the senator, get glimpses of him, and he glanced at her a few times. Gladys still sat at the piano playing hymns softly.

"Amanda." The voice came from behind her. Amanda turned.

"Bradley Washington," the young man said. "The senator told me I should introduce myself." He extended his hand.

Amanda extended hers. She wasn't sure what to say. She smiled, feeling herself blushing. "I'm Amanda Collins. But I guess you already know that," she said.

Amanda glanced at the senator. He showed that wonderful smile again. Then she glanced at Gladys. Gladys tilted her head slightly, smiled, and blinked her eyes, as if she were exaggerating a response to a romantic scene.

Oh, brother!

"Is it too late for a cup of coffee?" Bradley asked.

"No, I guess not."

As Amanda and Bradley walked up the aisle, Amanda heard a few notes of the wedding march played ever so softly.

I can't believe Gladys did that! I can't believe it!

CHAPTER 36

Griffin lay stretched out on his sofa, in his jeans and his favorite sweatshirt, his feet, in white socks, crossed at the ankles. One of those made-for-TV, loosely-based-on-a-real-rumor movies about the snatching away of a child had captured Griffin's attention.

The phone rang.

Griffin thought it was probably Ruth. Their conversation the first time they saw each other after it was all over flashed through his mind. They had hugged each other, saying not so much as "Hello." Then Ruth had spoken straightforwardly, as she always did. "Griffin, you and I have feelings for each other," she had said.

Griffin had said nothing.

"When Joshua graduates from medical school and Esther from college in two years, then perhaps. But for now, I intend to share my time with them."

"I have an idea," Griffin had said. "The Ozark Project."

Griffin remembered how Ruth had looked at him with a puzzled look on her face.

"It will be a book telling the truth about what happened, dedicated to Dr. Hegel. We can work on it together from a distance."

"I like that idea, Griffin," Ruth had said softly.

Or the caller might be little Tommy Jennings. Tommy had called twice since Griffin got home. He wanted to know how he could be a secret agent like his father. His best friend who was spending the night wanted to know, too. Griffin told him he'd have to wait, maybe four or five years. "If you're going to be a hero like your dad, you need a driver's license first, Tommy."

Griffin clicked the remote, turning off the movie, and in the sudden dead silence, he lifted the receiver.

"Hello."

"Hello, Griffin."

Griffin had hoped this call would never come, but he had known it would sooner or later. "Hello, Mr. President."

"I just want to tell you Constance isn't doing well. They've diagnosed her as severely depressed. She's on mind-altering drugs; might as well be lobotomized." The president's voice was soft, cloaked in a vanquished tone. He wasn't throwing up his hands now. No crooked, confident smile with these words. "She's frail and looks ninety years old."

"I'm sorry to hear that, Ashton. I really am."

"I don't think I'll run again, Griffin. The polls aren't good, and the national committee isn't backing me," the president said. "I hate to resign. Courtney Packard would be a worse president than I am. Wonder if that's possible. Might as well resign, though. Redden tells me the national committee is thinking about backing Gators for the nomination. Isn't that a kick in the pants!"

"Ashton, you don't have to talk to me like this."

"These religious right people, they have come out of a rock somewhere—"

There's more to that than you realize, Mr. President—

"People up here, they hold me in contempt, even ridicule," the president said softly. "People down there do, too; I know that. They think I believe in that secular utopian stuff Constance was obsessed with, or that I had something to do with those poor babies; that I could have stopped them from being—Redden tells me there's talk of Articles of Impeachment in the House. If it weren't for Speaker Jukali. . ."

"You'll come out of this all right, Mr. President."

"With a lawyer like you, I know that," the president said. "It's just the pressure. Can't sleep. No peace."

"Ashton—"

On the other end, nothing but silence.

"God is a God of second chances, Mr. President. Ask His forgiveness, and tell the people what happened. If they don't reelect you, go on with your life in Him. It is there and only there that you will find the peace you seek." The last image of Jennifer he had seen floated through Griffin's mind.

"I don't need your God," the president said. "I need the best political lawyer in the country, who happens to be the only friend I have left."

Silence.

"Griffin?"

"I'm sorry, Mr. President," Griffin said softly. "I can't help you now."

More dead silence.

Then Griffin Dowell heard a gentle *click* followed by a dial tone.

THE END

Would you like to offer feedback on this novel?

Interested in starting a book discussion group?

Check out www.barbourpublishing.com
for a Reader Survey and Book Club Questions.

ABOUT THE AUTHOR

Glyn J. Godwin holds a Ph.D. in food microbiology and toxicology and a law degree from Louisiana State University. He is currently practicing law in New Orleans, where he also chairs a community outreach organization that provides help to the poor.

Glyn lives in Louisiana with his wife, Trudy, and is the father of three grown children. *Body Politic* is his first novel.

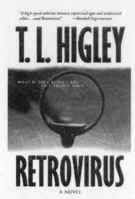
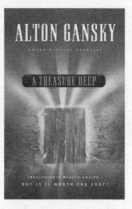